I0522769

MELODY

OF

MANA

✦ BOOK 2 ✦

MELODY

OF

MANA

◆ BOOK 2 ◆

WANDERING AGENT

Podium

In honor of my dear friend and mentor Jared,
who taught me that the most important step is effort

All rights reserved. No part of this publication may be reproduced, stored in a retrieval system, or transmitted in any form or by any means electronic, mechanical, photocopying, recording, or otherwise without prior written permission from Podium Publishing.

This is a work of fiction. Names, characters, places, and incidents are either products of the author's imagination or used fictitiously. Any resemblance to actual events, locales, or persons, living, dead, or undead, is entirely coincidental.

Copyright © 2022 by Michael Robert Taylor

Cover design by Podium Publishing

ISBN: 978-1-0394-1599-7

Published in 2022 by Podium Publishing, ULC
www.podiumaudio.com

MELODY
OF
MANA

✦ BOOK 2 ✦

CHAPTER 1

✦

END OF AUTUMN

Jackson's arrival and announcement caused what can only be described as a "significant disturbance" to that evening's events in the tavern. He'd successfully chosen everyone's conversation topic too. So once everyone settled down a bit, that was all I heard about for the rest of the night.

Part of the reason was that nobody had known just how bad the empire had apparently been. Sure, there had been rumors of revolts there, but nothing of magnitude. This level of surprise was not something that most people were used to. Normally, there would have been at least signs that they were about to fall, but the report from our newly arriving bard was that their army had been destroyed in one fell swoop. That was followed by city after city being taken down, ending in the fall of their capital.

Not even the messenger knew much here. Jackson knew what had happened and knew that it had been quick, but not the who or how. This was much to the chagrin of several of our patrons who'd bought him drinks in the hope of pulling out more information that he simply didn't have.

What he did have were reports of a few people fleeing across the border to seek safety from the new regime. Most of them lived nearby or were fleeing nobles of the empire. None of those trying to get refugee status were very welcome though, and the overwhelming majority had been quickly chased away. Our people were a little less than interested in helping those with whom we had just been enemies in a years-long war.

It was also apparent that the empire had done all it could to hide just how bad their problems were, even from their own people. Their fall had come so quickly after what seemed to be minor reports that it must have been covered up. Even the knowledge that their army had been destroyed was just now filtering across the border. I suspected that they'd hidden all the information that they could in an attempt to keep order. Hiding that knowledge hadn't helped them at all and may have, in the end, caused more issues since nobody knew what was going on until it was done.

It wasn't until the next morning that I got a chance to talk to the bard myself. It was unsurprising that Lucien had rented him a room, or that he planned to stay for the winter. Of course, I wasn't really looking forward to a full season of having to deal with his antics, but he could be a bit fun every now and then.

"Morning." I waved as I came down to the main hall.

"Mornin'. So you're here now."

"So I am."

"Working for Lucien?"

"Yup."

"In the capital."

"Uh-huh."

"And the Shield is okay with that. I remember you were with them last I saw you."

"Not at all, they're livid."

"Well, that's . . . good, I guess? Any word from your folks?"

"Nothing. Don't suppose you've heard about them or Mystien?"

"Sorry, no." When the aforementioned Lucien arrived, he looked between the two of us. "Okay, how did you two end up meeting anyway?"

"She showed up at my door. So she actually is that old coot's apprentice?"

"Oh yeah, I met her when she was just"—he indicated roughly knee height— "this big of a little monster." He turned back to look at me. "You scared the fire out of your town or something, right?"

"Okay, yeah, but that was my brothers' fault, not mine." Both men snorted in disbelief at that declaration. "I was minding my own business"—another snort—"and my brothers came up and threw a bug at me, and my spell went out of control."

"A likely story," declared Lucien.

"Yeah, nobody's going to believe that," agreed Jackson.

"It's the truth! It doesn't matter if you believe it or not." I didn't even have Dras to back me up anymore. Of course, he might have sided with these two jerks; that was a daunting prospect.

They shook their heads in apparent disbelief, with Lucien even going so far as to press my cheeks when I puffed them up. An action that got about half the staff laughing. Soon enough though, I did have to get back to work. Even as winter approached, there was much that needed to be done.

I ended up cleaning most of the kitchen. The room was rather small, designed to shove out high amounts of food in low varieties. There was an oven for bread and things like pies or casseroles, a stove optimized for making huge pots of stew, and a few small spits for meat. I didn't spend much time back here. I wanted to be alone today, and with how little food we put out in the afternoon, I could be assured of low traffic.

The cook who was working for the Starlit Sky right now was a tall, thin, and not particularly talkative girl by the name of Lude. With Lude and I thoroughly ignoring each other, we both got to enjoy the silence. So when she finally spoke while ripping up our day-old bread for stew, I was more than a bit surprised.

"You're the one who makes this, right?" She held up one of the loaves she was breaking into bits.

"Yes."

"Why?"

"Why what?"

"Why do you spend time and mana making bread. Isn't there some better way to use it?"

"At this point, my spell for that is really efficient. So it's not like I'm using very much mana. I've been doing it since I was a little kid."

She cocked her head, and a few strawberry blond strands fell over her shoulder as she made a face. "Why would you even learn that spell though? Isn't it hard to learn magic or something?"

"Have you lived in the capital your whole life?" Lude nodded in response, looking a bit confused. "During the war, the small towns and cities outside of the central area of the country were starving to death. There was no food, so I learned to make some. It really helped both my family and village."

"What? Don't they grow lots of food out there?"

"Normally, but not when too many people are called off to war; there's not enough people to work the fields."

"We never had that kind of problem. Sure, grain got more expensive, and meat was really hard to find, but it was never just nothing."

"The laws here are made so that there isn't too much scarcity around the capital. Probably because the rulers don't want problems here."

"Huh, I didn't know that. Well, at least the war is over, so your village can grow enough now." She smiled.

"Something like that." I didn't really want to go into all of it.

"Can you make other kinds of bread though? For a bit of variety?"

"I can change it up a little bit. Anything in particular?"

"Most of your stuff is the very fancy white bread. Having some of the darker bread would be nice for a few of our dishes. People don't like it as much, but the flavor is better for some things."

"Sure." I generally defaulted to something more like white bread from back home. Here though, that was considered rather high class. The more common folk ate mostly whole wheat and "meaty" breads. Mixing a bit in would be no issue at all.

After I finished up with my cleaning, we chatted a bit more. Lude was in her late teens or early twenties and part of the group that made up a lot of the temp workers in the city. Most women lived with their parents until they married, and she was no exception. But at her age and economic level, she still needed to bring in a bit of money. Working for Lucien was her solution. The pay was fair, the job easy enough, and she didn't really have to deal with customers. The last part was of importance to her because she was a bit of an introvert.

After work the next day, our newest resident came to join me for a late lunch.

"So, what's this I hear about you getting a boyfriend?" Jackson leaned over the table. "One going to the academy at that? I'll admit I was a bit surprised at first, but you did learn from the best . . ."

"You heard wrong. Anyway, is there a point to this?"

"All right, snippy. I've got a gig tonight that involves some light illusion work. Lucien said you'd been putting real effort into some of that kind of thing and might do well to have a bit of experience in the field. So, do you want to come?"

"More details please."

"Fine, fine. There's a merchant putting on a party. It'll be really swanky, lots of high-class folks. A lot of those guys aren't nobles but really like magic and have tons of cash to boot. Therefore, they often hire casters to come and put on some effects in the background. The pay is solid, and it's the kind of thing you only really see here in the capital."

"So, we'll just be tossing out illusions during the party?"

"We get to attend the party, too, if that's a bonus you wanted."

"I wasn't really thinking about that and don't really have a fancy party dress."

"Not a problem. I know a guy who can help. You'll be borrowing it, but it'll look good and so will you."

Now that was something that piqued my interest. After a few moments, I nodded. "All right, let's do it."

After I told Lucien that I'd accepted the job with Jackson, we were off. The streets passed by quickly as we climbed higher and higher into the city, moving just to the edge of the nobles' district. Eventually though, we came to a small, rather hidden shop. It was the kind of place I would have walked past without noticing. The small sign read Marcus's Fashion, and my companion opened the door like he'd been there a thousand times.

The store was bright and clean on the inside, with a surprising amount of mirrors. In the back was an area that seemed dedicated to cutting hair, while the front was obviously a tailor's shop. Upon hearing the bell, a man named Marcus came out to the front, looking us over.

He was tall and clean-cut, with sharp eyes that moved over us approvingly. His hair was jet-black, short, and well done. Perfectly fitted pants, vest, and shirt paired with the tape measure behind his neck gave him the look of a professional. A small woman followed after him. She gave me a bit of a frown.

"My, my, if it isn't Jackson. You're looking garish as always, and with a new friend this time? A bit young, isn't she?"

"An apprentice of sorts, and both of us need something on loan appropriate for a ball. I figured I'd bring her to the best."

"Flattery as well. You know it'll get you everywhere. Come on then. Let's see what we have to work with."

He motioned us both over and quickly began taking measurements. As the tape fluttered around, checking each body part, I had to admire his speed. It only took him a few moments to get everything he needed before looking at me again.

"Janis, hair and makeup on her." He motioned over his assistant who led me into the back of the shop while he worked on Jackson.

The current fashion, it would seem, was complex braids that pulled the hair up off of the neck. Janis didn't bother cutting my hair for this reason and just started working it. Her hands were firm and quick, but not rough, lightly tugging and pulling things until she was satisfied, then pinning them in place with care.

Makeup was, to my relief, minimal. Janis explained that some older women would wear heavier stuff, but for girls my age, that was considered poor form. Since I was already rather pale, a bit of blush and the smoothing out of a few blemishes were all I really needed.

As I finished up, I took a long look in one of their mirrors. I almost never got to see myself in one, and it was surreal to see how I now looked. I took my time, finally smiling as I decided that I really liked the whole thing.

When I returned to the front, I got to see Jackson paying for us and popping out for some reason or another. While he did that, Marcus was bringing forward two sets of clothes. He had a pale blue dress I was fairly sure wouldn't quite fit me. I marveled when he sang to it. The cloth subtly shifted and seams moved, pulling and expanding the dimensions to his desires.

"My family specializes in bardic magic that works on clothes. We've done it for generations, each learning what they can and passing down their knowledge." He looked up as he saw me staring.

"It's quite impressive."

"Thank you. Now, go and put this on." He handed me the dress, and I quickly walked over to a curtained-off area. Janis came to help me, a kind mercy as this particular garment was rather more complex than what I normally wore.

It still took several minutes to get all the layers tied down properly. When I finally returned, I found Jackson, dressed in similarly fancy clothing, waiting for me.

"I went and rented us a carriage for the night. It's not fancy or anything, but we can't well walk in these." He indicated our borrowed outfits with a flourish.

I felt myself blush a bit as I suddenly had the feeling that this was rather like a very awkward prom.

"If you can keep that up all night, dear, you'll be an absolute hit," Marcus said as he saw me reddening. Which, of course, only caused it to turn a deeper red. "No, no, too much, a bit less dear."

I had a feeling that I may have bitten off more than I could chew.

CHAPTER 2

✦

GETTING READY AND AN
EMERGENCY LESSON

The carriage that Jackson had rented was not great. The outside was clean and plain, with a coat of dark red paint and bare metal fixings. Inside was a bit nice, with cushioned seats and bars to hold on to while riding. I smoothed out the dress that I was wearing as I got in, looking over at my coworker for the evening.

I tried to begin conversation, but it died as soon as we left. This carriage had either no shocks, or very poor ones compared to a modern car, and talking while being shaken so was nearly impossible. I was bounced mercilessly about as we passed down the cobbled streets, internally begging for an end to the jostling.

Walking would have been completely impossible though, dressed as we were. We would have attracted far, far too much attention. I had no desire to get mugged, not that any mugger would have been able to take the two of us. It also kept us from getting dirty, something that was of great importance as we had to look presentable.

Eventually, we did arrive. It was still early, far too early for the party to have begun. Jackson was kind enough to lend me his hand as I was stepping out of the carriage and walking toward the large house. Servants were running about preparing things. Several were cleaning everything in sight; others were putting up decorations.

"So, am I not a bit young for this?"

"Certainly not. Larger events are reserved for those at or near adulthood, but this isn't quite of that level. These merchants want their daughters to attract rich noble husbands, so they tend to start them on the lower events of the party circuit around puberty. You will be among the younger girls here, but you definitely won't be the youngest."

"They're hiring us and this is a lesser event?"

"It's being put on by a merchant, not a noble. That alone puts it far lower in the rankings."

"Fair. Do the merchants often get their children married into noble households?"

"Depends on if the girl has any ability with mana. Lower-ranking houses or those a few generations removed from the main family may allow it. If the kid is a caster though, that changes things depending on how strong they are. Boys are almost never married into a noble household. Even if they are skilled, the best they could hope for is a position in a branch family."

"Good to know. What exactly are we doing tonight? Something specific I'd imagine?"

"I'm not actually sure on the specifics. The job explanation was for two mages able to do basic illusions. We'll find out when we meet the customer. Which should be right about . . ."

As we entered into the main door, we were quickly greeted by what I could only assume was the customer. His eyes moved over us with joy first, but his brow furrowed as it settled upon me.

"Ah, you must be the caster I hired. I am Ulbert of the Minhousen Company, and you brought . . ." It seemed he believed that I was here for pleasure instead of business, something that would need to be corrected with haste.

"An apprentice. She is being trained by my teacher and comes highly recommended. She'll be helping me tonight." Jackson seemed to understand my feelings, and his words put the man slightly more at ease.

"Ah I see, follow me please." He led us to a rather extravagant ballroom, easily large enough for two or three hundred people.

I was surprised at the display of money here. Building something like this in the middle of the capital had surely cost a fortune. Even if it had been around for some time, I could imagine that even maintaining it would be very expensive.

The floors were well-polished marble, white with scattered small light-gray inclusions. On the wall in brass sconces were lamps burning some kind of oil, odorless or very near, from what I could smell. The ceiling was high for buildings I'd seen in this world, perhaps thirty feet. The chandeliers though were dark, and I saw no place for candle holders.

"The first thing I need you to do is to put enough mana in the chandeliers to keep them active for the party. After that, our theme for the night is the coming of winter. If you have any ideas, I'd love to hear them, but I was thinking something snow- or ice-themed along the ceiling."

It took only a moment for us to find the recharging location for the chandeliers, and I filled them. Not much but enough certainly for a day. Jackson stood back while I did so, looking up and around. That alone seemed to mollify our employer.

"Any thoughts on what we should do, Alana? Surely, snow."

"We could do some lightly rolling light clouds or a night sky on the ceiling. I could also probably modify a sound suppression bubble to mimic how snow muffles sound."

"I would prefer a mix if possible," Ulbert declared.

"Very well then. Alana, handle the snow and the muffling, if you don't mind."

"Certainly." I quickly hummed a tune to start up the spells.

Expanding the soundproof bubble and weakening its effect to just a muffle wasn't that hard, nor was the actual snow illusion. Snowflakes always have been sort of indistinct unless you're very close, so mimicking them is fairly easy, even in a large area.

After examining how I had them moving, Jackson brought in the clouds. It was a lightly rolling bank above us, with a few openings to a dark night. He even brought in a small faux moon that shone down upon us. It was like being outside on a snowy night, except warm and dry.

"Oh yes, yes, this will do perfectly." He bounced on the balls of his feet slightly, his voice dying as it hit the walls of the room and my bubble. I was quite pleased with the effect.

Another man approached us. He wore the formal attire I would have associated with the rich but stood very rigidly.

"Let me introduce the master of ceremonies for the night, Hugh, one of my most trusted retainers." Ulbert nodded to the other man. "Alas, I've other things I must prepare, please consult as needed."

Hugh seemed a nice enough man, if a bit rigidly formal. He gave us a list of the dances planned for the night and led us to a small room to the side where we could rest until the festivities began. We had a couple of hours to rest now that we decided on our spells and the chandeliers were charged. It was important for us to have lots of mana so we could keep the illusions up into the night.

Jackson looked over the list of planned dances. "These are all fairly standard group dances. Looks like he mixed in about half for couples." He froze and looked at me. "I don't suppose you know how these go?"

"Oh . . . no, I don't."

"Okay, well, that's not the end of things. We'll run over them all real quick. If you're unsure, just follow the directions and what others are doing. We're lucky you're young. If you were even a couple of years older, we'd have real problems."

He started with the dances for couples, since there were more of those than anything else. These were mercifully simple, owing to the fact that many of those present were likely to be either young or inexperienced. The style was sort of like a Viennese waltz, though the order of steps was slightly different. I hadn't had much experience here but could at least process what I was doing. It took only a few minutes before he nodded, apparently satisfied.

"That will do for now. We'll work on these later if you want to join me for any more of these jobs, but for now it'll pass. Let's see . . ." He picked up the list, quickly going over it again. "When they call for Summer Flowers or Winter Flowers, excuse yourself; those are too complex for me to teach you in the time we have. That leaves us with the Diamond, a Couple's Arch, and Twin Circles."

He had to lead me through these rather awkwardly, as they were truly dances for large groups, some of it just didn't work with only two people. Again we were lucky that this particular party was not from a noble house, as they would put on some truly complex dances.

The Diamond, as one might suspect, started out in a diamond formation of eight, with pairs moving in and around one another to move the whole group in a clockwise direction. It was repeated for the whole song and was one of Jackson's favorites as far as ballroom things went.

A Couple's Arch was mostly walking elegantly, something I could at least passably do, and involved a lot of following those in front of me. It was the easiest, being that I wouldn't be leading. I just had to follow the leader and keep an eye on my dance partner. The couple who would lead would already be chosen, so there would be no issue.

Twin circles would take up most of the dance floor. Couples would form into concentric circles, moving outward from the center. The first would be small, and partners would face each other. Then another pair of rings would form outside of that, and another until all were involved. There was again a lot of walking, though the timing of steps and their length were important to keep organized.

Merchants liked to act as if they were of the higher classes, and some had astounding fortunes. But when it came down to it, magic was just too powerful. This meant that the nobility had far, far more time to practice overly complex social interactions. A merchant couldn't do that; they just had too many things to do. That meant they had to limit the types of dances they put on, a mercy in our case.

There were a few more rules that we had to go over as well. I was not to accept an invitation to dance more than once from a given man. I was unlikely to be asked, but to do so indicated a rather more than casual link between us. Only those near my age or having just reached adulthood should ask me to join them, but I was told to deny any older men who did. I was to try and socialize lightly with the other girls near the front of the room when dances were not being held, but the topics were to be inane, like dresses and weather.

I was not, under any circumstances, to reveal that I was a caster keeping the illusions going. We were too highly ranked by parts of society to be considered servants, so everyone pretended that we were guests, and a guest wouldn't reveal such. Everyone knew we had been hired, but that was considered rude to actually acknowledge.

Finally, there was a room to the side reserved for women and girls that would have some water, bathroom facilities, and a place to fix any hair/makeup/wardrobe issues. I couldn't hide in there all night though, because my spells would start to falter if I didn't keep mana flowing into them at least periodically. It was a good place to retreat to when the dances I had to avoid were announced though.

We finished up with these basics about the time that Hugh reappeared, telling us that the guests were going to arrive shortly and we needed to reestablish the magic. We arrived just before the Ulbert family, both direct and extended. It was considered good form for a few people to be in place before guests, and all was ready when the moment arrived.

The first wave of guests arrived in a large group; several of the girls let their eyes sparkle as they saw the illusions. One or two even tried to catch a snowflake on a daintily extended hand. It was good to feel appreciated.

CHAPTER 3

✦

A LONG EVENING

There was still a good amount of time to go before the beginning of the party, and I was expected to spend it socializing with the other girls who had arrived. Those who had come in already seemed to gravitate toward those they knew. The room had separated almost down the middle, with men on one side and women on the other, and a small area between the two where light conversation and introductions were being made.

I meandered over to several girls who were marveling at the snowflakes. The spell was drawing a small trickle of mana from me, but I could keep it up for practically forever. They gave friendly smiles as I came closer.

"The snow is amazing! How is it not melting and making a mess do you think?" one asked.

"Perhaps there's some sort of drying enchantment going on?" another commented, following a flake with her eyes.

"Father said something about warm snow once, but I can't remember the details."

"It's probably just an illusion, isn't it? I can't feel any snow touching me, and if you look at the ceiling, the sky definitely is one." I decided to give up the secret easily; these three obviously knew nothing at all about magic.

"I suppose that might be true, and the fake sky is lovely," the oldest of our little group commented, looking up.

I nodded, along with several of the others. Eventually, they did look back down though, the leader settling her eyes on me.

"I'm Quinta; these two are Julia and Armina." She pointed to her friends in turn.

"I'm Alana. It's a pleasure to meet you." I tried to fall back into the tone and mannerisms Mystien had me study all those years ago, but it was a bit difficult since I hadn't really been practicing.

Quinta was perhaps two years older than myself, with flaming red hair that draped down the front of one of her shoulders. She stood just a bit taller than the rest of us, perhaps owing to the small heels on her shoes. Beside her the other two looked like they could have been sisters, their hair chocolate brown and features quite fair, as was common among the wealthy.

"I don't believe I've seen you at any of the balls I've been to before, Alana." Quinta looked me over for a few moments as if trying to recognize me.

"This is my first in the capital, I'm afraid."

"Oh, that would explain it. Are you coming to the one hosted by Lord Johannes next month? I hear he's trying to find a wife for one or two of his sons. It would be best to be noticed early if you want success there."

"I'm afraid neither I nor my guardian have received an invitation as of yet. Perhaps I'll meet them here or there though." I needed to be as non-committal as possible when it came to this subject. I had no desire to get invites to parties thrown by the merchants and weaker nobles.

Julia had a keen eye for fashion and started pointing out the new trends in the dresses of some of the older girls. One, in particular, had managed to find a stunning violet piece that incorporated a few frills along the sides, which were gaining popularity. Other trends like overlarge padding on the bustle were now falling out of favor quickly and were only being seen on older women. I was thankful that my new dress seemed about average for what was expected, probably something Marcus had thought of.

As we stood back looking at the various people as they came in, one group threw me a bit. A man and three boys who could only have been his sons came in the door. The man was decidedly a magic user of some kind, as was the oldest of his sons. They were both quite a bit weaker in aura than I was, and the two younger boys had barely a flicker. I could see it, just barely, but it was one of those that meant they probably couldn't do anything.

The man's eyes scanned the crowd quickly. I could see when they fell on Jackson, and immediately I began suppressing my own aura. Not quick enough though, it would seem. The oldest son was already looking in my direction with wide eyes. He quirked his head a bit as he and his father exchanged words I could not hear. The other boys then perked up and looked over too.

"That's Lord Johannes; he's looking at us!" Armina excitedly whispered as a slight blush worked its way up her face.

As I internally cursed, the other girls around me began squealing in excitement. All of them were here in the hopes of being noticed. I, on the other hand, had no desire to be noticed at all. In fact, it took all of my effort to keep my face neutral as I had an across-the-room staring contest with the young noble boys.

Eventually, their father got their attention, pulling them away toward . . . Jackson. Naturally, he'd go straight to the other caster in the room. In the middle of their conversation, I felt Jackson's eyes flick over toward me too. We really needed to work on his poker face.

"Who's that man Lord Johannes is speaking to? I don't think I recognize him," Quinta asked.

"And what in the world is he wearing? It's the loudest thing I've ever seen!" Julia added in a small scandalized whisper.

Julia was, in my humble opinion, right. Jackson dressed like a man who puked and decided to dress in the colors that emerged. It did kind of work for him though. I dreaded seeing he and the small group of nobles move toward the area for the genders to meet, his eyes on me.

"Are they looking this way?" Quinta whispered.

"I suppose. I'll be right back." I groaned internally as I moved toward them, feeling like I was walking toward my death.

"Alana, this is Lord Johannes, and these are his sons, Dietrich, Rieg, and Armond." He turned to the nobles, "This, my lords, is Alana."

"A pleasure to meet you, my lords." I curtsied as we were introduced, even if it was absolutely the last thing I wanted to do to attract the attention of people at this party.

Each of the men nodded in greetings. There was a lot of hierarchical things going on here: who had to be introduced to who based on gender, rank, and all kinds of other rules I was only barely aware of. Regardless, after that, the lord and his sons quickly moved on.

As soon as they had, I hummed up a silence bubble around Jackson and myself.

"What was that about?" I asked as the sounds of the party faded, trying to keep my mouth as still as possible.

"Now that you've been formally introduced, it is not impolite for his sons to speak with you later tonight. It would also be quite rude of you to refuse light conversation or an invitation to dance."

I groaned loudly, knowing that it wouldn't escape the bubble.

"Be as noncommittal as possible. I'll have to give you some very basics on the etiquette of these events should you wish to continue working with me at them. We'll handle that later though." With that said, he left my little silence bubble, moving across the room.

I returned to the group of girls I'd been speaking with earlier, a rookie mistake. The three kept bright smiles on their faces as they all but demanded an explanation on the events. The simple answer that Lord Johannes realized he hadn't met me and arranged an introduction did not sit as well as I thought it would have.

All three had been introduced to him and his sons, at some point. They all also knew that he cared not at all about them; it had just been a formality. That kind of thing would be handled later in the evening by those who knew both individuals. The fact that he saw, was interested in, and acted to actually speak to me pretty much ousted me as a caster, though if I had to guess, only Quinta truly understood it.

I was saved by the dancing, which began before too many conversations and questions could be had. Everyone began to intermingle for a few moments before, choosing partners as they did. Armond came up to me at this point.

Armond and Rieg had to be twins if I was any judge, as their heights were almost identical. Both were close to my age, perhaps a year or less younger than me. They had dark brown hair. Armond's fell over his eyes, while Rieg had his cropped short.

"Miss Alana, may I have this dance?" His voice was smooth and kind as he offered his hand.

I lightly took it and quickly moved with him to the dance floor, a few moments before the master of ceremonies had called out Couple's Arch as the first dance. It was a group one, so talking would be minimized, and I knew it, so I was confident.

Armond made light conversation as we moved into place: the normally permitted subjects, how the weather was looking to be especially cold this year, a compliment on my dress. It wasn't until we were nearly in place that he started asking what I felt were the real questions.

"It is a shame I haven't seen you before, Miss Alana. Did you just move to Lithere?" He actually used the name of the capital, that was a bit unusual among my normal crowd. I'd only heard it in lessons with Mystien and in conversations where multiple countries were involved.

"A while ago actually, but I prefer to keep mostly to myself."

"Where from, if I might ask?"

"Out east, ah, it seems we are beginning." Using that excuse was magical, and soon enough we were working through the many motions needed for this particular piece.

It ended soon enough, and I managed to go back to join the chatting with the other girls. The fact that boys could and did now join us ended with me getting introduced and subsequently dancing with several others. Quinta's brother came by for one of those, as well as one of Julia's cousins or something, the relationship there was a bit unclear.

Rieg came by shortly after to ask me to join him for Twin Circles. That went much as it had with his brother, him trying to pry information out of me after small talk. I made another attempt at avoiding too much of that as well.

"It is surprising that your parents were not here with you today, Miss Alana. I should hope to meet them."

"Perhaps in the future they shall be, but they are unfortunately unable to be here tonight." That was technically true. They were unable to be here because well . . . they were out of contact.

"Oh, I see. Do I know them?"

"I find that unlikely, Lord Rieg." Again I'd managed to delay until the dancing started and postpone my suffering.

I hid for Summer Flowers, going into the room reserved for ladies as I'd been instructed. It was a good opportunity to grab a drink of water and use the facilities anyway. The latter part was a bit of a chore in a formal dress, involving a chair, several minutes, and a rather more fancy chamber pot than I was used to.

Following that, there were several more rounds of dancing. I again fled at the announcement of Winter Flowers as I saw Dietrich trying to approach me. I did all I could not to literally run, the idea of having to tell him no and violating some Byzantine rule of etiquette speeding me along.

Irritatingly, some girl of about eighteen, who I didn't know, approached me shortly after my arrival in the ladies' room.

"Are you quite okay? I believe Lord Dietrich wished to dance with you. You should hurry before they begin."

"Sadly, my history with Winter Flowers is poor"—*because it doesn't exist*—"and I was told by my dance instructor that I was, under no circumstances to dance it tonight. Had he chosen almost literally any other, I would be happy to join him. I can't well turn him down though, and I've no clue how to explain the problem."

I could have died right there. All I wanted to do tonight was make a bit of money, maybe have a bit of fun along the way. I had been woefully unprepared for what I considered my second worst disaster in the capital. Frankly, I might be willing to go fight the golem again if it kept at this rate though.

The girl suppressed a giggle and turned. "No worries, I'll take care of an explanation for you."

I didn't know if I should be relieved or more afraid. "Thank you."

When I returned, after hearing the call for an upcoming dance for couples, I was met by the young Lord Dietrich before I'd even made it all the way back.

"One of my cousins tells me you had a bad experience with Winter Flowers?" he asked as he neared.

"Something like that, Lord Dietrich." I could feel heat creeping across my cheeks as I tried to properly explain myself.

He seemed to take it in stride. "Ah, my apologies, I thought you were avoiding me for a moment there."

"Not at all. I merely wished not to publicly embarrass myself and you." That got a chuckle.

Of the three brothers I'd met, he seemed to be the most charming. He had a warm smile and his hair was longer, pulled back into a simple ponytail. If I had to guess, I'd say he was around a year my senior. Most of all was his confidence; he exuded it from every pore. This young man knew his place in the world and he fit there perfectly, moving past people with perfect grace.

"Well then, would you do me the honor of joining me for a couple's dance?"

"Certainly, Lord Dietrich."

"I don't believe I've seen you at the academy. Are you not planning to attend?" he asked after the standard handful of small talk questioning.

"Oh, I'm just a sliver too young to attend this year. Next year, I plan to apply."

It was at this moment that the music began. He wrapped one arm around my waist and led, quite a bit better than the other young men who'd joined me earlier in the night. This particular dance involved us being extraordinarily close, pressed together as we moved in circles around those older than ourselves.

"Oh, I see, I see. I shall look forward to it. There are several lovely places there. One particular nook is perfect for watching the sun rise. I hope you'll let me show it to you over breakfast one day."

Um, what? I mean, I liked breakfast as much as the next girl, but that was kind of a weird invitation.

"Perhaps, my lord. That does not sound unpleasant." Being noncommittal seemed best here, since I was a bit put off.

"Ah, but I'm getting ahead of myself. Is there anything you would like to ask me?"

"Why are you and your brothers paying so much attention to me?"

"That's quite simple. We know most of the magic users in our age range. Both our rivals and potential allies. A new individual is of great interest."

"Oh, I see."

"I don't suppose you'd be willing to join me in a bit of mischief?" he whispered to me, causing me to grin a bit.

"That would depend on what that is, Lord Dietrich."

He chuckled. "You see, I saw you before my father. Before you began suppressing your aura. He thinks, from what he can see now, that you might be interesting as a potential candidate to marry one of my brothers in the far future, and that I'm wasting my time by even speaking to you. I'd rather like to get one over on him, as I seldom manage that."

"And how do you propose to do that?"

"All you would need to do is stop suppressing yourself. I really would appreciate it."

I knew it was stupid, that what he was requesting of me was an absolute fool move. At the same time, the way he spoke, it was so kindly and warm. Even his aura was warm; it looked like leaves floating in the wind around him. In a snap moment, I let my suppression go, flooding out a trail of ethereal bubbles behind me, just for a few moments as we turned. The huge widening of his father's eyes was something to see as we spun past.

"Thank you, Alana, I really do mean it," he said shortly after I pulled my aura back in. "Will you be joining us at our ball in the near future?"

"Lord Dietrich, I haven't even received an invitation, much less considered it."

"Well, I will have to see that that changes then, won't I?"

After that display, the rest of the party was rather less eventful. I enjoyed a bit more until it was time to go and I joined back with Jackson.

"Well, that was wild," he said as he slid into the carriage after me.

CHAPTER 4

✦

A MONTH OF PREPARATION

The day after the ball, Jackson woke me up by pounding on my door. We'd basically gotten back to the tavern, coming in through the back door, and crashed. My rented dress was put to the side, since it was supposed to be returned later this afternoon. It wouldn't be a bad trip, and I had the day off anyway.

I yanked open the wooden door with all the viciousness that a thirteen-year-old could muster. Someone awakening me so early on a day otherwise reserved for rest and relaxation was likely to get screamed at.

"What did you do!"

"What?"

"WHAT DID YOU DO!"

"Jackson, it's way too damn early for riddles."

He waved a folded bit of parchment in front of me angrily. "It is also too damn early for me to be getting invitations to a noble's house for the both of us. Now, what did you do!?"

"Lord Johannes's son asked me if I was coming to their ball. I suppose he sent it upon learning I hadn't been invited." I tactfully left out the part where I'd told him I hadn't been invited.

"Which son?"

"Dietrich? The older one."

"Did he say anything else of note? Invite you to do or go anywhere else?"

"He suggested we have breakfast some time. I don't know what that has to do with anything though. I was noncommittal as you told me to be."

Lucien had appeared by this time, and I considered it rather fortunate that we were currently the only people staying here. A guest shouting at one of the workers early in the morning would look bad.

"What's all this about then?" the old man asked as he came over toward us.

"Some noble's son is trying to court Alana, and it seems she's TOO DENSE to realize it."

"He invited me to a public party and breakfast. It's not like that's a big deal or anything."

At this point, Jackson actually bonked me on the head with a closed fist. "He invited you to his house and on a date. The second of which you at least didn't accept."

"How is breakfast a date? Shouldn't that be dinner?"

"What kind of an idiot would invite a girl to dinner as a date? She's just going to go home and sleep. Isn't it better to wow her in the morning and have her thinking about it all day?" I had apparently missed some cultural stuff here, constantly forgetting that some things were just going to be weird. "And how are you going to attend a ball hosted by a noble family, Alana? You're going to need to be far more dressed up than you were for our little job last night."

Lucien looked like he had a headache. Jackson had a vein pulsing just above one eyebrow.

"Let me see the dress you rented," the older man finally declared.

I went and got it. It had been hung up, and I was fairly sure that it was nice enough.

"This will do, but you will need at least a necklace, hair decoration, and a bracelet to go along with it, all of good quality. Take this back to Marcus, and speak with him on the subject."

"How long do we have to deal with this?" I hesitantly asked.

"About a month." Jackson looked down at the invitations, handing me mine.

"You'll need to go today to start getting her ready. Alana, do you have more of that sugar?"

"Erm, yes?"

"Good, take it to market and sell the lot. You're going to need the money to pay for this mess."

"I mean, I could just not go . . ."

"No, no, you can't just not go. It will lead to some absolutely unacceptable social repercussions for me." Jackson was more than a bit irritated.

"All right, you two need to go and take care of this as much as you can today. Lad, since you're the one who took her there when she had no clue, you can take her to the market today and back up to Marcus's to talk with him. You know him better anyway. See what you two can do about accessories for her, too, so she doesn't look awful."

Jackson was pissed but went along with it, packing up our clothes in cloth bags and leading me off. Our first stop was the market, so I could sell the sugar I'd amassed over the past bit. I hated to see it go, but I really needed the funds. The price that I got was excellent, as it was more than most people could get and of higher quality. My familiarity with pure crystal sugar from Earth had really paid off.

After that, we returned to Marcus's Fashion whose proprietor met us when we entered the shop.

"So, how did everything go?" he asked as we handed over the clothing.

"The girl went and got herself invited to a noble's ball. Any advice?"

"Don't do that." The tailor answered quickly with a smirk.

"Any real advice?" I chimed in.

"You can get some decent jewelry from a place down the road for a reasonable price. I'll keep the dress in your size for now, and you can use it again. I would go for lapis in silver if you can afford it."

"And if I can't?"

"Definitely something blue. It'll match both the dress and your eyes. I advise silver or something silver-colored as well, for similar reasons. You could go with brass as well since it'll match your hair, but you would need a different dress."

Our trip to the jeweler was spent with Jackson glaring daggers at me. He was very stressed about this whole thing, and I was personally a bit tired of it. I was the one having to spend all the money to make this actually happen.

We took our time looking at different jewelry at the store Marcus had recommended, until I found some sets tucked in the back corner. The necklace was a simple pendant with a few small glass beads that were a lovely blue held in a silver wire. It included a pair of bracelets as well, some additional more dainty pieces that were almost too large in the same style, and a hairpiece that had small pins with little blue balls on each end.

The whole set looked almost like bubbles in light silver wire, or in other words, absolutely perfect. It would complement the dress and myself and had the added advantage of being one of the cheapest sets in the whole shop. Most people liked stones instead of glass. But in this case, it went so well with my aura that there was no issue at all.

When I worked it all out, I was actually a bit up on money. With the sugar I sold and the pay for the previous night's job, I had a hefty sum. Re-renting the dress was no small expense, though much of that was the cost of the deposit, which I would get back except in the case of disaster. The other expenses were comparatively small to what I had feared.

I walked through the market with Jackson and headed home; until that is, I was distracted by a flutist standing beside a small cart. It appeared he was advertising the pieces the man who owned said cart was trying to sell.

"Hey, Jackson, I've been thinking I need a hobby."

"Can you even play a flute? Anyway, for the next month, you need to focus on learning every dance I can force into your head."

"Oh, come on, you can't tell me you've never made flash decisions. As for playing, let's find out."

I watched the player for a bit, looking at his fingers. My first set of parents had decided when I was still in elementary school that I needed to learn an instrument. Pianos were large and expensive, and a violin was not only expensive, it tended to sound like someone was skinning a cat when played wrong. They had settled on the recorder as the safe option to force me to learn, the poor fools.

What had followed was a couple of years of pain for the entire house, though I did learn. Eventually, I traded it out for an ocarina and a concert flute at school. I'd not had a replacement ocarina since coming to this world, and I knew their making was a bit difficult—the holes had to be just right.

These flutes, on the other hand, seemed to be set up almost exactly like a recorder, and I was pretty sure I remembered enough to make it work. So I walked over to the merchant.

"How much?" I leaned over a few of his pieces, pointing out one that looked a bit more reddish than the others he had laid out.

"Two silver each. I've got three sizes."

"May I?" I asked. It would be impolite to not at least request permission and might get me in more than a bit of trouble.

"Go on." The man nodded.

I picked up one of them, the reddish one that I liked, and played through a scale. It was pitched in D if I still had any ear for that and made quite a nice sound. The fingering was ever so slightly different, being shifted just a bit upward, but it was easy to make the adjustment. I ran through one of my practice songs that I'd probably played a couple thousand times.

"One and a half?" I offered to the seller.

"You know, I've never heard that tune before. How about one and a half and you teach me that song?"

"Deal."

Jackson waited not so patiently as I ran through the tune with the merchant a few times, even letting his assistant come over and look. It was short, only a couple of lines, and catchy as well. As far as I knew, it didn't even have a proper name, just "Irish Jig." That was all that had been written in the book I had.

The days that followed involved me being forced into dance lessons for a couple of hours daily after my shift. Jackson would drill me until I could do it perfectly, often using the cook as his example and assistant. Lude seemed to enjoy this to no end, smiling happily as he twirled her around the floor. After that, I would spend the evenings doing some light studying and playing my flute. I wasn't nearly as good as Lucien was with the mandolin he brought out around the time I'd previously headed to bed, but I was passable.

Often, after all the kitchen work for the night was done, we would get together in the common room. It was kind of odd. I'd seen Jackson flirt a lot, chase skirts, invite women to his room to varying degrees of success, and generally sleep around while in Istlan. Here though, he seemed to actually be enjoying just talking to and sharing a laugh with Lude, a girl I think he wouldn't have given a second thought to just a few years ago.

For my part, I wished those two the best. I'd never thought of Jackson as one to settle, either in one place or with anything close to one woman. I remembered the lines of angry fathers and husbands, the long list of one-night stands, the fact that he openly admitted he'd happily knock a maid up if she just wanted that. Perhaps I was wrong though, or perhaps he and Lude could work something out, I didn't know. Lucien seemed to share my opinion, communicated through looks and nods only.

The time passed both too quickly and painfully slowly, and soon enough the evening of Lord Johannes's ball had arrived. We returned to Marcus to prepare and rent a much nicer carriage (which I was eating a bit of the cost on). He'd made a few additions to the dress to fancy it up a bit and quite approved of my choice in jewelry. His assistant again fixed up my hair as part of their service. All prepped and everything in place, we were ready, or as ready as we could ever be. I was nervous, excited, and a bit exhausted as the carriage pulled us into the evening light, hoping I was ready for what came next.

CHAPTER 5

◆

A NOBLE PARTY

The initial differences became obvious as we moved toward Lord Johannes's manor. First of all, we were going well into the nobles' section of the city, and the traffic around us showed it. People were finely dressed as they came in and out of shops, and few were walking. Some rode horses, particularly young men, and some were using carriages much like ours.

As we came to more residential parts, the houses and close buildings gave way to far, far, larger structures. The yards were still rather contained, but it was obvious these were buildings belonging to the very rich and very powerful. I could catch a few glimpses of the palace as we went along, though it was, more often than not, hidden from view.

I got more and more nervous as we neared our destination. Eventually, I could see what must have been it from the window. The house was huge, with large marble pillars out front that had been festooned with lights. I was fairly sure that was it because of the lights and because of the line of carriages.

I had completely forgotten that we were coming in as guests, and therefore were not coming in before the other guests. I looked over at my companion in our little vehicle.

"You look a bit nervous; I'm glad that has finally settled in," Jackson observed.

"How rich are they exactly?"

"For nobles? Not too bad, but this is the capital, and they can cause lots of issues for you if they so choose. Try not to look too nervous; that will only make you look bad. Be confident. As it stands, the two of us are more powerful than most lower-ranking nobility. It's their power and money that are the issue, not magical strength."

"Should I suppress my aura?"

"That's a coin flip. Hiding it for no reason might seem a bit rude, but it's also not uncommon. I'll leave the choice to you."

I mulled that over for a few moments while we waited for the carriages in front of us to make their way through. Eventually, I decided to let it be, suppressing it was hard and since Lord Johannes knew already, I saw no real point to it.

I asked to run over a few of the rules of interaction a bit more. It still came down to remaining noncommittal about almost everything and to be vague about my past. There wouldn't be any direct threats to me at a party, but there was no point in pointing out that I was from a poor peasant family from the middle of nowhere. All that would do is get me the kind of attention that I didn't want.

We disembarked when our turn came, and I got a full view of the entrance. The lights I'd seen from afar were small dim orbs, slowly floating around the front with warm, inviting light. Servants and the like ran to and fro, helping everyone out of their carriages and to the entrance where they were greeted and told the night's theme.

Themes seemed to be a running thing with balls as of late. The style had popped up a few years ago and caught on like wildfire. Now, every ball was expected to have some sort of thing going on in the background to add decoration, usually expressed through illusions. The contest to come up with the best was fierce, and those who could cast good illusions were considered must-haves at all parties.

Tonight's theme was the forest. As such, halls and the like had been decorated to seem like there were trees leading you through and into the main ballroom. Vines twisted along, appearing as if you might be able to pass through certain gaps that were, in fact, solid walls. They'd even added in a slight warm breeze and a woodland scent.

I gasped as we entered the main ballroom. The work was magnificent. The sky had complicated cloud formations and a few birds flitting across it. The sunlight pouring down as the light outside faded was striking and warm. I could even pick out a few bits of birdsong that I'd heard myself when out with my brothers.

We spotted Lord Johannes easily. He and a woman I didn't know were greeting all of the guests. She seemed about his age, and I was guessing was his wife. They smiled at Jackson and me as we approached.

"Ah, if it isn't Mister Jackson and Miss Alana. I'm so glad that you could make it even on such short notice." The man smiled at us with the trademark warmth his sons had displayed. I didn't think it was magic as such, just that they all had powerful natural charisma.

"Of course, Lord Johannes, we were honored at your kind invitation." Jackson smiled back, regardless of how much I knew he didn't want to be here.

"Well, allow me to introduce you to my sister, Geraldine. Dear sister, these are the two I was telling you about who made such a good impression at Ulbert's gathering the other day. Would you be so kind as to see to the young miss?" He quickly dragged Jackson off for some private conversation.

The woman looked down at me, obviously making her appraisals. She seemed a bit more harsh than the men of her family. Perhaps that was because she was used to girls trying to get their attention. I suspected that had I been a boy, Dietrich and his brothers would have been much harsher with me.

I curtsied to her in response. "A pleasure to meet you, Lady Geraldine."

She smiled, I'd apparently passed on some level. "You as well, Miss Alana. My nephew spoke quite highly of you, but I was rather loathe to believe him. I'm glad that I was mistaken." She slowly led me over to one side of the room, nodding toward a small bar looking area by the back. "We won't be beginning our dances for a while yet, but you should try one of the refreshments we've prepared. A rather new dish from out east. This particular version has some quite fanciful fruit mixed in." At this point, I could see Lord Johannes returning, and she nodded to me. "Alas, I've other guests to greet, but I do hope we can talk later."

As I moved toward the small bar, I took note of those around me. Many of the people here had magic of some kind or another, though I couldn't tell who had what. There were perhaps twenty casters in total, and only one or two with auras comparable to mine. One man in the corner had one that blazed like the sun and was painfully bright, and a girl around my age who gave off a sensual purple mist.

The people here were noting me too. I could see questioning gazes from several of the men on the other side of the room. The women had mixed responses. A few of the older ones were keeping a close eye on me, much as Geraldine had. Most of the younger ones, though, were sending outright hostile glares at me, as if I were some intruder there to steal their treasures. I supposed that to them competition for the limited number of noble husbands certainly was unwelcome. Not that I actually wanted one of those right now.

There was a small group of teens near the bar slowly eating small scoops of ice cream from cups. Their discussion was intense, each taking a bite then having words with the others. As I approached, the three brothers motioned me forward to join them. This seemed to be the area where socializing between the sexes was permitted at this party.

"Our father procured this treat and tells us that the flavor is a fruit, but nobody seems to be able to divine what kind. Care to give it a try?" Armond offered as the waiter prepared me a small cup as well, with what looked like a silver spoon in it.

"I don't see why not." I looked at the gathered group, recognizing Quinta and her friends from before.

The small bite I took flooded my mouth with flavor and nostalgia. The treat was perfectly smooth and firm, with a tropical taste that seemed a mix of all the things one would expect to find on a deserted island: mango and banana.

"Oh, that's a bit unexpected." I had to cover my mouth as I thought it over.

"Any guesses as to what it is? We're thinking something from overseas. Dietrich said he had an elven fruit once that tasted sort of like this." Rieg grinned as he put forth his opinion. I noticed his brother wasn't here just yet.

"It tastes like paw-paw, and I hate to tell you but that's from just a bit east. It might even grow nearby."

"You've had it before?" the girl with the purple aura asked.

I had to process this particular girl for a few seconds. She was, if I was any guess, almost my age, with thick brunette hair. Her dress was far, far simpler than I would have thought would be permitted here, and her only jewelry was a small pendant hanging from around her neck. That I recognized instantly with its man and woman motif as a symbol of the Order of the Lovers.

"Oh . . . Yes, my brothers knew of a tree and would harvest it every fall. It was a rather nice treat we only got a little of every year."

"In the fall? You mean it isn't a spring fruit?" Armond seemed quite surprised by that one.

"Yes, it produces fruit for only a short time in the fall. I only ever knew of the one place it grew though. It seems they grow near streams. I wonder wherever your father managed to get enough to make so much ice cream."

Everyone looked toward the waiter. Armond and Rieg both had raised eyebrows.

"The young miss is quite correct. Lord Johannes did indeed acquire this treat made from paw-paw fruit, a rather less common treat that grows in this region . . . and only rarely." I almost pitied him, having to work this closely to so many of the nobility. The gazes he got from some as he declared my success were not particularly kind.

After I'd finished the dessert, I quickly moved off to speak with others. I wasn't sure who all was here, but I was hoping that it would help to pass the time. As I was speaking to an older woman who it seemed was a merchant specializing in spices, I saw Dietrich enter from the side. After he shared words with his father and aunt, he scanned the crowd, giving me a small smile and nod as our eyes met.

I wasn't really sure how to feel about him. He certainly was charismatic, rich, and if I had to give an honest assessment, handsome. I suspected in a few years he would be a rival to many male models from Earth, and he certainly had a lot going for him. That said, I also felt like he was way, way too good at getting me to do things not necessarily in my best interest. Like revealing my aura or coming to this party.

As I was mulling this over, several heads turned toward the doors. The men near them first, those who looked like they were tougher reacted very fast, but it soon spread. There was the sounds of some kind of large clamor, followed by a bloodcurdling scream.

CHAPTER 6

✦

MANA-EATER

The scream was decidedly feminine, and as all eyes turned toward the doors, our blood collectively ran cold. What was the worst was that as everyone looked, the illusions started to fall, turning the room into night quickly. Even the lights that hung from the ceiling started to fade slightly, which seemed odd to me.

One of the men stepped forward; he had eyes like steel as he began to shout orders. He wore a silver jacket. "Men, cover the doors, physicals in front. If you have a weapon, draw it. Wizards, provide covering fire and shields, priests and bards on the inner line with women and children, support where you can. GO NOW!"

Men blurred as they ran to the fireplace to grab pokers. The bar and its stools were ripped apart with bare hands to form clubs. One man took a plate from a waitress and wrapped it around his fist like a gauntlet. I didn't know what was going on, but these men had been to war, had fought for years. I was now going to see them when they defended their families.

As the chandeliers began to fail, several sent up balls of light. When mine went up though, I experienced something completely new. It felt as if the mana was being sucked out of the light as it hung in the air, pulling the power directly from me. I was not the only one to feel this.

"Somethings pulling away my mana!" a woman just ahead of me yelled.

"Three potential monsters, two potential spells. Do not cast directly at whatever comes through that door, suppress auras." An older wizened-looking man near the first who'd given the orders for our orientation called out.

I pushed hard against my aura, suppressing it harder than I had in years until it was almost nonexistent. Jackson was just in front of me, looking in front of him as he pulled up a mace he'd gotten somewhere. His was nearly gone too. All the auras began to shrink down smaller and smaller, all but a few of the young, those who hadn't yet learned how.

Several of the older men were whispering to themselves. Most likely and worst-case scenarios, battle and retreat plans. They were spooked. Not much could mess with the spells of others, and all of those who could were powerful enemies.

We could all feel whatever was coming; it moved toward the front door of the ballroom. Inch by inch, it got closer, draining our magic bit by bit as it came. Everyone was on edge; everyone could feel their breath in their chest as something slinked ever closer.

The door opened.

There stood Armina, one of Quinta's friends. Her pretty pink dress and the bows in her hair marred by dripping blood and black ichor. From her mouth, her ears, her eyes, the blood and ichor also flowed. When she looked up, all that was where her eyes should be were a pair of black voids. She stood in the doorway looking at us.

The old wizened man didn't hesitate.

With a *thwump*, the wall nearest to the back line ceased to be. His other hand shot forth a light that flew through it. His voice was panic and despair as he began to yell.

"That's a mana-eater! RUN! Men, hold the line, hold if you want your families to live!"

Armina shot forward like a rocket toward the screaming old man, only to be met by the silver-jacketed man and the man who'd wrapped a plate around his fist. Several of the others ran forward to slam into her with whatever they had on hand. The mass of bodies swirled as panic gripped everyone.

It took me too long to move. A hand wrapped itself around my arm, pulling me away and toward the now missing wall. It was hard to run in a dress, but run I did. Terrified people were all around. I could hear a few cries, and as I got near the hole, a torso slammed into a pillar near me.

I looked up to see Dietrich pulling me along behind him, his face a mask of stone as we passed through the opening. We were one of the last and fortunate to be so. A series of *twangs* and *thunks* rang out, and the first few of the women and children to flee fell.

It was unclear who or where the attack had come from, but I paled as I realized that this surely was an attack. There could be no mistake; someone had loosed a monster on the ball and set to ambush any who fled. I didn't know who, how, or why anyone sane would have done such a thing, but I wanted to weep as I was pulled into the bushes, past a girl no older than myself laying with a quarrel protruding from her chest.

I struggled to keep up with Dietrich as he ran, finally letting go of my hand. The outfit I was in was in no way made for running. I took some heart in the fact that this was his home and he probably knew it as well as if not better than anyone else.

Eventually, he stopped in a small concealed alcove so that we could both breathe. I nearly fell over as the adrenaline pulsed through me. As I looked at the ground, I saw my shadows doing strange things and pointed my eyes skyward. There high above us a light flickered through a series of colors, brilliant where it hung in the sky.

"It's an emergency signal, highest priority if I remember right. There'll be knights here within the hour, we just need to survive."

"What, what was that thing that looked like Armina?" I stammered out.

"A mana-eater obviously."

"I don't know what that is."

"They're rare, and old . . . I'm not sure on the details, but they go after magic users. They're considered among the more dangerous of monsters."

"What do we do?" I whispered.

"Keep quiet, keep hidden, keep our auras suppressed."

I took his advice, and we rested where we were, both trying to bring our auras into nonexistence. It was a skill I hadn't practiced in a while; something I resolved to change if I made it through this. We hid in the alcove, peering at a small hole in the bushes as we waited for help to arrive.

I saw two men moving through the courtyard. It wasn't big, and through our hole I could see them nearing a fountain. As they did, another man came from the side, all moving toward the water feature. A hand shot forward pulling a form from the water.

"Well, well, well, look what we have here," the man said as he pulled up what seemed to be a girl in her late teens, "Not going to cast anything? Afraid our little pet might feel it and come out to play with you? I'm sure it will sooner or later."

I was frozen. If I used magic, would it draw the mana-eater? If I didn't, what would they do to her? Could I cry out or scream? What might they do to me if they found me?

"We don't have time for this. Look at the sky," the man who'd come from the far side said, pointing upward.

"I've plenty of time for a bit of fun," the first said.

I drew in my breath. It was hard to start pulling what I needed for a scream while keeping my aura suppressed, but I began the process. I'd wait until I was sure I had a good shot, and I'd let loose on the bastards. Damn the consequences. I could see Dietrich from the corner of my eye moving his hands forward to point at them, ready to set loose his own spell.

The first man's hand reached forward toward the girl's chest, but it never made contact. A small purple light smacked him in the back, and he popped like a balloon. The girl fell as blood and viscera sprayed the other two men and their would-be victim.

The two remaining men turned and raised crossbows but never got the chance to fire. As soon as the girl hit the ground, both Dietrich and I loosed our mana on them—a wave of agonizing sound followed by a burst of wind that took both men to the ground.

Both men were down for the count. As I rushed forward to try and help the now quite-in-shock girl, the priestess from earlier entered the little clearing with its fountain. Her face was a mask of rage as she approached the man nearest to her, holding her hand up as he clutched at his ears.

"Those such as you do not deserve to live," was all she said as she cast upon him.

It was not as explosive as her previous spell. It didn't need to be to have a profound effect though. I didn't think her target could scream, but his face said all it needed to about the agony that passed through him with the purple light she sent his way. It took a few seconds for him to die. When she finished, there was little more than a pile of organic goo left behind.

Added to my note to practice suppressing my aura was another to never truly piss off a priest. They were terrifying when they let loose.

The final man was trying to rise from the ground. He had been the one to tell the others to stop, so he might not die quite as horribly as the first two. Judging by the look on the young priestess's face though, he was still absolutely going to die. He crawled away as she came nearer and nearer to the man.

A small figure emerged from the bushes in front of him, looking down. The man looked upward. I'm not sure what was going through the mind of the mana-eater as its void-like eyes met those of the would-be killer, but for whatever reason, it made an errant swipe with an arm, and his head turned with a sickening crunch, body falling lifeless to the ground.

"Oh, shit," the priestess said.

"Oh, shit," I agreed.

The mana-eater looked up toward us. It had taken quite the beating. One of Armina's arms was gone, only a stub remained. Her dress was in tatters, bits and pieces ripped, cut, and torn away by whatever battle it had been in before finding us. Even its face was marred to bare recognition as it turned and stared at each of us, as if looking for the next thing it would call its meal.

"I do not believe we were done yet, young lady. Wherever have your manners gone?" the large man in the silver jacket said as he strode out behind the mana-eater, a sword raised high above his head.

I would have to learn silver jacket guy's name, because he was something else. He was turning and slashing as he went blow for blow against what was formerly Armina. The mana-eater was terrifyingly fast, and it seemed to take less damage than I would suspect from the few slashes that landed.

I fell back a bit as did Dietrich and the priestess. The girl we'd tried to help seemed to still be in shock and was staring at the pair of combatants with saucer eyes. She held tight to the young faith caster, seeming to tremble as she did so.

"You lot, fire, non-magical variety!" the man yelled as he ducked under a blow, the hand grazing his hair.

I looked at the other two to see if they had any ideas. The priestess looked at a loss. Dietrich, for all he wanted to help, immediately tried to light the grass with magic, a failing idea if ever there was one. The boy had a good heart, but he was perhaps not the brightest in the world.

This was complete crap. Where were we supposed to get something that could burn? If only I had a flamethrower, napalm, or heck even a Molotov cocktail . . . Wait that could work, maybe. I knew it well enough. I'd seen it made, tried it, smelled it, had it spilled on me. I even knew the formula from some nerdy T-shirt a friend had worn once.

"Burning summoned things okay!" I screamed as my idea took shape, feeling it all come together in my head. I felt so stupid, I should have thought of this years ago.

"Yes!"

"Get me a shot then." I brought my hands up and began to cast. I even knew the song to go along with it. Luckily, the translation was so simple I could do it on the fly.

"What do you do with a drunken . . ." As he kicked the mana-eater back, I forced as much mana into the spell as I could. This close to the monster it wasn't easy, but a spray of clear liquid flew forward, just like it had with the water. It even looked like water, not much more than would come out of a rather anemic hose, but a good spray for me, nonetheless.

"Fire, you idiot girl, not water!" Those words were followed by my call of "early in the morning" and a small spark woven into my spell.

I should have anticipated how energetic the fire would have been. I did not and found that it sent me diving for cover as everything in front of it just ignited. The blue flame seemed to travel almost instantly up the whole stream and onto the confused mana-eater, turning yellow-orange as it left the flow of alcohol.

I wanted to laugh at all the people who'd told me bards couldn't do combat magic, but it really wasn't the time. The creature screamed as it tried to backpedal, only to hit a bush. It was hurt, but by no means out of the fight yet. The little monstrosity was some other kind of durable.

That did mark the turning point though. While the monster charged, slashed, and dodged, the fire both injured and seemed to slow it down. I could now just keep my eyes on its movements as the man cut chunk after chunk away until finally managing to defeat the beast after several tense passes with his blade.

All of us currently alive in the little clearing by the fountain took a second to gaze at the burning corpse and the fire that was still going hot right near it. The man kicked the creature's body into the flames and looked at us after confirming that the beast moved no more.

"Can any of you heal?"

"I can," the priestess and I chorused.

"Good, come." It took her a second to convince the viscera-covered young woman to hold on to Dietrich instead, and I struggled for breath from the running and spell improvisation, a draining feat at the very best of times.

We passed a number of the dead on our way back. There were more young people here who'd lost their lives than I'd care to admit. We did stop to check those who lived, finding mostly survivable wounds. Once or twice, the priestess stopped at a person casting a quick healing spell to stabilize them before moving on. I was nearly out of mana and so let her take the brunt of the work as we headed toward the manor.

When we got there, we found a bloodbath. There had been perhaps two hundred people who were supposed to be at the manor, counting servants and non-casters. Of that, I guessed that perhaps half had perished. Most of the men had gallantly thrown themselves at the creature to buy us time and whatever injuries on it they could. They had taken the highest toll.

I found Jackson struggling to stand, a woman helping him move from person to person so he could heal them to stability. He'd taken what looked to be a hit to the ribs and just managed to keep his casting going. He nodded and pointed to the side of the carnage furthest from himself, telling me where to go first.

I found Lord Johannes and Rieg, bent down and holding Armond. The boy had taken a crossbow shot to the gut and looked as if he might die any second.

"Hold on, Son, the healer will be here any second, just hold on." The man wept as he held his child. His twin seemed unable to form words.

I stumbled to their side and began to cast, though I had to ask both father and brother to sing with me so that I could even do that much. I was running on fumes as I struggled to close up his wound. It seemed to take longer than it should have, but eventually it was enough and I could tell he would survive.

I had to drag Rieg with me after explaining that his brother would live and I needed his help. Dietrich had taken over helping the priestess as best he could, applying pressure to wounds and finding the most injured. When he'd come over before, his father had waved him off, pointing at the other girl without breaking from the song I'd had him singing.

As I worked on the next person, a group of men in full armor arrived, charging forward into the carnage as they looked for the source. I saw that a few of them had paused to process it all, before returning to action as they looked around.

"You lot, you're late. Send your fastest man to the Shield. Tell them the fighting is over and we need help here as fast as possible. Most of the victims are noncombatants. The rest of you, scour the grounds for enemies and hiding partygoers, particularly the injured."

"Yes, sir, Lord Fallon!" I'd finally learned silver jacket man's name. It seemed a bit odd to me that the knights obeyed him without any hesitation, but I was happy about it.

I finished up with my second patient and was having Rieg help me up to my feet when a hand fell onto my shoulder. "Cease casting for now, girl.

You've reached your limit." It was the old man who'd blown the wall off of the building. He was the same man who had an aura that was so bright it was unpleasant to look at.

"There are still people hurt," I said, objecting to his order.

His face was kindly, but his voice firm and commanding.

"If you overreach, you will do nothing but knock yourself out. At which point, you will be unable to do anything for longer than if you just rest. So you will rest, and when you've gotten enough of your mana back to be useful again, you will return to helping. Trust me on this, young lady."

I really wanted to fight against his judgment, if only because he was annoyingly patronizing. He was right though. I was on my last legs and before long would be out cold on the floor. With that in mind, I let him lead me over to a seat by the bar after I said, "Fine, I'll take a break."

"Drink something while you wait. It will help."

Shortly thereafter, he went to make the same declaration to the priestess. She'd had more mana to work with than I had on the healing and was working far faster through patients. I suppose she must have actually been around thirteen and not a reincarnated girl, because after a few comments I couldn't catch on his part, she began loudly telling him to mind his own business.

So he did, and after she'd finished with her next patient, she fell over unconscious. He floated her over to the bar where I was sitting, feeling like a dunce. After putting her down on the floor, the old man looked me over again.

"Stabilize three more, then another break. You two are still too young to keep it up like this. Good job though."

The knights had started organizing the injured while I was benched, and it was easy to find who I needed to work on next. Even as I started, a few priests arrived to help with the carnage, a most welcome sight. They could do far more than I could in the same amount of time and with the same effort.

When I'd done my three and returned, I found the young priestess just starting to wake.

"Ow. Who are you, and why am I on the floor?"

"Alana, and because you over-pulled on your mana and knocked yourself out." I knelt down beside her, knowing how unpleasant it was to have someone stand over you.

"Oh! I've got to . . ." she began as she tried to rise.

"Relax, a bunch of people arrived and are taking care of it." I put a hand on her shoulder lightly to guide her back down to the floor.

"All right then, I'll rest a bit if it's okay." It was not really okay, but she'd only be getting in the way. Regardless, she let me guide her back to a prone position. "I'm Kala by the way." I grabbed a cushion from one of the bar chairs for her head and sat with her for a few moments in silence.

The priests had everything well in hand by the time I returned to assist. Kala had passed back out, proving the old man right, much to my chagrin. I spent the rest of the night trying to patch up people as best I could until Lord Fallon gathered up Kala, Dietrich, and myself so he could converse with the old man, whose name I still didn't know.

"All right, care to explain what happened before I arrived?" the man asked as we went into a side room.

I finally got a good chance to look over Lord Fallon. He was well muscled and tall, seeming to loom over others. If I had to guess, I'd say his age was mid-fifties, but it was a bit hard to tell. His hair was dark with a few specks of gray seeping in here and there.

"A handful of men were attempting to rape a woman. I intervened. That was probably what got the mana-eater's attention." Kala was rather straightforward and to the point on that.

"I saw, and I saw what was left of them, not that anyone will complain." He turned from her to Dietrich and me. "You two, how'd you end up in the middle of that?"

"We were hiding nearby and also decided to intervene." Dietrich nodded along with my explanation, seeming satisfied with it.

"All right, fair enough. The guards will want to have a look and ask a few more questions, but that's most of what I need to know."

"Lord Fallon said you used some kind of liquid fire against the mana-eater. Could you explain that to me, please?" the old man finally asked from where he stood nearby.

I had to stop and consider this. Mystien had been very clear about me sharing secrets. That said, I didn't think a no would be well received. I needed to think carefully about how this could be abused, or used, by others, and if it was too valuable to explain. Or rather how I could explain it in such a way as to not have it be too big a deal.

"Um . . . that was just liquor. I summoned liquor onto it and lit it up."

"Liquor? Like . . . whiskey?"

"Yeah, it burns if you get the strong stuff."

"Huh, I'll make some notes on that. Did someone teach you to do that?"

"No, I kind of made it up on the fly. Wasn't even sure it'd work."

"I'll have some of the bards I know try it out. I'm not sure how good a combat spell it would be, but knowing that it could fight a monster like that will be helpful. Shame, food and drinks are a bard's domain, except water of course." He seemed disappointed. That was good, because a wizard definitely could summon ethanol, and I decidedly didn't want to see what kind of fires they could make with it. "Your name was Alana, was it not?"

I nodded at his last question, hoping I didn't get any more attention than I already had.

CHAPTER 8

◆

LIGHT SPYING AND THE WALK

The knights and guardsmen did indeed have a few more questions. They wanted to go over the whole incident about three times with me. It seemed they were interested in how I'd been invited to the party, by whom, who I had come with, where I had been for the attack, and particularly how many and who of the attackers I'd seen. I didn't get the feeling they suspected me of anything; they just seemed to want as much information about everything as they could get.

The whole thing took a couple of hours, and we were only a few from sunrise as they finally finished. One of them, a man with the distinct look of a father, took me back to my comfy corner to rest while they finished up with Jackson, apologizing for how long everything was taking. Seems that having actually been attacked by the monster, and survived, he had much more they were interested in.

I lay down in a quiet corner near Kala and nearly fell asleep. As I waited, I saw two figures I recognized come in the open wall and start looking around. One of them took a few moments to speak to the priests who were present, the other the guards. Following that, they met back up and walked toward the back, where one of the entry halls used to be.

Physically, I was exhausted; mentally, I wanted to sleep. That said, I wanted to know what those two were doing together and what all was going on. My mana had partially recharged so I hummed a few lines to toss up invisibility, then another to silence everything below my ears and followed after them.

They walked past the guards at the door the mana-eater had destroyed and into the hallway beyond. I hadn't come back here, but the old man,

Lord Fallon, and Lord Johannes were already there, along with several corpses in a rough circle and a small ceramic jar.

"So this is where it started then?" Emil said as he slid in, moving to the side as he looked at the scene.

"We believe so, though it's pretty likely most of the carriages were disabled and their drivers killed first. This is at least where they released the mana-eater." Lord Fallon shook his head. "Not that I know where in the world they even got such a thing."

"The host?" Emil inquired.

"A merchant girl named Armina, well liked. Appalling that they would choose one so young to act as its host." Lord Johannes looked like he was about to puke at the thought. "My guess is they thought it might cause a bit of hesitation on our part; nobody wants to put down a child."

"This is an absolute mess. It could have been much, much worse though. I'm truly glad the creature was defeated so quickly, and you have my personal thanks, Lord Fallon." The spymaster seemed genuine here. "As for the host, I'll see what I can do for her family. I imagine His Majesty will be livid on what has happened, and I'll finally be able to go in hard against the few rebel cells I've been investigating."

"That is not as much of a concern for me as where they got a mana-eater, Emil." The old man seemed a bit irritated at his unconcern with that.

"That is something I can actually answer. They stole it from us; it was taken about a month ago while en route to its destruction." That admission brought shock to every face.

"You were keeping a monster like that!?" This was the first thing Bishop Theodore had actually said since coming here. "Are you mad?"

"No to both of those. It was brought by one of the fleeing imperial leaders. He wanted to trade it to us for sanctuary. A true shame that he had a fatal accident on the way there." Emil sighed like he was discussing a tragedy. "So my men took it in; we were transporting it to a hidden sight where it could be killed without posing a danger to anyone when the storage vessel was stolen." He pointed to the jar, covered top to bottom in runes.

"Why was nobody told about this?" Lord Fallon scowled down at the man. I wouldn't want that look turned on me after seeing what he could do.

"Operational security. I can tell you now because though we failed, we were honestly trying to protect everyone. None of us are fool enough to try and use a mana-eater, not that the king would permit it even if we were."

Lord Johannes found a place and sat. "That is too much. There's no way a bunch of peasant and city-folk rebels could have found out about all of that and managed it."

"I agree; they had help," the snake-like man said, nodding.

"Perhaps the man who took over the empire? I've only heard a few rumors, but perhaps . . ."

Both the spymaster and the bishop shook their heads.

"He has respected all of the orders up until this point. Provided assurances and even took great care not to harm civilians. This does not match his actions so far," Theodore said.

"I agree. My reports indicate clean, precise strikes against the empire. This . . . this is messy. Killing a bunch of noncombatants at a party? Potentially releasing a dangerous beast? No, that does not match at all what I've seen. If this were one of his operations, I think we'd see a lot of dead soldiers, potentially with a spectacular show to go along with it."

"Then who?" Lord Fallon asked.

"I don't know. I can tell you why, General. It's well-known that you always attend your cousin's parties." He looked pointedly at the other man. "If I find out who though, rest assured that they will not enjoy it."

"It nearly succeeded too. If things had been not perfectly so, I'd be dead." The warrior now had a bit of a tired look.

"But it didn't. Now, gentlemen, if there's not anything else. I understand we managed to capture a few of the conspirators, and I, for one, would like to have a long . . ."

"Conversation?" the old man helpfully interjected.

"Torture session, a nice, long torture session with them." With that declaration, the man left, ostensibly to go hurt people.

"Most of the healing is done, but I'm off to check on the priests. Make sure they're all taken care of."

"My continued presence here seems to be putting you in danger. So, my friends, I think I shall head back home."

Lord Johannes looked to the old man. "If you'd like a place to rest, I'll do all I can to arrange it, though things are a bit of a mess now."

"Not quite yet. I'd like to have a bit more time with this containment vessel, not something I get to take a look at every day."

"As you wish. Inform one of my staff when you're done. I should see to the others who are still here." With that, the owner of the house left. Within a few seconds, the hall was quiet, and it was just me and the old man.

"I know you're there. Come on out."

I dropped my spells, allowing myself to be seen. I was still a bit shell-shocked by seeing all that had gone on.

"That was dangerous, Alana. Why did you think it was a good idea to come and spy on us?"

"Why didn't you tell them I was there?"

"Because it would have made them angry and not really changed much. Also I don't think you had anything to do with releasing this creature. I'd like an answer though."

"I recognized the bishop and spymaster and was hoping they wouldn't talk about me."

"From where?"

"The Shield considers me one of its wards, even if I disagree. I met the spy after someone had an assassination attempt on them. What makes you so sure that I didn't have anything to do with it? Not that I did."

"Because if you'd wanted Lord Fallon dead, all you had to do was flee instead of help him."

"Who are you?"

The old man chuckled. "You seem to like being secretive, so I think I'll hold off on letting you know that just yet, young lady. Know that if you try to spy on me again, I'll take it rather more personally though. Now I'd suggest you go back to where you were before young Dietrich comes looking for you."

I sighed. "I kind of liked him, but he's not very bright, is he?"

"No, he isn't. Rather charming though, isn't he? You're delaying, so go on now."

I clenched my jaw. Disobeying just to disobey would be stupid, and from the look he was giving me, might cause me more trouble than it was worth. I still hated that he was telling me to go.

"I don't like being told what to do. It's even worse because I have to keep going on with it."

"My dear, I already knew you were a bard, but if you don't like having to deal with some people, just don't. If they don't like it, tell them to go away. That's what's always worked best for me."

I pouted but began singing my spells back into place. Redoing all of this was costing me even more mana, but afterward I went back to my place beside Kala. She was still out cold as I relaxed and drifted off for a bit.

* * *

I woke up only a couple of hours later as the sun lit everything up. Most everyone had left by now except a few of the guards who were keeping an eye on the damaged house and one or two other casters who'd similarly fallen asleep from the work they'd been doing.

Dietrich was standing nearby, saying my name rather gently. "Alana, you really should wake up, I believe your tutor is currently talking to Father."

That got my eyes open. "About what?"

"Father wanted to thank the both of you for helping save so many people. The young woman beside you too."

"Mmm, leave me out of this," the priestess said as she rubbed her eyes. It would appear I was not the only disturbed from my rest.

"Well, if you wish, there's food, and I can arrange for rooms too. I don't know how things are with our guest quarters right now, but I will figure something out."

"That won't be necessary; we're going to be returning home." I was saved as Jackson appeared. His clothes were stained and torn in a few places, and he looked like he needed to rest in a bad way.

"My apologies then, Dietrich, but I think I shall be off. What of you, Kala?"

She rubbed her eyes again, looking about. "Oh, my escort for the night . . . didn't make it."

"Would you like to come with us then? We're heading out anyway."

She blinked. "Very well, it's that or go back with the Shield. Personally, I find them a bit stiff."

I offered her a hand, and the two of us headed out toward the exit. Jackson looked a bit exasperated as he followed; the poor noble boy didn't seem to be able to say anything at all.

It took me a few seconds to realize that the driver and horse were dead. We did find the carriage though, with a few nicks and the like in it.

"I bet we could ask Lord Johannes to . . ." Jackson began.

"Nope! I do not want any more 'debts' to him or any other noble. I will walk." Then I looked at Kala, realizing we couldn't give her a ride anymore.

She snorted. "You know, I kind of like that idea better anyway."

After smiling to her, I dove into the carriage to get my normal clothes. They were expensive to buy and I wasn't leaving them.

"I got some great advice last night."

"Oh? What's that? And from whom?"

"Some old guy, and it boils down to this. If you don't want to deal with people, tell them to get stuffed. By the way, you're going to be the one telling Marcus about the dress and dealing with the fallout, since you insisted that I come along and all that." I thought for a few more seconds. "Also, no more balls for me."

"I'm fairly sure that this incident killed the entire lineup for the year."

"Unsurprising."

The three of us walked down the streets in fully destroyed party regalia. We got all the looks that one might expect, but no guards who were on patrol decided to say anything. My guess was that they had been told something, or just didn't want to mess with a group of "nobles." Whatever it was, I was pleased by it.

As we left the nobles' section of the city, I heard Kala's stomach growl. Mine shortly joined her in agreement.

"Perhaps we should have gotten some food on our way out," she observed.

"Screw that. Jackson, you have any idea on drinks?" I said as I began to sing some sandwich-sized rolls and some cheese into existence.

With a sigh, he looked around. I'd apparently disturbed some deep thinking from the man. After a few seconds, he turned, went into a nearby store and came back out minutes later with a bottle of wine, which he promptly drank half of.

"Here, water it down. It's a bit early for drinking." He retreated back into whatever he was doing, drifting away from the two of us enough so that he was just keeping an eye on us.

I watered down the wine, and we passed it back and forth as we munched on our food.

"Is this what being a bard is like? Telling people that they can screw off while drinking watered wine at breakfast might be the most original way I've ever started my day. Could do without all the death though." I nearly spat out the drink at Kala's question.

"The death is pretty uncommon. As for the rest of it . . . I don't know, this is the first time I've done it," I coughed out.

"You're handling seeing so many die remarkably well. Most of the girls I know would be having a breakdown right now."

"My home was destroyed during the war. I've seen bad things before. How about you? How're you holding up?"

"When I first manifested my magic, I was near the battle lines. I ended up staying at one of the hospitals the Shield sets up for a few months, so I've seen worse."

The two of us decided not to dig into each other's pasts more than that and quietly walked for a bit. After a bit of consultation, Jackson and I decided to stop by the Starlit Sky before taking Kala home. It was somewhere we could actually take a break and get some real food.

CHAPTER 9

✦

A RELAXING BATH

The only people at the Starlit Sky when we got there were Luda and Lucien, something which I was grateful for. Partially because the latter was gazing daggers at everyone as we came in. While Jackson was getting the brunt of it, I was not spared the angry looks as I entered into the tavern.

"You were supposed to be back by midnight, not midday the next," was the first thing that came out of Lucien's mouth. It occurred to me that I was currently supposed to be at work.

"Er . . . sorry about that, Lucien. We got attacked and a lot of people . . ."

"I wasn't talking to you, girl. Jackson was supposed to be the more responsible of the two of you and make sure you got back safely."

"A monster attacked the party. You have my sincere apologies, but both Alana and I were needed for healing the injured guests." For once, Jackson didn't seem to want to give any lip. He was calm and contrite.

"How bad?"

"Bad, something called a mana-eater. It killed . . . around half of the people there."

"I've heard stories of um, but never seen one. Are either of you hurt?" The explanation took the wind out of Lucien's rage. He still seemed mad, but more controlled.

"We're fine, I got hurt a bit, but I don't think Alana got more than a few bruises." He looked at me questioningly.

"I'm fine. Jackson joined the men holding the monster back while we ran. A lot more things happened, but he did his best." The older man frowned, but nodded.

"And who are you? A priestess of . . . the Order of the Lovers?" Kala nodded. "Bit young, isn't she?" he mumbled at her confirmation.

Kala ignored his comment. "Yes, I'm Kala. Alana and I worked to help with the healing too."

"Well, you three look terrible. Go wash up, and I'll have some food when you're done. Lunch is stew today. Alana, you're taking the day off to rest. Though I'll want some explanations on things from you later."

"Okay," I chimed as I led Kala back to one of our open rooms, stopping by mine to grab one of my dresses and a towel for her.

The room was fairly simple, but I knew that this one had a washtub under the bed. It should be fine to use it so long as I cleaned it up later. Otherwise, there was a rather more simple bed and a small desk. The oil lamp wasn't kept filled, but that was an easy fix, and soon the little room was lit brightly. I hummed a few tunes for lighting the lamp and filling the tub, turning to talk with Kala as the hot water flowed. Getting it up to temperature was easy with my warming spell, something I'd been doing ever since I realized I could warm the water.

"Sorry if it's not all that fancy, but it's what we've got."

"Um . . . is that water hot?" she asked excitedly.

"Yes . . ."

"Is that a joke? We almost never get hot baths at the temple. It takes forever to heat the water. The best I get is lukewarm or maybe a pitcher or hot water to pour on myself." As she spoke, she began taking off her robes and putting them on the bed.

I thought back to my time in Istlan. That seemed to check out for orphans, but for priests too? "I thought that the temple would at least have hot water for priests."

"There are magical items that can do that, but priest magic can't, and spending that much money and mana on something just for warm baths? It's not really responsible so far as the temple is concerned, so they don't."

"But what about winter? Cold water could really mess you up."

"We can warm our bodies and keep sickness away easy. Heating water on the other hand requires tools, lots of fuel, or another caster. Um . . . sorry I didn't ask, do you mind if I go first?" At this point, she was down to her underwear, folding the other pieces and putting them to the side.

"Huh? I'm going to go bathe in my room. This one's all yours."

"Isn't that super wasteful?"

"I've been casting both water creation and warming spells since I was like . . . I don't know, four, so they cost me almost nothing now."

She gave me a bit of a look of confusion.

"The more you practice something, the easier it gets, right?"

"I guess . . ." Kala answered as she finished undressing and stepped into the tub, sitting down. It wasn't large, or deep, only about knee height and a few feet circular, but she could at least soak a bit.

"So . . . if you focus on some things a lot before moving on, you get better at them. At least that's what my first teacher taught me. He had me practice the same spell over and over until it was easy. Making water is basically free to me; heating it a bit less so, but it's not hard or mana-intensive."

"This is heavenly." She sighed as the warmth set in, steam filling the room slowly. I handed her the pitcher kept in the room so she could pour over herself if she wanted. "I wish I could do bardic magic."

"It's nice for things like this, but I can't pop a man like a bubble or stuff like that."

"Well . . . normally, I can't either. They have to be like really evil for me to conjure up that kind of power against them."

"Weird, anyway, I'll see you in a bit." She gave me a smile and a wave as I stood and headed out, satisfied that she'd be okay.

My own bath was extremely relaxing as well. There simply was nothing like hot water and clean clothes to refresh you after a long period of hard, messy work. I even took the time to soak for a bit. By the time I came back, Jackson was already at the bar going over the night's events in flowery words with an increasingly worried-looking Lucien.

"Where's the priestess?" the older man asked.

"Taking a bath. I imagine she'll be there until the water goes cold. Did you know they don't have a setup for priests to take hot baths?"

"I didn't. Anyway, I've heard Jackson's part of the story. What happened after the two of you got split up?"

"Um . . . okay, so, Dietrich pulled me out after the wizard blew the wall off the ballroom, and we hid after escaping from some men with crossbows."

"Dietrich being the noble boy who thinks he wants to marry you?"

"Yeah. So, as we were hiding, we saw some men catch a girl, and it looked like they were going to do some rather unpleasant things to her. Before Dietrich or I could get a good shot in on them, Kala blew up one of them. Some things happened, and the mana-eater showed up."

That got me some raised eyebrows from both men. It occurred to me that even Jackson hadn't heard all of the goings-on.

"Right as the mana-eater showed up, this guy named Lord Fallon arrived, and he fought it. I hit it with a new spell I made. Oh! I need to show that to you two; it's really cool and useful."

"Back to the point, Alana," Lucien said with a sigh.

"And he killed it. Then we went back and healed as many people as we could."

"What's the new spell of yours do?" Jackson asked as he was given a bowl of stew and started to dig in.

"It makes a spray of flaming liquid." I smiled as he nearly choked on his food.

"That's . . . important. Did you tell anyone about it?"

"Some old guy. It didn't look like I was going to have much of a choice on that though."

That got me sighs of exasperation. "Alana, did you at least get his name?"

"He refused to tell me."

"You're going to kill me, child," Lucien said, looking rather disappointed.

I shrugged. I wasn't even sure if another bard would be able to manage the spell fully with what I'd given him, or what I'd give these two. I did consider telling Lucien the deeper parts of it, but that would just raise a lot of questions that I didn't want to answer.

About that time, Kala returned looking deeply satisfied. She sat down and was fed a bowl of stew on the house. Lucien said it was for helping save people, but I suspected he was just feeling generous. I hoped that they would all get along, but regardless it was good to have a friend who wasn't a guy. I had lots of questions about her order, too, but those could wait for later.

Once we'd had a proper meal, I set off with Kala back to her home. I'd asked if she wanted to come with us, so I felt it would be wrong to just send her off. Jackson, on the other hand, had to go deal with the fallout of the previous night, talking to the rental people about the destroyed products and their dead employees. I didn't envy him that. But as the "adult," it was his responsibility.

The walk back to the temple district was pleasant. News about last night hadn't spread, so everyone was just going about their days as normal. It was good, really good to see normal people going about their business. It reminded me of how things would be fine in the end, no matter how crazy they got sometimes.

"I am *not* looking forward to my conversation with the head priestess," Kala said as we got near.

"Pfft, how bad could it be? You are fine, and you did a really good job. Basically, you spent your night being excellent. Even if you are a bit late coming home."

"She can be a little . . . traditional? Hmm, that's not quite right. She'll be mad that I didn't send word earlier, and probably have something to say about me taking my time to get back."

"Well, well, well, dear, I'm glad that you already understand." A rather matronly voice came from behind us.

We turned to find several priests. I had never seen four in any one place except perhaps at the Shield's temple in the capital. Kala's eyes nearly bugged out seeing them all arrayed there, with several non-caster staff aiding them.

"You know, I just got back from a rather urgent meeting about the party you went to last night, Apprentice Kala."

"I'm not surprised, it was . . . an interesting affair, Head Priestess."

"I'll be expecting a full report on it and your activities later. Who is the young girl with you?"

"Hello, ma'am, I'm Alana."

"A pleasure. Now, if you'll excuse us." I waved to my new friend as her order swept her off.

As they passed, I recognized the priestess who had given me my mark. She nodded at me as she went. I wasn't sure, but that looked to be a huge part of their order here in the capital, whatever the priests were going through now seemed rather significant.

I didn't even make it to the end of the block before I was approached by a familiar figure. The priestess my friends and I had gotten into a fight with stepped out in front of me, blocking my way. She looked . . . cross.

"Good morning, Alana. Bishop Theodore wishes to have words with you."

"I kind of expected that. Sadly, I have a busy, busy schedule today and must be on with it." I turned to step around her.

"You may come along the nice way, or you may come along the not nice way, but you will be coming with me. It will look much better for you if you come along nicely though."

I briefly considered introducing her to my brand-new flamethrower. I stopped myself, if only by a hair. It was too mana-intensive. I was alone on a whole street full of apparently pissed-off priests, and I could always light her up later. There were a few tense moments where the two of us stared at each other. Then I relaxed my posture a bit.

"Good choice. I believe you know the way?"

CHAPTER 10

✦

ANOTHER MEETING

The walk back to Bishop Theodore's office was silent. It seemed every-one had their hackles raised, and the priestess behind me wasn't really helping. I knew that she was waiting for me to give her a reason to drop me and just haul me off, and I was just waiting for a chance to see her jump off a cliff.

Eventually, I did find my way back to the bishop's office. The man himself wasn't there when I arrived, but I found myself a seat while my erstwhile companion stood behind me. It seemed she didn't trust me for some reason—like I'd attack her or something silly like that.

After a few minutes of waiting, a very tired, and again, quite cross-looking bishop arrived.

"There are literally tens of thousands of children in this city and, you, I am sure, are the largest headache."

"Good day to you too, Bishop."

"I understand you were at a ball that was attacked last night."

"I was."

"Where a number of people died rather violently."

"Yes, that is correct, Bishop."

"Our order was called to come and assist."

"I'm aware. I was healing people as best I could. I even saw you arrive."

"And you didn't come to say hello? I'm a bit hurt." The last bit was so dripping with sarcasm that I was actually surprised. Normally, he was just a smug jerk.

"You looked busy. What exactly can I help you with today, Bishop? Your . . . assistant? Was quite insistent that I come and meet with you."

That designation got me a nice sound of grinding teeth from behind. It was probably stupid to harass her, but . . .

"Good, I'm happy to get to the point. You remember our last conversation, yes? How I told you that, if I felt the need, we would be reevaluating your living situation? Well, based on last night's events, I believe we must now consider that."

"Explain your reasoning."

"I do not need to explain myself to you, Alana."

"You do if you want me to live under your nose without me setting said nose on fucking fire." The air could be cut with a knife. I knew they could and would, if needed, drop me as did they. But we all also knew that eventually I'd get back up, and when I did, I wouldn't be coming at them straight.

"Very well, you have now been at the site of an attempted assassination."

"Which I was decidedly not the target of."

"Involving extremely dangerous magic."

"Also not my fault."

"Your current guardians have even failed to keep you from such danger."

"That is a patently ludicrous accusation. No reasonable person would have expected an attack at a ball. Even if you were to tell me that you could, I wouldn't believe you. Because there was a priestess of my approximate age there as well. If the adults with me were being irresponsible, you need to go bother the Order of the Lovers about their foolishness too. I'm betting you won't." He was getting a little eye twitch. I knew I could win this argument if I could just keep him from coming down without explanation.

"Alana, I know you dislike me. Will you at least believe that I wish for your safety?"

"Dislike is a weak word, Bishop. You threw some of my most private business in front of my friends in a blatant attempt to embarrass me. I believe that you think you are doing what is best, but I also believe that you are a petty little tyrant and completely wrong."

He spent several minutes staring at me, thrumming his fingers on his desk. I could tell he was thinking, going over arguments and ideas in his head. I would wait; this was a game where I needed to bide my time and respond to whatever he came up with.

"There are so many things that I cannot tell you right now, Alana. If you but knew, you might agree to work with me, but you might also go and put yourself in even more danger. When you come of age, I will tell you."

"That explanation is just evasive and will not convince me."

"I'm aware. You wish to go to the academy next fall, yes?"

"I don't see what that has to do with anything."

"As one of the wards of the Shield, I can provide for your education. As a matter of point, we do have an agreement with the academy to have our spellcasting-capable wards attend if they show enough skill and can pass the entry exams. I've no worries that you shall do so."

"Are you trying to bribe me into staying at your orphanage?"

"That would be ideal, yes, but I'm wagering that you won't."

"You're quite right." I said as I nodded to the bishop.

"How about this then? We'll make arrangements for you to be paid for *if* you agree to stay at the dormitories there and have one of the professors appointed as your guardian while you attend. Until that point though, I want someone to be able to openly keep an eye on you who I trust as a responsible adult. They would basically be acting as your guardian until you go."

Now, it was my turn to think. That was not a bad deal and would make paying for school a non-issue. I had a few questions, but I thought there might be a chance we could come to some arrangement. Even Lucien had suggested that if they came to me with some reasonable compromise, I'd listen.

"I have some questions." When the bishop made a gesture for me to continue, I began asking. "Who would you be assigning to keep an eye on me until I attend? How would you have someone keeping an eye on me openly? How would the professor who would be appointed as my guardian be chosen?"

"Valid questions. While I would like to have a priest keep an eye on you due to your magic that is simply not feasible, so it would be one of the members of our staff. We would need to make arrangements for them to live with or near you, and you would have to interact with them often. As for what professor, I believe that generally a volunteer is sought, or if none is available someone is assigned randomly."

I already knew at least one person I thought would jump at the idea of having me as his charge. Not sure how I felt about that, but I liked him more than I liked Theodore, that much was certain. The rest didn't seem too egregious.

"Why are you spending this much time and money on me?" He was really bending over backward here. Even if he was supposed to keep me safe, this was just a bit insane.

"I have my reasons. Not the least of which is that you are a rather more potent than average caster with a habit of making . . . shall we say 'interesting' spells." He stared hard at me. "I think you have potential, young lady. Will you take my deal? Or shall we see how this ends if you don't?" The threat hung there for a few moments while we stared at each other.

"I will; try to find someone with less a stick up their ass than you. It would also be nice if they could play an instrument, as I think we'll be spending quite a bit of our winter playing at the Starlit Sky."

I could see the eye twitch, but he seemed to relax a bit. "I'll see what I can do, Alana. I really do not enjoy these meetings. So I will ask you to *not* cause any more problems, or get involved in any large-scale disasters until you've come of age. Or at the very least are attending the academy."

"I'll do my very best," I replied in a saccharine sweet voice while making my brightest smile.

After the irksome girl removed herself from my office and I could get back to the paperwork that needed to be done, I heard a slight cough. The now full priestess seemed a bit irked at me.

"Bishop, you can't let yourself be bullied by a child."

"Oh? How did she bully me?"

"Getting you to pay for her education, all of the kindnesses you're showing letting her stay at that tavern."

"Well, first thing, I have received no less than three requests to see to it that she attends that academy from those who have both the interest in her to know that she's one of our wards and the power to push a scholarship through. I bribed her with something she could have gotten without me. I got a full report on how last night she might have influenced bardic combat magic more significantly than we've seen in decades. That alone would qualify her," I chuckled. "Secondly, I will choose who keeps an eye on her. Did you know that Eleanor plays the harp? If anyone can both whip that girl into some semblance of shape and keep her out of trouble, she will be the one."

"Sir, Eleanor, that's just . . . a bit mean. You're right though . . ."

I nodded and began filling out all the needed paperwork.

When I finally made my way back to the Starlit Sky I was greeted to even more interrogation by my two teachers. First of all, I had to give a full demonstration of my new flamethrower. Both of them were nearly floored, as was I. The mana cost on that was still somewhere near my absolute limit. They made a couple of tries but got nothing nearly as effective.

Then I had to explain about my deal to Lucien. After I finished with the overview, he nodded.

"So, when should we be expecting your new guardian to show up?"

"I don't know. Tonight or tomorrow I guess?"

"You really need to learn to ask more questions. Will they be renting a room to stay here?"

"No idea."

"Come on, don't give me that look. I got a good deal at least!"

"I'll give you that. You at least managed to keep most of what you wanted. You're not being forced to live at the orphanage, and you've gotten school paid for. Were you going to stay at their dorms anyway?"

"I don't know . . . That would have depended on the cost. Dras is, and it will be far more convenient anyway, I suppose. Do you think the professor they assign to keep an eye on me will be a problem?"

"I don't know. Some of those types can be a little single-minded. They normally are safe people though and know a lot about magic. Anyway, first thing tomorrow you need to prep a room. Won't hurt anything if we end up not needing it. One of the ones down near you will probably be best."

"Okay, I'll make sure it's ready."

Bright and early the next day, I picked the room just to the left of mine and began cleaning. By time for breakfast, I was well assured that it was ready with fresh sheets, no dust, and everything just in its place.

As I was eating the mix of leftovers from dinner and warm bread, she appeared. The woman was middle-aged, with lines around her mouth and a rather large case for a harp. An older boy helped bring her luggage in and stood back as she marched up to me where I sat at the bar.

"I suppose you must be Alana, then?"

"I am."

"Good, I'm Eleanor. Know that I've been told you're a right handful, and I'll be having none of it. Now, where is our room?"

"There's one ready for you right beside mine. You'll need to talk to Lucien first though."

"That won't do at all. We'll need to stay together if I'm to keep an eye on you, no?"

CHAPTER 11

✦

THE IRRITANT

Eleanor seemed determined to be a pain in my neck. First she wanted us to stay in the same room, insisted upon it vehemently. Of course, because I was currently working, that meant I had to clean another room. I also had to go get all of my things and move them in, not that I actually owned all that much. Other than a few large pieces, most of my possessions could fit in a carry-able bag.

She complained about the size of the room, how it wasn't large enough for people to live in long-term. Of course, it wasn't really meant for people to stay in long-term, but that memo never seemed to land. Once I was done unpacking, she began with the questions.

"Is that all?"

"Pretty much."

"What about winter preparations?"

"Um?"

"Food, extra blankets, extra fuel for lamps, and the like!"

"You do know I'm a bard, right?"

"And?"

"I eat at the Starlit Sky when I'm working. When I'm not, I have simple meals of bread and cheese; sometimes I'll buy some dried nuts or something, but that's about it. I've got a spell to heat myself, so I don't really need more blankets, same for light. If I really need anything, there are a few places in the market still open, and as long as it isn't a blizzard, I can just go get it."

"That's very frugal of you, dear, but you still need to make some basic preparations. We'll go shopping tomorrow, and I'll show you what you need. Now, what all do you do for work?"

"I wait tables, make bread or cheese, and charge magic items."

"You can make both bread and cheese?"

"And a few other things besides, yes."

"You'll need to go over your spells with me."

"No."

"Excuse me?" She seemed aghast that I would defy her so openly.

"No, that's rather personal. I'll tell you about some of them, but some are simply not your business. As far as things you should know, I've already told you about heating, bread, cheese, and light. I can also do water and sugar, and I can do some things to defend myself."

The woman pursed her lips but held her tongue. "How much do you work? And when?"

"One day off, two days on. Normally, morning shift, from before we open to anyone other than overnight guests until just after lunch. If things get weird, I'll work nights every now and then." There was no harm in telling her that; she'd see it soon enough.

"Hmm, what are the meals served here like?"

I went over the normal menu. It was mostly soups and stews with seasonal fruits and veggies when available. Winter was a bit more limited because everything had to be stored, but that was normal for everyone.

"That's not terrible, though I'd like to see more greens . . . You don't seem to be malnourished at the very least. I'm thankful for that, too many children in the last few years . . ." She looked a bit sad at that thought.

I understood that concern. I'd seen too many starving faces and would be happy to never see another.

"Anyway," she started up again, "ground rules. You will keep your things in order and clean. Your bed will be made every day after you get up and you will be back in it before the final bell rings for the night. I expect you to keep yourself clean, as well as your clothing, as much as is possible."

"Pay attention, Eleanor. Look at my things. They're already clean; I'm already clean; my clothes are already clean. With heating magic, I can wash and launder as needed without your input and far more regularly than would otherwise be possible. Also, you can't hear the temple's final bell for the night without going outside, and if you plan to sit outside through winter . . . well, you have fun with that. I do not need your input on these things at all."

The temples in the city ran a series of bells to indicate time. Sadly, they weren't particularly loud, so if you weren't outside or in their district, it wasn't all that useful. It should have been possible for them to make louder ones, but for some reason they didn't.

"Your magic has gotten you through this far, dear, but the lack of anyone actually keeping an eye on you had led to you being in danger. If it were not so, I would not be here. So the backtalk will be unnecessary."

"You are here because Bishop Theodore is an asshole, and for nothing else."

"The foul language can go as well, young lady, and I'll not have you talking ill of the bishop. His concerns are keeping the country as stable as it can be."

I snorted. "If you'll excuse me, I've got to get back to work." With that, I left her there.

I convinced Lucien to give me my old room as a place I could study at a low rate for the winter. He grumbled but understood when I informed him that if he didn't the chances of both me and the Shield's servant making it through the winter were near zero.

I understood what she was doing. She wanted to establish herself as some kind of authority. Problem was: she really didn't have a leg to stand on there as I was already quite capable of taking care of myself quite well. My hope was that she would get the message sooner rather than later and leave me mostly be.

I actually did go to sleep pretty early if I had work the next day, so we didn't run into any issues the first night. It was weird to think about, but I'd never realized before how easy it was to wake up when you wanted. There were a number of methods the people of this world used. Of course, the wealthy had forms of clocks, but most used one of a few rather more simple methods. Mine was to manage my water intake and time getting to bed. I always woke up on time because I was rested and simply needed to find a chamber pot.

We'd had no issues so far, and by the afternoon I was hopeful we wouldn't. Unfortunately, our first argument started due to weather. I'd not objected to her little shopping trip because I had a few things I needed to pick up anyway.

"Alana, it's time to go." Eleanor stalked up to me a few minutes after my shift had ended.

"I'm ready."

I got a raised eyebrow. "You will be once you get a shawl or the like; it's too cold to wander about without one. Hurry along and grab one so we can be off." To be fair, it was rather nippy out.

"Heating Magic" I spoke slowly so that she'd let it sink in.

"It is foolish to waste mana when you can just grab an extra layer."

"It is foolish to be uncomfortable when the spell is nearly free."

We spent several moments glaring angrily at each other before we were interrupted by Jackson's chuckle.

"Better be careful, girl. She might put you over her knee."

I looked dead on at the man. "The first person who tries to strike me will be the last." That threat seemed to cool even him for a moment.

Eleanor huffed. "Fool boy, beating a child doesn't work. Makes them afraid and teaches them to use violence to get their way." That was . . . strangely progressive for a viewpoint.

"You're all being foolish. Eleanor, the girl's a mage, and a rather good one. She doesn't need your input on her day-to-day activities." Lucien said as he appeared beside us.

"Thank you."

"Girl, stop arguing and go get another damn layer; you're wasting everyone's time."

That got a satisfied "humph" from Eleanor.

"Jackson, stop picking fights. Because if you succeed and you start going at each other, I'll have to get involved." He took a moment to glare at us each in turn. "And *nobody* will enjoy that."

I didn't think I'd ever seen him look at me that cross before and quickly went to get a poncho, only grumbling a little. I had a shawl but was still feeling just a bit contrary. When I got back, I saw him and my assigned minder in a glaring contest. Apparently, she didn't like that I'd listen to him but not to her. Too bad for her though, Lucien was way scarier than she was and actually had taken care of me when I needed it.

Our shopping trip went relatively well. While Eleanor was busy lecturing on oils and blankets and how much of what was needed for each person in a household, I bought the few things that I actually needed. Some of her info was useful, but I wasn't buying for a household, I was buying for myself.

No, our argument came afterward. I decided to follow Kala's lead and have a long and steaming hot soak. The tub had been moved into the shared room, but I threw up an illusion for privacy. As I was sitting there enjoying my bath, Eleanor walked through said illusion, ostensibly not realizing why I'd put it there.

"What in the . . . oh goodness, excuse . . . what's that on your leg Alana?" She went from confusion to embarrassment to accusatory in under three seconds flat, quite impressive.

"A Lovers' Mark." I didn't even look up. The hot water was just too good.

"I . . . you're thirteen! You shouldn't be having . . . relations with anyone."

"I'm aware of that, and I'm not."

"Then why do you have that?"

"Because I might not have the option to get it in the future, and as insurance."

"Alana, one does not put sheets on a bed nobody will sleep in." That was a surprisingly good saying, and one I'd never heard before.

"They do if sheets are a product that's hard to get. I'm surprised you didn't know I had it, Bishop Theodore did. Now if you don't mind, I was rather enjoying my privacy."

"I DO MIND . . . Why in the world would Theodore know anything about . . ." She was getting rather flustered, something that I was happy to allow.

"You'd have to ask him. Are we done?"

"We are most certainly not! Good grief, could you at least cover yourself?"

"Well, I did put up an entire wall to do just that. You seemed to realize your rudeness in walking through it for about half a second."

The poor woman looked like she had a headache. "You're actually not wrong there. We'll continue this conversation when you're done." She left before I could have the chance for a good denial.

I soaked for a long, long time, but all good things must come to an end. Eventually, I got prepped and dropped the wall to find her sitting on her bed. I decided to sit opposite her for what would undoubtedly be a long talk.

She kept saying things like "Alana, sex is a very important, personal thing" and asking me if I was sleeping with anyone. The latter was asked no less than half a dozen times, until I finally snapped at her. She didn't seem to believe me on that account, sure that I'd been hooking up with someone. Eventually, even her long wind faltered, and I left for dinner.

Dras arrived in the middle of my meal. It took him a moment to scan the Starlit Sky before he walked up and sat. I hadn't realized how tall he'd gotten, but I suppose he must have hit his growth spurt at some point.

"Look at you! Long time no see," I offered as a greeting when he joined me.

"Yeah, no time really to travel much. Sorry for not coming to see you sooner. I've really been unable."

"I understand, school must be rough. You got a day off or something?"

"Yeah, some of our classes cover social activities. They say it's important to know because a lot of us are nobles, and a lot of us will end up dealing with nobles, or something like that. We were supposed to go to some event tonight, but everything got canceled. There was a monster attack or something."

"Yeah, I know. I was there."

"For real? What happened?"

"Well . . ." I spent several minutes regaling him with the tale before we were interrupted.

"Alana, who is this young man?"

"Dras, my friend."

"Is that so?" Eleanor looked down at him appraisingly.

"Oh, hi. Yeah, I'm Dras, nice to meet you." He held out his hand.

"And you as well. I'm the guardian assigned to keep an eye on Alana by the Shield."

"Pfft, I see your bishop made good on his threats."

Eleanor didn't say anything but glared angrily and found a nearby seat. At some point, Dras had to leave as he had class the next day. I did a bit of light studying—no point letting him get ahead of me or anything—then began to play with the other musicians for the night.

As a marked surprise, I was not told to go to bed. Eleanor did motion to me about the time, but when I ignored her, she simply left by to go and sleep. It was a bright ray that told me that perhaps she would learn to act reasonably.

I nearly snapped when I was pestered out of bed at my normal awakening time the next day.

CHAPTER 12

TRUCE

I had gone to bed early after being woken up on my day off. This was not due to some contrition on my part, nor tiredness from lack of sleep. No, I was angry, I really, truly hated being awakened when there was no point to it. I even tied a string around my wrist so that I would remember when I inevitably woke up early.

Upon my return to the world of the awake, I looked around. Eleanor hadn't stirred yet, and so I hummed a few different spells into existence. First came a bubble of silence and darkness around her, then another bubble of silence around our room. Now safe to act, I retrieved my flute from its place among my things and went to stand in the middle of the room. On a whim, I put up a bright ball of light in the middle of the room, just for good measure.

I dropped all of the protections from light and sound around her and launched into a flute variation of the bugle wake-up call. I'm quite sure that the influx of sensation was jarring, to say the least. Eleanor nearly jumped straight out of bed.

"Good morning, Eleanor!" I cheerily chirped.

"What were you thinking?" she nearly screamed.

"That I prefer not to be awakened on my days off. Shall we continue bothering each other's sleep, or would you like to call a truce?"

"And you woke everyone up for that?"

"Only you."

"That was very loud, Alana. You certainly woke everyone up."

"There is a bubble of silence around the room."

I could see the twitch in her eye. "I see."

"So, do you wish to continue our fighting? Or can we come to some understanding?"

"I believe you already had an understanding with Bishop Theodore, did you not?"

"Certainly, that I would allow you to be my guardian until such time as I go to school. That does not mean that you and I have to get along though. It will be easier for both of us if we do, so I would prefer to."

"You are completely reasonable and unreasonable at the same time."

"Thanks?"

"Not a compliment. Very well, what do we need to do to not be at each other's throats for the rest of this year?"

"Let's start with not waking each other up for no decent reason."

"It is important that you keep a schedule, Alana."

"I do. You also need to accept that I can, mostly, take care of myself. There are times when I may need help, and if I do, I'll come to you. But for just going about my day . . . I can do that without you being all over me."

"For some things, you certainly are, but you have some very concerning habits and situations, young lady, and you need to accept that I need to keep an eye on you because of those."

"Like what?"

"Let's start with your boyfriend. You're very young to be in so serious . . ."

"I'm going to stop you there. Dras isn't my boyfriend; he is a friend. I'm also not having sex with him and don't plan to. You can accept that, or you cannot, but it is the truth."

She took a few seconds to stare at me. "I find it hard to believe, but you don't look like you're lying. We'll put that to the side for the time being then. I'm also concerned about your habits of preparing for the future and your finances. You have a good amount of earning potential even at your age, and I want to make sure you're not making a mess of it."

"I'll go over my savings and stuff with you after work if you're that concerned about it. As for standard winter prep, I've already told you that most of it just doesn't matter to me. I can make up for the most important parts with magic."

"Your magic helps you a lot, but you need something to fall back on in case you end up having to use lots of mana on other things. I agree that you don't need the same preparation that most do, but you should have at the very least some things set back just in case. That is the very basics."

She seemed exasperated but actually concerned about it. "Fine, on my next day off, I'll get some extra stuff just in case. I think it's a waste though."

"You need to think about the things you buy. What will you do when you have a family if you're not thinking about that? You may be fine, but what about your children, or husband? Will they?"

This world was one in which it was pretty much taken as a given that I would, at some point, settle down and have a family. Few were those who never did, and as a spellcaster, there was even more pressure to make lots more little spellcasters. I wasn't entirely sure how I felt about that, but I could see myself at some point wanting kids.

"Those are valid concerns. I'll consider it."

"At least I don't have to worry about your cleaning. You do that rather well for someone your age."

"Yeah, I made a spell for that a while ago. I don't use it on clothes, but for the floor and stuff it works fairly well."

She sighed. "Don't want to do anything the old-fashioned way, I see?"

"I do not like assigning myself more work than I have to do. If I have a resource, I will use it."

"Fine, well, let's get breakfast then. No point trying to go back to sleep now."

That afternoon, I had another visitor in the form of my new friend Kala. She strode in just after noontime with my folded-up dress for me.

"I see you escaped the other priests." I gave her a smile as she handed it over.

"It was a grueling affair, but eventually they decided I wasn't actually in the wrong. I still had to go over everything about a dozen times though and got chewed out for not sending word that I was okay when I had the option."

"Boo on responsibility."

She snorted. "Some things we must be responsible for, but there are others where I think we could relax just a hair." Her fingers held up in front of her face to show a small bit.

We found a booth and ordered a bit of food. "So what do you lot do at the temple all the time."

"Depends. There's plenty of work for older priests either helping people or maintaining everything. There's also a lot of . . . clerical . . . work."

"Ugh."

"For apprentices like me though, we study and are drilled on things like healing and how our magic works. Lots of stuff on philosophy and how to act too."

"How'd you become an apprentice anyway? Be a priest and what . . . submit an application?"

"All priests are taken in by one order or another. Once your abilities manifest and are recognized, you are given plenty of time to meet with a few different priests and decide where you want to go, but you have to go somewhere. Most girls end up joining the Order of the Lovers, because we do so much that helps women in particular. But it's not a hard-and-fast rule, we have priests as well as priestesses."

"What if they don't?"

"Don't what?"

"Choose an order."

"You have to."

"Really?"

"Yeah. Priest magic is like scary dangerous if you don't know what you're doing. You can kill yourself or a lot of other people without meaning to. Also, if a priest is not right in the head, they have to be disabled and restrained, though that is mercifully very, very rare. Something about how we are makes us like grouping up and keeps us on the right path."

"Huh. I never really had that kind of issue. What made you choose how you did?"

"Well . . . the Shield was the first to take me in. They're really strict and military-like though, so I never really liked them." I understood that. "A couple of the other orders had people I talked to, but they just never felt like a good fit. The Order of the Lovers though, I spent some time with a priestess and went with her as she helped a few women who were pregnant or trying not to become so. It just seemed right. Don't bards have some form of that too?"

"Not really. I was hiding my abilities until I got found out and a local wizard took me in for some basic training. Eventually, he introduced me to Jackson, the guy over there in the five-colored pants." I pointed out the man in question. "He trained me a bit, and I trained myself a lot. When I got to the capital, Lucien taught me some, too, though most of that was to do stuff on my own. I think bards are pretty independent. We have friends and stuff, but I've never seen any kind of formal grouping."

"That matches the stereotypes, yeah."

"Everyone kind of says that. Says we're flighty, a pain, and a bit of flakes."

"Yup, that's what bards are like."

I stuck my tongue out at her. We laughed and exchanged a few jokes. There were a few really dirty ones from Kala, seemed the Order of the Lovers really liked those. Eventually though, she had to leave. A brief hug and promise to meet back up later, and I had my meeting with Eleanor.

Finances were not particularly fun or public to go over, but we did back in our room. I had in total around fifteen gold coins to my name, a frankly absurd sum for most children. A gold coin was a lot of money, enough to buy a large animal like a cow or horse, though quality would vary. Depending on the local market, you'd surely get a good one for that amount.

There were thirty coppers per silver and twenty silvers per gold, but prices in this country and world were a bit wonky. Food prices had been higher during the famine, but at normal rates, a copper could get you a meal with a small ale or a strong drink at a tavern. Things of less value than that were normally grouped together or bartered for. Peasants made a few coppers per day.

I was making between one and two silver coins a day, depending on the amount of things I had to do with mana. Charge rates on "most" magical items were standardized based on the runes on them, filling one rune was normally three coppers. That was about the equivalent to a day's charge for a Lovers' Mark. Mana was just as expensive. A few minutes of work from me might be a week's worth of labor for a farmer back where I came from.

A rune worth of mana was a sort of weird amount to measure too. It was more than some of my simpler, more practiced spells, but less than some of the more complex ones. That all depended on a number of factors involved in the casting, not some set price.

My sugar though sold. It was an expensive luxury item that only the wealthy really used. There were also very few sources for good quality sugar, of which mine was. If I spent all my time just making sugar, I could increase my income to easily five silvers a day. Something I might have needed to do if I were having to pay to go to the academy.

The tuition was twenty gold coins, twenty-five if you wanted to stay in the dorms. That amount was insane for most people, enough to buy a house and furnish it well. People in the city though made more than the villagers and had more expenses. I was at least glad to hear that the tuition covered all four years, even if you had to pay it up front.

I was glad that the Shield was eating my cost and a bit unsure of how to keep my money. There were no banks in this kingdom. Someone had attempted to make a few, but they'd either failed or attempted fractional banking. The practice had been seen as hugely immoral and was now severely illegal. For now, I supposed that I'd have to just keep my money or put it into some form of hard goods.

I thought about that as I drifted off to sleep that night, tired from all the day's activities.

CHAPTER 13

✦

WINTER PASSING

After a bit of time, Eleanor and I managed to relax our relationship just a bit. She was still a bit of a pain but didn't get into every inch of my business so long as I at least pretended to think she might have a point.

As the end of fall passed into winter, the few people who were still coming to the Starlit Sky fell to almost none. Jackson was staying for the season, much to Lude's joy. He seemed to be spending more and more of his time with her, and she didn't mind since there was little to do. I even had plenty of time after the basic daily work was done. We had lots of breaks between recharging magical items. Jackson joined Lucien with charging the few Lovers' Marks that still needed it. Even the brothels mostly shut down for the season, with only a few still running at all.

So as three bards were locked in a tavern with plenty of time and nobody to really disturb them, the predictable happened. Music on a frankly insane scale was played. We played during the day when we had time. We played all through the night. Any time that anything was being done, singing, playing, and humming for new tunes was also being done.

My erstwhile guardian even joined in to an extent. She had some songs she knew and would bring out her harp in the evenings. She even taught me the basics since we had plenty of time and I was happy to learn it. Unfortunately, she was painfully formal. We bards tended to a bit more musical tastes that were foolish or group songs. Even pop tunes seemed to be roughly appropriate—anything that was fun to sing together. Learning from her was a bit stifling, but I did learn plenty.

Dras came by only one more time, since he was having his nose pressed hard to the grindstone. Kala was a far more frequent visitor, managing to come in about once a week. After a few of these visits, I got permission to go and visit her. Pretty much anyone was welcome to come to the temples for business, but personal visits were a bit different.

So I took to visiting her. Even in a blizzard, I wasn't too much bothered because I could make myself warm. And since I had a bit of time, I even worked out a basic spell for keeping myself dry. It was far more rough than a lot of my magic, but it served a good purpose in that I could probably walk through a rainstorm now and come out with little more than ruffled clothing. I could also use it to clean up spills. Sadly, it could only do so much at once, and removing large quantities of fluid wasn't really possible yet.

It was near midwinter when I came by giving a smile to the poor attendant who'd been assigned to let people into the temple on this particular day. I was quickly led to one of the rooms that was being used for some of the daily work that the priests had to do. Most of that was recharging the magical items used in the temple.

The room itself was not particularly large. It was perhaps the size of a large bedroom or living room and had a roaring fire happily crackling away on one side. I wasn't sure why, but the temples seemed to be really opposed to using magic for convenience.

"Hi!" I waved to Kala as I entered. "Not bothering anything, am I?"

"Not particularly, no. Just doing some studying while my mana recharges."

"Prepping for the entrance exam then?"

"A bit, but most of this is on how things at the temple are run. There's a lot of background work that nobody ever sees."

"Sounds . . . kind of boring actually."

"But important."

I nodded in agreement. "Yeah, I suppose it is in the long run. Anything else going on?"

"Nah, just charging up some of our tools."

She showed me the tools in question. They were mostly for checking on the health of a pregnant woman and could give all sorts of information based on what you looked for. These were spells that a lot of the priests already knew, but having the items on hand meant that even a non-priest could do it, and they could save mana for other tasks that would be done during the heavier working seasons. There was one thing that did strike me though.

"The capacity on these is insane, isn't it?" I was no expert but had charged a good few items in my time and had a feel for how much they could take.

"It's really high, yeah. Most of our stuff is built that way. We charge it up in winter and then use it as needed for a couple of seasons afterward. You would not believe the number of pregnancies we get during spring and summer."

"People locked in their homes with nothing much else to do? I think I probably would." That got me a laugh.

She led me over to a small bench near the fire where we could chat, bringing the items that she had to work on and placing them on a side table. For the next couple of hours, we just talked about our days, sharing jokes while enjoying the afternoon. I even helped with recharging the tools. I had plenty of mana, and there was no point letting myself top out while some was needed.

Eventually, she put a pot of herbal tea over the fire so we could have something nice to drink. The drink itself was fruity, if a bit bitter, and they only had cream to add. When I summoned a bit of sugar to sweeten it, Kala sighed deeply.

"You're going to have me all spoiled with sugar and the like."

"Sugar is an important part of tea, without which it just isn't complete."

"It's also dumb expensive, Alana. We use honey every now and then now that there's tons of it coming out of the villages to the east, but it's just not the same."

"Is there really tons of it coming in now?"

"Well . . . it's still not all that much, but it's way more than it used to be I'm told. Seems some of the farmers have found a way to keep beehives or something. I don't know all the details."

I briefly thought about my brother. He'd loved to keep bees and all the honey and wax we'd gotten from them, thanks to his hard efforts. That, of course, reminded me of his death.

"Something wrong?" Kala asked, apparently reading the look on my face.

"Ah, I was just thinking about one of my brothers for a moment there."

"He's . . ." She didn't have to finish.

I nodded, not really trusting my voice.

Kala put down her drink and reached over, pulling me into a hug. She held me like that on the little bench for a while. It had been a long, long time since I'd cried about losing him or about missing the rest of my family, but she said nothing as I let silent tears fall. I ended up getting her robes all messy.

Eventually, it passed. One could only be so sad for so long at a time, and I'd used up my tears for the day. When it did, she gave me a small smile as I wiped away the last drop. Then she began to speak.

"I had no brothers, but I have a sister. She's still living somewhere near our old village from what I hear. Dad got called into the war and . . . well, soldiers die." Now, she was the one who looked sad. "At some point, there was a battle near our village. I wasn't at home when the empire's soldiers came. They went house to house, killed the boys and the older women. The younger ones though . . . They take slaves, did you know that, Alana? When I got back, I found her in chains. The things they'd done to her and the others . . ."

Her voice was shaking a bit, and it was my turn to hug her as she continued. "And when I saw it . . . I'd been hiding my magic for a while, careful to keep the few things I could do secret for fear of being taken away. That day, I let loose on them. I knew they were evil, monsters in the skin of men. Killing them was as easy as breathing."

She cried quite a bit, eventually settling her head on my lap as she did so. This wasn't a happy time, but there was something deeply comforting about it. We'd both been through so much, seen such horrors. Certainly, others had seen similar things, or perhaps even worse, but we were alike in our ways and understood each other's hurts. This was something I couldn't share with the others around me, and having someone who understood, someone I could lean on without holding back, was a true blessing to me.

So we mourned. We let each other have another to lean on while they processed until we were both done for the time being. Then we just sat in companionable silence for a while, curled up and watching the fire as it burned.

Eventually, we were interrupted by the head priestess coming to check on progress. She took one look at the two of us and quirked an eyebrow.

"Is everything okay?"

"It will be, Head Priestess," Kala answered.

"Very well then. If you're sure." She gave the item we'd been recharging a quick look over and raised her eyebrows.

"Ah . . . Alana helped me fill it . . ."

The older woman looked over at me with a kind smile. "Thank you for contributing dear. You two . . . take care of yourselves."

We nodded as she left, wiping away the last streaks on our faces. After looking at each other for a moment, we both laughed. If I looked half as bad as Kala did, I must be a total disaster, and I reckoned she felt the same.

"Oh no! The tea, and after you put the effort into making sugar for it." Kala despaired over the now ice-cold drinks.

I suppressed my giggling for long enough to cast the spell to heat them back to steaming, only to fall back into it at Kala's declaration of "That's so unfair!"

After finishing our drinks, I actually paid attention to the sounding of the bells and nearly bolted off the bench. It had gotten well past time for me to head home, and if I didn't soon, I'd be walking through the dark. After one last hug to my friend, I rushed out into the snowy cityscape and hurried on my way.

The walk home was peaceful. As the sun set and the lightly falling snow killed all noise, I strode along the roads. It was almost like a scenic painting as I made my way home to the Starlit Sky and its warm, often loud interior.

Winter continued in that pattern until the season finally broke. Kala would visit me; I would visit her. I introduced her to the idea of hot, spiced cider, which we drank while at the tavern. At the temple, we'd sip on warm tea, enjoying the fruity sweetness. I even taught her a few of the dirtier songs that Jackson liked so much and really pissed off Eleanor.

I was happy to finally be fourteen as the first blooms of spring started to show in the little green areas around the city. The last of the snows melted, and birds again returned to their singing, letting everyone know that the time for quiet rest had finally finished, and that the time to begin working in earnest had begun again.

Social visits didn't stop with the flood of activity, but they were just slightly less common. Both Kala and I had jobs to do, and even if travel was easier, we two were busier.

CHAPTER 14

COCKTAILS AND HANGOVERS

Other than the influx of work, spring brought with it a host of things. Most importantly to me was the food. While it wasn't quite as good as summer food, spring food actually had some fresh ingredients. It was sad to say, but most of what we ate over the winter were stored products or things made from them, and it really put a damper on my mood sometimes. The coming of spring brought salad, sprigs of veggies, and even a few different fruits.

So one morning I went to see Lucien. There was a lesson I needed, and I had something I would trade for it.

"Hey, Boss!" I chirped as I came over.

"What do you want?" He easily read me.

"I'd like you to teach me to add sound to my illusions. I need to take them to the next level before my exam."

"You could figure that out on your own you know." His normal method was to tell me a general idea of what to do and leave me to it.

"Sure I could, but if I had someone explain the basics to me before going off and trying to make it work myself, it might speed me up a bit."

"It might, but you might learn something new. It would also take hours that I could be doing other things. You could ask Jackson; he hasn't buggered off yet."

"I could, but you're the best at illusions."

"Flattery will get you nowhere."

"How about a trade?"

"What do you have to trade?"

"A few new drinks."

He had to think on that one for a few moments. "Bring me an example later and we'll see."

There are a handful of basic things one needs for a cocktail. I now had most of them, even if I had to improvise a bit. With the various things I could make using magic, I could easily enough whip up a small batch of cherry syrup. Add to that a few early citrus fruits that were being brought into the city from warmer parts of the country and a bit of mint, and it was easy enough to make some light drinks. Sadly, I didn't have tonic water of any kind; it was something I might have to work on.

The first drink was a rather potent cherry lemonade. I made a full pitcher as it was easier to measure it that way. The amount of summoned alcohol was not terribly much per volume, but it just didn't need to be. That was followed up with me making a batch of cherry cordial. It would take time to make but would be well worth the effort. I ended with a very, very rough approximation of a cocktail called Blood and Sand. For that, I had to sub out most of the ingredients, but we had several whiskeys and a high alcohol wine or two, so it was not too bad.

I had to be careful when making these. I was still tiny and not fully grown, and the last thing I needed was to get fall-over drunk trying to figure out how to remake cocktails from Earth. Eleanor had been backing off a bit as of recently, and me inebriated would probably turn that on its head so fast I might get whiplash. I also really didn't like being drunk, and even worse were the hangovers.

That night, I presented my creations to Lucien. He looked over the three drinks while giving me a bit of a look.

"What in the world are these?"

"Drinks, they're sweeter. I think a lot of women will like them, even if they will be a bit pricey."

"So should I guess there's lots of sugar and alcohol in them?"

"Yup."

He took a few moments to try each of them, though I warned him the cordial would take some time to come together.

"Not bad, though I'm not sure how popular they will be."

"What's all this then?" Eleanor asked as she came over, looking at the two of us.

"They're drinks. Want to try?"

"Very well, I suppose there's not harm in that." With a look at each, the rather annoying woman decided to try the lemonade. "Oh, that's not bad, that's not bad at all."

"Well there's a pitcher of it there, but I wouldn't drink all of it, Eleanor."

Lucien and I slid down the bar a bit so that we could continue our discussion in private.

"See, even she likes it. There's decidedly a market for them. Even if they are a bit expensive," I pointed out, trying to get the best price.

"All right, I'll give you that much. You just want to add sound to your illusions then?"

"Yup, yup."

"It's easiest if you have a sound you can move to where you want it to go. Otherwise, you need to know the sound you're making almost perfectly."

"Fair enough, and that should work for most of what I want to do."

"What are you trying to do?"

"Heh, heh. Don't worry, just a joke that's been a long time coming."

He explained to me how he did it. Which seemed a rather inefficient method of hearing then making what he heard appear somewhere else. That wouldn't quite work for me. I knew my voice sounded different to me than it did to other people. When I asked, Lucien didn't actually have a solution to this issue, so I tried to come up with one of my own. He apparently didn't have a good way to project his own voice other than to make it louder. I wasn't sure if he was lying to me about that to make me do my own work or not, but some of his insights on using an "ear" as a receiver were nice.

This information and considering my own changes that I'd have to be making to the spell took a while to go over. I knew passing off how to make the drinks even though he hadn't helped me much was a bad deal, but Lucien had been a friend for a long time, and I was going to give them to him anyway.

By the time we'd finished, Eleanor moved over to us. She squinted as she looked at me and sat down.

"Alana."

"Hm?"

"How . . . how strong is that lemon drink?" she asked, slightly slurring.

"Um . . . pretty strong why? How much did you . . ." I looked at the half-full pitcher and began to laugh.

"What's so funny?" Lucien leaned over.

"Oh, don't worry. It's going to be a good night."

"Alana . . . AL-a-NA, you never pay attention, pay attention." I almost felt bad for her. If nothing was done, she'd certainly be feeling this in the morning.

"Eleanor, you're drunk. Get some water."

"Fine, fine . . ." She didn't get up to get water, so I kindly filled her cup with some.

"Drink, you'll thank me for it in the morning."

"You waste too much mana. Spending it all here and there on things. You should use it smarter." She did, in fact, drink now that she had something in her glass but still babbled on about my failings. She'd been on me a bit recently about how I shouldn't just use magic to solve as many problems as I could.

"So . . ." Lucien now took his turn to ask. "How strong is that stuff?" He then took a chance to look back down at the recipe. "Oh, oh dear."

"Should we get her sobered up now or wait till morning?" I asked, trying not to laugh.

"Honestly, I don't care."

I opted to wait. Watching my normally cross guardian bumble about was a source of untold amusement for me. Eventually, it was time for bed though. It took a bit of cajoling from both Lude and I, but we managed to convince Jackson to haul her back to her bed and help her lie down. He asked why I didn't do anything about her drunken state, but I just shrugged.

The next morning Eleanor rose from sleep with a groan.

"Good morning," I said as I went about getting ready. I had the day off.

"Ugh. What in the world happened?"

"You drank a bunch. I did warn you."

"Of the lemonade? It didn't taste that strong though, and I didn't drink that much." I slid a bucket over as I saw her face, and just in time. She spent several moments emptying her stomach into it.

"It's the sugar; it hides how strong it is and makes the hangover worse."

"Good grief."

"I could help a bit, but you went on a whole thing about me wasting mana last night." Her glare met my shit-eating grin.

"Alana."

With a last laugh, I began to cast the poison removal spell. Alcohol was mostly just a poison, and a hangover was at least partially that. Getting the small quantity of alcohol she hadn't yet digested out was easy. Of course, many of its by-products were also a problem. While I didn't specifically know those, I could imagine that they were there, and I knew they were making her hangover worse, so pulling them out was my next step. That done, I could only do one more thing for her.

"Here," I said, putting down a pitcher and glass with cool water in them. "Drink up. That's all I can really do for you."

With the toxins gone, all she had to work through was the dehydration. It ended up with her getting a nice quiet morning while I went to my old room to practice my magic.

I worked on a receiver/broadcaster model for my sound spell, not unlike a telephone. Half of the spell "heard" something, taking in the sound waves, while the other half put out a copy of them. I could also alter this to make sounds from my imagination rather than the receiver, but that was really difficult and not quite what I needed. It took me most of the day going between casting and studying to get it to a place that made me happy. But by the time I was done, it was at the very least workable.

Eleanor found me at dinner, parking herself across from me.

"Last night was a bit of an embarrassment. I hate to say that I was taken completely off guard by that drink. I thought it was more akin to a beer or cider than hard liquor."

"I could tell, but you were well and drunk by the time I realized your mistake."

"I would prefer it if we didn't speak of it again."

"Okay, if that's what you want. Jackson might have words for you later though." I felt that was an empty threat, but it did get a good look on her face.

"What? Why?"

"Because he's the one we got to carry you to bed and dump you there." I tried, and failed, to keep a straight face as I said it.

The flare of embarrassment on her face was perfect. I knew I was being a bit pointlessly mean here. I could have sobered her after she fell into bed or before. The poison removal spell would have stopped it dead in its tracks, ceasing the drunkenness and preventing the hangover. On the other hand, it was really funny to me, so . . .

"Why Jackson?"

"Because I'm too small and Lucien is getting on in years."

At my answer, she put her head down on the table. I patted her on the shoulder a bit. It wasn't that bad. Sure, for about as long as I'd known him, Jackson had been a playboy, but he wasn't evil or anything, and he probably wouldn't even mention it if she didn't. I imagined he'd had to been thrown into a bed once or twice in his long career of drinking and chasing women.

So far as I knew, the man never did say anything to her about it. For the rest of the spring though, she ended up studiously avoiding anything she wasn't particularly familiar with. Not much else of note happened for the season other than a few visits from friends and a good bit of hard studying. By this point, I could almost quote the study book line for line, it was kind of sad.

✦

CHAPTER 15

JACKSON'S EXIT AND EXAM REGISTRATION

Spring rolled on into summer, and one day Jackson made his exit. He didn't say anything to me personally. He was just there one day and gone the next. It was my understanding that he had some words with Lucien before leaving; he did have to pay for his room and the like. Lude joined me at the bar that evening after we both finished up for the night; she seemed unbothered.

"How're you tonight?" I asked, keeping an eye on her mood.

"I'm great. How about you?"

"Fair enough. So . . . um, you and Jackson then . . ."

"Yeah, he's got some things he needs to take care of. Then he's coming back."

I seriously doubted that. "Yeah . . . he does seem to come and go, doesn't he?"

"Mmm, yeah. I don't care though. I don't even care if he goes for other girls, so long as he returns to me." She had a dreamy look in her eyes. It was honestly a bit creepy.

"Well, he'll come back here eventually. If nothing else, he and Lucien are friends."

I left her to her daydreaming to prepare for the inevitable tide of angry husbands and fathers. We even took bets on how many would show up. Several of the bar staff made a pool for betting and chose numbers. Based on previous experience, I chose five, putting up a small jar of sugar as my wager.

To everyone's surprise, Lude won. Not a single man showed up to complain about Jackson's behavior, nor to beat him for cavorting with their wife/daughter/friend. To say that both Lucien and I were surprised would be an understatement; perhaps Jackson had really changed.

Around midsummer, Kala sent me a letter asking if I'd like to join her for going to register for the academy. I responded with a fervent yes, as we'd not had nearly enough time to hang out recently. I'd been tied down with work, trying to build a bit of a cushion of money and she'd been slammed, too, with making preparations.

Late summer and early fall were the busiest time for the Order of the Lovers, as many women would, if able, choose to give birth as near as possible to one of their priests. It was considered good luck. It was also rather smart as they tended to be highly trained in midwifery and able to heal injuries dealing with births unlike any normal person could. While infant and mother mortality might be horrific in many parts of the country, the presence of one of their priests dropped that number to near zero.

When the day came, Kala and one of the older members of her order stopped by the bar to pick up Eleanor and myself. It was considered proper to have someone acting as your guardian apparently, though not an absolute rule.

The two of us hugged and then began our normal chatting.

"How's things?" I began.

"Oh, you know. Marks, babies, the works. You?"

"We had a couple of good bar fights recently. Let me tell you about them . . ."

The walk up to the academy was rather uneventful. I wasn't overly surprised to learn that Eleanor knew who they'd sent with Kala, the temple district wasn't all that populated when it came down to it. They talked behind while Kala and I held hands, leaning in to spread what little bits of gossip we'd been gathering.

Eventually though, we had to split up, as registration for the exam was done by caster type. I was surprised that they had a section for physical magic. Apparently, they didn't come to the academy for much but attended a few classes, with formal training in a nearby barracks. The arena that we used for entrance exams was part of the facilities that had been built partly for their use.

Eleanor had to split from me to go do some paperwork on her end, something about finding me a guardian when I got in. I was glad to see her go as I walked down the hall toward the bard area. It was a small hallway with a line on the floor leading to a door.

The room was a bit on the opulent side. It had thick green carpets and a number of couches we could wait on. There were perhaps a dozen of us in total of various looks. Most were rather fancily dressed, obviously nobles or some shade thereof. Some of these were clearly wealthier than the others, and all of them seemed to have a servant attending them. There were also a few who looked rather less well-off, though still rich if I had to guess.

I'd worn my nicest dress. It was the one that I'd gotten from my work saving Prince Lief, though I'd had to have the seams extended to their very maximum width to make it fit properly. Even now, I doubted that it would be long enough for too much longer. I still felt far underdressed for the occasion.

"A servant? Why are you here? And not even in uniform." A boy with a frankly uninteresting aura asked. He looked both weak to me and like he was glowing a dull gray.

Maid outfits seemed to be a multi-versal truth, as all those here were wearing one. The male servants had on similar clothes of black and white one might expect of a butler. I could only assume that was what he was referring to.

"I am here to register for the exam," I explained simply.

"Pfft, you've no aura; begone, Commoner."

"I'm simply suppressing it. That is to my understanding common practice."

"Completely?" The boy began to laugh, which spread to several others.

I was happy to see the little bits of practice I'd slipped into my daily routine after the incident at the ball had paid off. I could still detect it, but it seemed this little idiot was having a hard time.

I considered letting it loose and giving them all a real showing. Honestly though, who cared? I was going to ace this test. I was going to slam their fat little noses into the academic grindstone that was this school and teach them a real lesson about learning. I'd been through more formal schooling than all the little noble brats in this room could even dream of, and I knew the materials for this test like the back of my hand.

"Discipline is important." I simply shrugged and sat down, causing those who'd been laughing to bristle a bit.

The boy, in particular, seemed to take this a bit personally. He clenched his jaw as he rose, advancing toward me with a few stomps.

"I'll teach you to respect your betters." I could see him breathing in to scream at me as he came.

Unfortunately for him, I was quite a bit faster. With a hummed note, I threw a bubble of silence all around his throat and mouth. I practiced my spells every day. I used magic as much as I could. His little show was a joke. I could have responded with something significantly nastier, but just shutting the little shit down was enough for me. Technically, he could still cast, but without hearing himself sing, I doubted he would realize that fact.

He tried and failed again and again. I didn't say a word as I watched him breathe in and scream himself hoarse. It was dead silent. Those who'd been laughing before had shut up in a hurry as they saw that display.

"Well, I can see you don't have anything to teach her then. Best if you sit down, isn't it?" A masculine voice uttered from one corner, out of which strode a man in rather formal-looking robes.

I hadn't seen this man before and wondered if he'd been using some form of camouflage or invisibility. It was possible he'd just been really good at remaining unseen too. I looked him over and then the corner. He was tall, dark-haired, and moved as if everyone in the room were already his students, glaring at each of us. The corner I saw had some kind of weird optical effect going on. My guess was that it was either something he'd done, or something about the room itself.

"I am Professor Magnolia. I also happen to be the nominal head of the bards here at our most esteemed institution. Allow me to point out that if either of you had actually managed to harm the other, you'd have been instantly rendered unsuitable as a candidate. Magic, particularly combat magic, is not something to be used lightly."

Professor Magnolia moved to one side of the room. He sat down at a desk there and began to take out bits of paperwork. "I'm going to need you to come up one at a time to answer a few questions. Don't worry I'll put up a muffling spell to keep your answers private. Miss, I would appreciate it if you took whatever you'd done off of your fellow prospect."

"Yes, sir." I nodded and dropped the spell.

We were called forward in order of status. I suspected he knew what nobles were here or could tell by their clothing their rank. I would, of course, go last. The idea of equality was completely foreign in this world, and I could understand it. Either you could do magic or you couldn't, there was no equality in that, and magic was a powerful tool.

Eventually, it was my turn though. When it was just myself and the professor left in the room, he looked up, motioning me over to the desk.

"Name?"

"Alana."

"Place of birth?"

"Orsken on the Forest. It doesn't exist anymore as far as I know though, sir."

"Not a problem. Parents' names."

"Verren and Amara."

"Very good, if you had any teachers, I would like to know their names."

"My first teacher was a wizard by the name of Mystien"—the man's brows rose at that—"followed by a bard named Jackson, and another named Lucien." He gave me a hard look after I'd finished.

"Normally, at this point, I'd ask you to demonstrate some small spell, but I think you taking the little lordling down a notch will more than suffice. That was a good response by the way. What did you do?"

"Um . . . zone of silence around his mouth and throat. Nothing terribly complicated there."

"Ah, it was just localized. There are a handful of ways to get a similar effect, but I can see that working quite well."

After being dismissed, I returned to the main entrance. Several groups were forming here with a few of what I could only guess were current students filing among them. As I found Kala and Eleanor, a familiar voice greeted me.

"Hey there, figured you'd be in today. Long time no see." I turned to see Dras standing there in what must be his favorite robes. They looked terrible, if rather comfy.

"Oh? A friend of yours, Alana?" Kala asked as she came over to stand right next to me.

"Yes, this is Dras. I told you about him. Dras, this is Kala. We met awhile back and she's a good friend."

The two looked at each other for a few moments. While Dras had come up to join us, it was Kala who seemed to be staking her claim as my best friend right now. I liked them both, but it was true that there were some things Dras would just never get . . .

"Yeah . . . anyway. We don't have classes today, so I thought you might want to . . . get some lunch or something after you'd registered for the exam . . ." Poor Dras seemed at a loss on how to deal with Kala.

"Let's all go," I suggested, forgetting the constant pain in my neck who was nearby.

To my relief, Eleanor waved us off. Leaving us to what had to be one of the most awkward lunches I'd ever been to. The place was one near the school and a popular hangout for the students. The food was good. Also, neither of my current companions said more than three words at a time to each other. They'd apparently decided that rivalry was the way to go. I felt like that would get tiring in a hurry, but that would be a problem for another day.

CHAPTER 16

TAKING THE EXAM

Fall came, and the studying became real. It was either Kala or Dras or both at all times that I wasn't working. Once the exam was just a week away, I took the time off to just study. If I didn't get in, I would be amazed. As it stood, Lucien accepted my leaving with little more than a chuckle and pat on the head.

On the night before, Dras came down to join Kala and me. We spent the evening relaxing again and chatting about whatever came to mind. I appreciated that he was keeping this tradition alive, and as the sun set, we all went to rest for the coming day.

I woke up early—insanely so—and found that Eleanor was still sleeping. With little else to do, I slipped out of my room and headed toward the main room. I wanted to see it, to take another hard look around the place that had been my home for so very long. As I came in, I found Lucien there, leaning on the bar and doing some light cleaning.

"Woke up early?" he asked with a grin.

"Yeah, nerves."

"Alana, I've known a good few casters. I've known bards, wizards, and clerics of all types. So, as someone who has seen plenty of people who've gone to that school, allow me to tell you. You're going to be fine. If anyone I've ever known was ready for that exam, it's you." He gave me a kind smile and motioned me to take a seat by him at the bar.

"I know that I know what I need to. I'm also fairly sure I'll destroy the practical."

"How's that thing you were preparing for that going?"

"I got it down; it'll be great if it works."

"Odds on that?"

"Fifty-fifty, depends on one big factor. That's out of my control though, so who knows."

"Well soon, you'll have a proper teacher. I'm sure they'll be able to help you get it going afterward."

"You're a proper teacher, just a rather unconventional one."

"Alana, I take in strays every now and then, but I'm no professor. You and Jackson are my only two real students. Even then, I only took you on because you reminded me of my old friend."

"And Jackson?"

He gave me a real deep look, and I nearly fell out of my chair. "Does he know?"

"I'm not even sure. Could get a priest to check or something if I really wanted. He's the right age through, and from the right neighborhood. I can't deny that he certainly acts like I did too . . . Enough about my past though. You've got a future ahead of you. Do you think you're ready?"

"As I can be, not just in an ability way either. I like it here. It's comfy, but I need to get stronger. When I come of age, I need to go and find my family. I'm betting they're still out there somewhere. I just don't know where yet."

"Bit surprised you're waiting that long."

"I don't really know where to start. I'm hoping that they come and find me, or Mystien comes to visit you. If he does . . ."

"I'll get word to you, and I'll let him know where you are."

"Thanks, for everything."

Lucien smiled at me and patted me on the shoulder. He then made me a frankly huge breakfast with most of my favorites. I was surprised he knew them, but we'd lived in the same place for so long I really shouldn't have been.

Before long, the Starlit Sky was abuzz with the morning crowd. Eleanor rushed me off to get ready before it got too late. Even as I was doing that, I could feel the butterflies in my stomach. When I returned, I found Kala there, along with an amused-looking Charles. His big eyes taking in everything around him.

"Surprised to see you here," I said as he came over.

"Hey, hey, we're friends."

Were we? I only saw the guy like once or twice a year outside of him coming to get his injuries mended up. Charles was weird about the social stuff though, so he might actually consider me his friend. I mean, he did tell me when I was being stalked.

"Well, sadly, it's time for me to go on . . ." I looked at him and he shook his head.

"Sure, but we'll see each other again. I mean, you're not even leaving the city, you can visit the Starlit Sky pretty much any time you want."

I felt really silly in that moment about being all tied up in leaving. Sure, the Starlit Sky had been home, but it was just going to be a short walk away. Even Kala shook her head as she looked at me.

Our walking chat up to the gates was at least fun. Kala had apparently been saving some of her best jokes for this very trip. It worked to relax me completely by the time we arrived.

"Alana, I know you don't like me, but good luck, dear," Eleanor said as we split from the adults with us to go to the actual test.

Kala had a few who had come to cheer her on in the practical as well, and they gave her a wave. Lucien had opted to stay back, something about not liking the nobles' section of the city.

It was easy to follow the crowd to our testing room. I'd thought that we'd only have a few people based on what I saw yesterday, but it seemed that I had been mistaken. There were easily three hundred candidates filing into the large hall used for the written test. I didn't think there were this many in the capital itself. My guess was that nobles from all around the country sent their kids to try and get in.

"Welcome to the written examination for the Bergond Academy of Mages." A familiar old man spoke from the front of the room. His aura was still a bit unpleasant to look at for too long, but I thought he was toning it down a bit. "Though we more often refer to ourselves simply as 'the academy' here. I am Dean Lorrae, and fifty of you will have the privilege of being my students. First, you will take the written portion, and those who pass will undergo a practical examination afterward. Attempting to cheat here will result in immediate failure. You are here to show us your abilities, and your abilities alone. Find your seat. Once we begin, you will have until the sand runs out."

At the front of the room was a desk with a rather large hourglass on it. I wondered if they used that rather than a clock for some practical reason, or just because someone thought it was a good visual. My desk was near the back, quite far from it. As were all the desks of what could be considered lower-class folk. Not that that bothered me in the least.

We began as soon as the hourglass was flipped, and as soon as I began to dive into the test, I relaxed. It was easy as pie. After years of study on the material, this was a bit of a joke. Even the prose and rhyme parts were nothing major for anyone who'd been forced to sit through language classes for as long as I had. The math was laughable, nothing more complex than the most basic algebra and geometry.

As I was around halfway through the math section, there was a loud *bang*, and one of the students on the other side of the room was launched backward from his chair. He was quickly removed from the room by an irate-looking Professor Magnolia.

"That's our one for the year. We've never had a second, but do feel free to break the record if you were planning on it. For those of you who are smart though, back to work," the dean declared.

I finished early and ended up sitting there for a good bit of time. That was after I went back over everything twice, just to check. There were one or two more who had finished as well, though most were still bent over their papers and scribbling furiously.

When it ended, there were only a few who hadn't yet finished, and the lot of us were quickly instructed to form into groups. Since there were so few bards, we ended up as a group. The priests were much the same, but the wizards . . . The wizards had to consult a list, and then go to their assigned section of the room. They had the rest of us thoroughly outnumbered.

Our time spent waiting was filled with nervous glances around, the tapping of fingers, and one rather annoying noble giving me a glare. It wasn't too long though before Professor Magnolia and my old doorway guarding acquaintance walked up to us.

Professor Magnolia took out a piece of paper and looked it over briefly. "June of Estri, Omar of Mintra, Lora of Lithere, and Alana of Orsken, you may stay. The rest of you may now leave."

Most of our little group rose and began departing. I was glad to see that the boy with the gray aura was among those leaving. He, on the other hand, seemed to have something to say.

"The common girl passed?"

"Her score made yours look like the scribblings of a small child. Now go."

"Professor Rooke, there's no need to be impolite," Professor Magnolia stated.

"I've no use for those who can't pass that test—particularly when they let themselves be blinded to their own failings by the illusion that their birth should do anything other than require their excellence." Professor Rooke seemed far more harsh in this setting than I'd ever seen him before.

"Now, go. I've far more interesting things to be on with." Yes, he seemed particularly cross for some reason.

The students who'd failed quickly fled from his presence when he turned to give them a look that might be capable of literally wilting flowers. One that he then turned on me. I was unsure what I had done, but it seemed there was something.

After they'd left, the two professors took out June and Omar. My guess was that they'd take us in order that we were called on the list, meaning I was thankfully last. I took the chance to begin quietly humming several spells into place, one after another until everything was right where it needed to be.

"He seemed pissed." Lora leaned over after they'd left. If I had to guess from her clothing, she was fairly low on the nobility totem pole.

"Yeah, that's an understatement."

Professor Magnolia came back first and gathered up Lora for her practical. He dropped off June at another waiting room to the side as he came; she seemed in good spirits. Professor Rooke, on the other hand, pointed Omar off to the exit as he came in, before he came striding up to me.

"Alana, I'm a bit miffed at the moment, though not at you."

"Oh . . . I suppose that's good then, Professor . . ."

"Did you know that I came to join the duty roster for the odious job of testing applicants who show almost no talent just to see you in action?"

"Um . . . you did say you'd administer my test last year, sir, yes?"

"Good. Then I don't suppose you can tell me why the dean has decided that you passed your practical already then?"

"Oh." I understood now. I'd convinced him to come and test me himself and then had shown Dean Lorrae enough magic that he didn't feel the need to test me further.

I'd literally kept him waiting to see me cast for a year, gotten him to take a job he hated, and then been pulled away before he even got a look at my magic. I'd be a bit grouchy at that level of tease too.

"I . . . suppose that the dean saw some of my magic a while ago and made his decision there . . ." I could see his eye begin to twitch.

"Well, I am still quite curious as to what exactly you showed him."

"You could still run me through the practical, sir . . . I prepared specifically for it and all."

"I was hoping you might agree to that. Did our esteemed dean"—I could nearly taste the sarcasm in the word *esteemed*—"let you know that he'd passed you?"

"When we met, he didn't even tell me who he was."

"That . . . is a bit unsurprising. He rather likes his jokes."

As we walked past the man in question, he looked up at me, and then he looked *at me*.

"Eh, ha, ha, ha, ha," he laughed as Professor Rooke passed.

"Something funny, sir?" the still slightly irate man asked.

"Don't worry about it, lad. You'll like it."

When we finally made it out into the arena, coming in through a side door, Professor Rooke had on an actual smile.

Once we'd found a good spot away from the other examinations, he turned to look at me.

"All right, Alana, you may begin when you're ready."

"Oh, I began some time ago, Professor," I said with a smile.

"What? . . ."

When the illusory me that I'd made while waiting for him to come administrate my test poofed, and I appeared some twenty feet behind it, I got to see him actually begin to laugh. It took him a good fifteen seconds to stop.

"Okay, how'd you do that?" he said, wiping his face.

"Invisibility and illusion mostly. I used a silence bubble over my mouth to hide the sound of myself and a sound-moving spell to make my voice appear from the illusion's mouth." That got me another round of chuckles.

"Quite good and the footprints?" He pointed to the places in the sand where my double's feet had landed.

"Just a simple movement spell."

"You're quite the bold girl to go and pull that on me. Good job on the casting, multiple spells like that can be hard to work out. What else have you got?"

Most of my other spells weren't all that impressive to him. Though he gave some good reviews on my sugar summoning. The big show was the flamethrower, which I saved for last. It was too expensive mana-wise to use earlier. Even if the cost had dropped significantly for me, it was still a monster.

After that, there were indeed a few small questions on mana regulation and group casting, nothing complex though.

"Well, sir, did I meet your expectations?"

"And exceeded them, Alana. If you'll come with me, we'll go join the other successful candidates." There were a few still testing as he led me back in and to the waiting room.

CHAPTER 17

✦

ANNOUNCEMENTS, PARTIES, AND LETTERS

When I got to the room for passing candidates, I found Kala waiting for me. I was glad she passed even without me going to the extremes I'd done with Dras. I would have if she'd wanted it, but that had never been requested. We smiled at each other, and I nearly fell into the chair next to her.

"How'd it go?" she asked as I flopped down.

"Well, I'm wiped from all the mana I used, but very well, you?"

"I did well enough. The written was kind of hard, but I think I aced the practical."

We chatted about the exam and its results, and eventually Lora was let in as well. She looked ready to collapse and nodded as she passed me. I hadn't had more than a few words with her, but she seemed personable enough.

As the room began to fill slowly, I looked around at who had made it. There were quite a few fewer commoners here than there had been in the beginning. All but the priests and one other person were dressed as nobles. Everyone was also exhausted-looking, running through all of your spells in front of a teacher was no easy feat.

We spent a good long while waiting, and after a bit, a group was led in to join our own. This room had apparently been designated "passing" with another put to the side as "potential" for those who'd done not quite well enough to grab a spot for sure. The failing candidates had been shown the door.

"Greetings, everyone." The dean looked around as we all rose at his entrance. "I'm glad to see you all here and eager to continue, but there are things that must be done first. You'll each be provided with a list of needed materials and your time for uniform fitting. There will also be a few meetings with the professor in charge of your group; information will be provided to each as you exit. Classes begin a week from today."

I had to split from Kala and join with the other bards as we went to see Professor Magnolia. He was in a corner and gave us a big beaming smile.

"Three is an excellent crop this year; some I don't even get one. Allow me to congratulate each of you on your hard work and success. We'll have one class that will be just for you girls and focused on making sure you've got some basics down during your first year, then we'll be moving you onto bigger and better things. That's for later though, for now, schedules."

He handed each of us a small booklet. The meeting and fitting times were all written on a scrap in the front, while the rest was dedicated to rules and a rough map of the campus. There wasn't much to the rules. Stay in uniform during class and on days when we had classes, with a few exceptions. Don't attack other students or teachers. Don't damage the campus. There were also some rules about keeping the dorms in order and where we were allowed to work on new spells and items, but nothing odious. Appended was a section for rules for servants. We were apparently allowed to bring one, and they had their own guidelines.

The more concerning thing was the list of things we needed. Most of it was basic, but near the bottom was listed attire appropriate for social gatherings. I hated the idea, but apparently they did require it.

Professor Magnolia had a little speech that sounded like nothing so much as a regular greeting before he released us. The other students had gotten their information and were going now, too, and I was ready to head out.

I found Professor Rooke talking to Eleanor as I exited the room. He had apparently finished rather earlier than the rest of us had and taken to speaking with my current guardian. I wasn't sure if that was to be expected, or if it boded poorly for me.

"Greetings again, Alana, I'm glad to see Professor Magnolia didn't keep you too terribly long," the man said as I came over to them.

"Ah, there you are, dear. This kind gentleman was telling me how well you did. He's even volunteered to be your guardian for the time you spend at school."

"I'm quite grateful for that, Professor." It was painfully obvious that he just wanted me close by to try and observe my magic as much as he could.

I got the feeling he knew that I was doing some out-of-the-box things and wanted in on that while the getting in was good. Frankly, I was going to hide a lot of it from him, at least in the specifics on what I was doing. Some of the thoughts I had told me that a wizard with even a fraction of the limited understanding of physics and chemistry I had would be far, far too dangerous for me to loose upon this world.

"Well then, when exactly do you have your meeting with Professor Magnolia? I'd like to have a few words with you before you go to that. Eleanor and I will have to get all the forms in order, and we need to discuss your classes and preparation."

"It's two days from now, sir." I brought out my schedule to check, and it was there, in the morning. Apparently, they gave higher-status students what were considered more convenient times, later in the week, and later in the day. Most had celebrations to attend.

"Then let us meet tomorrow afternoon. We have much to discuss." I made a small mark on my schedule before Professor Rooke bid us farewell and left to attend to his own business.

"Are you okay with him as your guardian, Alana?" Eleanor asked as I walked back to the Starlit Sky with her. It was nice that she was taking my opinion into consideration for once.

"I am. I suspect he's just interested in my magic, but he seems like he's a decent enough person. If things go wrong, I'll contact either Theodore or the dean. My experiences with the latter say he's someone I can trust."

She snorted. "You would actually contact *Bishop* Theodore?"

"He's a jerk, but if I were actually in danger I think he would probably step in. He's also powerful enough politically to handle it. I would be loath to owe him any favors though."

"You're right about that at least. If you were in danger, the Shield would try to protect you, as we do with all children in your situation."

When I opened the door, I was greeted by my friends and pulled into a party they'd thrown together for me. It wasn't some big noble fancy get-together, but everyone had chipped in a bit. Dras was pulling out a few small presents he'd bought. He got me some pens and the like that I'd apparently need for classes. Lucien and Lude had handled food. Charles and Meg (though I didn't know her past our one conversation) had shown up. There were also a few of the neighborhood folks here, regular customers and some of Dras's friends.

I hadn't known, but it seemed that Lucien had taken my idea of making sugar to Lude and been doing a bit himself, the scamp. He let me know that as he passed out a small amount of ice cream. He also told me the tools for that had been hard to get. People weren't sharing it freely it seemed.

There was also a slow-roasted beef dish, the sauce for which was sweet and mildly spicy. Lude just winked when I asked her what the recipe was. Seemed she had some surprises for me yet.

Charles looked like he was suffering through a social anxiety attack. His little brother sat with him and chatted lightly to help him along. I joined them when things settled down, and we sat in silence for a bit.

It was well into the afternoon, and we were all roughly done. The Starlit Sky had to be ready for the dinner rush, and everyone else was good and partied out. I was considering making a quick trip to offer congratulations of my own when a rather confused messenger in clothes far, far too nice for this part of town appeared at the door.

"Er . . . I'm here looking for a bard?"

Both Lucien and I raised our hands in greeting. Relieved he came over to me.

"May I please have your name, Miss?"

"Alana . . ."

"Ah, excellent. Lord Johannes wished for this to be conveyed to you." He held out a letter written on thick parchment with a rather complex seal plastered on the opening.

"Oh . . . thank you." The young man nodded to me and left.

With a shrug, I opened it, curious as to what he wanted.

Dear Alana,

Word has reached me that you have passed your exam. My congratulations. When I heard this, it occurred to me that I had failed to offer proper thanks to you for your actions on that most disastrous night. It is therefore in the spirit of thanks and of joy that you shall soon find your proper place among the finest casters of our esteemed nation that I have made arrangements with the finest tailor I know of. Please accept this small gift from myself and my house.

Thank you once again,

Lord Johannes of House Kiedern

I called over both Eleanor and Lucien. Not sure how to and if to respond to this letter. They both took time to look over it and the directions on the back. I recognized the location of Marcus's shop there.

"What are your questions?" Lucien asked first.

"What should I do? Should I go and accept whatever 'gift' he has arranged, or not? What are the repercussions of doing so? Will I owe him any favors if I do? Will he cause any problems for me if I don't?"

"Good questions. He's labeled it as a gift and one in thanks, so you *shouldn't* owe him anything if you accept. If you don't he might try to send you something else, or who knows. Nobles can be kind of weird when they feel they're obligated to someone. Also, he's definitely trying to get you on his side, probably hoping you might end up with his son or something."

I'd already come to the conclusion of the last part and nodded along with him. Then I looked to Eleanor. She read the letter a few times with a rather furrowed brow. We didn't get along much, but she did know her stuff when it came to handling issues.

"Alana, I would like to have one of the priests look over this and advise before you accept or decline this 'gift.' I think that the wise position."

"Why one of the priests?" I was glad she was at least asking my permission to do that rather than just trying to force it, but she wouldn't be my guardian for much longer anyway.

"Several of them have been to the academy and have some training when it comes to the etiquette of the nobility. I'm not sure on the proper response, but one of them certainly will be."

"Perhaps I should ask Professor Rooke as well? I would imagine he has a good idea, and he'll be my acting guardian soon enough."

"Good thought on that one, dear. He's surely someone who'd want input as well."

Eleanor was eager to go and take the letter to the Shield, and I wanted to go and see my one friend who wasn't here. We both headed down to the temple district, bidding our current party goodbye. She requested that I stay at the Temple of the Lovers until she returned, something that I could easily agree to.

Kala's party was still swinging as I came in. It was a bit smaller than mine, but it seemed the priests took one of their apprentices getting accepted as a big thing and had gotten tons of good food for those who were coming in and out. We hugged and excitedly chattered about how awesome school would be as I took a few small bites of a really wonderful little tart.

Somewhere nearby, a couple of men poured over the letter for a bit, discussing every phrase before deciding it was innocuous enough. Those of the Shield knew how much of a pain nobles could be. Not even they knew that another letter had been sent over to the Order of the Lovers that was very nearly word-for-word for another young woman.

CHAPTER 18

✦

MEETINGS

Alana, you're oversleeping. Wake up or we'll be late to our meeting with Professor Rooke," a voice sounded, causing me to sit bolt upright.

Normally, I hated being awakened, but I'd had trouble sleeping last night after all the partying. For once, I was glad that Eleanor had bothered me. As these thoughts passed through my head, I rose, stumbling around for my dress and shoes. If I was late, I was sure to get chewed out, and that would be a horrid first impression to someone who would soon be both my legal guardian and teacher.

"Thanks for waking me!" I shouted as I pulled on my clothes.

"My, the surprises never cease. Remember the letter Lord Johannes sent you."

It was only a few minutes later that we left the Starlit Sky. I was still struggling to get my hair into a proper shape as we walked. About halfway there, I remembered that I'd forgotten breakfast and summoned myself a bit of bread and cheese. I might have died of embarrassment if my stomach started growling in the middle of things.

I was flustered, and Eleanor looked a bit disappointed in me as we finally came to the gates. They were closed, unlike the day before. We were met though by a man in servant's garb, who allowed us in and led us toward Professor Rooke's office. A bit unexpected, but not unwelcome. I made sure to memorize the route in case I needed it later.

Upon our arrival at the solid wooden portal, the servant knocked. I was nervous but also very excited by the prospect of coming to school here. All of the hallways were stone, but clean beyond almost anything in this world and beautiful. There were small columns and art in the hallways. I even passed a few magical items in cases, though I didn't know their function.

"Enter," the voice from behind the doorway bade us.

Professor Rooke's office was easily the size of a large bedroom. On one side, a small fire crackled, keeping any of the oncoming chill at bay. There was a comfy-looking chair for reading beside it. The walls were lined with shelves, each loaded down with a variety of raw materials. There was even a shelf dedicated to books, though it was easy to see that there was some magical effect on it, presumably to prevent anyone from messing with them. It was also very bright, light from a number of oil lamps stationed along the walls.

Behind a large desk sat the professor; there were two chairs before him. Behind and to his left was another large table that was covered in runes in amazingly complex patterns. He gave a smile as we came in and motioned to the chairs.

"Please sit. We have quite a bit to discuss."

After we found our seats, Eleanor asked, "Where would you care to begin, Professor?"

"The paperwork for the Shield, of course. It is what I need you here for most."

What followed was not unlike a parent-teacher conference. I was expected to sit quietly while the two of them filled out all the forms needed to have my guardianship transferred over to Professor Rooke, at least temporarily.

I took the time to examine his aura. It was odd, looking like a number of different symbols coming and going, almost like they were being written around him in the air. It was also definitely suppressed, being that I could only make it out if I paid close attention to him.

"Well, that's all of it. I'd like Alana to remain with me at the Starlit Sky until she moves into the dorms, if you've no objections?"

"Of course not. Alana, is that all right with you?" The professor looked at me with a raised eyebrow.

"I'm quite fine with it, Professor."

"Good. Then, Eleanor, while I do not mean to be rude, my charge and I have much to discuss. I would like this meeting to be private."

She gave a brief nod after seeing my smile and left.

"Now, let's get down to the actual reason for this meeting. Are you fully prepared right now to move into the dorms?"

"Mostly, sir. I don't have many things to pack."

"What about your maid?"

"I . . . don't have a maid?"

"Alana, you are allowed to bring one. I encourage you to do so."

"I'm not sure I really need one though? Do I?"

He rubbed his temples for a moment. "Alana, do you know the purpose of this school?"

"To teach magic, isn't it?"

"Partially, but not entirely. Our true purpose is to raise those who will be leading the country. Teaching magic is a part of that, but teaching the proper behavior and forming valuable connections is another. On a purely time basis, you will struggle if you don't bring a servant to help with things like basic cleaning and clothes. You will also miss the chance for a good connection there."

"I mostly use my magic to clean, Professor."

At my statement, he picked up a few papers from his desk, rolled them together, and hit me on top of the head, only hard enough to make me nod a bit.

"Umph! What?"

"That was for saying the dumbest thing you've ever said to me. The amount of mana you use will easily allow you to hire a maid, with plenty to spare. You also missed the second part, Alana, to form a connection."

"I don't understand. Could you explain what you mean?"

He grinned at that. "Certainly, admitting ignorance is the first part of learning by the way. That's one of the most important lessons you'll get. Don't forget it," he said before launching into his explanation. "Most servants are young adults or older children from lesser noble families. Perhaps they're a branch of a true noble family, or perhaps a child who never properly manifested magic. Are you familiar with the term *minor talent*?"

"I am not."

"Have you noticed how some people seem to have an aura that is barely there, or seems to try and flash through every now and then?"

"Yes."

"These people have what is called a minor talent. They're not full casters and cannot see an aura in the same way you or I could, but they do have a tiny amount of mana. Enough to use one or two very simple spells or bolster their physical abilities slightly. Many children of weaker nobles are born with this, and while they are not a caster, they can grow and potentially become one."

"And these people often become servants?"

"To nobles and casters, yes. The common belief is that being around more mana makes awakening as a caster more likely for one of them. There are other methods, but they're highly dangerous. They can also learn to make magical items, though they're slow at it and never advance far down that path. As one of the benefits of being a servant to one of our students, they're permitted to attend a basic class on magical-item creation, something rather hard for them to get access to outside of these halls."

"Okay, I can see why they'd want that. If I had to work as a maid to maybe gain magic and item creation, I definitely would."

"Female servants will also often try to form relations with some of our older male students. There are some rules on that. For example, if a maid were to get pregnant before her charge's final semester, it would cause rather severe fallout for her and potentially her family."

"Wow, it's great to know that I'd be hiring a woman who will drive herself to get knocked up by one of my classmates."

"Alana, noble families are concerned with the magical strength of their members, first and foremost. This holds at every level of wealth and power. Because magic is power and power gives wealth. Do not forget that. Noble women will seek a partner strong enough to ensure their child is stronger than they are. Noble men will seek a woman whose children will bolster their family. They will go to great lengths to this end. You will have suitors just because of your abilities."

"The one boy from the exam might disagree."

"Yes, Professor Magnolia told me of the initial incident, and I saw its follow-up. There are a few, but only a few like that. There are only a few because within a few generations his family will weaken if they behave like that young man did. He is a fool, and while there are many students who are barely worth my time here, there are mercifully only a few like him."

"So . . . if you think it's best, I'll get a maid then. What is the method to go about hiring one?"

"Normally, you would seek someone who's related, or who's related to a friendly family. I'll ask my wife to gather candidates, and the two of you can meet with them and decide. On the subject of other things you need. What is your clothing like?"

"I have a few dresses not unlike what I'm wearing, and one that's a bit nicer. Before I forget, Lord Johannes sent this to me the other day." I passed him the letter, which he read over several times while thrumming his fingers on his desk.

"You should accept the gift. You'll need more and better clothing, and if you don't, he might try to repay you in some other way that would be a pain."

"That is what the Shield advised too."

"There are a few other concerns, but most of those can be handled as they come. Professor Magnolia knows his business when it comes to recommending classes, but I'd like you to take at least the class on the Atali language. We have a visiting professor for the next few years, and it's a chance most don't get. It's tangentially related to the runes used in item creation and may be useful to you." He made a few notes for himself. "Anything else?"

"Not that I can think of presently, no I will take care of all the things you mentioned as soon as I can."

"Good, see you at the beginning of the semester then." He waved me from his office, and I fled a bit exhausted.

I received a letter from his wife that evening with an address and time. It was after my uniform fitting and meeting with Professor Magnolia, which was a small mercy.

My meeting with Professor Magnolia was actually significantly calmer. There were a few classes I was required to take. Magical-Item Creation had both a practical and theoretical side and was one of them. There were also required classes for all bards, and general spellcasting. On the less magical side, I was told I was going to be attending mandatory social classes, which included some ball attendances and general math and history.

I also had to choose three instruments, since I was a bard. I went with flute and harp (since I already knew at least the basics) and Atali dance. The last was a class exclusively for girls being taught by the visiting professor that I'd been told about.

Finally, I had to choose elective courses, of which I had three. One of those spots was taken up by Atali language, which I'd been advised to take. The other two I picked were on magical materials and combat spellcasting. Professor Magnolia did his best to dissuade me from the final of those three.

"Alana, the combat spellcasting class is seldom taken by girls and particularly bards. I really rather think you should take the healing one instead. It would help with any medical issues you encounter and is rather well received. You could also go into summoning. We cover some in the bardic classes but you've already shown great skill in that area."

"Professor, I've already had far, far too many times when I've been unable to defend myself. I'm no expert healer, but I can handle most emergency situations. As for summoning, I mostly use that for convenience or combat."

"Fine, if you're sure that's what you want. I do want you to know that they'll be treating you rather roughly there though."

"I understand."

The classes I was taking were as follows.

Magical-Item Creation (theoretical): Professor Rooke

Magical-Item Creation (practical): Professor Hern

General Bard: Professor Magnolia

General Spellcasting: Professor Klien

Proper Etiquette: Professor Sasha

Math and History: Mr. Ilvern

Flute: Mr. Hansel

Harp: Mrs. Nadia

Atali Dance: Professor Etia

Atali Language: Professor Etia

Magical Materials: Professor Hern

Combat Spellcasting: Professor Endel

"Professor, why are some of the teachers Mr. or Mrs.?"

"Because they are not casters in their own right, merely experts in their field. Do not think that means you may disrespect them though, doing so will result in immediate and harsh punishment."

As I poured over the painful-looking list of a dozen classes I fully understood why Dras almost never came to visit. This much studying would be enough to crush anyone. I contemplated how best to study for all of this as I drifted off. It was early, but tomorrow I'd be getting fitted for my uniform, and I was beat from the meetings.

CHAPTER 19

✦

CLOTHES, CLOTHES, AND MAIDS

I finally arrived at the uniform fitting. It was interesting in that I had no idea what our uniforms actually looked like. The shop I was going to was obvious, due to all of the carriages out front and the large number of important-looking people wandering around. Sadly, Kala had a different day for her fitting, so I was on my own for this little outing.

A few gave me looks as I walked past and into the shop, right up to the counter.

"My name is Alana. I'm here for my fitting."

"Ah lovely dear, you're the last. This way please." The woman led me into the back, where some seamstresses were taking measurements on the various girls lined up and lightly chatting.

"Stand here please, Miss Alana." Within moments, one of them was seeing to me.

"Did she just say Alana?" One of the girls in a rather more fancy outfit looked over at me.

"Um . . . hi." I smiled at her.

"Are you the one who came up with the fire spell? My uncle was telling me about that. He said it was a rather new one."

"I am. Who is your uncle, if you don't mind my asking?"

"Lord Fallon." A few more of the girls were paying attention to us now.

"I met him only very briefly. I'm surprised he remembered me."

"Oh, my little sister is a bard. He was hoping that she could learn to do that. Thought it would make a good impression when she goes to apply for her spot in the academy. I don't suppose you'd share how it works?" Her eyes were gleaming as she asked, almost predatorily.

"As I told your uncle, you just summon very high purity liquor and light it. It really is nothing too complicated. The other bards I know have a hard time with it though."

The girl pouted. "She couldn't get it to work quite right. I was hoping there was something more."

I tried to shrug only to be glared at by my seamstress. "I'm afraid that really is how it works. Even I have a really hard time with it. The mana cost that first night almost dropped me on the spot." That was mostly true. It was harder than most of my other spells and far more mana costly. I was bringing it down though, slowly but surely.

"A shame, but it is what it is. I'm Pinea by the way, a pleasure to meet you."

"And you as well."

Her acceptance of me seemed to encourage the other girls too. The subject of most of our discussion was the uniforms we'd soon be wearing. While I thought they looked fine, most of the young noble girls who generally wore skirts to their ankles were a bit scandalized.

The uniform itself was based on the armor worn by the few female mages in the kingdom's army. This was generally only worn while on guard duty to one of the women of the royal family or while in dangerous situations. Due to the fact that there just weren't many women in the kingdom's army, and those who were soldiers were heavily, heavily discouraged from dangerous situations, it was rather a rare thing to see.

On the back wall was an example of both our uniform and an unenchanted version of the armor for us to understand this. They stood side by side, the placement of their seams nearly identical. Even the skirts were the same "short" length, going only to just below the knee.

While ours was made of cloth, the armor was mostly enchanted leather. It was supposedly made in such a way that if anything should strike it, it would harden like steel, providing excellent protection. There was a cuirass, gorget, and helmet, with spaulders over the shoulders and an armored skirt. Almost every inch of skin was covered by it. The boots were calf height and well made.

We had no gorget, though the uniform did come all the way up to the neck. The helmet was, of course, excluded as well, having no purpose in classes. The lacing in the front mimicked the armor's design too. I noted that it was modest, simple enough, and looked very warm. There were even stockings to go with the uniform, and the thick cloth that would cover us was dyed a couple of lovely blue colors.

"Yeah, the skirt is a bit shorter than normal, but it's not that bad. With the stockings, your legs will be covered anyway, and those shoes look excellent and extremely comfortable." The boots on the uniform were the same as the military ones. They were light and supple and seemed wonderful to run around in.

My appraisal got a few grumbles.

"What about the top though?" one girl asked as she appraised it.

"It's high-necked, but the cut is really good. I think we'll look great." That part at least met with widespread approval. The seams followed the curves of the body, which gave good emphasis to all the places they might want to show off if they were after a husband.

It all ended rather quickly. We mostly were just being measured, with a few rounds trying on test sizes to examine potential issues. That done, the lot of us went our separate ways.

I personally had another thing I needed to take care of while I was up in this part of town. When I came into his shop, Marcus looked at me harshly.

"My, my, my, look what the cat dragged in."

"Destroying that dress was hardly my fault."

"I'm aware, but you could have at least come to me afterward."

"Eh, that whole week was insane. Everyone wanted all my attention, and I was in a mood to tell all of them to shove it."

"Well, in that case, it may have been best to avoid my shop. I was enjoying the headache of so many very lovely outfits destroyed by that incident. The fact that the entire season was canceled nearly tanked my business. Still, why didn't you send Jackson?"

"My apologies. As it is, I got a note from Lord Johannes."

"Yes, he's paid for you to get some new clothes. Five outfits in total."

That would easily double my wardrobe. I could also look forward to really, really nice clothing.

"That's a bit much though, isn't it?" I was confused at the sheer scale.

"My understanding is that you saved his son's life, as well as the lives of many partygoers. Good job on that at least."

I nodded and began thinking about what to get. Marcus took me through a number of different shades and styles, sample pieces he had or other people's clothes they hadn't yet picked up. I needed one formal dress, which was my first pick. I went with a lovely midnight blue cloth and a rather standard style, no point in looking too out of place. For my day-to-day clothes, I got several different sets, in blue, two different greens, and a yellow. More color could only do me good.

He agreed to have me one of the green ones ready by the next day. Something I was thoroughly grateful for. I had one more major operation left before I was actually prepared to begin school.

I was nervous when I arrived at Professor Rooke's home. I knew inside and waiting for me was some woman who I didn't know who would ostensibly help me find a maid who would, I hoped, serve me while I was very, very busy taking classes. I stood there alone, waiting. Eleanor had offered to come with me, but I'd said no. Soon enough, the good professor would be my guardian. If I couldn't trust him to get me through this, what could I? He'd nearly insisted that I undertake the task.

I was led inside by a maid who'd come to the gate to greet me. The walk up to the door was my first jarring event. Rooke's house was even more ostentatious than Lord Johannes's had been. We passed through a garden with neatly trimmed bushes and a pair of bubbling fountains. The stones were white and cleanly swept beneath my feet as we moved along, quick steps leading me to the huge double doors.

As I entered, I tried to not gawk around like an idiot, but it was difficult. I knew that the professors were likely nobles and possibly extremely rich, but this was on another level. The entry room had warm cherry-looking wood floors, with several alcoves for art spread about. I got the chance to examine one while the maid went off to find the lady of the house.

The piece was exquisite. A life-sized marble statue that had been painted or dyed somehow. While the figure's skin was still the pale white of the stone, the clothing had been gifted with marvelous colors. If I squinted, I thought I could even see a weave to it. The man stood proud with hand raised. When I looked up, I saw an even more shocking thing. Someone had replaced his eyes with emeralds. I tried to understand the amount of money invested in this one item but knew only that it was far beyond me.

"It's lovely, isn't it?" The soft voice from behind made me jump a bit. Of course with Lucien around I was as used to it as I could be now.

I turned to find a young woman, perhaps in her late twenties. She wore a fine dress of deep red, which went well with her dark hair and pale complexion. It took me a moment to realize that it was because of a sheen in her hair, something red shining through the deep brown.

"Yes, ma'am, it is. The eyes particularly are striking."

"One of my husband's forebearers. That man lived about two hundred years ago, he was an arch-mage of some kind. My dear husband keeps it where he can see it all the time, to remind himself of what he aspires to. Ah, but where are my manners, you may call me Amelia."

"Is that so? Professor Rooke hasn't told me all that much about himself, so I only know what I've seen."

"Oh, then this is a rare occasion for me. What is your impression of him?" She quirked her brow, moving forward a bit.

"He seems to be irritated, quite a bit, by those who don't strive. There's not a lot of tolerance for those who don't show skill either. That said, he has shown me kindness, even if I did something that irked him."

"That's not a terrible assessment. I will say that even those who lack skill will not gain his ire too much. As long as they keep working toward their goals." She took a few moments to think, then gave me a smile. "That's not why you're here though. I've been asked to help you find a proper maid, and so I shall. The candidates will be here shortly. Do you know what you wish to prioritize in your search?"

This seemed like a first test, but it was one I was not unprepared for. "I'm inexperienced in much of noble culture, so someone who can aid me in that, along with normal work might be best. Professor Rooke also said that this was a good chance to gain connections, but I'm not sure where I should try to gain those. I was hoping you might have thoughts on that. Since I know that those with a minor talent will likely value working for me the most, I think that I should aim for that as well."

She laughed. "Oh, that's fairly well thought out. I can see why he likes you. Let's interview them then, and we can talk about it afterward."

I interviewed ten girls. All of them were just of age and quite proper. Of them, six had a minor talent. Of those six, four were from branches of noble houses. The other two were from mothers who'd served in one but were not a member themselves. One of those four I cut out myself; something about her was just too haughty and it felt wrong.

"What are your thoughts, Alana dear?" I was asked after the last one left.

"I think either the Sarah, Daisy, or Emma would be best. I'm not sure which of them though."

Lady Amelia put three sheets before me. She'd had these three girls picked out already. "If you look at their references, you'll see that Daisy simply has none; this would be her first major job. For that reason, I would recommend against her."

I nodded. "Then Sarah or Emma. How would I go about making that choice? Both seem to have good references, and they both strike me as well prepared."

"Emma is the proper choice. Her family has some connections to mine. Even if she's just the daughter of a baron's second son. If she grows, it will reflect well on you, Rooke, and myself."

"Did you have her picked out from the beginning?"

"Naturally, Alana. I've gotten reports on most of these girls from their former employers. I also know enough about family lines to know who's who. I am a bit surprised you didn't pull out Irina on your list of potentials."

"Something about her seemed off."

"Good intuition. I'm told you rather embarrassed her cousin during the exam. I didn't think she'd come to the interview, but . . ." The older woman just shrugged.

"Was this all just a test?"

"Of course not. It was partially a test. I wanted to see what my husband saw in you, and I did. But I also showed you how to choose a maid."

"And I suppose that since you arranged it, and you're already well in with Emma's family, that getting her the job will gain you connections too?"

"Certainly. Use what opportunities you can to build relationships with those who can benefit you. Emma's family is not a major player, but they've done well by our family in the past, and this is their reward. Hopefully, that relationship will deepen through this, and all will prosper—even you, since you are being associated with both Emma's family, and my own."

"Lady Amelia, I feel like trying to manage all of this will be a true trial."

"Don't worry, dear, it will come with time." She patted me on the shoulder and gave me a kind grin.

I spent the rest of my day learning how to do the proper letters accepting Emma. As well as one to Professor Rooke to thank him for his aid. That evening, I made one for Lady Amelia in the style I'd been shown. She didn't tell me to, but I wasn't so truly dense as to not know to do it.

CHAPTER 20

ARRIVING AT THE ACADEMY

I sat on my bed. Today was the day, the day that I left the Starlit Sky, Lucien, and Lude. I would even miss Eleanor, just a bit. I had packed most of my things, not that there were many. I'd made it to the bottom of my trunk. There I found an old spindle, the same one I'd had with me all these years. I nearly broke down seeing it, but with some effort managed to keep myself together. I rolled the little tool in my hand as I thought about it for a while, smiling at all the memories, all the places I'd been. I packed it away again, knowing that I'd have to keep it.

Dras showed up to help me get my few things up to the school. I knew that he wasn't allowed in the girls' dorms, and that Emma would meet me there to put it all away. I didn't have much to take in truth, only a handful of clothes and personal items. It all fit in a few small bags.

There was a bit of light chatting as we made our way to the gates, but not too much off that. I was feeling more contemplative today than I had in a while. Eleanor walked alongside, reading my mood and letting me to myself, I appreciated that. Eventually, we did make it though, and she would leave me here. I turned to her as I came up to the gates, and we took a moment to look at each other.

"This is it then." I decided to speak first.

"It is, assuming you don't find your way back to the Shield's care. Know that we are there, Alana, if you need it."

I nodded. "I'll keep that in mind. Thanks for dealing with me."

She smiled, patted my head, and left.

"Well, no use standing out here; let's head in." Dras smiled as he hauled up my bags.

As we approached the gates, there was a group of maids waiting, from which one broke off.

"Greetings, Miss Alana, may I get your bags?" Emma spoke, giving a smile as she approached the two of us.

"Certainly, Emma. This is my friend Dras; he's also a student here."

She gave a bright smile as she moved to get the bags, which the young man handed over without complaint. If I had to guess, Emma was only eighteen or so, and even at her age, she still had to look up at Dras to see his face.

The school was laid out in a sort of plus shape. The first building you entered was mostly offices for professors and the like. By going through it, you could reach the school proper, a large round building where the different classrooms were located. I was taking the average number, but unlike my wizard friend didn't end up in some of the weirder esoteric magical ones. Opposite the offices was a small library with laboratories for research and projects in the back. My practical class for Magical-Item Creation was there as well, which seemed sensible. The other parts of the plus were made by the dorms, girls on the right, boys on the left.

We made our way slowly to the door to the dorms. It was a massive oaken thing, easily ten feet tall and quite wide. There was a line on the floor over which men were not allowed, excluding professors and some special cases. As we came to the line, Dras stopped, keeping a distance back.

"Well, this is where I leave you two. I'm not sure exactly what will happen if I try to cross into the girls' area, but some of the others have told me it's 'painful and funny to watch,' so I'll be off."

I wondered what exactly it did do now. I'd have to ask, or wait until some blowhard boy decided to find out personally. I imagined that there was some equally unpleasant fate awaiting any girls who tried to enter the boys' dorms. Not that I had any intention of ever trying to go there.

"Well, let's head on in then." I turned to look at Emma and give her a smile as we passed the door.

Our dorms were an enormous complex. I knew there were only around two hundred students here, and this was absolutely insane. This building could have easily fit four or five times the number. On the ground floor was the communal baths and a few other public facilities, study rooms, and the like. Above that, there were four floors, one for each year. First-year students were, of course, on the top and had the longest walk to get to anything else.

Once we got all the way up, I looked about. There was a central opening on all the floors to let in light from above, with our rooms circling around it. The first thing that struck me as odd was the room placement; some of the rooms were much further from the others.

"Are the rooms different? Do you know, Emma?"

"Of course they are, Miss. Their size is based on social rank and to an extent family wealth."

"I don't suppose you know where mine is?"

"Naturally. I arrived early this morning to get everything in order for you."

"If you would then."

Emma led me to the far side of the roundabout. I was about as far as one could get from the stairs. Over here, all of the rooms were spaced evenly. My guess was that these were for those not of noble birth. Something that seeing Kala coming out a few doors down seemed to confirm.

"Hey there!" She nearly skipped over to join me, slowing only to smile at Emma.

"Hi, how's it going?" I said as I opened the door. My maid's hands were full, and there was no point in making her wait out here while we talked, so I led the way in.

Then I did a double-take. This room was huge. It had a desk to one side, tucked under a small window. Along the wall near it was a fireplace, with all its associated fixtures. The opposite wall had a curtained bed in a pale periwinkle and a setup for dressing and hair. I could see doors off to the sides, too, that led to some other rooms. This place had to be as big as a good-sized apartment would be back on Earth, and it was just for me.

"Yeah, I kind of felt the same way when I saw mine." Kala had gotten annoyingly good at reading me as of late. "Yina is getting all my stuff put away now. Not that I have nearly enough to fill it out."

"Yina?"

"My maid, it's tradition to bring one."

"I'm surprised the temple was willing to spend money on that." I knew how much I was paying Emma. It wasn't that much to me, but it was more than a great many made.

"She works for the temple, Alana. She has a minor talent for healing, so if she grows into a proper caster, she'll probably become a priestess in the Order of the Lovers."

"Ah, I see." They were putting Yina here in the hopes that she would grow. Everyone won from that scenario. "Aren't healers really needed though?"

Kala shook her head. "They are, but minor talents aren't all that potent. She can heal only minor injuries; it's useful, but not something in high demand. I do hope she gets stronger. What about your maid?"

"Ah . . . I don't really know Emma well yet. Professor Rooke's wife helped me find her. She seems quite reliable." I responded in a rather low voice. It was kind of weird to talk about someone I knew was just on the other side of the room.

"Well, you have time. Anyway, I'm off to explore the baths. Word is they're wonderful."

Kala rampaged off to find herself the washrooms. She did seem to love a good bath. While she was busy, I began to explore my own room. I was still unsure on how to speak to Emma, so I just started looking around.

First I found a lavatory. It was smallish but well appointed. It even had something akin to a toilet, which I had to check out. They'd figured out how to run a pipe down to catch waste, and how to install a stopper and water tank, but not a U-bend quite yet. This led to an absolutely foul odor every time you tried to flush. That said, an actual toilet was probably one of the best things I'd seen in years. Beside it, there was even a small apparatus that worked like a bidet. It also drew from the water tank, which I supposed Emma was filling, so I didn't mess with it too much.

The other door led off to another bedroom, this one much smaller and plainer. It looked rather like my own room back at the Starlit Sky, and I quickly closed the door. As I did, my maid looked up at me.

"My apologies, I didn't realize they'd put you a room beside mine."

"Miss Alana, these are your rooms, and you are my employer. You have every right to go in there if you so desire."

I cringed at that thought. The idea of someone I worked for just barging into my living space rankled on a visceral level.

"That's . . . I don't think I would want anyone to do that to me, so I won't to you."

She smiled as she hung up the last of my clothes. My uniforms were already in the room, and I really wanted to try one on, but I would hold off until classes tomorrow.

"Thank you. By the way, are these all of your clothes?" She seemed a bit concerned.

"I've got some more coming soon. They should be in in a few days. Until then, I have classes, so it shouldn't be a problem, should it?"

"Not at all."

"So . . . we don't really know each other, do we?" I awkwardly tried to break the ice.

"No, but we know some things, Miss. You've read my résumé, and I've been told a bit about you from Lady Amelia."

"True, but . . . um . . . do you have any hobbies?"

"Well, I like embroidery. I do that when I've exhausted all my mana on practice." She showed me the edge of her apron. On it I could see lovely designs that I'd missed before in the same color as the cloth, small flowers and vines moving along the very edge.

"Wow, that's pretty good! What kind of magic do you do?"

"Oh . . . I only have a minor talent for water . . . it's nothing much, but . . . it's good for cooking and stuff. Water isn't considered all that interesting." She went over to one of the buckets by the fireplace and put forth a small stream from her hand, rather like a faucet. "I can only do a few gallons at once, but it's something."

"Don't knock water. It's one of the first things I learned to do. My first teacher was a water specialist wizard, and he was crazy cool. It's useful too!"

She blushed, and after a bit more light conversation, we got back to setting everything up. It was an all-day affair learning the campus, and I wound up walking far more than I hoped I'd have to most days. When I finally got back to my rooms (nearly saying some rather unladylike words after the third flight of stairs), I was exhausted and basically fell into my bed.

Emma gently woke me the next morning. There was much I had to do before class. First was getting dressed. While the uniforms looked good, they were also rather complex, and I was nowhere near used to having someone help me get dressed, so the whole affair was rather more difficult than I would have hoped.

For my hair, I was told, in no uncertain terms, that leaving it loose simply wouldn't do. After a bit of discussion, we settled on a simple waterfall braid. It looked fancy enough that I wouldn't irritate the noble girls but didn't take so long that I would have to wake up before dawn just to get ready.

Breakfast was simple and served in a small communal hall on the first floor. I was so rushed that I hardly had time to enjoy it. The toast and fruit did serve as a good pickup for the morning though. Sadly, before I even made it through my entire plate, people started leaving. With a sigh, I joined Kala and the other girls in my year. Our first class would be altogether, and we were all looking forward to Professor Rooke's first lecture.

Shortly after, we found our seats. As expected, mine was rather near the back of the large hall, its massive blackboard covering easily half the room. Kala was right beside me though, so I had that going right. We exchanged a few hushed whispers before the man himself marched into the room and looked out at us.

"Good morning, Class. Let us begin with the basics."

The basics of runecraft. Who can tell me what runes are?" After waiting for a few seconds, Professor Rooke pointed randomly at a boy near the front.

The lad looked nervous but began. "The runes are magical symbols that . . ."

He didn't get the whole answer out before Professor Rooke harshly answered "No. You." A finger went toward the next nearby student who paled.

"They're the symbols on magical items, Professor. I don't know much, but it's something to do with them controlling the item I think."

"Better. Who can tell me where and when they originated?" After a brief wait, he indicated another of the students near the front.

"I . . . am not sure, sir."

The professor patted the boy in the shoulder, rather than giving a stern rebuke. Then he turned to me and locked eyes. "What do you know?"

"Very little. They serve as indicators on magical items of their power level and are somehow related to the Atali language."

The professor returned to the front of the class and began looking at all of us. His gaze swept over each and every student. That done, he returned to his lecture, the chalk flying up behind him and beginning to write on the board. The symbols it wrote were noticeably runes.

"This runic script, if it were inherently magical, would turn my chalkboard yellow. It is not. The runes are themselves no more magical than any other writing system and are, in fact, a language of sorts. This language was constructed by the elves some five thousand years ago . . ."

He launched into the story, or what was known of it at least. Five millennia ago, a great king came to power among the elves. He was a genius the likes of which the world has never seen since. His greatest invention was something called a core. The creation of which allowed the creation of magical items. Before mana had been only able to be used on-site. The storage and ability for even those not gifted in magic to use the power was a game changer.

The elven king took over the continent he was on and expanded his reign around the world, forming an empire the likes of which the world had never seen before or since. Eventually though, he passed, and over time his dynasty weakened. None of his children were blessed with his mind, and the low birth rates of the elves finally allowed every other people to kick them back to their own homeland. A few had tried to invade the elven continent, but there were still items from their great king, and those could turn fleets and armies to ash.

A core was a magical construct and a very small one at that, barely visible to the naked eye. It came in three types or levels: apprentice, journeyman, and master. Each was composed of a number of parts, one that understood the runes, one that held what they were currently doing, and finally one for storage. The last stored both the information of what rune was what and the blueprint for passing on the core.

"Each of you will learn to make a core. You will do this by constructing it inside of your own brain. It is not an ideal location, but it is the one that the spells used to pass it on and put it in. You are heavily advised to not try and make any alterations to it, or it will not function properly."

That seemed insane to me, to actually build something in my own brain. He then went on to explain how there were a number of commands and control sequences that we would either have to memorize or keep a record of. The core itself did not tell you those up front, at least not in any way that anyone knew of. Much was poorly understood about it, and while there was much innovation on how to get them to do things, this was accomplished by learning what commands did and then kludging them together.

"For now, begin memorization of the runes themselves and these three command sequences." He wrote the listed bits on the board. Each was very similar, indicating a color change with the first bit and what color with the second.

Before I knew it, the class was done, and we were off to the practical. It was held in the library and laboratory wing, and we walked there as a group. Apparently, it was tradition for every class to go straight to the practical side after finishing up with the theory for the day. My guess was that they wanted us to jump in while everything was still fresh in our minds.

"Greetings, everyone," Professor Hern said as we all filed in.

The room where our practical took place was huge. All around it, there were small workstations, which I was eager to get a look at. In the middle was a large demonstration table. I didn't see supplies out, but there were drawers and closets abounding throughout the room.

"First thing first. Everyone find your assigned workstation and familiarize yourself with what is where. You don't need to know what all of it does or what any of it does. We'll handle those questions later. For now, I'd like you to just see where it is—everything is labeled. I feel like I must say this, because I really must. Do not attempt to use tools before you've received instruction in them, and always follow your safety protocols. You'll be learning those too."

I made my way around, guessing correctly that I would be near the back. As I looked over the various parts of the workstation, I noticed some rather interesting things. First of all, everything, and I mean everything had a label on it, and said label was easily visible. On the desktop were circles of runes labeled things like "Metal Manipulation Array" and "Wood Manipulation Array." Each was on a separate slab of wood embedded into the desk, and I suspected they were magical items of some form.

The drawers were also labeled by what manner of tool they had, and I had a whole tool-shop worth here: drills, files, hammers, and more. Two of the drawers had small locks on them. One was labeled "Materials" and the other "Projects." I knew the combination to neither, but suspected that I would find out more soon.

"All right, everyone, you lot look settled. Now, first off, there will be no playing around in my class. What we are doing here may be fun, but it is also deadly serious and deadly if done carelessly. Two, you are forbidden from using any tool that I have not signed off on personally. Once you've demonstrated that you can safely use it, then we can get to the practice portion. Any questions?" He waited a few moments as he scanned the crowd. "No? Good."

He then began to go over the tools one by one. This was a laborious process that involved all of us pulling out the tool as he explained how, and importantly when, to use it. There were like nine different types of hammers, and all of them were for different stuff. Some were obviously bigger than others and made of differing materials, but I had no clue what was for what.

He demonstrated each and then had us mimic his movements, assuring us that in time we'd all get it down perfectly, that he'd see to it. That sounded more like a threat than anything to me, but at least I was assured that he took his job with no amount of humor.

This whole chore went on for the period. By the end of class, we were exhausted and all looking forward to lunch. As we returned to our dorms and fell into our seats, the talking began.

"Well . . . what did you think?" one girl down the table asked her neighbor.

"That I'm more qualified to be a carpenter than when I woke up. We haven't even done any magic yet!" her partner replied.

"Sounds like you lot just got back from Hern," an older girl said as she plopped down next to them.

"Is he always like that?" I ventured to ask as I leaned a bit nearer.

"Yeah, when you're working with new stuff, but not for no reason, yeah? I made a dagger last year that was amazing. It has an enchantment that will clean it for almost no mana. It also involved me working with liquid iron. Do you know how hot that is?"

"Very?" one of the others ventured.

"Yes, very. Long story short, some of the stuff you use in that class is dangerous, very dangerous. So sit through the boring bits."

"I think we have another helping of it tonight." Kala peeped up as she looked over her schedule. I was sure we did, but was so not looking forward to it that I hadn't dared to check yet.

There was a collective groan from our group. Each year was broken into two main study groups, with an alternation of core classes. Well, some alternation, for the bards and priests, we were all in the same group; our groups were just too small for us to break up for core classes. That meant that classes like Magical-Item Creation and General Spellcasting were always going to be our little group of twenty-five.

My next two classes were Flute and Harp. Those both went rather swimmingly. The instructors were both experts of a level that I couldn't really follow, but they understood the methods and techniques far better than I did. Mostly, I went over different pieces that I knew and started working on reading this world's musical notation. While I could play a bit, that last part was one I really would have problems with.

It occurred to me that an astounding amount of what I was learning was going to be different languages. That was odd, and I wondered for a minute if there was some linguistic aspect to magic. Then I thought about it more. It didn't matter what I was playing when I cast, just that I performed. The intent and performance were the important part; the method was secondary. The runes were also apparently not magical at all, but rather some weird kind of input to the interface that was the core. So the magic relation to linguistics didn't seem too likely . . . shame.

I mulled this over as I found my spot in the practical room. We were all in a bit of a sour mood as the professor came in and moved to his spot.

"Good, you're all here. Now, I know that what we've been doing so far isn't too fun." That was an understatement. "So I've got a surprise for all of you. Something you can do on your own where you literally can't hurt yourselves. I wager that you'll even find it interesting . . . for a while at least."

That statement got us all perked up as he led us out and down the hall to another room. This one was unlocked and apparently open to our group at all times. That was a bit of a relief, since this seemed to be our current project.

My breath left me as I came in. Now this was a magical classroom. The walls were all black, as were the floor and ceiling, some kind of obsidian if I had to guess, or something that looked like it. On the floor were twenty-five rune circles all around a central pedestal. In the very center, there was floating a small light, pulsing out along lines into the floor.

"This, everyone, is where you will be building your core. Pick a circle and stand in it. Once you're all ready, you can kneel. The spell will take you inside yourself and show you where and how to build, just follow its directions and all will be well. I will be checking to make sure you have correctly followed the spell, but if you screw it up, you'll know. The spell will kick you back after an hour, or if you are disturbed."

I wasn't too sure about that last part but joined my classmates, none-theless. I stood inside the circle of runes, looking down at the pulsing lines of power below me. I was nervous as I knelt down, my stomach all in knots.

Instantly, my physical form fell away. I found myself seemingly inside myself. The sensation was truly difficult to explain, but I could see a faint outline making some form of lattice in front of me. It formed a complex web of interconnecting parts with little balls and lines.

This was obviously what I was here to do, and one of the little balls was lit up. These seemed to be some kind of node point, with the lines moving around one another in three dimensions connecting them. I tried focusing on the little ball and found that it pulled a bit at my mana. I fed a bit in, only a tiny, minuscule particle, hardly enough for me to notice. The ball became physical rather than outlined, and around it a crystal formed. So this was the beginning of making a core . . . interesting.

CHAPTER 22

✦

THE CORE

The core was an interesting piece. Each line and orb I added expanded the crystal structure slightly and formed a web within it. I could see and feel these in ways that were rather unusual and could tell that the whole thing was sort of impossibly complicated. I could also see where signals would run down each line and where the orbs met looked like a switch.

I was never all that into computers, but I'd had a friend who was, and between him and the insistence of the school librarians, I began to recognize Boolean operators in the structure, if only because signals could be sent down the lines. The first I saw was an "and" operator, and it just went from there. Soon I was seeing "ifs" and "nots" here and there.

This isn't to say that I could actually tell what this whole mess was doing, I couldn't, but I recognized that it operated on the same principles as a computer from Earth. It also let me conceptualize things as operators, a task that once done meant that I could just make the operators. That was some kind of weird bardic hack I think. I understood what one thing was, what it meant, and what it did, so I could just put that through rather than a single line or junction.

Professor Hern was absolutely correct too. If we made any mistake, the spell itself seemed to light it up bright red and release a slight nagging feeling. It must be checking against something else that everything was where it was supposed to be and then telling us. That was a really neat little safety measure.

I built and built until I suddenly found myself thrown out of my mind space. I was again kneeling in the little circle, waking up with all the others. My knees really hurt too. Professor Hern was there waiting for us; he seemed to be going over paperwork while he waited. As we came out, he looked up.

"Everyone stay where you are for a bit longer. I'm going to check on your progress."

He went person to person, giving advice. Nobody had managed to screw it up. Most hadn't gotten much done though, and he told them that they needed to keep at it. Eventually, he came over to me, placing his hand on a particular point on the circle.

Immediately, we were back at the core. I could feel him there, too, looking at it. After a few seconds, we popped back out and he looked at me.

"That's . . . how did you get so much done?"

"Sir?"

"You look like you've been working on it for a week or so. What happened?"

I just shrugged. "The structure just repeats a lot, so I made the repeats instead or the basic structure . . . if that makes sense."

"You've a free period after lunch tomorrow, do you not?"

"Yes, sir . . ."

"Good, come to my office. I'd like to talk about this a bit."

Shit. I knew I'd screwed up somewhere. I didn't know if they knew what all those junctions were for, or what they were doing, and that concerned me. What would they do if they found out? I began to thoroughly consider how I would answer questions that I knew were coming.

After our final class of the day, I stumbled back to the dorms with Kala. She'd convinced me that I should absolutely try out the baths. Seemed to be a bit of a thing with her, but I needed one anyway. Sitting on the floor for an hour concentrating after all the rest of the day had been unusually physically draining, even if it took almost no mana.

Upon informing Emma of my plan, she brought my clothes, towels, and the like. She and Kala's maid insisted on joining us, even though neither of us thought it necessary. It looked like they were supposed to at least escort us and assist with the washing . . . I was told it was a multistep process. I didn't really feel the need for them to do that, but when in Rome I suppose . . .

The idea of Rome was actually quite accurate. The baths were, in a sense, extravagant. First you undressed and washed at an area not unlike a shower, only buckets were used instead of faucets. From there, you moved into the baths proper. These were more like heated soaking pools; there were a few different temperature pools depending on what exactly you wanted, from very hot to just slightly warm.

The maids helped at the washing stations to get our backs and help with hair, which nobody sane in any world washed every day. I felt my nerves melt as Emma ran a cloth covered in hot water over my back. I was happy to let her do that, though both Kala and I refused to allow much more than that, instead releasing our maids.

The soaps were simple, but well made. The foam from them pleasant as I scrubbed myself. Once that was done and I rinsed, we headed toward one of the pools.

"Hot? Medium hot? I don't really want cool." Kala looked between the pools.

"Medium. I can see how much steam the hot is putting off. While it'd be nice to soak in that, we wouldn't be able to for too long." Kala pouted at my statement, but joined me anyway.

We were not alone. The medium was the most popular of the three. The water was still hot, quite so, but it wasn't sauna hot. There were three or four older girls with us, chatting as we joined.

"You two new?" one girl asked, leaning over.

I nodded to her as I settled in.

"Excellent! What do you do? Who are your families? Are you betrothed?"

Kala and I looked at each other, and she went first.

"I'm a priest, my family isn't really of note, and no."

"Bard, and the two others are the same for me too."

"Oh wait, are you the girl who shut down that prick Johnathan?"

"If he's the one who tried to scream at me during the exam registration, then yes."

"That's great! I'm Lapia by the way. That boy was trying to court my sister, but now that he's failed his entrance exam . . . Oh! Is it true that Rooke dressed him down in front of everyone too?" This girl seemed to really hate that guy. I took a few moments to wonder what he'd done to piss her off so bad.

"That's totally true. It was brutal," another girl from my year, Lora, said as she came to join us. "I was there. If Rooke spoke to me like that, I think I might die on the spot."

"You don't want to go down that route, trust me. Rooke is . . . well, he's not bad if you're trying to learn, but if you slack off even a bit, he'll rip you to shreds." Lapia leaned back as she spoke, seeming to carefully consider her wording.

We chatted about the different teachers for a while. Apparently, Magnolia was good, if a bit of a flake. While he knew his stuff, he often got sidetracked and led you down a weird path. Lapia had a good amount of experience with him since she was a bard in her third year. There were only three girls that year, and none in the year ahead of us. Apparently, sometime soon, we first-year bard girls would be getting a lesson from some of the older ones.

As things went on, I found myself slipping down deeper into the water, letting the heat take me. Kala poked me after a bit, making me wake from my stupor. After sticking my tongue out at her, I sat up straight and paid attention. Not long after that, I returned to my room, falling out cold as soon as I hit the sheets.

My next day consisted of general classes on spellcasting and bardic magic. Professor Magnolia began by handing out a list of spells we had to learn as part of his program.

"Sir, why do we need to learn to summon paper and ink?" Lora pointed toward the list that she'd been handed. "At least one food item as well?"

"Ah, because they are vitally important to the work that most bards do. Paper and ink end up being what many of my students produce for their fellows and are also important to a lot of clerical work. As for food, well . . . It's highly useful for when you're traveling or to feed yourself in an emergency."

"Okay . . . how do we become familiar with those though? I mean, I know what paper and ink are kind of like, sir, but probably not enough."

"Good question! We'll be having demonstrations on their creation. It really is quite interesting . . ." He spent most of the rest of his lecture wandering from one tangent to another on that subject.

After lunch, there was no getting around my meeting with Professor Hern. I walked to his office, still trying to work out what I would tell him. I settled on the truth, to an extent. Lying might be found out later. If I just told him that, I wouldn't answer some of his questions now, so it would probably work out better.

Professor Hern's office was quite unlike Professor Rooke's. The fact that the madman had somehow added a forge to it was the first hint. Everything was overtaken by tools and projects. Everything seemed to have a place, but there was just so much of it. I found it claustrophobic.

As I came in, I saw Professor Rooke sitting in one of the guest chairs. He motioned me to the one beside him as Professor Hern settled in behind his desk.

"You know, Rooke, there really is no need for you to take valuable time out of your day for this . . ."

"Alana is my charge, so it is, of course, my responsibility to oversee any important meetings she has. Certainly, you wouldn't gainsay me that?"

These two had smiles as they spoke, but they couldn't cover their rivalry. Each seemed eager for information, happy to learn something that might surprise them. It was like being a small fish between two giant sharks.

"Fine, fine. Unless you have some objections, Alana?" Professor Hern looked at me with a glint in his eyes.

"I'm happy to have Professor Rooke stay." Having someone who could oppose him was useful. In fact, the idea that these two might end up getting in each other's way and spare me did flit here and there.

"Fine then. You said that you realized that the structures in the core were repeating, and that helped, no? My understanding is that many bards have realized this, but without some deeper understanding of them, they can't reproduce the whole blocks. They can see, but not understand, not know really. We wizards face a similar problem in that we don't know what they are as such.

"If you don't understand, then I don't think I should explain that right now."

"Care to expound on that, Alana?" Rooke was giving me a rather more harsh look than I'd like. Professor Hern had apparently decided to join him.

"I'm not saying that I won't ever, but not right now. My first teacher told me not to tell people too many conclusions that I came to if they were outside of the usual, and I wouldn't want to disobey him in that. I need to think about what I say and if it could cause any large upsets."

Neither of the two seemed happy with that explanation. I had to give it to them that they'd at least held off on immediately coming down on me though. Professor Rooke, in particular, seemed to chew over the words for a bit.

"This isn't the first unusual thing you've come up with, is it?"

"No, sir."

"The flamethrower, why it doesn't work quite as well for other bards is one, no?"

"A couple of my spells. That is one of them."

"I'd really like to know that one, Rooke. The girl could speed up our training significantly if she'd tell us." Hern seemed to want to press the issue. By the look on his face, I knew that Rooke showing up had been squarely to my advantage here.

"I agree, but her insight could have a large effect. Ruminating on it isn't a poor idea. Alana, what would you need to feel comfortable explaining your little secret to us?"

"I think I first need to understand what it will do to magic item creation in general. As well as knowing what effects it could have that I don't intend. Basically, I need to learn a lot more about that before divulging anything."

"I understand your concerns, Alana, and while it will personally be a pain . . . Well, we'll see to it that you learn as much as possible about magical items, won't we?" Hern looked over as he spoke, getting a smile from Professor Rooke.

That night, I got a lecture on what they understood as the basics. They knew that the structures formed things that would only pass on a message if it was powered a certain way. On the other hand, they didn't know the purpose of that. They had all the pieces they needed, but nobody had made the leap that it was doing very basic math and making true/false declarations on if/then statements.

There were a few theories that included those elements, but theory alone wasn't knowledge. It is for that reason that people had been trying to prove things for a long time. There were some hiccups though, primarily in that there was no way to get at the raw information easily. Even if you could, it was still a monumental quantity of data to try and work by hand. There seemed to be some odd blockage as well in transferring it over, but I figured I'd get on that later.

I was also instructed to finish my core as soon as was actually possible, causing me to frown the whole way back to my dorm.

Over the next couple of days, I got to go to several new classes. Math and History were about what they sounded like. I found the history lineup to be rather interesting, but the fact that the math we would be covering was shockingly basic was tiring. Proper Etiquette came next, and for the first day of that we simply had tea as the professor observed us, taking notes. Professor Sasha taught the class, and I really had no idea what to make of her. She was from the wizard program, specializing in some kind of light magic.

I freely admit that I was excited most about my Atali classes. Something that only overflowed when I realized that our teacher was an elf. She was not quite as ethereal as one might expect, her ears not quite as long. Her first class went over the basics of the alphabet, which I recognized as belonging to the same as the runes, a small mercy. It meant that I only really had to learn one of them. She also gave us a few words to learn but seemed rather disinterested in her own subject.

Dras joined me for this one, while Kala had some other class on healing or something for that period. We sat beside each other since Professor Etia hadn't given us any assigned seating.

"So, how's it going?" he asked as we finished up. It was rude to speak in class and just wasn't done.

"Pretty good. I have a feeling Rooke and Hern are going to pummel me with information though. How about you?"

"Oof, yeah, those two are rough. I'm pretty good; my pyromancy course is finally heating up." He gave a smile like he was actually proud of that statement.

"Ugh. That joke must have been made a thousand times."

"True, but it's still good. We're going over how to get flames hotter right now; it's fun and consists mostly of trying to keep the flame steady while you add air to it. Simple in theory, but the practical aspects are a bit harder on the fly."

I nodded. "Basically making a furnace with nothing to contain it?"

"Yeah, the heat flows out really fast though, so it's a pain. That and keeping it from just growing."

We took a few moments to banter as we cleaned up on the subject of fire. I didn't really know all that much from a practical standpoint. Or at least I didn't know what I knew that would cause problems, so I pretended not to know anything.

"Any other cool classes you're taking?" Dras asked, I forgot that I'd never actually gone over my schedule with him.

"I think Atali Dance will be fun. You in that?"

"My adviser told me it's mostly a girl thing . . . there are styles for men, but they're not all that popular apparently."

"Huh . . . I've got that and another class, Magical Materials . . . oh, and Combat Spellcasting too."

"I've heard the combat class is brutal. They send you out with some of the knight apprentices and stuff for games. I wanted to take it, but there was just so much else, you know?"

I shrugged. "The bard course is a little more sparse I think, because there's not many of us. Magnolia tried to get me to take some advanced healing, but I just wasn't feeling it."

"Fair. Well, I'm off, catch you later!"

I was happy to see him. Also really glad that we'd finally get some chance to talk. I hated it, but over the past couple of years, we'd not really seen too much of each other, and having a class together would finally help that, if only a little. I ruminated on it as I made my way to lunch. Kala joined me there as well as Lord Fallon's niece Pinea.

"So, what's next on the schedule?" Kala asked as she plopped down.

"Atali Dance, you?"

"Oh, the outfits for that are absolutely scandalous." Pinea leaned in as she spoke, bringing her voice down. "I signed up for it too. It's going to be wonderful."

"I'm taking Advanced Healing, but be sure to show me all the moves you learn," Kala chuckled.

"I'll be sure to. Care to help me practice, Pinea?" The girl nodded vigorously at my suggestion.

"Of course. Elves live for like ages, particularly the more pure-blooded ones, so it's ancient and really cool stuff. I got to see one of the performances a couple of years back at a party It was wild. I thought my chaperone was going to die where she stood."

"Pure-blooded ones?"

"Uh . . . yeah, pretty much all elves are like part human or something now. Not sure on the details."

Okay, so that was neat information. I now wanted to go and see what I could learn on that. Maybe ask someone. That was something I could put a pin in for the time being though. Because in front of me was Pinea, who was practically vibrating with excitement. Kala looked on at the worked-up noble girl before turning to me and shrugging.

"I've never seen it. Though I'm feeling like I might have missed something fun now."

"You have!"

"Regardless. It's about that time. Care to walk there with me, Pinea?"

"Yeah, of course!" Pinea practically pulled me down the hall on our way to the room assigned for this class.

It was a room full of girls. I supposed that the various advisers had pushed the boys away, though I didn't know why until Professor Etia entered the room. She was in what could only be described as a belly dancing outfit. From head to toe, ten out of ten would absolutely agree that this was an outfit for belly dancing. Several girls looked like they needed to pick their jaws up off the floor as she moved before us.

"Greetings, everyone! I'm so glad so many of you have come to join me for this wonderful class." Her earlier disinterest in teaching us had disappeared like mist on the wind. "In this class, we'll be learning traditional Atali dance. It's enjoyable, excellent exercise, and those of you who are bards will find it works great for casting as well! I'll show you a few things, and then we'll begin with some basic exercises!"

She activated a small magical item that played music and then began to dance. My understanding of the costume was not mistaken at all. This was something I'd expect to see from the Middle East, or at least something that someone would think would come from there. I pondered all I had gotten myself into. The culture in Bergond was what one would call "highly conservative" when it came to clothes and dance. Even trying to wear that, and dance anywhere even vaguely public might cause a ruckus. Then again . . . it did look fun. She also said it worked well for casting. . . .

I soon learned that there was much to this that I hadn't known about. Things like posture, position, and all that good stuff. After the demonstration, Professor Etia spent most of the remaining class forcing us into proper posture and then showing us only the most basic of moves. It was fun. Pinea, in particular, seemed to be having a wonderful time.

As class ended and everyone made their way out, I stayed behind a bit. I had a question I wanted answered.

"Professor, you said you could use dance to cast magic?"

"Ah, you must be one of my bardic students. Yes, though you're nowhere near that yet." Her accent was subtle, a small extension of her a's and y's.

"I'd heard it was possible but never learned it. Do you have any advice?"

"Hmm . . . it will be easiest when the dance comes naturally to you. When you move with the flow rather than some predetermined way, it will work best."

I nodded at the statement. "So you're a bard then?"

"Indeed I am. I will say that I find most of your bards here in Bergond a bit strange, but things are like that. Now, if you'll excuse me, I need to go change before my next class."

The rest of my day was a bit boring. There was a lot of studying, because I really needed to show well in these classes. I also spent a bit of time practicing what we'd learned with Pinea before dinner. Kala joined us and looked a bit shocked at what she was seeing and very interested in us showing her what we'd learned.

After dinner, I had to go work on my core. I made a point to spend a bit more than average time on that task, if only so that I didn't start getting angry letters telling me to hurry up from Professor Hern. That was something I was thoroughly expecting at some point in time. The task there wasn't hard, per se, or magically draining. It was mentally exhausting though, and by the end of it, your legs were really sore.

I slept well. It was really clear to me why I got so few visits once Dras had started his classes. I had just begun and I could hardly imagine having any free time at all. One blessing was that there was no homework. You would either study, or you wouldn't. Of course, this wasn't a school slackers could get into, and even those from really high noble families were pushed hard to achieve. This led to hard-core study groups on our off hours.

My final day of new classes began with Magical Materials, taught by Professor Hern. He informed us that most of the materials we would be dealing with in our first year were not, on their own, magic containing. Rather these were those used in the creation of magical items and we'd be going into far, far deeper detail than most would get.

Metals were of great importance in this class as they tended to act as magical conductors and were therefore excellent for building a number of things. Silver was the best, though gold would be used if something had to last for a long time, being that it didn't corrode, a real problem when dealing with higher energies. Copper was considered good, too, but iron was not. Iron, on the other hand, could be made insanely durable to a lot of forces and was cheap, so saw a lot of use, particularly as a covering to the underlying structure.

We didn't need to know the exact properties of them for now, but Professor Hern gave us a few simple to follow examples before letting us go for the day. I gathered that we'd be learning quite a bit more about the various metals at length before we moved on

My final class was Combat Spellcasting, something I was wildly excited for. When I got to the class, there were a number of tough-looking boys about. A few girls were here and there, but each of them looked hard as iron too. It was a bit intimidating.

Our teacher walked in, and he was huge. The man had broad shoulders and bulging muscles and looked out at all of us. I thought he should have had scars, but with the level of healing magic available to those who could afford it, I suppose that was foolish.

"Greetings and welcome. In my class, you will learn how to fight, how to use your magic to defeat your enemies, and how to prevent them from taking you down too. There are some simple things, methods and the like that I will teach you. There are a number of things I shall warn you against. There are also a number of things that you will need to figure out for yourselves. War and battle are chaos, and you must understand this, internalize this, make it your own. The methods that work one day may not the next, and you must be able to change on the fly. Any questions?"

His eyes eventually fell on me and I saw a slight grimace. "You got the wrong class, girl?"

"No, sir."

"You sure? You don't look like one of mine. Didn't your adviser tell you anything?"

"He advised me against this class, sir, but I insisted. I want to learn to fight properly."

He sighed. "You ever been in a fight girl? Killed a man? Faced down a monster?"

"Yes, yes, and yes, sir."

That got me a few surprised looks. Even our esteemed professor quirked his eyebrow a bit. "Well, then, let's see what you can do."

CHAPTER 24

COMBAT SPELLCASTING

Professor Endel decided that we all needed to be judged for his class before we did anything else. To that end, he led us to the arena and had us ready for one-on-one fights.

The rules were fairly simple. We were to fight to disable, not to kill, so fire and other often lethal elements were banned, as well as going all out. We had to stay in the arena until one of us won. We were allowed a wooden weapon if we desired, and a strike from it was to be considered as if delivered for real. Most of the students didn't take a weapon, and my choice of a dagger and mace was considered deeply strange.

I was, of course, in the first match, and soon found myself opposite a boy from the wizard program. Endel stood to the side after a brief overview of the rules and yelled "Go!" I opened with a focused scream; it was fast even if I didn't expect it to do much.

The wizard boy seemed to be expecting that and threw up some kind of shield. It worked partially for him, but him being distracted gave me plenty of time to start casting. While he was trying to recover from the partial blast, I threw up invisibility and my standard bubble around my mouth.

Wizard boy had recovered by this time and was looking around for me, seeming a bit confused. I had to be careful as I moved so as not to be seen, changing position only when he was looking away and very slowly then. After a few moments, I decided to sing in some fake footprints running around on the other side of the arena. It was just my movement trick from the exam, simple and easy to do.

The hard hose of water slamming into the wall there was a bit alarming. I could practically feel the force where it hit. While he was looking that way, I slowly, slowly crept closer. If I could just get within reach, I'd just use my dagger and be done with it.

My opponent was now shooting all over, here and there as I closed in. As I rose the little wooden tool, he released a big wave. Perhaps he sensed that I was closing in on him. Perhaps he was just searching. I honestly didn't know, and it didn't matter much as I was swept off my feet and far back, slamming hard into the ground.

"Cease!" Professor Endel called as I rolled to a stop.

He moved out onto the sand and toward the two of us, giving me a moment to catch my breath and get back up as I dropped my spells. I also cast the drying spell, since being soaked was no fun.

"Not bad, to either of you. Girl, do you have any attack spells other than the scream?"

"A flamethrower, but fire was against the rules."

The professor took a second to look at a piece of paper from his pocket, and I could see him visibly flinch. "Well then, Alana, we'll need to work on that. The stealth approach wasn't bad, but we will really need to beef up your direct attack and defense." He then looked at the boy. "Lad, you did well near the end, but you let her lead you around too much. Think about countermeasures to stealth on your own for now; we'll be discussing that later on in the class. You were on the right track with the area attacks."

I hummed a light healing spell as we returned to the stands to watch the next bout. I'd taken a pretty good hit there and was currently on my way to some lovely bruises, which I didn't need. After I'd finished, the boy I'd been against looked over at me.

"So . . . how close were you?"

"I was right next to you. You got me as I was setting up to jab you."

"Nice. I'm Troy, good to meet you."

"Alana, the same. What was that shield you used?"

"Oh, I was just trying to put up something to block sound. Figured you'd go with sonic attacks."

"Yeah, the easiest bard attack is just that scream."

"What about like . . . water or air?"

"They don't really work. Who knows though? I bet Professor Endel knows of something that will."

He nodded and we watched the rest of the fights quietly. There were a number of different approaches on display, some far more effective than others. The boy who soaked everything and then dropped the temperature like a stone was particularly good. Both myself and the priests who'd opted for this class got a good workout on healing by the end of it.

Professor Endel looked over all of us at the end of class. "Not bad, not bad at all. I want you lot to consider all that you saw and did today. Think about what worked, and what didn't, and what could work better. While I have much to teach you, you also have much to learn from experience, and considering that experience will lead to you learning faster those lessons that will keep you alive. In our next session, I will be having a discussion with each of you on what you learned today, so be ready."

Our next day was designated as a rest day, and while I couldn't speak for everyone, I was sure ready for it. Of course, not much resting was done by most students. Everyone seemed to be either heading to one of the many places throughout the school to study their various subjects. A few of the older students even took the time to work on personal projects like magical items or spells.

I was no exception, having tons of subjects and not nearly enough time for them. Being that most of my subjects were something I could spend an hour or two on with ease every day. I was fortunate that at least I didn't need to study math and where I was now I could easily do my instrumental classes.

I spent all morning studying my different classes one by one, eventually being joined by several of my classmates. They were of limited help, being that most of them were wizards and the bulk of their classes were focused on things like rudimentary and often wrong physics or natural science. The company was nice though.

Dras joined Kala and me as we went over our runes. He could now talk to us about that kind of thing, and together we went over several of the sequences we'd been told to study. None of these were overly complex commands, but it was fun, nonetheless.

He was currently reviewing a far more in-depth sequence and trying to figure out how to get it to work in an item. It was another lighting enchantment, as those were rather popular for testing. There was no real risk of explosion, and the mana cost on smaller ones was so low that it wouldn't break you to keep it going as long as you felt like it.

As I pored over what he did and he explained what each part was, I nodded along. There were commands governing frequency, intensity, and color as well as a simple on-and-off one. The sequence ended by simply running through the different patterns in a cycle, but the goal was to get the cycle to run in a certain way.

I would love to say that I instantly understood Dras's work and could tell him how to do it, but I didn't. The runes and command structure were simply too different from anything I'd seen before. I did get that one of the variables was based on frequency per second, but honestly, everyone understood that one. There was another that was using numbers to represent light. I was pretty sure I'd seen something like that in high school physics, but I couldn't remember too much about it. When I asked, Dras just kind of shrugged, seemed it was just one of the things that had come pre-done with the whole magical item system that nobody really understood too much about, but everyone knew just worked.

My afternoon and evening were spent on dance and light music, followed by a couple of hours spent meditating to continue building my core. I was speeding along compared to the others in my class on that front. At least that's what Professor Hern told me when he came by to check on it. It took most students the better part of a year to form the apprentice level of their core, but it seemed I might manage in just a couple of months, if my speed held.

My week complete, I finally stumbled up to my bed and fell in. As far as first weeks of school went, this might be the most intense I'd ever had. The topics were a mix of old and new, but the sheer number of them and the difficulty, both physical and mental, was on another level. Practice for Atali dancing alone probably counted as a decent workout.

The following week during our class on bardic magic, Professor Magnolia grabbed us all up and began to hustle us toward the door.

"Come, everyone, we're going to one of the nearby workshops. We're going to see paper made firsthand, and you need to pay close attention."

"Um, sir, is there any reason we can't have them come to us?" one of our bolder students suggested.

"There certainly is. The equipment to make paper is rather larger than most would like to admit. We went through all the trouble of having the shop made, and even getting it approved to run in the city every now and then, just so that you lot could go and see it. Now, come on."

I didn't understand that as we were rushed toward the gates. When we got there, the whole street was empty. Not slow, dead empty. I could see on the ends, a few barriers and guardsmen pointing people around. In an instant, my hackles raised and I started prepping for some attack.

"Where is everyone?" I asked, already pulling magic to hide myself so I could flee if needed.

"Huh? Oh, there are a few classes going to places on our street today. In the past, we wouldn't have bothered but . . . with what happened last year and the continuing unrest, the headmaster decided to organize our outings in such a way that the road could be shut down so we can go in peace."

"Isn't that like . . . really obvious and going to make us a huge target?"

"Indeed, it would, but don't fret. Now, off we go."

His ending made it clear that he was done discussing it. Of course, it also made me want to panic even more. I hated the idea of being bait, particularly for anyone as insane as the current flock of rebels seemed to be. That said, I knew that this class was mandatory, and complaining would only get me in trouble.

I lamented that I didn't know any spells to shield myself, even if they were suboptimal, I'd still need to pick those up. I concentrated on that and scrutinized all around me for any sign of movement as our little class walked down the street. June and Lora were both looking at me like I was crazy, but they hadn't been on the receiving end of two botched assassination attempts.

It was only when we came up to the paper shop that I was able to take a deep breath and relax. I immediately regretted that decision. It hadn't occurred to me that we were going to a paper manufacturing shop, and that the professor had informed us that it only ran on certain days. I understood now why that was.

The place was rank, absolutely, positively, foul. As the door opened, I feared I might cough up my breakfast. I was fairly sure that old-style paper mills from Earth didn't smell this bad, but this one certainly did.

Lora didn't manage to keep herself as steady as the rest of us and bent to empty her stomach in the gutter. It wasn't dignified, but I understood. That, of course, led to two others joining her. And with the sound and the added smell, even I couldn't hold it in. Within moments, the whole class had begun to thoroughly toss our cookies in the street.

"Gets 'em every time," our professor chuckled from the door. From his tone, I could tell he was breathing through his mouth.

CHAPTER 25

✦

PAPER

We toured the paper shop as quickly as we could get the adults to take us through. I felt sick the entire time, as did everyone else. The owner, I understood, had simply built up a resistance, and, of course, our jerk of a professor knew not to breathe through his nose. There were magical items on the doors whenever the shop was active that served to push the air inside and down into the sewers. That was surprisingly well-thought-out compared to most uses of magic I saw.

The smell itself was from a plant known as rotweed. Rotweed was useful in that it sped up the decay process of organic things; it also smelled like rotten meat mixed with feces and fresh baked bread. The last part served to make everyone slightly hungry, which the body fully rejected. The stuff seemed tailor-made to inspire sickness. It also made it possible to break down the plants used in paper into their fibers quick, fast, and in a hurry. It even gave a fairly good color, not pure white, but close enough.

This meant that good quality paper could be manufactured. The issues were thick though. Making paper anywhere even near the vicinity of a city was strictly banned, excluding special shops like this one. It was almost impossible to find people willing to work in such shops as well, meaning they had to be well paid. A few nobles had tried in the past to force the work on to some villages, but that had ended in a lot of their peasants fleeing the area. This meant that while papermaking was simple in theory, in practice it remained an expensive product—expensive enough that young bards were encouraged to learn to make it for themselves and their peers.

Once the plant's bark (a mixture of two small trees and a woody bush) was broken down thoroughly by a rotweed and water slurry, it was washed and run through a rather intricate process to make the paper itself. It was cool to watch. The process took two weeks to go from plants to sheets, most of that was drying though.

After we finished with our tour, we were given a few sheets to feel, smell (once we were out of the shop itself), taste, etc. I was fairly sure we all had a bit anyway, but this stuff was fresh and of the highest quality the shop could produce, so it was nicer than what we were used to. We were told that we had a week to make something acceptable, and that if we failed, we'd be having to come back and observe the shop again. That threat was enough to make us all take the assignment with utmost seriousness. All of us looked at one another with the grim hardened faces of those determined not to fail.

After our release, we three girls hurried back to our dorms. We collectively smelled like death, the lingering stench of the paper shop grasping onto our clothes, shoes, and hair. Professor Magnolia had made sure that his class had been scheduled such that we had plenty of time to wash and eat afterward, which we all agreed to do as a group. I arrived around the time Emma was putting away laundry.

"Oh goodness, what is that smell?" were literally the first words out of her mouth.

"Professor Magnolia surprised us by taking us to a paper shop today. Please bring some clean clothes to the baths if you would. I really don't want to touch anything until I've washed. Also if you could, prep to wash this uniform."

"Will it come out?"

"The smell is supposed to leave with water and just a bit of soap. It gets on everything though."

"Understood, I'll meet you at the baths."

I met Lora and June there as well. All three of us furiously washing ourselves while June chewed on a small bit of the paper we'd been given. After three separate washings, we all felt that it was safe and went to one of the tubs to soak as we talked out where to go on our project.

"Okay, I think I'm going to try to summon some," June declared as she settled in.

"If you bring that stink into this tub, I swear I will stab you," Lore responded.

"Ditto." I gave her a nasty look as she brought her hands up and concentrated.

Slowly, a sheet formed there. It was squarish and of the approximate right size, but it looked a bit too rough and slightly more yellow than I'd really want. There was no accompanying smell though, so I counted that as a win. June gave it a hard look over as she held it, frowning slightly.

"Needs work," she declared.

"All right, my turn." I pulled my hand up and thought.

I'd handled literally thousands, potentially tens of thousands of sheets of notebook paper. So I thought of that, of the smell, the weird taste everyone ended up learning, the feel of it. I also thought about how it was structured, thousands of tiny fibers all compressed in a random way. I tried to picture all of these things as I pulled my magic together with a simple tune.

The sheet I held there looked like standard college rule. I'd even put the lines on it by mistake, but hey, nobody was perfect. As I looked it over I noticed a few imperfections, little changes that made it look just slightly more like the paper we'd been given. The way the grain stood out just slightly more, the barest hint of roughness.

"Okay, that looks pretty good." Lora leaned over to look at it, the warm water lapping around us.

"Better than mine for sure." June nodded. "What's with the lines?"

"Those weren't intentional. I guess they'll make it easy to keep an even spacing though."

"May I?" Lora asked, holding out her hand.

"Go for it." I passed over the sheet. It was starting to get a little wet from the bath and steam anyway.

Both June and Lora seemed to like my version, thinking it was a bit nicer than the paper we'd been given at the shop. I was taking that as a pass. I ended up making a few more sheets, with and without lines for them to check out as well. The spell was still inefficient, but one or two sheets at once wasn't very much anyway.

"What are you picturing when you summon this?" Lora finally asked.

"So, paper is just a really dry, pushed-down bundle of random fibers, right? I just kind of pictured that. The fibers also need to be really white and kind of random. Other than that, focus on the feel and stuff."

They each gave it a few more tries, eventually getting something rather like what I'd made. It was around this time that a few more girls showed up. One made her way over to us with a scowl.

"Hey, you three, no summoning crap in the baths; you'll make a mess." If I had to guess, she was a third- or fourth-year student and looked none too pleased with our antics.

"Oh, sorry . . ." June whimpered out. Lora and I both tried to look contrite.

"Don't do it again." With a snap of her fingers, all of the sheets we'd made went up in a quick burst of flame, not even leaving ashes.

After she'd turned and left us, I looked at the two others. "Well, with that I think I'm done. See you in class."

Emma met me at the washing area, seemingly relieved that I'd managed to get the smell gone. She quietly helped me dress and gather my things before prepping for the rest of my day.

"Thank you. Have you started learning about magical items yet? Professor Rooke said that he held a class for the servants."

"Oh yes, it's all quite interesting. It's a wonderful way to spend my time when I'm done with all the work for the day."

"I'm glad you have some time for it."

I was still faltering in my conversations with her, unsure of what to say, if anything. Did she even want to talk to me? Was there even any way I could ask that question? Honestly, if I didn't have to have a maid, I didn't think I would. She didn't seem to mind talking though, not that I thought she'd show it if she did.

After a few more grueling days, I found myself back in Combat Spellcasting. We were each given a number of documents to read over while Professor Endel met with us privately. I tried to go over what I'd learned, but it was mostly just repeating what I already knew. The busywork was at least interesting, some notes on basic tactics for spellcasters on the battlefield.

"So, what are your thoughts on your performance," Professor Endel began when I first sat before him.

"I know my power is lacking and I badly need to improve my defense. It's my opinion that I should continue to use tactics that focus on stealth, since in a forward-facing fight I'm highly unlikely to win. I already knew most of that though, sir."

"Your power is not lacking; your speed is. There is a significant difference in the two, and that is a mistake many bards make."

"So, it's not that I can't manage to cast strong-enough spells, but that I can't cast them quickly enough? How do I fix that?"

"You don't. It's the weakness of bards, but you can compensate. Magical items are not a bad way to go, but they tend to act as a crutch if used in learning. You need to learn to lock down your opponent long enough to get going. Illusions are also unaffected by the bardic slowness, and I know you can use those. You showed it quite well."

"So . . . once I put up illusions, I start prepping defenses and attacks, then release them when they're ready?"

"Indeed, or you can get somewhere where your opponent cannot get to you while you cast. It might do well for you to learn a bit about weather control. The cost in mana is often obscene, but the effects are something else when wielded by someone who knows what they're doing."

"There isn't a class on that, is there, sir?"

"No, it's mostly bardic so there wouldn't be many students, and it's also rather specialized. Professor Magnolia might know some, or have some books on the subject he'd let you read though. If not, you'll have to figure it out on your own."

"How do you know about it?"

"Seen it on the field. Some bard from Ermath whipped up a storm over one of our formations and started dropping lightning bolts. It was something to see."

"Sounds terrifying."

"Eh, I was fairly far from that point. The poor peasant troops broke and ran though. They had no way to deal with that."

"What about the bard in question?"

"Got too big for his breeches and stepped out in front. Caught a fireball to the face. That's another good lesson for you. Always keep your head down; you're a target. Now, off you go."

I nodded at his wisdom before leaving.

Dras came to meet me after that class, looking as tired as I felt.

"Is it always like this?"

"Pretty much, yeah. You get used to it though. How're things going?"

"Mmm, all right I suppose. Professor Endel suggested I learn about weather magic."

"Sounds cool."

"He said it was mostly bardic, but I think my old teacher could make it rain . . . I wonder if that was an actual storm or him just summoning a bunch of water really high up . . ."

Dras shrugged. "You'll have to ask him the next time you two meet then."

I frowned, wondering when in the world that would be. "Yeah, if I ever see him again."

CHAPTER 26

✦

CORE COMPLETION

My classes proceeded at an exhausting pace. I was both exhausted and feeling like I was barely moving forward as winter came. Each had its ups and downs, and each felt as if it was getting harder.

My General Spellcasting class was straightforward. At this point, we were mostly still covering the basic techniques. The General Bard one was much the same. We had another field trip to learn about ink, a process that didn't smell bad at all. My non-magical classes were what I considered my rest periods. They were not held as high in regard by most students and were fairly straightforward. Atali Language and Dance were at least fun, and I even felt like I was starting to enjoy them. I was even enjoying Combat Spellcasting, not the least because we weren't having any more fights for a bit. Professor Endel had decided to run us through some basic shields. I had learned a really simple one that deflected physical projectiles. It was painfully slow to get up but was really something.

My Magical-Item Creation and Magical Materials classes were the outliers. Hern seemed to think that I was purposely dragging my feet, so that I wouldn't have to decide if I would explain my trick in speeding up learning about the core. The truth was that I'd had to slow down as I hit the parts that looked to be dedicated to memory within it, as they were a bit different in structure. I was still going fast though. I was also starting to see something about the command sequences for the runes that was really nagging me. I felt like it was staring me right in the face, but I just couldn't place it.

I sat happily in Rooke's theory class, ruminating on all of this. He was going over another basic sequence that allowed an item to change color based on temperature in a given spot. It was useful in that it functioned as a thermometer and also brought in the commands for temperature. We'd had to learn the structure for "observe," a rather useful one that came up in many diagnostic items. It could be repeated multiple times to give information on several variables. Professor Rooke seemed to think he'd covered enough on the subject for the day though and invited questions.

"Professor, how will we know when our cores are ready?" Pinea asked when called upon.

"Oh, has Hern not told you? I suppose he might be keeping it as a surprise, but . . . The last bit is fairly obvious, it is considered the piece that really makes the core function for making items and allowing you to remake cores yourself. You'll also receive a message."

"What sort of message?" another student asked, perking up.

"That's the thing; nobody knows what it is. Everyone has some theory, ranging from a simple confirmation that it's active to some profound secret about the core itself. They're all just theories though. I'm interested to hear if any of you have ideas when you get to see it. It'll only happen once, so pay attention."

Well, that was cool. Some mystery announcement that you were ready to go and make items sounded like somebody's idea of a prank. There was a very good chance that it was some in-joke, or had no meaning at all, and the ancient elven king who put it there just decided to screw with people millennia in the future.

As I packed up my things, I had to start thinking about other items though. First was that we had reached a point in our Proper Etiquette class that the professor decided we needed some actual real-world experience. She'd therefore arranged for the school to put on a small ball of sorts. That was apparently not ideal by anyone's reckoning, but most parties for nobility were still nixed since the rebels who were still alive were making moves in other provinces. The capital was quiet on that front though. I'd been told that. His Majesty had gone nuclear on all those involved after the mana-eater incident.

The school dance, because I really couldn't think of it as anything else, had therefore been declared. Some had escorts and dates already, but a lot were scrambling to come up with someone to go with them. It was considered good form in this circumstance for a young man to ask his intended date by letter to join him for breakfast that morning five days prior to the event. The idea was to woo her there, then allow her to stew through the day until the event, or something like that.

I was unconvinced about the whole breakfast idea, but that wasn't my main problem. My main problem was that apparently word had gotten around that I could summon pure white, high-quality paper. This meant that literally half the male students were requesting it because they wanted to make the best impression possible. There had been a number of incidents from young men already, and it was becoming a real pain.

The smart ones were grouping together with one another and finding someone's sister, cousin, or whatever who could ask me for an order in the girls' dorms. Some were also sending notes, which I then had to sort out for what, how much, and to whom. A few were asking me between classes as well. These made up the bottom rung, as that was considered both rude by the nobles and annoying by me.

The good news was: after consulting with the other girls in our dorms, I'd come up with a price that shocked my sensibilities. I think some of the girls were telling me to set it so high just so they knew the boys were spending a lot of money on them. The male half of the student body didn't seem bothered though. I myself couldn't complain too much because I was making an absurd sum.

A small cough stirred me from my reverie. As I looked up to meet the eyes of Professor Rooke, I froze for a second. He looked oddly pleased.

"Yes, Professor?"

"Professor Hern informs me that you're nearing completion of your core. He said you'll be done with the apprentice level sometime in the next few days if you continue at your going pace, even if you have slowed down as of late. I wanted to congratulate you."

"Oh . . . thank you."

"Once you have, you'll be able to make your first item. Have you thought about what you want that to be? I normally consult with my students much later. But you're rather early in your education for making something, and your first item should be something special. Many like to make something that they can keep as a memento or use daily. I myself made a small lamp of which I'm rather fond."

"I haven't actually put much thought into it. Something small and useful would be nice though. Maybe something I could wear? I'll have to think a bit on it, but maybe a light source would be nice. For a second there, I thought you might be coming to ask me about my growth like Professor Hern has." By this point, we were alone in the classroom, all other students having headed off for their break.

He nodded. "Is Hern pestering you often then?"

"About every three days or so, he asks if I've learned enough to decide," I admitted

"I will tell him to cease. Alana, in the future, kindly come to me with things like this. I am your guardian after all." He saw my confused look at that and raised an eyebrow of his own. "What is that look about?"

"I'm just surprised. I thought you'd be pressuring me to tell you too. You seem to . . . almost not be bothered though."

"I am patient. While I greatly desire for you to let me in on your little secret, I am willing to wait. Professor Hern's approach is more likely to drive you away. If you need to see what it could do before you tell me, I shall show you, and that will take time. I'm willing to invest that time, Alana, because that investment is one I believe will pay off well."

My real concern at this point was the idea of hacking a core, particularly one that was inside of someone. I was still learning about all of the inputs and outputs and didn't think that was possible, but I was still trying to figure it out. The core was in the brain after all and seemed to have some form of interaction with it. That meant that messing with it could be insanely dangerous. My question was though: Could someone else force that interaction from outside?

"Well, thank you for that, Professor. I am trying to figure it out."

"I'm glad. Now, best not be late for anything. Off you go."

I sat in the core building room in my circle, working away. I dreaded the idea of going back to my dorm and resting because tomorrow was when all of the date invites would be sent out. I had no idea how many, if any, I was going to get.

For that reason, I was on my second session, and I saw the last piece. The final bit that needed to go in to finish off this project. I could feel it and even understand it. The rest of the core had been methodical, built block by block. The rest of the core felt like it was fashioned by the hands of a wizard. But this, this was bardic; it couldn't be anything else.

There was a ball of intention right at the center of the core. All the rest of the pieces had been built around it, leaving only this bit of magic. It was so different, it was nearly jarring and so beautiful. I understood it as I looked at it. I understood it as it showed me how to make it because that's part of what it did.

As I formed it, I felt it flowing through my core. The bits that had been little paths of light flared to life, lighting the whole thing up as it flowed. It was astoundingly beautiful to watch, a work of art and science all in one, all coming together. The light of the last piece worked its way out methodically, flowing through all the paths I'd made like a lightning bolt.

This bit of magic had only a few functions, but they all melded wonderfully together. First, it allowed the mind to interact for some very limited purposes; this was only able to show how to build/grow it and to work on the final function. It was where the little light that had shown me the way to build my core had come from, where the magic that let me float in my own mind originated.

Second, it detected faults. The core knew what it was supposed to look like and how it was supposed to function, and it showed me that its advancements were nothing but that, no addition of function, only addition of speed and ability. It also knew when things were wrong, and if they were wrong and tried to work incorrectly, it would retaliate, breaking itself. This magic protected the core and assured that if it were transferred, it was transferred correctly.

Thirdly, it could read the runes on an object if they were connected to the core properly. I understood that because the spell was becoming part of me. I even understood how to link them; it was a surreal experience. Someone had managed to learn to do this manually and shoved that knowledge into this magic.

At this point, the final function appeared before me. Now, it was ready as it was finally complete and able to function itself. Within my mind space, a small board appeared. I knew that I could make symbols on it, but not what for. I suspected it could also display information. A suspicion that was quickly confirmed as words in a language I'd not seen written in years appeared upon it. Two simple words in my first native tongue that sent me into instant shock.

"Hello, World."

CHAPTER 27

THE DEAN'S OFFICE

I raced back to my dorm, heart pounding in my chest. Hello. World? Hello, fucking world? It was a joke, how was I even supposed to respond to that? I had so many questions that were rushing through my mind.

I stopped dead in the hallway. There was nobody I could go to about this, nobody to even ask. If my family were here, it'd be worse, but even without . . . I just couldn't bring this up; it would make too many questions. I'd never told anyone that I was reincarnated, that I'd lived another life. How could I? Lucien would probably have some advice, but I don't know how he'd respond to me having the mind of an adult. Rooke? Yeah, that was a joke. I'd never let anyone within the nobility know about this. That'd be insane. Kala? Dras? Both bad options, who knows what they'd do?

I leaned against the wall briefly trying to straighten out my thoughts. The cool stone felt good to press against.

"Are you quite all right, my dear?" The voice stirred me, making me turn quickly to see Dean Lorrae looking me over.

"I'm . . . fine, sir, just heading back to my dorm."

"You young people always seem to think you're much better at lying than you are. I don't suppose you'll actually tell me what's wrong?"

"Um . . ." I tried not to look at him as I worked on coming up with an explanation.

He sighed. "I must at least know if there is a danger to you or any of my students. Or if you're being harassed in some way."

"No, sir, I don't think there's any danger, and nobody has done anything inappropriate."

"Oh? Not even Professor Hern? I hear he's been pressuring you quite a bit to let him in on some technique involving building your core. Actually, I witnessed him being dressed down for it by Rooke in the staff room, but don't tell him that."

"Wouldn't he already know if you were there?"

"You're not the only one who knows how to make yourself invisible, Alana." Dean Lorrae gave me an impish smile as he let me in on that secret.

I chuckled, "Well, he does want me to tell him how I've been building on it so fast."

"Understandably so, but you seem to have some reason for not telling him. I would like to speak with you on that, if you don't mind too much." He turned and motioned me to join him. It was clear that his intent to speak with me was less a request and more an order.

I felt like I was going to my own execution as I marched along the halls beside him. There was no way I could tell him the truth, and I thought he would eventually demand my method for speeding up the core-building process. Of course, I could now answer that well enough.

Even if they learned a bit about the core, there was no way they'd be able to abuse it. The final little bit would see to it that any attempt at hacking the core itself failed. To undo that, they'd need to remake the whole thing from the ground up, and frankly I didn't think anyone in this world had the ability to do so. If someone out there did, they certainly wouldn't need my help to do it. It was in my opinion, therefore, safe to explain that it was made of logic circuits, at least on an individual level. It might still lead to massive upheaval though, and I wasn't sure I wanted to be responsible for that.

Eventually, we made it to the dean's office, and he opened the door. His office was massive, easily the size of a house back in my village. It had bookcases, all sealed with some magic or other that was easily visible along two of the walls. The back wall was home to a number of tools that I now recognized as being used to make magical items, along with a filing cabinet of the kind used for material storage. There was a massive desk, covered in drawers with two chairs before it, as well as two couches off to one side.

Dean Lorrae lead me over to the couches, taking a seat on one and indicating that I should take the other. He stretched back a bit, letting the cushions form around him until he seemed at ease.

"Now, what are your concerns about sharing your method?"

"At first, I was worried that someone might use them to attack the core itself. Now I'm worried about what releasing that knowledge could do to the rest of the world."

"Is it dangerous in and of itself?"

"Not as such, but speeding up the making of the cores and giving insight could have massive implications. I'm not sure I want to be responsible for what might come of it."

"Most people your age wouldn't even consider that. It's valid, allowing the training to be shortened could have large-scale implications, depending on how easy your method is. It could also upset the balance between countries. It's rather difficult to say on the long-term effects of introducing new knowledge."

"Are you encouraging me not to?"

"Not at all. I'm actually of the opinion that you should tell us. My point is that there is research going on all the time that could have huge implications if successful, but we still do it. We still work and strive to share knowledge with the world, even if that knowledge could fall into the wrong hands."

I frowned. "Not all knowledge should be known by all people."

"True, very true, Alana."

"What would you do if you learned some secret that could upset the world?"

"I have done so on multiple occasions, to varying levels. There are texts, very old and rare ones, that detail techniques of magic that most casters of this age do not know. Some that contain the knowledge for spells of great power. These are passed down from dean to dean of our school and used to protect it, or tell others when the time is right."

"Will you tell me what you know about the core. The things that others might be a bit surprised by?"

"Hmm? That's an interesting one, but I'll share some insights." Dean Lorrae stroked his chin. "First, there are a number of commands that make no sense in any language. While Atali has some of the words used in the rune sequences in its language, most scholars suspect this is because the adapted those from the runic language. Basically, it came first and added a lot of words to Atali. There are also commands that lead to menus in another language. I and several others suspect that this is important, but we've no way to translate them. There's no point of reference for what they say."

"They bring up pages in another language? What are they?"

Lorrae waved and two words in Atali script appeared in the air. As far as I knew, they had no meaning in Atali, but if you sounded them out phonetically they were roughly the words *guide* and *help*. Then it popped into place: a lot of the commands that were runic sequences in Atali script spelled out English words phonetically, which made good sense. There were parts that were still nonsense to me, but they probably meant something to someone who knew about coding.

"You're staring at those as if they're something more. I will say that while that knowledge isn't common, at all, it isn't secret either. Anyone who studies the core could have told you; most just think it's irrelevant and would distract you from your learning. So do try not to lose yourself in figuring them out."

"I'll keep that in mind, sir."

"Also, the message that appears when the core is first finished. There are a number of theories, but I think one speaks above them all."

"What is that, sir?"

"How much do you know of Ristolian?"

"I cannot say that I have ever heard of him."

"Then we'll need to reevaluate our history course. He was a magus of his age and quite amazingly powerful. A wizard through and through who performed feats I would personally have loved to witness. When he first finished his core, he did so with a number of his fellow students around him. It is reported that he fell on the floor and began laughing. When asked why, he simply responded that it was a joke. I think he had some insight that we do not, perhaps he cracked the language of the core and understood it for what it was."

Well, that's three. If he actually got it, then there was a nearly 100 percent chance that this Ristolian was another reincarnated person. Being a wizard probably let him use what knowledge of the modern world he had to beat up physics like it owed him money.

"What happened to Ristolian?"

"Nobody knows. Around the time he turned forty, he just disappeared. While he was reported to be amazingly powerful, he was also a bit of a nut. Perhaps he ran off to become a farmer or something. Based on the stories about him, I really wouldn't be surprised."

I had lots of questions about the who and why of people being brought to this world. I also had no way of finding the answers, but it was nice to know that I wasn't the first. At some point, I'd have to go and learn about the others. Probably a good place to start by looking for stupid, powerful spellcasters who came up with potent magic.

I sat in contemplation for a good long while after that. Dean Lorrae seemed to be amicable to wait for me to think about things. It was truly annoying how some people could do that, just wait while you thought about crap. Like they knew disturbing you would only cause them more problems.

"I still think that I will hold off on sharing my technique for now."

"Are you still considering it dangerous then?"

"Less so than before, but there's something else."

"What's that then?"

"I think that there's no reason for me to share it; it doesn't benefit me. I keep meeting all these nobles who only do things that help them and theirs. But this doesn't aid me, only those around me."

That actually got him laughing. "Now, that is a good answer, Alana. You should only share things if they're harmless or useful to you. We'll make a proper noblewoman of you yet." With that, he waved me off, and I finally got to head back to my room.

I stared up at the ceiling as I drifted off. There was much to consider, and I had the feeling that the list would only be growing from now on.

I awoke the next morning to a cheery and smiling Emma.

"Good morning, Miss Alana. You've received several letters."

I resisted the urge to beat my head on the wall. I'd totally forgotten about the bloody dance and the incoming invitations I'd been hiding from while working on my core. I had to read all of these dumb things and come up with answers. Then word them properly and go with Dras in all likelihood.

I took the stack and looked at the names, Dietrich, who I hadn't really spoken to at all in the academy, two boys from upper years who I didn't even know, and Troy, the boy from my Combat Spellcasting class. He was a bit of a surprise. I blinked and looked again. I flitted through them a third time before looking at Emma.

"Is this all of them?"

"Of course."

I frowned; there was no letter from Dras. Had I done something? Had he forgotten to send it? Maybe he didn't want to go to the dance at all? That was understandable. I'd have to find some way to find out.

CHAPTER 28

LETTERS, DECISIONS, AND ROMANCE

I filed Dietrich's letter, as well as those from the boys I didn't know under T, or in my case F, for fireplace, and got on to reading Troy's. It was fancy and floral, and he had really rather nice calligraphy, surprisingly so for someone as into combat as he seemed to be, but I supposed that was likely part of a noble upbringing. I kept that for the moment, as while I didn't really know him all that well, he seemed like a genuinely decent guy.

It was unsurprising that most girls got multiple invitations. In our school, there were certainly more boys than girls, nearly a two-to-one margin among the wizards. While we bards had an all-girl class, which was a bit odd. The priests were nearly equal in their makeup, and when added to the bards, made up a small minority of the school.

My understanding was that the pressures were very different for men and women in noble society. Everyone wanted more magic, but to inherit a noble title one was almost expected to attend the academy if they were a caster. This was because of the hard-core education that went on (compared to the rest of the country) and the connections one could gather. The magic was important, but political power was no joke either. And being able to potentially find a marriage partner from your peer group was a big plus.

While the boys wanted the titles and were encouraged to go get them, girls had very different pressures put upon them. It was well-known and established that if the parents were magical, their child had a much better chance. Having both was not needed, but if both were able to use some form of magic, then the chances of their child being so as well went through the roof. Women were the limiting factor in the equation, and as such were heavily pressured to get married and procreate.

This wasn't to say that noblemen were disparaging to their counterparts. Few boys in our school would have the gall to tell one of the female students to "know her place" because of her sex or something like that. From what I gathered from my classmates though, a girl's mother was far more likely to try and steer her daughter toward things like financial and household management, or learning about the complex web of merchants she'd need to handle. Since the academy focused mainly on magic and its associated crafts, that led noble girls elsewhere.

Commoners tended to be a different story, depending on their level in society. It wasn't as bad as most of Earth's history was depicted as in movies and the like, but it was there. Magic though changed things; if a girl could set you on fire or throw you bodily through a stone wall, you'd do well not to be too discriminatory to her.

I thought about all this as Kala and Pinea joined me for breakfast. They both seemed rather pleased this morning.

"So, how many did you get?" Pinea opened with.

"Four, though two were from boys I didn't know."

"Dras and Dietrich then?" Kala asked. "Obvious choice between those two."

"Not one from Dras."

"He's one of the commoner boys from the year above us, right?" Pinea leaned over, looking at us. I wasn't sure they'd ever met.

"Yeah, specializes in fire magic mostly," I informed her.

"Mmm, I think he's in one of my classes. Seems nice."

"Eh," Kala still didn't seem to think much of him.

"So, Kala, how about you? Any good invites?"

"I'm passing on those for now."

"Um . . . then who are you going with?"

"Myself? What about you, Pinea? Get lots of letters?"

"Only one important one, but a couple of others too."

Pinea had other things she had to do, so after eating Kala and I walked to class ourselves.

"You really not going with anyone then?"

"I'm going with me. To be honest, I'm not all that interested in spending time with boys."

"I understand. They won't give you trouble at the temple though, will they?"

"There are many kinds of love Alana. Sexual, parental, that between friends, romantic, all of these are love, and our order supports all of them. Even if we mostly focus on the sexual stuff when helping others. They might care if I told them I never wanted children, romance, sex, or friends, as we're supposed to experience all types of love we can, but I do at some point, so it's no issue."

I think I understood Kala well, but this was something I'd never learned about her before. We just didn't talk about romance and that kind of thing very often; there were far more interesting subjects.

"Would you like to come by my room after classes? We can study or something, and Emma's got the afternoon doing some of her own business, so it'll be quiet."

"Sure, see you then."

We split to go to our respective classrooms. I had a busy day today and looked forward to having some time at the end of it to relax. That thought would carry through the afternoon with no issues, and since I'd finished my core, I didn't have to worry about working on that at the moment.

At least that's what I thought until Professor Rooke asked me to have a word after class.

"Alana, how are things coming along? I'm well aware of your progress in classes, but otherwise."

"You're aware of my progress in my classes?"

"I am your guardian, as well as a member of faculty. Your grades and the opinions of your teachers are no mystery to me. You still have not answered my question."

"Well enough, I guess. I haven't gotten to all of the things I need yet, but I'm making good progress. Still need to ask Professor Magnolia about weather magic, but otherwise, well."

"You always seem to forget about making connections. Is that to irritate me intentionally?" The man looked hard at me.

"That's going well too. It's slow, but it should be, shouldn't it?"

Professor Rooke grinned. "Sometimes. Have you decided who you're attending our ball with?"

"I'm working on that. The person I thought would ask me has not, but I don't know why."

"Interesting. If you need any advice, do feel free to come to me. Now onto the meat of the matter." I felt my stomach drop as his face fell to a much more serious expression. "Hern is getting more and more irritating; he seems to think you should have well finished your core. Have you?"

"Yes, sir."

"Good. Do you feel you still need to learn more? If so, please tell me specifically what you need to make your decision."

"I do not. From what I saw in the last bit, I'm fairly sure that it's not possible to do too much damage to a core, and if you did, it wouldn't work, would it?"

"No, at least not as far as I or anyone else know."

"You could have explained that at some point to me."

"Would you have believed me? It was easier to let you see for yourself, to let you achieve a more visceral understanding, like all of us who make one do. All it took was a bit of time." He smiled slightly. "Alana, patience is a virtue that it is important to learn, both for you and Hern. It will improve your work quite a bit."

"I think Professor Endel had a lesson sort of like that . . . He said I wasn't lacking power, only speed."

"Professor Endel knows his business, and he's right. Now, back to the subject at hand. Will you teach your method for core construction?"

"I will not. I had this conversation with the dean last night."

"His view on you refusing?" He seemed genuinely curious about that, and sharing that wouldn't hurt me at all.

"He laughed, said I'd make a proper noblewoman yet."

I could see Rooke's eye twitch, his voice dripped with sarcasm. "Certainly, that would be his opinion. Very well, I'll inform Hern of your decision."

"Will there be problems from that?"

"Perhaps, but it is best to deal with that when it comes." He shrugged, taking this better than I could have hoped. "That done, we can now work advancing your core. If you continue at your current pace, you might well have all three levels by the time you graduate. It would not only be a first for our institution, but would be a good mark for your future."

"I'll have to sit in that room for the next several years?"

"Hmm? No, you now have everything you need. That array is simply to help those without a core. If you concentrate, your core should have everything you need, though having another example on your person will be useful. I'll have an example core sent to you."

"Thank you, sir." He nodded and dismissed me.

* * *

Classes for the rest of the day were rather less eventful, and after we'd finally finished Kala joined me in my room. We sat around going over some of the basic things we'd had to do this week in our more general courses and chatting about our plans for our next actually free day. Eventually, I made my way back over to my desk and Troy's invitation.

I looked at it and considered. I didn't really want to go with him, but it was expected by most of my classmates that I'd go with someone. Then I looked over at Kala, and I remembered that first morning after we'd met. Had I actually been telling people to shove off with their expectations? Well, not always. I was getting better at it though, my interaction with Rooke being some evidence of that.

"You know what, Kala. Screw going with any of these idiots. Who wants to wake up early just to go on a date anyway? That's just annoying."

She began laughing, "Decided to join me on the 'no boy' list then?"

"Yup. I will say though, look at Troy's handwriting. I'm jealous; it's just too pretty."

She came over and looked at the letter. "No lie." Once we'd both had our fill, I chucked it in the fire like the others, and the two of us found a comfy spot to sit.

"So, what's the plan for that day? I'm completely free now."

"Want to hang out? Oh, we can watch all the people who're doing their dates. Put on our most comfy clothes and laugh at all the fancily dressed folks who woke up too bloody early."

"Sounds like fun. I'll get some sweets."

"Oh, yours are the best."

"It's practice, Kala."

"And ready access to dumb amounts of sugar."

I crinkled my nose at her for a moment. Then she surprised me by leaning in and pressing her lips to mine. I froze, startled.

She pulled back and looked at my shocked face. "I'm sorry, I didn't mean to . . . I just thought maybe . . ."

I looked at her; she seemed like she was about to bolt from embarrassment. "Kala, I like you, but . . . I don't really think of girls . . . sexually."

"Well, mostly, I just want someone to . . . be with. I think I'll get a husband one day, but when I do . . ." She seemed to consider her words. "It'll be more like a business transaction and sex too. I care for you though. I thought you might feel the same?"

She moved to get up, but I pulled her back gently. I didn't kiss her, but I did hold her, and she held me. We stayed like that for a long time, wrapped up in each other's arms. It was nice, if a bit different from what I'd done before. Kala was warm, soft, and comfy.

Eventually though, we did need to talk. It took a few hours for us each to go over what we thought. It was a whole thing I was a bit new to. Kala felt that romance and sex were two vastly different things, and I couldn't say I really disagreed. Eventually, she proposed that we pursue the former without the latter. A suggestion I happily agreed to.

CHAPTER 29

✦

WEATHER AND THE DANCE

In the time before the dance, my lessons really started to get interesting. Combat Spellcasting particularly was moving on to a subject I hadn't even known existed yet. The ability to resist harmful magic. This we were told was an imperfect, but highly useful skill for every would-be battle mage.

It was much like hiding your aura, only in reverse. Rather than pulling your own strength out of your surroundings, you had to try and flood them with a dense layer of your own power, one that stuck as closely to you as possible. This made you highly visible when you used it but would reduce the effectiveness of offensive magic to a degree.

The word *reduce* here was key as well. It didn't outright stop you from being hit; it only made the hit from the spell hurt less. It also didn't seem to function against every type of magic. Summoning, for example, went straight around it, which explained the high propensity of mages to use water in combat rather than fire. It could blow through the resistance with ease. We were also told that much like its sister discipline of hiding our aura, those who used physical-type magic could learn it almost instinctively and to a much higher degree than we were likely to ever produce.

Professor Endel had us working in pairs. We would alternate between casting very weak attack spells and trying to reinforce ourselves against our opponents. I'd been avoiding Troy since my decision not to go with him to the upcoming dance and had therefore grabbed some boy whose name I didn't know for this exercise. He was currently hitting me with waves of concussive force roughly strong enough to knock me over if I didn't resist, an exercise that was not going particularly well on my part.

I let out an "Oof!" as once again I fell over backward from the invisible blow.

I lay there on the ground for a bit, thoroughly considering the idea that perhaps this class had been a mistake. I was currently covered in small bruises, mostly from where my backside had met the floor and felt downright horrible. That said, I could tell that I was slightly improving, being that now I was only being knocked over and not thrown. I was also able to notice my aura pushing back against the spell a bit now; it was nice of it to finally join in and help.

"You done over there?" the boy called after a few moments.

"Not yet." I brushed myself off and rose from the floor, launching a small, concentrated scream at him as soon as he signified his readiness.

A couple more passes and he asked for a break, turning to me as we sat down and started sipping on a bit of water.

"Nice scream there," he commented. I'd healed his ears twice now, because he wasn't any better at this than I was.

"Thanks, it's not super useful if you really want to hurt people though."

"Yeah, maybe not, but still useful. I'm guessing it's cheap mana-wise too?"

"Middling, why do you ask?"

"Oh . . . you're just throwing them like it's nothing." He seemed to be examining me as we talked. "What's your aura like when you're not hiding it or pushing it out like you are now?"

I blinked at him. I was currently just letting it loose. That was something I seldom did, but being as tired as I was, it was a bit relaxing. Like getting into your pajamas at the end of the day. Keeping it tamped down a bit was no longer too hard, but it was much more like wearing a slightly uncomfortable bra.

"This is what it looks like when I'm not doing anything to it."

"Oh . . . I just thought . . ." He looked a bit embarrassed by the question.

After that, our conversation died down just a bit. We were by no means the first pair that took a break, and soon others were joining us. It seemed that some of the class was beginning to run out of mana through the constant casting exercise, something that was not particularly unusual. Most students didn't have a huge amount of mana in the first place, so using it quickly like this was rather rare.

Our conversation died there. Professor Endel came back up before the class and gave another short refresher on technique, giving general corrections on some of the issues he'd seen while we were practicing. He seemed to be more in favor of actually letting us just experience things rather than trying to lecture too much on what to do. It made the whole class more like a gym class from my first life.

I was asked to say after dismissal and happily complied. Several times had Dietrich tried to come and talk to me, which I'd studiously avoided, even resorting to invisibility once. Troy looked like he wanted to talk as he gathered up his things, but upon seeing that I was staying, simply smiled and waved before he made his way out.

"So, how go your attempts at learning weather magic?" Professor Endel began, looking at me closely.

"Not particularly well, Professor Magnolia doesn't seem to know much about it personally. He knows it's possible, but not much about how to do it." I'd asked him a few days ago, only to be disappointed that he'd never really studied that particular branch.

"I'm unsurprised. Have you worked on trying to figure it out on your own?"

"Er . . . not really, sir."

"Why not? Did I not tell you that it would be an excellent route?" He looked down at me disapprovingly, like I'd failed some sort of test.

"It has just been a very busy time recently . . ."

"That will never change. I want you to at least put forth some effort to this though; your current spell list is simply not going to be enough for you to continue in this class. Learning basic weather control will expand it both rapidly and in a way that will help you. As such, I expect you to begin soon, because if you don't, I will have you removed from my course. Am I understood?"

"Yes, sir . . ." I resolved to take action as I tried not to imagine the embarrassment of being removed from any class by the teacher.

"As it is currently winter, I've taken the liberty of reserving one of the larger of our rooms for you to practice in three days a week." He handed over a slip of paper detailing the reservation schedule and noting the location.

"I . . . you didn't have to do that, Professor."

"No, but I want you to succeed. I seldom have bard students in this class, and even more seldom any with any potential to actually use their magic in interesting ways. So, you will not be permitted to keep me from seeing whatever absolute nonsense you manage to come up with when you try. I simply won't have that." Did he seem . . . giddy? While Professor Endel had a hard undercurrent of harshness almost all the time, it looked like he was about to start smiling. Maybe he just really liked seeing people cause mass destruction in innovative ways . . .

Since my first scheduled time was that night, and I was fairly sure that Professor Endel was going to be checking if I had used it or not, I found myself going to his reserved room. The room itself was huge, if rather empty. My guess was that it was used for purposes similar to that which I ended up here. Sometimes you just needed a lot of space to work a large bit of magic, or perhaps a place for many people to work together.

There was no time like the present to begin, so I tried to think of where to start. Water, wind, and heat tended to begin the forms for any bit of weather type systems as far as I knew and I had at least some basis in those. I decided to start with water first, since it "should" be the easiest.

I thought that mist would be a good starting point. It was mostly water, could obstruct vision, and I thought learning it first would probably help with things like cloud formation later on.

My progress was, as always with a new spell, a bit slow. I did make some mist though, and by the end of the allotted time, the room was quite full of thick fog. It really was much like making water, something I knew a good bit about, and I just had to make it into tiny droplets and get it to hang in the air. I was even fairly familiar with things like mist and fog from just my day-to-day experiences.

At least a simple drying spell could clean up the pea soup before I headed back to the dorms to crash. As I walked, I wondered idly if that could be used for some part of weather manipulation too. Sadly, I didn't know too much about that kind of thing. I knew that storms were mostly wet, hot air moving upward then cooling, but as far as serious mechanics went, I really had no clue. Perhaps for something involving lightning? If I figured out that one, I was sure Professor Endel would leave me alone . . . for a while at least.

The morning of our school dance, Kala and I sat around in our most comfy outfits watching the chaos. It was rather like a train wreck or some natural disaster. Girls and their maids were all hurried to get everything perfect for that morning, each running around like there was a huge rush.

Instead of joining, Kala and I simply sat and ate some light breakfast, sipping tea and eating toast as girl after girl went into what looked like a mild panic attack. One even spilled a bit of tea on what I assumed was one of her nicer outfits and had a near breakdown in the dining hall.

"Wow, that looks insane." Kala watched as the girl in near tears was hurried off by her maid to find something else to wear.

"Yup, aren't you glad we are skipping it?"

That got me a snort. "So, no plans for going and trying to woo each other with fancy outfits and morning plans?"

"Well, we could do that, or we could just make cookies instead."

"Oh, now that's an idea!"

Consequently, that morning was spent in Kala's room on what was ultimately a rough approximation of gingerbread. It seemed the right time for it, and I was feeling rather more festive than usual, so we worked together, chatting as we tried to bake on a fireplace that was in no way made for our use.

The ingredients included more spices and sugar than any normal food eaten in the capital. Things like ginger, allspice, and cinnamon were available, if not overly used. What really caused issues though was my insistence to make a basic frosting to decorate the cookies. The fact that it was mostly sugar and really there just for decoration nearly sent Kala into a lecture on wasting magic. That was until I pushed the spoon covered in the sweet gently to Kala's lips.

"Okay . . . it can stay," she muttered after tasting what was my best attempt at a Swiss meringue. "Only because you've already made it though . . ." After that, she took said spoon and licked it clean.

Most of the rest of the day was spent getting ready for the ball. Regardless of how little I was really interested in going, we still had to. So I reluctantly split from Kala to go and prep for it. Emma had already prepared my clothes and thought of several different hairstyles she really wanted to try out, so it wasn't like it took too much effort on my part anyway.

Because of the rather more unusual nature of this particular event, there was no real order to entry. There was no family that you needed to meet and greet and no strict formalities of who would arrive when. That was excellent so far as I was concerned because it meant that Kala and I arriving a bit late was not of any note. It also kept anyone from asking about our dates for the evening, which was nice.

The room we were using as the venue tonight was absolutely massive. I was unsure what its normal purpose was, but for tonight it had been bedecked with one of the most complex sky illusions I'd ever seen. There were even a few auroras moving here and there across it as a primary source of lighting.

Kala and I both joined in a number of group dances; they weren't particularly romantic, but they were fun to do. About halfway through, I saw

Dras dancing with the same girl over and over again. Some blonde in his year who was snuggled close to him as she could be.

"Seems like your friend has developed a bit of a tumor," Kala observed, a slight sour note in her voice.

"His business then. Are there drinks? I rather think I'd like one." I hated to admit that I was a bit jealous and a bit hurt that he hadn't even told me he was with someone, but I was.

Kala just pointed to a small setup on one side of the room, and I went to go grab something. Really anything to distract me would do fine. As I approached, I saw our dean, who gave me a mischievous smile and a nod, his eye flicking over to where Kala still was.

As I considered throwing some form of spell at the old jerk, Professor Endel came in the doors and beelined for him, a small envelope in his hand. As the older man flipped it open and began to read, I saw his face fall. He went from his normal self to looking suddenly very, very old. His eyes darkened and fell a bit, and he looked deeply sad.

"You should make an announcement," Professor Endel said, his voice just at the edge of my hearing.

"And ruin a perfectly good party? This may be the last one for a bit and I'll pass. No, set up for an assembly of the students first thing tomorrow morning."

/ CHAPTER 30

◆

ALL ACROSS THE KINGDOM

The ball went off without a hitch. It featured dancing, a bit of light conversation, and some refreshments. All in all, it was rather nice. The little interaction between the dean and Professor Endel was a bit disconcerting, but there really was nothing I could do but wait till the next morning.

That evening, Kala and I stayed up late and watched the fire burn down while we lightly chatted. It reminded me of the times we'd had just before coming to school. I missed Lucien briefly, wondering what he must be doing right now. He was probably serving drinks or something, singing and laughing. I considered telling Kala about the conversation I'd overheard, but there seemed no reason to worry her about something we could do nothing about.

In the Starlit Sky, the only sounds were whispering and the sound of a few grown men weeping. Several sat at the bar with drinks in hands, looking hollow and broken. The proprietor sat near the back, trying to compose a letter for his former student. He'd failed again and again to put his thoughts into words, eventually scribbling down a rough note telling her to keep well. He then moved on, trying to come up with what he should tell his other former apprentice. Leaving nothing for him was just not an option.

Across the city, the headquarters of the Order of the Shield looked like a kicked-over anthill. Assistants ran to and fro through halls with stacks of papers and messages between the various priests. Coordination would be key they knew; it was their duty to keep things as protected as possible, and they would follow it. The bishop himself was packing for his own mission. It pained him to have to leave their main base in such a hurry, but there was news only he could deliver, and it would have to be done in person.

His assistant was given a ream of pre-prepared notes. This day had been certain to come he knew, even if he dreaded its coming. The woman looked over them before she nodded and wished him well.

In the city of Istlan, Father Mannory read all the news available to him. With him were several of his fellow workers. He struggled to compose himself as he looked around at them. Gigi, one of their oldest girls sat in a corner, she'd managed to read his papers while delivering them and looked nearly in shock.

"I'll tell the children. Most of the younger ones won't understand, but we need to keep a close eye on the older ones. Keep everyone together; we'll weather this."

All of the brothels in Hazelwood were closed. Most of the taverns and inns had shut their doors too. Some were on the street confused, trying to figure out what had happened, looking in windows and for those they knew frequented these places.

Behind the doors and thick curtains in The Scarlet Harlot, boxes were being loaded down to the basement. A veritable train of men passed each along and down, pushing them onto carts in a hidden tunnel far below.

Veska pointed at things one by one, before looking to one of her men. "How goes it?"

"Well, ma'am, most of the girls are already out of the city. A good few of the men too. Once we've gotten everything cleared out, we'll be set, but . . . Are you sure this is needed? There hasn't even been any incidents yet."

"Orin right?" she asked.

"Yes, ma'am . . ."

"When 'incidents' start, there is a good chance this city won't be standing. It wouldn't if I were in charge. Now, get everyone and everything out, preferably before the town guard notices."

"Yes, ma'am." He frowned a bit, not that long ago some of those had been his men.

A boot fell upon a tuft of grass, crushing it into the dirt.

"I used to live here, before . . . so long ago it seems. There is where

Sorren's house was; he was ever generous, a friend to all of his neighbors. There, see, that's where André lived; his daughter was supposed to marry my son." The words stopped for a moment as tears were blinked away.

Before Verren was the waste that used to be Orsken on the Forest. Now vines grew over the burned-out remains of houses and walls. The fields, left to go for so long without a plow, now were tall with grass and small bushes. It was a ruin if ever there was. No more did fires burn in hearths, nor candles or lamps light the evening. Only the cold light of the moon and stars lit this place now. Only the dead and the animals that had come to seek what paltry shelter there was called this place home.

"Do you know the reason for this? The crime this village committed? They tried to live in peace! Tried to feed themselves and take care of their own! This is what the kingdom did, the empire as well. While their highest rulers sat back in comfort, they sent men to do this to those who sought no harm to them. That my friends is why we are fighting, why I brought you here tonight. So that we may all be reminded what our mission is to destroy."

Verren turned, looking out upon his assembled men, his mail gripped tight to him as he rose to his full height, spear shining as he thrust it up. "Now let us do so! All hail, Lord Durin! All hail, the Lord of Shadows!"

"ALL HAIL!" The roaring cheer that went up was repeated again and again in ruined villages and upon deserted battle-sites across the kingdom of Bergond that night.

CHAPTER 31

✦

EMERGENCY POLICIES
AND CORE DIVING

We were all called down to the assembly, held in one of the larger halls of the building. Once everyone had arrived and found their places, Dean Lorrae stood in front of the students. He looked over us, letting his eyes rove between our slightly concerned faces.

"There has been a declaration of war upon our kingdom by the so-called Shadow Empire. We currently know little in the way of information beyond that, but I am told that diplomats are meeting to arrange the rules by which both sides will conduct this conflict." Sound in the room died as shock descended upon the students; many seemed not too bothered, while a few were nearly visibly shaking from this announcement. "As such, we will be changing our schedules to match the current situation. All students not currently enrolled in Combat Spellcasting will have a once-per-week lecture on the very basics of self-defense. All those who are capable of casting healing magic and are not in an advanced healing course will be given a once weekly class on basic battlefield medicine. It is my sincere hope that these will not be necessary, but it is our duty to best prepare you."

After the dean stepped down, he was replaced by one of the other teachers who continued with the organization. For today, all classes were being canceled in favor of a series of lectures on school safety and emergency procedure. We would also be getting talks on how this development could more directly affect us.

We were separated into smaller groups first. Professor Sasha, our Proper Etiquette teacher was in charge of my particular group.

"In the event of an attack on the academy, you are to evacuate through the standard emergency exit located in the center hall of the school."

Our school was basically a big plus sign, so finding that location would be easy regardless of where you were. There was a large circle in the very center, which, in the event of an emergency, could change into a spiral staircase. This ostensibly led out to a safe location, one that we were not told of, just in case.

"I should hope that it is not needed, but I'll be showing you some secondary emergency exits. These are specific to each group and are *not* to be shared with your classmates until and unless you must use them. Also, since we'll be putting our protective enchantments on their highest setting, all students will be required to add mana to them."

We were taken around by Professor Sasha to the emergency exit locations; these were hidden well behind cabinets and art pieces. Opening one was fairly easy. All one had to do was place a hand upon the exit and push a small quantity of mana into it. This would set off alarms in the school, of course, and they had their own protections on them. The most notable of which was a complex series of runes around each exit that was supposed to prevent ingress to the academy. These doors would get us out, but only out.

As for adding mana to the school's defenses, that was simple enough. Every morning just before our first class, there would be a professor waiting near the exit to our dormitories. A small array on the wall there would allow us to put mana into them and record how much we did. There was a daily minimum of three runes' worth, not much for me, but quite a bit for some of our weaker students.

"So . . . what does it do?" I asked as I took my turn trying out the array.

"The full scope is undisclosed obviously," Professor Sasha intoned. "I can tell you that it projects some form of shield around the academy that stops at least projectiles and most harmful spells. It's incredibly expensive to keep going, but in times like these . . . well, we're one of the most defended locations in the country, second only to the royal palace."

I had my doubts about that. There were probably some military installations that had superior defenses. This was where a lot of noble heirs were though, so whatever we had to keep us safe was probably quite substantial.

Once Professor Sasha had finished with us, we were taken to meet back with all the other girls. I recognized the priestess who was here to speak to us as from the Order of the Lovers. She stood in the center of the room and waited for us all to arrive. There was a bit of chatter between us as one group after another joined us, slowly filing in.

She began by giving us a lecture on the realities of war, particularly the danger associated with being caught in the siege of a city. Sexual assault and rape were not uncommon in these situations, and it was therefore important that we know and understand what to do if the city were attacked. Escape was to be prioritized, to either a protected or hidden location. If that was impossible, we would need to determine if fighting or surrender was the superior option. In either case, we needed to make sure our opponents knew that we were casters.

The last part was important for a number of reasons. First was that most of those who would be any real threat to a magic user were magic users themselves. Establishing that we were likely nobles or related to nobles would make them more likely to want to capture us unharmed as bargaining chips. Similarly, this protection was also offered to their side. A nobleman wouldn't often wish to harm the daughters or wives of an opposing nobleman, for his opponent might respond in kind.

The other reason was also purely practical. Pairings of magic users often produced children who were magic users, and the limiting factor in how many of those children could be made was on the number of women, not the number of men. Since a country could live or die on how many mages it had, nobody wanted to waste those potential children. This as well would buy us at least a modicum of protection. So long as we didn't pose a threat, we were likely to be spared and kept in far better conditions than a normal prisoner would.

It seemed that they brought in the priestess for this lecture as a matter of policy. The Order of the Lovers dealt with most matters concerning sex in this world and consulted for any talks on the matter. The various orders also tried to negotiate rules for war in such times. Of course, those weren't always followed by the soldiers on the ground, but in theory there were supposed to be agreements on how war between countries should be conducted.

The former empire of Ermath had not wanted to agree to many rules, particularly in the case of non-magical individuals. They had a policy of enslaving most of those they victimized, which they used to justify their actions. From my discussions with Kala, I understood that this was a real point of contention between them and the orders and had led to them being rather hands off when Ermath got brought down.

The Shadow Empire was a bit of an unknown to those who lived in our country though. The priestess giving the lecture indicated that they had in the past followed most or all of the policies that the orders had put forward. For this war, it was still unclear how they would behave, but we could consult with one of the priests when all of that was settled.

After a brief break for lunch, we received our new schedules. Our additional classes had been fitted onto our normal week, adding them as super-late on a rotating day. It was inconvenient, but my guess was that was the only way they could work them in without completely redoing everyone's schedule.

Kala had an additional lecture to attend, but my day ended early. That was a welcome break at least and would give me more time for my current personal project. Upon my return to my room, I collapsed onto my bed and fell into a meditative state, accessing my core.

I was slowly, slowly working my way through the "guide" and "help" sections that were built in. The going was slow, complicated by the fact that I didn't have time, or the proper note-taking abilities for it. There were some serious issues, and I really wanted to beat whoever wrote these pages.

Issue number one was that the whole navigation of either "help" or "guide" was bonkers. There was no search function (so far as I had yet discovered at least); it wasn't even divided up into pages, just one massive mountain of text for each of them. Sure there were sections, and even a table of contents, but they were practically useless, since whoever had decided what went where had a system that I was guessing made sense only to him.

It also seemed to be written for someone who already understood the material. There was jargon and directions that only made sense with context strewn through the "guide." If you didn't know where things went in what section, the "help" page was useless too, because it was divided by action and issue rather than alphabetically like any sane person would. Add to that the random comments like "this doesn't work well, but it works" and "I need to fix this later" that were just jammed in, and it was like reading somebody's personal notebook.

I couldn't even take notes. If it was possible in the core, I hadn't yet reached the directions on how. If I tried to in the real world, I'd have to write in English, revealing that I understood these sections, or in the Common Human Tongue, and there was no chance that I was writing some of the insights that I was gleaning in any way where someone could get hold of them.

All of those issues aside, I was learning things. Rather than play around with light like most of our classes were doing, the writer of the "guide" began with moving parts. These were simple motions, isolating one part and having it spin or move forward and back. The directions may have been filled with jargon and nonsense, but once you made it through that, they were at the least precise. What did what was clearly defined in the runic system. There was even a definition page included that had the numerical values used for defining things. As far as I could tell, things like the speed of light and the like were correct and listed in metric. There were measurements for that, temperature, force, and a whole list of others.

I also learned some of the issues that who I assumed was the ancient elven king was having. According to the notes, there were several things he'd tried and failed to do. It seemed that the cost of light increased with frequency in such a manner that high energy/dangerous forms like X-rays and gamma rays were for most purposes infeasible. Some elements were also listed as highly difficult to make. Metals and the like were known for being very hard, but so was anything with a crystalline structure. He seemed to have tried to make a few heavy radioactive substances, too, all of which he'd thought he'd done, but in quantities he couldn't detect.

There was a special note on antimatter. It looked to be impossible, or at least nearly impossible. An experiment was described that was trying to make one positron. The definition was given, and everything was hooked in only for the spell to consume mana endlessly. All attempts after that had been canceled; there were easier fruit closer to the ground to pick.

After some time reading through the "guide" and coming up with my own mental exercises to do, I was jolted back to the outside world harshly.

"Miss Alana! Are you okay!?" Emma was shaking me lightly and yelling.

"Huh!? Emma, what happened?"

"Are you well? I called to you several times, but you didn't answer. I can call for a priest . . ." She seemed genuinely worried.

"Oh . . . no, I was just in my core. I'm fine."

"Well, you gave me quite a scare there. I thought you might be hurt."

"No I'm fine, really."

"If you're sure, Miss. Dinner is soon by the way; you mustn't forget to eat."

"I won't, thank you." I rose as Emma gave me one last look and hurried off to her other duties. I really needed to find a way to keep aware of my surroundings while reading.

CHAPTER 32

✦

SELLING THE SECRET

The next few days of classes were fairly standard. Well, everyone was stressed as all get-out, and there was only really one major point of conversation, but beyond that fairly normal. Magical-Item Creation finally got to some really cool things. We started talking about the various parts of magical animals and how they could be used. Turns out, most monsters were chock-full of mana, and once you got their bodies, you could use them for a whole bevy of different things. The fact that they had mana in them, and were able to conduct it, meant that they could be used to improve the efficiency of magical items by leaps and bounds.

My work on getting weather magic down was progressing, albeit slowly. I could get most basic things working now, slowly building up winds and water, but the growth rate was abysmal. It would take forever to get to nice huge storms. It was enough for Professor Endel though, who came by to check on my practice a few times. I was even thinking about lightning now, but I wanted a safe way to practice that before I tried to make any.

It was around this time that I was called to the dean's office. It was a simple enough thing, but when I arrived there, I met with him and both Rooke and Hern. The three of them were sitting around the dean's desk, conversing lightly as they waited for me. Another figure was there, one I recognized. The royal servant Emil sat nearby, waiting as well.

"Greetings, Alana, please sit down." Dean Lorrae motioned to an open chair near Professor Rooke.

"Is something the matter?" I looked between the gathered men a bit nervously.

"Not as such, but we do have some important things to discuss," the dean said, looking down at me from his spot. "Though I doubt you will be pleased with it. As you know, we are at war." I nodded at the dean's statement as he continued. "As such, our country needs every advantage that it can get. Mister Emil here is a representative of the royal family, one who has been placed in charge of acquiring potentially useful information."

"We've met. Am I to assume that he wants information on core building?"

The man himself smiled. "Quite so. It is my understanding that you have no issues sharing it if you were to be properly incentivized?" The way he said the last bit nearly sent a shiver up my spine. I didn't know if he was actively trying to be threatening, or if it was just force of habit at this point, but he could certainly scare most people with ease.

"I . . . do not. What is the proposal?"

In answer, the man produced a rather sizable sack of coins. I could hear the metal jingling as they rubbed against each other. While it was interesting, money was not really a problem I had most of the time.

"We are willing to offer one hundred gold pieces, with additional monies possible if it turns out that the information is of military use." That was a . . . sizable amount, enough for me to retire on with no further questions. That said, I could make sugar, which was basically a money-printing machine.

"Money is nice, but there are other things that would be more welcome."

"Such as?"

"Safety and privacy. Regardless of how things with this war turn out, I honestly want very little to do with it. I can use the gold, but I'd rather be left alone, than much else. So whatever amount you offer has to come with promises that you won't go bandying my name about."

"I can agree to that easily."

"And the rest of you?" I gave a look to the three teachers, Hern in particular.

"I don't know why you would think . . ." he began.

"Because you've been pestering her about this for some time, you dolt," Rooke cut in. I really wanted to give him a high-five, but he probably wouldn't understand what that was and this truly wasn't the time.

"I would also like to not be bothered about other things I decide to research until such time as I'm prepared to reveal them publicly." Since most of the things I was investigating at the moment would probably never reach that point, this was an important clause.

There was a series of nods, and I doubted that it would hold up forever, but buying myself a bit of peace while I was still in school was worth sharing this little tidbit.

"All right, let's hear it then." Hern, in particular, seemed excited.

"What do you know about how the core works?" I asked. "Rather, about how it understands things on the basic level."

"It uses a series of inputs that are either on or off to give a particular output. Through some effort, it is able to tell that parts of it are doing basic math as well. Certain series of inputs are giving known outputs. Its internal workings and the like are still a bit unclear though, particularly when it comes to more complex interactions," Rooke rattled off. That was pretty good all things considered.

"So . . . yeah, it's always doing math, for everything. The math it's doing is a bit different though, hmm . . ." I had to take a few moments to think about how best to explain.

"Alana, we understand math, please get on with it," Hern said.

Buddy, I've seen your math classes, and you guys don't even know about imaginary numbers. Seriously, most of what you know could be found in The Elements and a bit of basic algebra.

"Fine, it's converting logic statements into math and then solving them. That's the basic trick as to how I made so much progress. I didn't bother visualizing each connection, but rather thought of them in terms of the statements they represented."

"What?" Dean Lorrae looked at me as if I'd just said something incredibly silly.

"It's easier if I draw it out . . ." Within a few minutes, I had diagrams drawn for the group. The professors looked like they were nursing headaches. There was also Emil, who was going over each bit with a fine-toothed comb, and Dean Lorrae, who was laughing like a madman.

"So . . . it's not that everyone didn't know what these pieces were doing, rather that you were just thinking of them as . . . if, not, and the like?" Rooke was massaging the bridge of his nose.

The pieces that I'd drawn out to explain were well understood. They already knew that if in one of these you put in a "yes" and the other a "no," what the answer would be. The only change that I'd honestly made was converting them into Boolean logic, which wasn't a big one but was a shift in paradigm. It was also like pointing out that you could see your nose if you tried, but that you just ignored it most of the time.

"It's obvious. I can't believe that you made us jump through so many hoops for this, Alana," Hern said.

"I'm unsure whether to be proud or irritated," Rooke added as he opened his eyes to look at it again, only to go back to rubbing his nose.

"Is it useful?" Emil asked, squinting at the diagram like it had personally offended him.

"To a bard? Certainly, changing the way they conceive of this would have the same effect it had for Alana here and massively speed up the growth rate of their core. To a wizard . . . probably not as it is, though it is a new way to think about the cores and how to use them. If we do more research about it, we might gain some insights." Dean Lorrae wiped tears from his eyes.

"I'll take that as a tentative yes then. How many bards do we have that this could help? If it speeds up magical-item creation . . ."

"There are perhaps two hundred or so bards in the country who are capable of making magical items. If you decide to teach all of them, it will speed it up a bit, but in my opinion, it will be mostly useful for growing the core inside one's self. Making a copy for an item is rather more fast than building your own," Hern pointed out. He seemed to be the most versed on this kind of thing.

"That's rather disappointing. Well, you don't win every time, but at least that's something." Emil packed up my diagrams and a few notes that he'd made before pushing the bag of money over to me.

I smiled at him trying to move it into my lap only to find out what I should have already known. Gold is heavy. "Thank you."

"I can't believe you're actually paying for that, or that we even needed it at all," Hern grumbled.

"It is important that the royal family keep its agreements to the letter. While the information wasn't what I was hoping for, it is useful, and if there are any more useful insights young Miss Alana gains, I hope that she will share them with us in the future." He smiled at me.

My best guess was that he was wagering that I'd come up with some more helpful shift in thinking. The things I'd shared with them, like the flamethrower and this weren't something that was impossible for them to know, but just weird for them to think about. A lot of important things were like that though; they were things that were easy to find out, or kind of obvious, but that nobody really pointed out to others or used.

I had to be careful here and consider my actions. I knew that it was often very minor changes in thinking that ended up having massive changes to fields, but some of that also took a lot of time. If I restricted myself to very few and very minor insights, then it was probably fine for now. I just needed to act with care.

Relativity was a good example of how a minor shift in thinking had a big ripple. Einstein's tram ride while looking at a clock was a perfect showing. Had he seen anything that someone else hadn't? No. Did he have access to some unusual information? No. Did his minor change in thinking have a big effect? Absolutely.

I wanted to avoid things like that, at least for now. The fact that this society was still thinking about a lot of things in a rather medieval way while I was thinking like someone from a much later society made that hard though. I had no idea what minor things might make big changes, and that meant that I needed to stop and consider everything that I said that wasn't just parroting what they were telling me.

I was dismissed. It seemed that those four had been going over a lot of other information as well. My impression was that Emil was here to coordinate with them on research they were doing personally and what they might do for him and his part in the war effort.

I returned to my room to put away my money. While I did that, I went over the things I'd learned from the core so far. These were things that I knew I would be holding back. I felt the need to learn them so that I could use them for my own gains, but the idea of sharing them with others was right out. It would probably be advisable for me to not use them at all until I'd graduated and this stupid war was well and over.

I sighed in relief as Emma was about some other business. It gave me time to hide my gains and lie down to enjoy a bit of personal studying. I looked over the small command sequence I'd written out, a brief and simple setup for a lamp. After a bit of prodding, I'd even managed to get one of the older students to show me how to set up an on/off switch. It would all fit into a small container that I was currently considering for materials.

CHAPTER 33

STARLIGHT AND SILVER SPHERES

My first Healing class came by soon enough. I knew that the name of the teacher was Professor Londa, but little else. It was only once a week, so no big deal.

The classroom was one of those set up for more practical work, with tons and tons of room. I stood by with the other bard girls in my year, not that there were all that many of us and we chatted while waiting. Neither of them had opted to take any healing classes either, instead focusing on other subjects.

Soon enough, Professor Londa came in. She was perhaps in her mid-thirties, with a slim figure and dark hair, currently bound up in a tight, severe bun. Everything about her gave off the feeling of a rather stereotypical cross teacher. Every one of us quieted as her eyes flitted over the room.

"Good morning, Class. Here, you will be learning the very basics of what you should know for healing. We'll be covering a few spells, as well as proper triage. The latter subject will take most of our time and while I don't expect any of you to excel, you do need to earn at least passing marks for my class. Questions?"

She had each of us fill out a few brief questions, mostly on what healing we knew, and then we all had to demonstrate. An older one-armed man was brought in.

"This is Roon. He has so generously offered to help us with learning your basic spells. As it's best to demonstrate on a living target, and you lot will be expected to work on humans, he's an ideal candidate."

I could feel my own eyes go a bit wide at her declaration. I wasn't sure how they'd found some poor guy to act as a literal guinea pig, but that was a bit insane. Was she actually going to cut the man up, or poison him, or infect him with diseases? Where were the cute little mice that I'd learned on?

Apparently, she did intend to do all of those things. When the first student came up to demonstrate, she took a small knife and made a cut across Roon's hand. He winced, but seemed otherwise fine with the situation, which didn't make me feel any better.

The line went on and on until it was finally my turn. I'd managed to find myself at the back, status being the main determining factor in things meant that I almost always was in these things. By the time I got there, there was a small mark on the man's hand, where the skin had been broken and healed so many times.

"Are you ready?" the professor asked with a quirked brow.

"Yes."

She pulled the knife once more over his skin, splitting it and letting the blood flow. I immediately launched into my standard healing spell, knitting it back together as quickly as possible. I watched as the flow stemmed and stopped, and the skin regrew again, smoothing out as if it had never been there in the first place.

"Acceptable, please return to your spot."

She spent the rest of the class going over the basic theories involved in healing magic. Most of this was a review, or just completely wrong from what I understood from my previous life, but I took notes diligently anyway. While it was no longer than a normal class, the whole process was exhausting.

That evening, Kala and I were headed up to one of the towers we'd learned we could get access from the roof to watch the sun set. I'd prepped some snacks and blankets so that we could have it rather like a picnic.

She told me about her day as we stood there watching the sky go from blue to pink to deep purple, finally letting night settle in as the golden orb sank below the horizon. She'd had to go down to the temple district to handle some things with her order. The whole trip had apparently been long and involved a stop at a lovely little shop she wanted to go to together at some point. It served some kind of hot fruit drink that she'd really liked.

We found a nice place to lie down, and I responded in kind. She listened as I told her all about the Healing class and the one-armed man who served as our training dummy. I got the feeling that she understood my concerns, nodding along until I'd finished. By that time, the stars had come out and decorated the sky with their pale lights.

"That's rather normal, Alana. You have to practice on humans for some things. Animals work for when you're learning the very, very basics, but humans are quite different, and you'll eventually need to work on them too," she said after I'd finished, wrapping a blanket around the both of us and snuggling in close.

"Maybe, but it seems cruel," I said, pouting.

"Not at all. It takes a lot of time and mana to fix something like a lost limb, just because of how much is gone. That man is likely a volunteer who's being repaid by having his arm restored. Commoners can't often afford that kind of investment, but taking a few weeks where you're given minor injuries? It's really not the worst deal for him."

"So . . . is that normal?"

"Mmm, yeah, most classes have one such person at a time. That or someone who's got a child or something in the same boat. They don't use the children themselves, but a parent can volunteer."

"I see."

Kala shook her head. She could be a little cold toward those she didn't know sometimes.

We lay there for a good while, looking up at the stars. Without things like electric lights, they were truly magnificent, and the few times like this that I'd taken to just stare at them had never disappointed. You could even see something that looked kind of like a purple and yellow cloud that stretched across the sky. I'd heard that the Milky Way was like that, too, but I'd never seen it before.

Eventually, a light snow started to fall. A bit strange as the night was rather clear, but not impossible. I took a few moments to sing up a light wind to keep it off of us and a drying spell to be rid of it completely if it landed anyway.

"What no warming spell too?" Kala asked when I'd finished.

"No, the cold is nice, and with the blanket it's fine." I also wanted an excuse to keep close, as I absolutely loved cuddling.

"You know this is fairly impressive magic, right?"

"It's not like I'm making it stop snowing."

"No, but it's clever, and the control is really good."

"Mmm well, feel free to keep complimenting me."

She laughed, and we went back to watching the sky. The added snow really made the view that much nicer, and when the moon joined us, it seemed to make the falling flakes glow a pale white. We stayed like that for a long while, until it eventually got late and we had to return to our dorm.

* * *

The next few weeks were hectic. They were spent mostly ironing out my weather magic and the other spells I'd learned since coming to school. We also spent a lot of time learning about forming magical items.

There was a certain trick to the shape of magic items. While they could be any shape and still work, there were some that ended up being slightly more efficient. This had to do with a number of factors involving the materials used and the amount of mana you were adding to something, as well as how it was being expelled. Geometric shapes were favored, of course, particularly if they could be made into regular 3-D ones, but this simply wasn't practical for many uses.

While going through these, I finalized the design for my light. The item itself would be a small sphere of silver alloy, something rather like sterling silver. Silver was perfect for many applications due to its insanely high mana conductivity and only avoided being used due to price. The alloy was a nice middle ground for this, not too pricey, since the item would be small, but highly effective.

The sphere would be held in a small lantern that had a plain white fabric covering. It looked rather unassuming but should put off a large amount of gentle yellow-white light. It also didn't put off any heat, and so it would serve me well.

We'd moved on to actually forming things in the practical side of Magical-Item Creation. The circles on our desks allowed for the visualization and molding of materials to a certain degree. It was limited, as they were mostly set up to make the geometric solids that were best for items, but after you made something into the general shape using them, you could easily form it into other shapes. I used my practice time in class to form the lamp's cover, which Professor Hern allowed after looking over my designs.

For the item itself, I approached Rooke. I'd finally finished up my sequences for it. It was a standard lighting enchantment with an on-and-off function that I'd set up to work on voice commands. The last bit I'd had to pull the details on out of the "guide" section of the core. I'd checked with older students to see if that was a normal thing to have. It was, and I tried to get them to show me how, but most of them had told me that it was beyond my level of training.

Voice commands weren't all that difficult to set up in all honesty. Well, the training on how to do them might be a bit weird, but my personal reference source made it rather simple. The "guide" for all of its weirdness was rather clear on directions such as these, telling you what commands for simple operations like that were, and what each part of the code for it was. An on/off switch using verbal commands was even one of its example exercises.

I handed over the code I'd written down to Professor Rooke and watched as his eyebrows rose right at the end. It wasn't all that long; the whole thing fit easily on one sheet of paper.

"You put in voice commands?"

"Yes, I wanted a way to control it without having to fiddle with the item itself. I'm going to put it in a holder and having to open that up to mess with it would be a bit of a pain."

"Those are not normally covered until much later in your education."

"I asked a few of the older students to help me a bit. Is that a problem?"

"Not at all. It's just a bit more than most people try for their first item. Everything here looks good to me, though your choice of command words is a bit strange. 'Illuminate' and 'deluminate' are certainly original."

"I like them." I also really happened to like films from the early 1990s, but he didn't need to know that.

"Fair enough then. What shape and material will you be using?"

"For the sphere, one of the standard silver alloys. Professor Hern already agreed that those should work well."

He nodded. "Yes, for simple emanation effects like this, a sphere will be best. Spending the extra to make it out of silver is a good choice, too, even if it's a bit on the costly side."

I shrugged, it wasn't like I was short on money or anything. I could have made it out of pure silver with no issues, or even gold if I'd really wanted to. That seemed like a bit of a waste, so I had not bothered.

Professor Rooke had a few more questions about the overall design of the holder and the like. He seemed at least satisfied that I'd put proper thought into this after looking at the designs. By the end of the meeting, he nodded and gave his blessing to go ahead and make the item itself.

CHAPTER 34

MAKING A LAMP AND
A GROUP PROJECT

First of all, making a core once you have one is simple. There is literally a menu control for it. Once you've put that in, you mostly just have to go through the core and build, which is both monumentally faster and easier than the initial core building. That whole process took me maybe two or three hours. Then I just had to place that onto the desk we used in class and form the item around it.

When I went to actually make my lamp, most of the process should have been underwhelming. Since the shape involved in the item was so simple, making it was almost automatic I did replace the number they were using for pi, 3.141818 with the proper first hundred digits, because I'd been taught the song so long ago. Humming that while making a magical item was, in retrospect, probably not a great idea.

I winced as I looked at the lamp. It was . . . perfect, far, far, too perfect. You don't really notice how imperfect most spheres are until you hold one that is very, very nearly perfect. For that reason, the whole damn thing stood out like a sore thumb. I was divided between redoing the whole thing and just leaving it, and eventually decided to leave it since nobody would be looking at it anyway. I also thanked myself for doing this while nobody else was working in the same room.

I sighed and connected to the core inside the sphere by placing my hand on it. From there, putting in the actual codes to make the thing work was also straightforward, I just had to copy them in line by line to the menu. I checked it over three times to make sure I'd gotten it right, then finalized. That actually locked the item down, keeping me and anyone else from ever accessing that particular core again. This process also wrote the runes on the outside of the item. I knew that it was possible to make these read as something different from what the actual code was, both from my work in the "guide" and my classwork, but I didn't know how and it seemed like a bother anyway for something like this.

And . . . it was done. I had a sphere with runic text all along the outside, going top to bottom in a little spiral. Putting a bit of mana in it was easy enough, and once I'd done so, I uttered the command "illuminate." The level of light it gave off was determined by the core. After watching it for a bit, I said "deluminate" and put the dang thing away. I'd mount the sphere in its housing later.

There were so many more things to try out now. I'd managed to make my first item, and it was simple but pleasantly functional. I also had an idea on something I could make that I would absolutely have to keep quiet about and would have to manage its "hiding the actual runes" function.

It was a week or two into spring that I was informed that my weekly Healing class would be canceled. That was a cause for celebration, until I was informed that Professor Endel would be taking all of his Combat Spell-casting students for "exercises" instead, joined with a number of those seeking to become knights.

I'd made steady progress in most of my subjects. I was able to communicate a few simple ideas relatively well in Atali, and now actually dancing regularly rather than just a few simple exercises. Our general classes were still focused on things like hammering out some of the issues commonly found in spells, along with going over how to manage multiple spells at once. I found those classes particularly easy exercises since I regularly kept two or sometimes three spells going at once.

As the day of our "exercises" dawned, I found myself bleary-eyed and slightly irritated by my poor breakfast. We'd all been awoken early and had to hurry down to the courtyard where we were outfitted with mildly enchanted practice armor. It didn't seem like much, but I knew from both my work on magical items and experience wearing it in class that it could keep us much safer than it appeared.

We were quickly loaded onto a number of carriages. As I was getting on, I saw other students, in armor not too dissimilar to our own being loaded up as well. That was unusual, and I cocked my head trying to look before Professor Endel gave me a look and I hurried along.

Our ride was bumpy, and we were all tired as we flew down the streets and out the capital's gates. It hadn't really occurred to me that I had stayed in this city for years without leaving it. As we moved past fields and the like, I tried to catch a few glimpses, if only for nostalgia's sake.

Before long, we reached our destination, and as the sun actually properly rose into the sky, I stared wide-eyed at the walls. They weren't tall like city walls, but they did cover an enormous area, and they were decidedly enchanted, though I couldn't tell to what end.

"Who knows where we are?" Professor Endel asked once we'd all formed up.

"Is this the Junkyard Copse, sir?" Troy asked.

"Indeed it is, my boy, and do you know what it is?"

"Um . . . a place for the disposal of broken and aged magical items?"

"Correct again, at least partially. What I have behind me here is an area full of broken and terribly aged magic. Normally, magical items remain rather stable, or when they break, they do so in a way that releases all of their contained mana at once. Unfortunately, this is not always the case. Sometimes they . . . leak and are considered too unstable to safely destroy. This is particularly the case if their purpose is unknown. If they're made of old and degraded materials produced by magical plants or animals, those must also be disposed of if they cannot be repurposed."

I looked behind him. Calling this place a copse was a rather generous use of that word. It had to be at least a few hundred acres if what I was seeing was right. I could see a few trees poking up above the walls. There were also a few questions running through my mind.

"So . . . they just throw them in there then, Professor?" Asking was often the best way to learn things.

"Not exactly, Alana. Certain magical plants and fungi are grown around them that gradually leach out the mana. They are then used as materials for new items. The downside is that all of this mana in the environment tends to create monsters." That statement got a few looks from his class. "Now don't worry. This place is managed, so anything that does pop up in here is going to be small, or it'd have already been taken out. That said, there are a few smaller monsters in here that you lot will be sent in to hunt down. You'll also be on the lookout for certain magical substances that are useful. Once everyone is here, we'll be dividing up into teams, and each will be sent into a different section to see what they can. If anything does go wrong, there will be several more experienced individuals, professors from our school and trainers from the knight program around."

"Um . . . another question, Professor. What happens if a magical item is not properly disposed of?"

"Most of the time? Nothing, maybe it makes a colony of some kind of mildly magical plant or glowing fungus. Sometimes though, something nasty grows around it. Some of those magical plants can establish and grow beyond their normal bounds, too, forming really dangerous areas and leading to much larger monsters. Ask Professor Hern if you want more details, or Professor Empia."

I didn't know Professor Empia, but it was something to look into another time. For now, I could see more carriages arriving and others being unloaded and given a similar talk to ourselves. I recognized two different groups from our school. One was definitely most of the priests and bards I knew. The other I didn't really identify any overriding group dynamic. It was mostly wizards and a handful of priests though. All of them were dressed in a slightly lighter version of our protective gear.

There was also another rather larger group disembarking. Of note on their side was their much, much heavier duty armor, along with the fact that they carried weapons. Their group as well seemed divided into two. One was much more heavily armored, wearing large steel plates that covered almost everything and carrying a sword and shield. The other seemed more lightly so, wearing mostly mail with inlaid plates and carrying a longsword and bow.

Numbers were assigned randomly, and we each met with our groups. As I approached, I tried to gauge each of my teammates. There was a girl who was decidedly a priest. I was pretty sure she was a year above me and she was rather plain, with pitch-black hair. We had a reedy-looking boy, also from my school, who I'd seen in General Spellcasting, but I'd never learned his name. The two knight apprentices were both boys: a tall, handsome lightly armored one with flowing blond locks, and a rather short and stocky one who looked rather like a turtle lumbering along on only its hind legs.

"Hello, everyone, I'm Etta. I'll be healing you if you get hurt during this excursion. Don't take that as an invitation to do stupid things though." She seemed . . . acidic, like someone who would help you only after telling you what an idiot you were.

"Morning, I'm Glen. I'll be taking point." The turtle-looking guy was rather short on words, but his voice was at least pleasant.

"Wonderful to meet you all, I'm Ethbert. It'll be my pleasure to be taking out as many things as I can." He sounded . . . almost stereotypically like a haughty noble, guess looks weren't everything.

"Oh . . . I'm Ean. I suppose I'm here to help identify anything we come across. I guess I'm good at knowing my plants and beasts . . ." Reedy boy seemed nice enough, if a little lacking in confidence.

"Hi, I'm Alana. I suppose I'll be your combat caster. I do mostly illusions and weather magic, though the latter can be a bit slow to wind up. Don't suppose any of you have been in here before?"

Only Etta had it seemed, and after a few questions, we learned what to expect. It seemed there really wasn't too much, some birds and giant bugs, with the occasional mutated boar. The plants were what we'd really want to be on the lookout for though, as gathering them was our primary objective. To that end, we'd need to go slow and be thorough with our work.

After introductions, the assembled instructors brought out a rather large map. The copse was laid out in something like a leaf pattern, with paths as the veins dividing the different sections. This made it easy enough to find a path and the edge of our area. Each group had one area, which we were expected to remain in for the duration of the exercises. When it was all over, we'd be informed by a voice amplification spell over the entire area calling us back. Our main objective was to gather what we could from the area and get any experience in actual combat we could.

"Any questions?" one of the instructors asked.

"What do we do if something does go wrong?" one of the priests piped up, looking on thoughtfully.

"If it is your group and you can get to a path, do so and retreat. If you cannot get to a path, send up some form of light spell and we'll investigate. If it's not your group, but you think another is in trouble, stay within your area and keep yourselves safe until the issue is resolved."

That seemed to be the only one anyone had. This was all rather straightforward, even for a student exercise, and I frankly suspected that the place was being a bit undersold.

As the doors finally opened and our groups were let in one by one, I breathed a sigh of relief. "At least it's not underground."

"Claustrophobia?" Ean asked, rubbing his chin.

"Not at all, just that every time I end up underground, it all seems to go wrong." That got a laugh from my group.

✦

CHAPTER 35

STORM IN THE JUNKYARD COPSE

We trudged through the paths until we finally came to our section. Said paths were actually very clean-looking, and for some reason nothing seemed to bother us while we were on them. While that seemed a bit odd to me, others in the group didn't seem to think it was out of the norm, so I just went with it.

The area we'd been assigned was probably twenty acres total, in a triangular section. It spread out from the point we first arrived at and could only be described as dense. I looked to the others for how they wished to tackle this particular problem, but there seemed to be no consensus. Ean was in favor of going straight in, as he said most of the plants he thought would be best for us to find wouldn't grow too close to the path. Ethbert, on the other hand, was in favor of circling around the edge first, as to scout out any potential beast tracks. While both ideas had some points, Ean was making significantly more sensible points.

"Ethbert, are you a hunter?" I asked when I'd finally gotten tired of the back and forth.

"What? Well, I dabble of course." He seemed a bit confused by my question.

"Then we should go with Ean's plan. He claims to be an expert in this kind of thing. His job is to help us with beasts and plants while we deal with the fighting."

That seemed to settle it, and while Ethbert was a bit peeved by the decision, he was overruled by the rest of the group. We dove in at the smallest point and began a snaking search pattern through the wood. It was painfully slow-going, with rather thick underbrush until we got well away from the path.

A few hours in and all of us were tired. We'd found a few good plants but nothing else, and it was getting rather exhausting to walk all this way. I made some mental notes about getting better hiking shoes specifically for this class around the time we decided to take a short break.

"What?" Etta said, most of our group had turned to her as she pulled out a bit of jerky and began to munch. "I told you, I've done this exercise before. Learning to bring food is part of it."

"The rest of us were not informed of that," Ethbert stated, getting a grunt of approval from Glen.

"That is unfortunate, but I'm sure you'll do better next time."

"Did anyone else bring anything?" I asked, stretching a bit.

The answer to that from our boys was a resounding no, but a few songs later and we all had cold water and a rather plain sandwich. It was in times like these that I felt better about my lack of direct combat capability, because the lot of us would have just gone hungry had I been a wizard.

A half hour after our little break, we found a clearing, in which was our first real enemy. Across from us, and about fifty feet away was a dog-looking beast, covered head to toe with spines like a porcupine. Its muzzle was buried in a deer carcass, ripping and tearing the thing apart. My first move was to put a sound dampening barrier between us.

"Okay, it shouldn't be able to hear us. Ean, what in the world is that thing."

"Spine-wolf, highly aggressive, highly resistant to direct magic attack. It can launch some of those spines so watch out for that. There are a few of the spines on its underbelly that are white. We want those; they're good for making items."

"Dangerous?" Glen asked. He was more the quiet sort, so speaking up caught me a bit off guard.

"Commoners with shields and clubs could take it out; it shouldn't be a problem for us."

After a few moments to form a plan, Glen and I, covered by silence and invisibility, would move to flank the beast. He was to be the initial attack, charging headlong toward the spine-wolf and doing his best to draw its ire while Ethbert closed in from behind. I took a few extra moments to toss up some spells, before tapping Glen's shoulder, our signal for him to go.

He was nearly on top of the beast before I couldn't maintain the invisibility. I'd not worked too much on keeping others unseen and found it much more difficult than doing the same to myself, and anyway, he was supposed to be drawing attacks.

As Glen charged, the monster jumped back, spinning its tail forward in an arc and throwing a hail of spines. They peppered the forest around me, slamming into trees with a wicked *thunk*; a few even bounced off of the shield I'd set up to keep myself safe, giving it its first live test.

While Glen weathered the storm, Ethbert closed in from behind like an arrow. He blurred a bit as he ran from the trees to the monster's side. His longsword flashed in the sunlight as he struck, sending a spray of red out from the beast's back leg.

It was a good blow, but not enough, and the spine-wolf turned again. This time, the rain of missiles flew toward Ethbert, who promptly ducked under the attack, only a few slammed into the armor covering his biceps.

While it was distracted, Glen had closed in. His attack did not have the speed of Ethbert's, but it frankly didn't need it. The blow was titanic, cleaving through the spine of the monster in the middle of its back and out through the chest. He sliced through the spine, ribs, and shoulders; I was guessing he got several internal organs as well. The legs were still held on by the skin, but the spine-wolf's head, neck, and parts of its upper body flew right off. Had that been a man, he might have been able to go through him, horizontally.

I hurried over as I saw Glen helping Ethbert to his feet. Blood was flowing freely from where the latter had been struck by the spines, several having pierced the lighter mail he was wearing and sinking deep. The young man just clenched his teeth and began walking toward Etta.

We found her over Ean, who'd been hit several times as well. He had three of the projectiles lodged in his leg, with another in his upper arm. Needless to say, Ean couldn't really stand and looked like he was in rather severe pain.

"You knew it could throw those. Why the fuck weren't you behind cover?" she snapped as she ripped one of the spines out of his leg. Her other hand slammed a healing spell over the wound, not seeming to really care that his eyes rolled back in agony at the pull. "Waste of mana . . ."

When she saw Ethbert's injuries, she immediately moved to treating him instead. She was no more gentle than she had been with Ean but didn't seem nearly as pissed about fixing him up.

"Are you just leaving me here?" Ean asked as she moved to the armored lad's side.

"Your wounds are not critical, and we'll need our fighters up if something else happens. So shut up, and I'll deal with you when I get the time."

I considered dealing with Ean's wounds myself. On the other hand, she was right; his wounds wouldn't kill him, and I did need to conserve mana just in case. In the end, I decided to let the generally angry priestess deal with it.

Etta was absolutely brutal in her behavior. She seemed to be of the opinion that if we screwed up . . . that was our problem, so long as it didn't endanger our lives or our mission. That did not particularly endear her to anyone, though I suspected that she didn't honestly care. Ean, in particular, seemed a bit peeved by her, understandably.

It took a while, but eventually everyone was healed up and ready to continue. The spine-wolf spines were easy enough to harvest. Mostly, you just ripped them out of the thing's skin once it was dead. Ean wrapped them in cloth and put them with the other items he'd been gathering.

About the time he finished, there was a noise like thunder crashing nearby and an actinic blue flash off from our side. It was followed by another, and another, and another. As I spun my head, looking for what was going on, I saw from the middle of the clearing something pop up, flying into the air. In an instant, I recognized the method of attack properly, my brain catching up to what was going on.

"GET DOWN!" I screamed, grabbing the priestess and the wizard as I flung myself to the dirt.

The earth-shattering noise and bright blue flash as the lightning bomb went off drowned out the rest of the world. Even though we were low to the ground, I could still feel the lashing of electricity against my skin, burning and charring as it passed over me.

It passed quickly, and I knew I'd survived the initial assault, albeit very injured. As vision returned, I could see the weak wards of our armor an angry glowing red. Those had probably had a fair hand in keeping us alive, being that the whole clearing was covered in scorch marks. Even the trees had been broken, their sap vaporized and the bark blown apart. I knew I wasn't the only one to have made it, too, judging by the choking, pained noises from around me.

I also heard more explosions; one came after another almost like a chain. I could see a few here and there, but mercifully there were none close enough to finish us off. Though there were definitely more in our section of the copse, as well as in those around us.

I was hurt, badly so. I could tell the places where the lightning had run over my body, burning it like a brand. As I gasped and tried to stop myself from sobbing, I looked at my allies. Etta and Ean had both definitely made it. Etta was rolling a bit, seemingly unable to do much through her pain. Ean . . . Ean was having a bad day; he currently looked like he was in the middle of a seizure. My guess was that my training pushing my aura out to defend against harmful spells had helped me significantly.

As for our two knight apprentices, they were a mixed bag. Ethbert was on the ground, unmoving. I couldn't tell if he was alive or not and had other issues to sort before checking. Glen, that crazy bastard, was trying to stand up. He looked to be having a hard time of it, but he'd somehow managed to weather that storm the best out of all of us.

The first step in triage was understanding the basic situation, if possible. I'd managed that and moved to the second step. I was a healer and very injured, so I needed to get myself up ASAP. I wasn't even going to try and sing with how messed-up I was, but I could hum, so hum I did. I focused on the areas that hurt the worst. Before anything else, I needed to be able to think and to cast. Glen briefly tried to talk to me, but I flailed an arm at him to shut up. I was busy.

Once I had myself in a state that I considered . . . acceptable, I stopped and looked over at the other member of my team. "What do you need?"

"Personally healing, and we need shelter in case there's another hit."

"Etta is next on the list. I could move where I'm at right now, but we could kill the others if we move them."

"Ethbert is worse off."

"Ethbert can't help anyone else though; she can. Basic triage, get your healers up first."

Etta was still shaking. From the looks of it, she was still doing well enough to stay alive and conscious, but probably too injured to think straight. Fixing that would be my first priority.

CHAPTER 36

✦

PAIN AND INSANITY

I couldn't see the state that I was in, and Glen was covered by his armor, but the other three were badly burned. Most of the hits had landed on their backs and limbs, charring skin and muscle and doing who knows what to the internal organs.

Etta was my first target and I needed to work fast. Glen was right and we needed some kind of cover. Add to that that there was no way I could get everyone up quickly on my own, and I needed to hurry in a bad way. As an added incentive, I was still hearing loud explosions and other noises in the distance.

There were lines crisscrossing across the other girl's flesh, looking like the patterns of roots from a tree. I slowly began my work, trying first to make sure that all of her organs were working before hitting her skin. She was still awake, and once I got her fixed up enough, she should be able to do the rest on her own, at least that was the hope.

While I worked, I tried to look at the still down members of our team. Ean seemed much like Etta and myself, save that he was marginally worse off. Ethbert, on the other hand, seemed to have taken a blast full on. His once handsome face was crisp, with a few bits of bone sticking out here and there. I was unsure if he'd survived, but if he did, he would need significant work to be back to his old self.

It took almost a full minute, but eventually the priestess's breathing slowed down a bit, and she seemed to be coming back to her senses.

"Etta, can you hear me?" I asked, continually pumping mana into the healing magic now flowing over her.

"It hurts," she whimpered in response.

"I know, but we need you to get to work."

She nodded and slowly moved her hands up to her own body. I breathed a sigh of relief when I saw a faint light start to emanate from them and flow over her. Even a poorly trained priest could do far, far more than I could in the same time, so I left her to it.

I gasped in pain and had to stifle a scream as I tried to rise. I could feel the damage to my back but hadn't realized how bad my legs currently were. Hot tears flowed down my face as I tried to catch myself from falling, only really able to crawl.

"Glen, help," I pled.

The warrior in question had been keeping an eye on things, vigilantly looking this way and that for any threats. At my words, he pulled me up and led me over to our other fallen knight apprentice. Each step was another round of intense pain for me, and I could tell by the look on his face that he was hurting bad too.

When I finally got over to Ethbert, I basically flopped down beside him. The good news was that he was alive. The bad news was that he was only barely so. As I pushed my magic into him to fix him up I got a sense that several of his organs were currently failing. My first job then was to get him as stable as I could.

I was beginning to flag a bit as I heard noises from behind me. Our actual healer had finished with herself and was now reaching out to heal Ean. I was glad for that, because while I didn't know what he had, he was a wizard, so I would think there was something. He was also likely to be able to function under her ministrations far quicker than under mine.

When I heard said wizard speak the words "I feel like I'm going to die" from behind me, I nearly laughed.

"You aren't just yet, though you will need more healing later," Etta responded.

"For now, we need to get out of the big, open field and to some form of cover. I'd rather not take a chance with another one of those," Glen said.

"Ethbert is still in no condition to be moved, and I don't think he'll be helpful for quite some time. Anyone got an idea?"

"There's a place where a creek has carved out a little ditch on the far side of the field. We should go there. As for how . . ." Glen was a wealth of things right now. I had heard more words from him in the last few minutes than the rest of our mission combined.

"I've got it." Ean waved his hands, and a soft light flowed around our downed companion, carefully lifting him off the ground. With a few repetitions, our casters had the same under them.

Whatever spell it was, its effects were perfect for this situation as well. The dim light it formed held me not unlike a couch, soft but supportive as it ferried us across the field. I relaxed, letting my head rest on the magic, breathing a sigh in relief.

The creek bed turned out to be a great place for cover. The little winding trickle had sliced a ragged but nearly sheer face in the clay nearest the field. The other side was also fairly steep, but not more than about forty-five degrees. As for the drop, it was perhaps five feet, quite well enough for us to hide in while we tried to patch up.

Etta took a look at things once we were there and decided to change her tactics. She began some kind of large-scale healing spell. It wasn't as powerful as a single-targeted one, but as the magic flowed over me and cooled my scorched skin, I wanted to hug her.

While she was doing that, I switched to putting up the projectile shield around us. It wouldn't stop another lightning bomb, but who knew when there would be some other attack? Ean joined in the shielding. From his brief explanation, I gathered that he had some that could act against heat and cold. Nothing for electricity, but I'd take what I could get.

Glen gathered a few fist-sized stones from the creek. At my quirked eyebrow, he simply informed me that while he wasn't fast, he could throw pretty hard. Based on what I'd seen him do to the spine-wolf, I wouldn't want to be on the receiving end of one of those. The shield I'd put up also let things out, so no problem there.

Once we were all able to move again, even though doing so hurt, our priestess began working on Ethbert alone. She was pumping spell after spell into him, trying to do all she could for the fallen boy. I personally couldn't see too much of the results, but my guess was that he was getting his insides put back together one piece at a time.

"That's it, I'm out," she panted after a few moments. "He'll live if we can get him more help, but I'm totally dry on mana. So don't get any more hurt."

I briefly considered taking up the cause and doing what I could for him, but my mana reserves weren't in great shape, and I wanted my shield up. I could still hear a few sounds of fighting, and that worried me. Coming to that decision, I clenched my teeth and went to keep a lookout.

It wasn't long until there was a crash and a figure flew into our nearby clearing. She was decidedly female, with some kind of head and face covering and a number of glowing ropes of magic floating around her. I could also hear her laughing like some kind of psychopath, giggling happily as her ropes pulled her at a rapid speed into the field.

She was followed quickly by Professor Endel, who looked absolutely livid. He, too, had some form of flight spell going on that made him look as if he were hovering just above the ground.

"Awww, did I hurt your cute, little students?" I heard her yell at the enraged instructor as he came nearer to her.

"Perish!" was his only response.

A brilliant red orb flew from our professor, beelining for the woman. One of her many ropes intercepted it. When the two met, the ground shook from the explosion, which even sent my hair flying back from my distance.

I didn't see how she'd managed it, but somehow one of her ropes had gotten behind him. As he was a bit distracted, it grabbed the teacher by the neck, lifting him up. He responded like most would and lost his concentration for a moment, and that was all she needed. Within a second, more ropes had reached out to bind him, looping around limbs and body.

"GOT YOU!" she cheered in a saccharine voice, closing in and saying other things I couldn't make out. She walked up to him, one hand running down her stomach as she did reaching for the area between her . . .

What the fuck!? I didn't know who this girl was, but she was obviously nuttier than squirrel crap. My mind made up, I breathed in, gathering and focusing as much mana as I could. It was time to send out a good scream in her direction.

Before I could strike, Glen moved. His fist-sized rock hurled forward like a bullet. Sadly, one of the ropes managed to intercept it, almost as if automatically. The resulting explosion reduced the projectile to nothing but dust, but it did distract her for a second, causing her to look our way.

That was when I let loose. I gave all I could to the spell, trying to pump power in and bring it to new heights. She fell for only a second, but it was enough for her ropes to briefly disappear and drop Endel to the ground. They were back a moment later, but small wins.

"Dammit!" she screamed. She pointed at us and sent one of her ropes, only for it to be blocked by Ean with some kinetic spell of his own.

Glen launched a few more stones to keep her on the defensive while I threw some illusory ones toward her. Those were cheap, and while my initial attack didn't seem to do much, if one of Glen's landed, the fight was over.

We continued on like that for a few seconds before more figures came from the forest. My heart briefly sank. That is until our enemy began to scream in incoherent rage and launched herself away from them, fleeing back into the woods while dodging and intercepting more attacks from the newcomers. One, which I could only assume was from a priest, barely missed her, instead striking a tree and causing it to wither into a blackened husk in an instant.

As she fled the field, several pairs of eyes moved to us. Some of the other instructors seemed to recognize us before any attacked though.

"Students!" one of them yelled.

"I'll take care of them and Endel; the rest of you, after her," the priest said loudly enough for all of us.

The remaining teachers needed no prompting and rushed after the assailant. While I hoped they got her, I gave it mixed odds at best.

The priest came over to aid us, though he was sparing with magic. He was worried about more attacks but made sure all of us were at least going to be okay. That done, we kept sheltering in our little divot for a while.

From that point, we didn't see any more direct action. The instructors had chased down crazy girl until she'd fled down some pre-prepared tunnel. Nobody had been stupid enough to follow her into what was obviously a deathtrap. Eventually, we were gathered up with the rest of the students, who all looked brutally rough, under the supervision of the combined teaching staff.

Our group had been one of the closest to one of the bombs, and so had taken a rather bad hit. Not the worst, as there were a number of deaths, but bad enough. Most of the students capable of any healing, myself included, were soon running on nothing but fumes as we waited for our professors to find us a truly safe way out.

The main entrance was just assumed trapped, and after a good bit of discussion, a hole was broken through the wall so we could get out and to get support in. We were all hurried back to the city and into the hospital run by the Shield. As soon as we got there, I found the nearest bed and promptly passed out.

CHAPTER 37

✦

THE SHIELD'S HOSPITAL

When I awoke, I found a familiar figure sitting in the chair beside my bed.

"Eleanor?"

"Hello, dear. I thought you'd like to see a friendly face when you woke."

I wouldn't exactly call our relationship friendly, but we did have some form of understanding. We'd also spent a good amount of time together, so of those here she might well know me best. I looked her over, then gazed around me. The hospital was still a bit busy, but the worst of it had passed. It was now night, the windows showing a deep blackness outside.

"Well, yesterday was . . ." As I thought about it, I tried moving, noting that my wounds were gone. My armor also seemed to have been taken off and put beside my bed.

"Quite bad as I understand. As for your wounds, one of the priests saw to them while you were sleeping."

"Yeah, do you know about one of the boys in our group, Ethbert? He was looking quite bad."

"My understanding is that everyone in your unit survived. Not something that could be said for everyone. That said, I'd like you to tell me what all happened if you could." Eleanor seemed slightly more calm than usual, as if worried for me.

I recounted the tale: how it had all started normally, then how we'd been hit with that explosion, and the good work from everyone who had brought us to somewhere with cover. When I got to the part with the fight with the crazy woman, I saw Eleanor's eyebrows raise. Then I finished, told her how we'd been brought here, and I passed out.

"I won't hide this from you, dear. The woman who attacked you; everyone wants her. I don't expect you to know too much, but if you think of anything . . . The Shield wants her, the kingdom wants her, everyone. In her attacks, she's been indiscriminate, children, priests, noncombatants, commoners, and nobles . . ."

"I understand. Wait . . . attacks? As in plural?" I saw Eleanor flinch at my question.

"The authorities have been trying to keep it quiet, but over the past few months, there have been . . . quite a few in the capital and surrounding cities."

"How have I not heard of this? Why do you think it's the same person?"

"Because, dear, you've been at the academy, where information is easy to control. As for your second question, I don't know, but all of them are . . . big, loud, and tend to cause rampant destruction. I don't know all the details, since much is being hushed up, but I know it's been quite bad."

"Okay, is there anything else?" I was already exhausted, and I'd just woken up.

"Several things. The first is that you will need to talk to someone about all of this." At my quirked eyebrow, she explained. "Alana, it's not the first time someone had tried to kill you. You were horridly injured and saw others in the same state. Perhaps you feel fine now, but that's not something that's going to last forever. You need someone who can listen to you when you need to get that out."

I . . . well, I'd not had any experience with that from my last life, but I knew that it could cause problems. Even now, I was pretty much ardently refusing anything that took me underground after all the pain that that had caused me. Though that felt more like stubborn superstitiousness than anything else.

"I have a couple of people I'll seek if I need it."

The older woman gave me a rather tired look. "Very well, there are also a few other people who want to speak with you. Are you up for that?"

I nodded, and she went to go find whoever it was. I had a few minutes to myself while she did. It was nice, calm, I could just stare at the ceiling and let myself relax.

There was a knock, and the door opened before I could say anything. I found myself staring at a man in formal attire. "Good evening, Alana, I've a few questions if you don't mind."

The man was one of the investigators assigned to this case. He asked for the same general breakdown that I'd given Eleanor, along with asking if I'd recognized anything. That one I did have to respond to.

"Mmm, a few years back, there was an attack involving lightning that I saw the edges of. It would have been . . . four years ago? The day of the entrance exams to the academy. I saw some of the explosions that day, and they felt very similar to the ones that hit us today. That's why I got everyone down. I'd seen those from far off before and knew they were bad."

"Interesting, did you see the source at that time?"

"No." I shook my head. While I didn't go too deep into it, I was sure his report would eventually reach those who knew just how close I'd been to the previously mentioned attacks. Letting them know that whoever did this was the same as who attacked the prince at that time could be helpful.

"All right, if you think of anything else, please let me know."

"Yes, sir."

A bit after he left, Professor Endel came by. It was hard to read his mood. I knew he was probably less than thrilled by the fact that his attacker had gotten away, but he'd also survived the experience. He moved to pick up the armor that was sitting near me, looking deeply at its damage. One of his hands ran over the places where the lightning had struck me.

"It's hard to believe that you survived this." There was a scorch mark that went through the entire chest piece, in one side and out the other. "Did you know we recently changed some of the standard warding on our student armors?"

"No, I didn't."

"We did. That madwoman who hit us isn't working alone. In the last couple of months, there have been . . . too many incidents where we've been hit, many involving those lightning bombs. Dean Lorrae thought it was just a matter of time before someone attacked our students. Needless to say, neither of us thought that our pupils would be in danger at that location. It's highly managed, even warded to keep things in and out."

"How bad was it?"

"Our academy lost six, which is almost unheard of. The knight apprentices . . . well, we did offer to change theirs as well, but they refused. I imagine that they'll ask us to now. They lost twelve."

Six out of a class of only fifty was certainly significant. Even losing one would be a big deal, but that many in that violent of an incident. It would shake our class deeply.

"That many from the knights? One of ours took a bad hit, but the other nearly remained standing."

"Ah, I met him. His armor was his own, not loaned. His defense is also rather thick." He sighed. "That aside, I'd like to personally thank you. If your group hadn't intervened, I very well might have died back there. The lot of you did an excellent job in a situation that was well beyond you."

"Not going to ask me to recount everything that happened to you?"

"I'm sure you've gotten enough of that already and will more in the future. Your classmates will be curious. As for telling me about things . . . Alana, many soldiers have issues after they've seen battle. Of them, many are both older and better prepared than you students were. I'll tell you as I've told all your classmates that I've spoken to already. If you need anything, do come and see me."

"You're the second person today who's wanted to have that conversation with me."

He chuckled, a kind of rough, tired sound. "Good, I'm glad that you have someone who cares about you. Now, you lot are getting tomorrow off of classes to rest up, then we'll be seeing you all back, bright and early."

With that, he left me, taking the destroyed armor. I was a bit surprised that we were getting anything with how hard the students were driven, but I supposed that it was probably a good idea to get a bit of time to organize our thoughts anyway.

Since I didn't feel at all tired, I opted to do a bit of looking through my core. This incident had proven to me that sooner or later I would need to make my own defensive gear, and I was betting that there were hints in there. The issue of finding them would be my first challenge, of course, but once I had, we could dive into that.

There were indeed a number of things within the "guide" and "help" menus relating to making defenses. Sadly, they were much further along than I'd yet managed to get and quite a bit more difficult. They were also strewn about with the large amount of jargon that whoever wrote these seemed absolutely in love with.

Finding those sections and doing a once over while pretending to sleep took a good part of my night. I did come out a few times to check on the world at large and after a fair bit of work found that the sky was quickly brightening.

I stood up and stretched. At some point in the night, someone—my guess was Eleanor—had left me a rather simple dress at my bedside. Which was nice, because my current clothes were a bit . . . rough and would decidedly attract attention if I walked around in them. After changing, I poked around a bit to see what all was going on. I personally planned on going back to the academy today regardless of how everyone else felt about it. There were some other things I needed to do as well.

As I poked around, I found Eleanor, who now looked exhausted, talking to one of the priestesses. She waved me over as I looked her way.

"I'm glad you found the dress. We've got a few headed back to the academy in just a bit."

"Thank you for letting me borrow it, but if it's all right, I would like to run some errands. It'll give me a good chance to clear my head too."

She seemed a bit concerned, but she seemed to realize that if she said no, I was just going to go back out anyway. "Very well, but be careful."

I nodded and headed out, my uniform tied in a small bundle. I'd walked the lower parts of the city a near endless number of times, and as I began, I found myself taking my normal route from the temple district straight to the Starlit Sky. That seemed as good a place as any to start, particularly if I wanted to unwind a bit.

The Starlit Sky was as it had always been. At this time in the morning, that was rather slow. Sadly, Lucien wasn't there today, as he'd had some business elsewhere, but I left him a message that I'd stopped by to say hello and wished him well. After that, I chatted to some of the regulars and staff I knew and had a good breakfast. The food wasn't as high quality as we got at the school, but it was homey and rather nostalgic.

Afterward, I opted to take a walk through the market. It was early spring and the perfect time for seeing what fresh things were being brought in. There were early fruits and fresh meats. I saw a ton of the handiwork people did over winter being sold, small woven, knitted, and the like pieces of varying quality. There was even a bit of carved art and small jewelry for sale, not that I needed any.

As I passed by the edge of the district, through the area where more industrial things were sold, a man unloading a small cart tripped and spilled the contents of the sack he'd been carrying. Small white crystalline stones scattered everywhere.

"Sorry, Miss," he said as they spilled almost atop my feet.

"It's fine. What are those anyway?"

I didn't recognize the word he used at first, but he told me they were used for a few things. Mostly, they were used by tanners or dyers, after being ground into powder. I nodded, it was clearly alum then, though I'd never seen it as anything except powder, and then mostly for pickling. I began to let my mind wander as I turned to leave, alum was such a weird word. It sounded almost like aluminum or "alu-min-i-um" as the Brits seemed determined to pronounce it. I stopped and turned . . . could that be because it came from . . .

"Actually, sir, could I buy a bit of that?"

CHAPTER 38

✦

RETURNING AND BREAKING THINGS DOWN

I had an idea. Well, somewhat of a theory I needed to test, but this would work. It would require a little caution too. I was unsure of exactly what I was and would be working with, so I would need to do the proper setup, and that in and of itself might take a hot minute.

Metals were, for the most part, impossible to summon, at least in metallic form. So what if I could kind of bypass it, not summon the metal but rather draw it out? If I could, and this alum actually contained aluminum, which I was unsure of. Then I could possibly end up with something really useful.

I'd never seen aluminum in this world, which was a bit of a shame. It was easy to mold, great for pulling away heat, super light, and while I didn't know the alloys, some of them were really strong too! It was the perfect thing to use for a number of cool applications if I could get it to work.

That would be a problem for the future though. Mostly, because I was greeted by a number of concerned friends as I entered the gates of my school. I'd been so distracted by my new idea for a cool toy that I had totally forgotten about them for a bit.

First came Kala, who just booted everyone else out of the way. She ran up to me and gave me a hug.

"I was so worried when I heard the news, but they told us we couldn't go anywhere and the school was locked down for a day. Everyone who was outside had to stay out or be held off campus until it was all over."

"Yeah . . . I understand that, are you okay? Nothing happened here, right?"

"No, everything was fine. It was just a bit of a shock. That kind of thing just doesn't happen to students normally."

While we were talking, Dras came over. I hadn't spoken to him much in the past couple of months. That wasn't his fault so much as mine. Since the whole thing with the dance I'd been a bit standoffish, and now he was here, looking rather regretful.

"Hey . . ." he said, scratching his hair.

"Hi . . . it's . . . been a while since we've talked, huh?"

He nodded, giving a sad sort of smile. "We should though, when you're ready to."

"Yeah."

"Hey, what you got in the bag?" Kala interrupted us, pulling us back from that painfully awkward mess.

"Oh, right!" I looked down at the medium-sized bag of alum I'd managed to buy. "I saw something on the way in and had some ideas. This is for a project I'm going to do later."

"Anything I can help with?" she asked.

"Not really. It's not even a big deal." It totally was, but I wasn't going to say that outside of anywhere I didn't know was quite private.

The three of us found a quiet room where I got to once again recount the story of the attack for more people. I was rather tired of that by now, but the whole school was curious, and I felt like I should at least tell these two. Kala because we were going out and Dras because . . .

"Dras, it was them. The ones who did the attack on the day we first came to check out the academy."

He nodded. "Yeah, I thought it might be when you brought up the lightning bomb. You're sure?"

"Very, and there's some insane woman leading them. Be careful; she almost took out Professor Endel in a fight."

"No kidding? That's nuts, he's like, a trained battle-mage, and good enough to teach here. They don't hire anyone who's not the best."

"Wait, what am I missing?" Kala leaned in, glaring at both of us.

Dras looked at me, as if he wanted me to explain. Well, whatever, of the two of us, I was definitely the better storyteller.

"A few years back, we came to see the entrance exams for the academy. During that time, there was an attack, and we fled down to the city underground, ending up way deeper than we should have. We met a few monsters, a couple of golems, and helped get our friend Charles out of there. You've met Charles, right?"

"Quiet guy? Pale with eyes that look like he's constantly on alert?"

"Yeah, same guy. He was trapped down there for years. We helped him get out."

"Wow, no wonder he seems a bit off. You're likely to go crazy with complete isolation like that."

"Be nice. He's a really good guy, bit weird, but really decent," Dras said in defense of our friend. My expression must have told Kala how much I agreed with that; Charles had helped me out a couple of times when I didn't even know I needed some help.

"Fine, fine. So, what's the plan now?" Kala asked, her eyes sparkling.

"We keep our heads down and try not to end up in any more terrorist attacks?" Dras gave what might be the best practical answer I'd ever heard from him.

"I have to agree with Dras here. They're out of our league, but we should put some effort into learning how to protect ourselves. I could walk you two through the magic-resisting exercises if you want. It's not hard and it might save your life. I also want to learn about making some other defenses. I'll show you when I'm about ready."

That got a series of nods and we decided on our "rest days" that we'd have a small study session on those. Both of them were excited as getting access to new techniques was often really fun, if quite difficult. This particular one wasn't secret or anything, but most people never bothered learning it. I mean, how often are you attacked?

During the week leading up to our first practice session, I got to work on my aluminum project. I was pretty sure that there was aluminum in the alum, like 60 to 75 percent, but there was almost certainly other things as well. To that end, I wanted to set up my workspace.

There was plenty of area in one of our labs where there were configurations for carrying fumes away, as well as preventing splashes or explosions. These were things that could happen when magic went very, very wrong, particularly with items or certain magical ingredients. So taking a spot in one of the rooms with lots of protections in place was easy enough.

It was rather like a chemistry lab, only all of the science stuff was replaced by fantasy equivalents. There were beakers and the like, but they looked crude with corks and open flames. Glittering solutions were in the cabinets that I didn't have access to. There were even a few cauldrons of various sizes. It was clean though, more like an alchemist's lab than a witch's hut. I supposed that made sense since what was done here was far more formal, and nobody would allow dirt in our pristine educational institution.

I found one of the tables that would work for what I was up to. The enchantments had blocks for splashes, and one that would purify and remove all gases that came off. I would have to power these myself, but that was no big deal. It was a bigger problem that I'd had to choose a time when there wouldn't be anyone around, and that meant it was late at night.

The spell I would need to design now would be simple enough in what it would do. I needed to separate out all the different elements into their pure forms. A few questions told me that some wizards had worked on similar things when messing around with metals and trying to get alloys to revert back to their original forms. Unlike those, I was not trying to pull out a known from the alum. My goal instead was to pull out everything based on atomic weight.

I hummed, focusing on my goal. I pictured myself pulling each and every one out, sieving them by the size of their atoms. It was imperfect, but I'd sorted plenty of things before, so this shouldn't be too terribly difficult.

Problems started quickly. First was that a lot of whatever made up this stuff was some form of gas. I could tell this because it was steaming its way out of the stone, making it smaller and smaller. It wasn't too mana costly, but I was losing so much to whatever gases were getting pulled away that I really worried about what I'd end up with. Second was that all that gas leaving at once was making the sample I was using move a lot. That was solved with the simple movement spell I'd been using for years.

I watched in horror as my sample shrank and shrank. Finally, to my great relief, it started to move apart into . . . three large blobs and a few very, very small ones. When it was all done, I had two metal samples and one that was a bright yellow stone. The yellow stone was obviously some form of crystal. It looked weird on the tabletop, and I honestly had no idea what the heck it was.

The two metals were my other head scratcher. I didn't know what they were exactly, but my guess was that one of them was the aluminum I was after. With no other options, I took some tongs and picked both up, looking them over. Since that did nothing, I moved on to poking them. One was way softer than the other, and at that point I thought I might have my aluminum. Well, the only other experiment I could think of was to test their density. Aluminum was known to be one of the lighter metals at least.

When I put a small bit of what I thought was aluminum into the water I was using, it appeared that it was far less dense by weight than anything we were using in class. That was a good sign in my book. The other piece . . . well, it caught on fire and flew around the little container of water. That was both good and bad. It was good in that I now guessed it was some form of alkali metal, but bad in that that shit was dangerous. I found a small phial with oil to store it in, since I was fairly sure that's what my high school chemistry teacher had done.

I tossed out the trace elements, not knowing what they were and honestly not wanting to screw with them. I now had aluminum, some alkali metal (I was fairly sure), and some unknown yellow stuff. I considered what I knew about them, and how I could use them.

While I had some ideas on uses for myself, there was the issue of how rare they were. I hadn't seen or heard of aluminum, so . . . I figured I'd ask. I took the time to form it into a small block with a bit of heat and some of the metal-molding spells that were fairly standard issue in our labs, no problem. The next morning, I took it to someone I knew would be able to identify all the stuff I'd made.

Professor Hern was surprised when I showed up at his office. That had nothing on how he reacted when I told him that I'd found some interesting samples while browsing the market. I did leave the alkali metal behind. I was worried about how dangerous it could be.

"Well, this is just sulfur, nothing too special, but very pure. It's also been shaped nicely into a marble for some reason. Interesting, but not overly valuable." The crystal seemed to be something easily explained enough.

With the second, we had a very different issue. He took a sample and his eyes went wide. Probably because it was so light. After asking if he could re-form it, he melted it, changed the shape, tested density, tensile strength, compressive strength, seeming to get more and more wide-eyed with each one. He pulled out an old tome from behind his desk and went over it as well, even running mana and heat through the sample using one of his tools, each time going back to his reference book. Finally, he stopped and looked at me.

"All right, you said you bought this in the market?"

"Yes, sir," I lied.

"Do you know what it is?"

"Some weird metal?"

"Alana, this is sky-metal. At least as near as I can tell." His eyes were intense, like someone who'd walked into his yard and found a diamond sitting there.

CHAPTER 39

SKY-METAL

I watched as my several gram bomb exploded in Professor Hern's mind figuratively. He was tapping his reference book repeatedly as he waited for my response.

"Okay, what is sky-metal? Why is it important?"

"Excellent question! Do you know why we use leather for making most war-mage armors?"

"Well . . . it's readily available, and you can enchant it."

"No, well, sort of. It is enchantable and replaceable, but the main reason is it has good strength versus weight ratio. If a mage were to wear iron armor or the like, they would be harder to hurt, but much slower than they already are. Since only very thick, very enchanted metal would be good for stopping an actual knight who got too close and that would make your average caster unable to move, we instead make armor that can stop blows from non-magic users while providing some magical protection."

"Okay . . ."

"Sky-metal is a game changer when it comes to that. It's not quite as magically conductive as silver or gold; it is nearly as good though. It differs more in its weight, sky-metal is extraordinarily light, and those two things make it one of the best, if not the best material for making armor for war-mages. It's soft certainly, but that is easily remedied with a few basic enchantments; the same spell we use on leather would be far more effective on this."

"What are the other ones? Not magical materials?"

"No, no, no, you absolutely don't want a magical material as your armor. If the magic is somehow disturbed, the results can be quite bad.

Those are used mostly in static items. The only other known material that could compare would be primordial-metal, though that is even rarer and not anywhere near as conductive." He blinked, as if he realized I'd gotten him off track. "Sorry, where were we then? Ah, yes, do you have any more of this?"

"Sorry, no." That was technically true. I did not have any more metallic aluminum laying around.

"The merchant who sold it to you, do you know if they did?" Professor Hern looked like he was nearly salivating.

"I highly doubt it. Not that I would even know where to send you. It was just something that caught my eye as I was walking down the street. If he had a shop, I don't know where it is." Another truth . . . technically. I hastily told him what street I'd bought it on, well, the alum at least. The last thing I needed was Professor Hern poking too deeply into my business.

"I see . . ." He had re-formed the metal into a ball and was playing around with it in his fingers. "There are some more tests and the like I'd like to run on this. I've never actually seen a sample in person before, and it's a rare chance. It will also allow me to update some of our reference works."

I considered that for a few moments. "I don't mind you keeping it for a while, mostly since I don't have anywhere to store something that rare, but I would like it back at some point."

He gave me a few promises to that effect before sending me off. I could tell my professor was a bit too excited for this, but it would keep him out of my hair for a while. It was my guess that he'd find some reason to go into the market and search it bottom to top for more aluminum, but he'd probably be disappointed.

I, on the other hand, had some things to deal with. Other than my many personal problems, I now had a new project. Aluminum-enchanted armor would be on the docket so that the next time I knew I was going into a fight, I would go in hard and fast. There was no way I'd be sharing this with the teachers though; it was way too big. As a matter of point, I was going to hold off on making any more aluminum at all until Professor Hern had his chance to waste a bunch of his own time. Hopefully, I wouldn't need it too soon.

The next day, I had Atali Language, and I went to class with a whole stomach full of butterflies. Dras and I had yet to have our talk, and that was something I knew would have to happen. We needed to go over where we were and what had happened. Certainly, I knew we'd drifted apart, but it had been rather more extreme than I'd realized. I hadn't even talked to him about his girlfriend.

We still sat near each other in that class and even talked lightly sometimes, but nothing like we did when we were younger. I sat there, barely paying attention as our teacher went over several terms I'd already put to memory. While I was still trying to think of what to say, class ended.

The two of us waited as everyone left, packing our things but keeping to our seats. Even Professor Etia eventually made her way out; she did give us a look before leaving.

"So . . ." he tried to start.

"Yeah."

"When is the last time we really talked, Alana?" Dras looked out across the room, seemingly at nothing. "I mean really talked, like we used to."

"We chatted a bit when I first came to the school . . . even then though, I think we were . . ."

"Mmm, I suppose I let myself get too caught up in my studies, forgot my friends."

"I mean, I didn't really try too hard either. So don't blame yourself."

"It's always been like that, hasn't it?"

"What?"

"I'm two years older than you, Alana, but I've always been behind. Even when we were really young, there was so much you knew that I didn't. You're a better mage, better at math, better at almost everything. I feel like you're always the elder in every situation."

"Is that why you didn't ask me to the school's ball?"

"What? I didn't even know you thought of me like that. I mean, Dietrich has been practically gushing over you since he discovered you existed. Several of the other boys like you too. Besides, I'm dating Clarissa anyway, have been for like almost a year."

"Okay, first, Dietrich is nice and all, but he's sort of an idiot, and I can't stand that. Two, you've been dating someone for almost a year? Why did you never tell me?"

"What, of course, I told you . . . erm . . . oh, oh maybe I didn't. We really do need to talk more."

I wanted to hit my face on the desk. That was huge. How did he not think to even tell me? We sat right beside each other in class and chatted. How had it never come up? What even, dude? Do you not think your personal life is something I'm interested in hearing about? Actually . . .

"You . . . you never do talk much about yourself and what's going on with you, do you?"

"Nah, not so much. Mom always used to ask me every detail about everything, then get mad at things she didn't like, you know? So I guess I just try not to go into personal stuff."

"Details she didn't like . . . like me?"

"Oh, she still hates your guts. I don't think she knows you go to school with me though."

"Does she know about Clarissa?"

"Absolutely fucking not." We both got a chuckle at that one.

"We should hang out more."

"Yeah, there's a few small events going on in the knight's school soon, I hear. They're catching a few beasts and letting the students fight them for training. Do you want to go? Well, I think I'd need to bring Clarissa so she doesn't get all jealous, but . . ."

"That's fine, let's do it. Mind if I bring Kala along?"

"Kala? Why?"

I looked at him and raised an eyebrow. It took a few moments for him to get it, but when he did, his eyes got a bit bigger.

"I'm honestly surprised it took you so long."

"I mean . . . that's a new one for me. I didn't know you liked girls."

"I don't, I like Kala, and probably not in exactly the same way as you like Clarissa."

"Um . . . okay. Wait, why did you want me to invite you to the school ball then?"

"Because I thought you probably would. Nothing was likely to happen because we're not like that, and you're a nice enough guy."

He responded by flicking me on the ear . . . hard. "Do not play games with boys, Alana. If you are or aren't interested, make it clear, and make clear what you want. Going to that ball together would have been announcing ourselves as an item, which would have pissed off Dietrich. That's something I would have had to deal with. Which I would have, had I been single and you just told me what you wanted."

I rubbed my ear and pouted a bit. I suppose just expecting him to invite me had been a bit rude on my part, particularly if we both knew I wasn't interested.

"Sorry."

"Forget about it. You've been there for me for a long time, Alana.

You're like a big sister or something. I could never really think of you like I do other girls."

There was a bit of a lull for a while, both of us thinking about all we'd learned about each other. It was nice and in some ways reminded me of all the time we'd spent studying and hanging out. Eventually, we did pick it back up though.

"So, watching knights fight monsters?" I asked.

"Hey, don't blame me. I understand it's something a handful of nobles do for fun and to see how the new students are coming along."

I rolled my eyes, and we headed off to our next classes, making jokes on the way.

Classes for the rest of the day were rather uneventful. When I returned to my room though, I found a most unwelcome surprise. Professor Rooke was there, as was another professor whose name I did not know. She stood off to the side while he spoke with Emma, seemingly awaiting my return. Several of my personal effects were laid out, uniforms and the like, it was also obvious some of my drawers had been opened, some still were.

"What is this?" I asked my voice quite a bit sharper than I normally would speak to a professor. "Men aren't even allowed in these dorms, Professor Rooke, and what have you done to my room?"

"I received a number of disturbing reports, and it was determined that searching it was necessary."

"You had no right to go through my things." I could practically feel my magic rising as my anger peaked. The bubbles that constituted my aura seemed to cover me in a thick layer protectively, bursting out a bit as I released my control and pushed, seemed my training had paid off some.

"I did not search your things, Alana. It would be improper for a man to go through a lady's possessions. I waited outside while Emma and Professor Lur did. You will also find that I had every right, as your guardian, to authorize such a search."

I could have almost spit fire at him. With magic that was really an actual option too. "Reports? What reports?"

"Well, the most alarming would be that you have been spending hour after hour lying seemingly unconscious on your bed, failing to respond when called. I would think that you might be trying to work on upgrading your core, but according to Professor Hern, you seem to not be progressing on that much. You've also appeared with a sample, albeit small, of an extraordinarily rare material. Oh, and let us not forget this." His voice was acid as he reached over and opened my lamp, revealing the actual magical item inside. "I'm not sure what is going on with that, but whatever it is, is really, quite decidedly not standard."

"Oh." I looked over to the sphere that seemed to defy reality itself, still there, still looking too perfect, too . . . almost wrong.

"Oh, indeed. While I've agreed not to pry into your research, at least some of that needs explanations."

CHAPTER 40

✦

CONFRONTATION

I needed a few moments to think, to organize my attack. In that vein I decided to go for the lowest of hanging fruits.

"The sphere is research that I'm not yet bringing forward. In fact, most of what you're on about is."

Rooke looked at my lamp. "I am inclined to believe that this is research, but my main concern here is if it's dangerous."

"I doubt that."

"I do not, because everyone who so far has looked at it gets the feeling that it is . . . off. What even is this thing?"

"You can surely understand the rune sequences," I huffed. They were written right there on the surface.

"There are ways to hide the true ones . . ."

"No, it's just a lamp."

"Then why does it . . ."

"Personal research, but harmless personal research. Which I will expect you to stay out of as per our agreement."

"Very well, I can ignore that so long as you don't do anything dangerous with it. It was incidental for us to find it anyway. The main concerns are your bouts of unconsciousness and the fact that you are appearing with unbelievably valuable materials that your explanation for is nonsense."

"Well, as for my lying unconscious, that is me doing research on my core, and it's also none of your business."

"Research? Without taking any kind of note or anything? Not recording any result? Even if it were in code in some manner that only you could understand, that would make sense. But you've done none of that.

You've just spent hour after hour lying there. That is the appearance of narcotics."

"Oh yes, let me take notes, because my room is so secure from intrusion. I'm sure nobody would barge in and search through such things." I let the sarcasm drip for a few moments. "As for what I'm researching, that should be obvious, it's the core. Which you already know I've spent a lot of time thinking about already. Since you've searched my room and found that I don't have any narcotics, that should do away with that suspicion as well."

Rooke picked up the phial that contained . . . my guess was potassium . . . and put it on the table.

I opted to head him off. "Another sample I acquired, and not one I would advise consuming. I opted not to tell Professor Hern about that one because I don't think it useful."

"Oh? And what would happen if it were consumed?" Rooke looked doubtful.

As way of demonstration, I walked across the room, picked up a cup from my bedside, and filled it with water. I then used a minor movement spell to toss the metal sample in, wherein it immediately started spewing out fire and sputtering around. "That's what happened while I tried to measure its density. Sadly, I have no more of it, or I would invite you to have a bit."

Rooke actually seemed a bit put off as he looked down at the glass. I'd managed to easily demonstrate that the metal wasn't a drug. I'd also destroyed it quite nicely so he couldn't look into it any further.

"Very well, on to my final concern. The appearance of these materials is so far outside of the norm that I cannot ignore their making their way onto our campus. Do you know how rare sky-metal is?"

"Obviously not, that is why I took the sample to Professor Hern."

"It is uncommon enough that he has never seen it before. Professor Hern has seen diamonds the size of your thumb, pure gold plates inscribed with magic, magical items the likes of which you can hardly imagine. Never has he held a sample of that material. My understanding is that he thought that it might be a legend, only put in his reference books because others had it in theirs. Here you show up though, with a sample you 'bought in the market off of a merchant you didn't know.' It's not believable."

"I did buy it off a merchant whose name I do not know."

"Alana, that's bullshit." He seemed actually irritated by that answer.

"The truth is often stranger than fiction, Professor. That you cannot believe it is not my problem. Do you have any other concerns that would cause you to go through my things?"

"The bouts of torpor were our main concern. Those alone were enough." Professor Lur spoke up finally, she'd spent the entire time sitting in the corner rather quietly.

"Care to explain?"

"There are . . . certain narcotics sometimes used by young wizards in an attempt to boost their power. The main side effect is visions that incapacitate the user for a period of time. Well, that and the fact that they tend to be fatal."

That sounded like some kind of psychedelic, not something I wanted. "There are drugs to make your magic stronger? That seems . . ."

"Did you miss the part where they are often fatal to the user? Every few years, the school sees someone try, often someone who has failed their entrance exam before and wants that bit of extra boost to get through. They almost invariably perish from that effort."

"I'm already more powerful than most of my peers. I've no need to kill myself trying to gain more."

"Indeed, you are. A girl from no noble family who is stronger than most. That does nothing to allay suspicion. In fact, it serves as a point of concern," she continued.

"Well, if you lot must know, I've been looking into two pages in the core that Dean Lorrae told me of." I waved a hand to bring up the codes for the "guide" and "help" functions. "It was my understanding that these were well-known enough to exist and they are extensive."

"You're looking into those? Have you learned . . ." Rooke began.

"There's no context, Professor. Whatever code or language they're in isn't ours, and it's not Atali. Similarly, there doesn't seem to be any parts that are in either of those. Trying to gain insight is going . . . slowly. There's also an absolute mountain of that documentation, whatever it is, so trying to sort through it even lightly is daunting." That should be enough to get them off my back, and I even managed to put in that I was going into the core, but implied that I wasn't learning anything, a total win for me.

"Well . . . it seems I owe you an apology then, Alana. I oversaw a rather serious invasion of your privacy. I do hope you'll understand my reasoning and forgive me." Rooke lowered his head a bit. While he spoke the words, I was still pissed.

"I understand, if you have any further concerns, do try speaking to me first, Professor." I let my tone tell him just how agitated I was. "As for the moment, I've a number of things that must be taken care of."

"Oh?" Professor Lur looked a bit confused.

"Why yes, firstly I need to retrieve my sample of sky-metal from Professor Hern, since he clearly can't be trusted with it. Then . . ." I looked over at my maid, who was trying to be as inconspicuous as possible. "Oh, Emma, there you are. I have no need of a maid who cannot maintain my privacy. Get your things and get out by the time I return." I turned back to the two teachers. "Then I need to go complain to the dean about people getting into my research. Finally, I need to see about finding a new maid. I would appreciate it if you lot could close the door on your way out." With that, I turned and left. The last thing I needed was any of them coming up with something I'd actually done wrong, or some suspicion that I couldn't easily deflect.

Professor Hern and the dean would have to come first. I needed thinking time. My main problem was the maid issue. I'd seen through her work how much I actually did need one while here, a few days wouldn't be an issue, but long-term it would be a problem. Where to get one who wasn't a spy was the problem though.

Asking Kala if she knew someone was a decent option, but I couldn't be sure her order wouldn't send me somebody to look over me. For the same reason, asking the Shield was a low option on my list. They would certainly have a spy who they would send me, and probably would be happy to do so if I requested. As for others who might help . . . I knew most of the other bards in my year fairly well, but probably not well enough. Pinea also might know someone, but it might be the same issue as I had with Rooke. She was a rather high-ranked noble, so she'd have connections, but anyone she helped me find might really be in it for her and her family. The only other nobles I really knew well were Dietrich's family, and that was a hard no.

Hern didn't even question anything. As soon as he saw me and the angry face I was making, he just handed over the little ball of sky-metal. I could, and would, test it later to see if I'd lost any in weight or volume, but I was fairly sure he wouldn't be that bold when he was clearly in the wrong. I wasn't sure how mad I should be at him compared to Rooke, but I wasn't all that surprised he'd told the other professor.

Dean Lorrae was also in his office when I came by. It occurred to me that I didn't know when any of my teachers actually went home, or if they did, but I managed to catch him.

"Good evening, Alana. I suppose that your presence here and that angry look on your face mean that Professor Rooke didn't find anything incriminating?"

"Correct. I am quite irritated that after violating my privacy, he found and questioned me on my research."

"Understandable, then does this have to do with the sample of metal you 'found in the market,' dear?" I could practically hear the finger quotations.

"Why does nobody believe that?"

"Because it isn't believable. I've seen plenty of strange things though, so it's not a big matter. Since you're angry about his questions, what exactly would you like me to do?"

"Do you have any advice on how to keep people out of my things?"

"Certainly, there are a number of magical chests and the like that can be opened only by the one registered as their owner. Can you find the issue though?"

"Anything you give me you will probably know how to bypass?"

"Mmm, quite so. My advice would be to think of something yourself. That will probably be the most secure."

I wanted to beat my head on a wall. He wasn't wrong, but that also didn't mean he was being particularly helpful. I would have to come up with something—something only I could follow if I really wanted it to be secure. That would be an absolute pain too.

I briefly considered if the one who'd made the core had the same issue, and what his solution had been. I knew there was no obvious answer, but I'd look and see if he had any advice on locks and the like that I might find useful later. There was probably something buried deep in there that would help.

"Any ideas on where to find a maid who would actually be loyal to me and not someone else?"

"That's probably impossible, Alana. Everyone has their own interests, and you don't have nearly enough connections to get someone from your family or the like. No, I would take a different path."

"What's that then?"

"Find someone skilled, and accept that they are going to report on you to others. If you go into it knowing that, then you need only hide the things you want hidden. You can even feed others misinformation if you do it skillfully. It's what I do, and it is quite fun," he said with a chuckle. Dean Lorrae might be a bit weird and very prone to bouts of laughing at others, particularly Professor Rooke, but he did know a whole lot of things.

As I left his office I had new things to think about. I would need a new maid. I could—and should—use this to build a connection between me and others. All I needed to do was accept a lack of trustworthiness.

CHAPTER 41

✦

VARIOUS ARRANGEMENTS

Pinea was now the obvious choice for helping me find a new maid. We got along, and forming a connection with her would be best. Her family was a big player, which would be good. I also happened to personally kind of like her, she was wild, and a bit pervy sometimes.

Setting up a meeting with her was my first goal the next morning. For that night though, I was glad to find that Emma had smartly gotten herself from my rooms quickly. It took me a while to make sure everything I owned was still there and in its proper place. They had at least not stolen anything nor moved any of it so far. All my things were in place, clothes in the closet, money in its place (I did count that one just to make sure), spindle still at the bottom of its trunk. All done, I collapsed into bed.

Luckily, I had Atali Dance the next day, which both gave me a good chance and ended up putting Pinea in a great mood. We would sometimes practice a bit together, so it was easy to tell that this was by far her favorite subject and one that she put her all into. I suspected that she'd bought her own dancing outfit already, even if we'd not been told we would need one just yet.

"Hey, Pinea," I called her over after class. We were both a bit sweaty. Even if it hadn't yet been a year, we were constantly getting better and better and now able to do at least basic dances.

"Oh, did you need something?" she asked, tilting her head a bit. Pinea was a bit weird, but she had the mannerisms one would associate with being high class down to an absolute T, though she normally fell into a pervy manner when speaking about dancing or anything even a bit risqué.

"Yes, actually. I was hoping you might assist me in getting a new maid."

"A new maid? Whatever happened to your old one?"

"I relieved her of duty for invasion of my privacy," I flatly replied, still a bit sore on the subject.

"How horrid, of course that's unacceptable. I have some connections that could be leveraged to find you some candidates but . . ."

"But?"

"I would want something in return. A favor in the future, nothing major. I've got some ideas for projects, and while I can handle the ones I have now, I'm not sure that I'll be able to do all the ones I work on in the future without help. If you agree to help me on one of my future projects, I'll help you find a maid."

That . . . sounded like a deal to be weary of. "What exactly would you need?" I narrowed my eyes as I looked her over.

"Goodness, Alana, I won't ask anything terrible. You're one of the best in our classes with the different rune sequences, and you know more than I think you're letting on. I'll ask for some basic help with something like that. If I were to ask for something bad, it would only serve to damage my own reputation."

I had to take a few moments to think this over. It really was a 'I'll help you now, but you'll owe me one in the future.' I didn't think she'd go overboard. If she did, I could refuse her, though I'd lose another maid for sure if I had to. As long as she didn't ask me for anything illegal or too dangerous, I was fine with it.

"As long as you don't ask anything dangerous or illegal, I'm fine with helping you on some personal project in the future."

"Oh, nothing like that. More like something like this."

She pulled a sheaf of paper out and let me look over it. It was a design for a small magic item that was supposed to light a room. This particular variation had a number of settings that would allow it to glow brighter or more dimly, based on what the user needed. I could understand it easily enough in that it was close to what we were doing in class. I could also see that she'd already completed the sequences she'd need.

"Sure, if it's just a small item and it's harmless, I will happily help you with something like that."

"Good! It'll be a few days before I can get some candidates together. How about I set up interviews on the next off day?"

"That should work fine. See you later, Pinea."

She waved as she turned and walked off. We'd spent a good bit of time and both had more classes for the day.

* * *

Choosing a new maid was a fairly normal process. Unlike my last time, I now knew what I was looking for. Rather than in someone's home, we met in a nearby restaurant, whose proprietor was only too pleased to let me rent a private room for the occasion. From the four candidates Pinea found, I ended up picking one named Dora. She was seventeen and from one of the branch families attached to Pinea's.

"Is there anything I should know, Miss? Or anything you're rather particular about?"

"If you notice me doing something strange, and you have questions about it, just talk to me."

"Whatever else would I do, Miss?"

"Ideally nothing unless you already tried speaking with me on it."

"Of course. If you don't mind my asking, could I have your schedule? It'll let me make sure that everything is as it should be for you."

That was a simple enough request, and I supplied her with my normal daily and day-off schedules, which she looked over before nodding and assuring me that everything would be in order.

I was surprised the next day when she woke me up. My morning routine was far smoother with her than it ever had been with Emma. My clothes were hung by the fire to warm while my hair was done and I washed my face. I even found that she was an expert on helping me with the uniform, merely asking me to hold still while she put it on me.

Bishop Theodore had made his way across the country. He'd had to work hard and pull every favor he could to make sure that nobody knew where he was going or who he was trying to meet. If the wrong people did learn, then things could get rather sticky for his charge and for himself as well.

To that end, he was traveling with only two others. They'd disguised themselves as merchants and were making their way east. There had been one incident with a small group of bandits, but the poor men hadn't expected to find a caster powerful enough to drop them all with a wave of his hand. Their bodies had been easy enough to dispose of, and their loss was no great one to any civilized person.

He approached the border between the two countries carefully, sticking to roads that were well-known and making sure not to try and hide his presence. When he finally reached it, he was stopped at a border station, where his credentials were checked. He used a false name, but for priests traveling from one country to another, that was no big issue, and he made clear that the one he gave was false.

"And your business, sir? If you don't mind my asking." The guard was polite. He stood straight in his jet-black leather armor, a halberd held lightly in one hand.

"Oh, nothing much. Due to the wars, we run a number of orphanages. There've been some issues I need to discuss with my counterparts. Once this war is over, we want as many of the children returned home as is possible."

"A noble goal, sir. I wish you the best." The guardsman handed back his papers and let the bishop pass. Everyone knew that the orders kept the peace and were neutral, as much as possible.

From that post, it was easy to find the nearest place that hosted his order, and he'd moved there with all haste. It was a good trek and took him to the nearest city, but if that was where he needed to go, then that was where he needed to go.

Rooke sat before his grandfather. He felt almost like a student he'd had called to his own office to discipline. The old man was in his seat behind his desk, flipping through a number of files. The information he'd compiled hadn't been much, but it had existed.

"You moved too quickly, my boy, and with too much aggression."

"Perhaps, but my hand was forced when the asset came to us . . ."

"That's a poor excuse. You could have ascertained if your charge was involved with anything dangerous in much better ways. What of our asset anyways?"

"I found her a new assignment. It will keep her out of the way. Luckily, Alana didn't see the need to have her or us punished for our overreach." Incidentally, having her sent to serve as the mistress of a minor noble was both what she wanted in the end and a wonderful way to get her out of the picture.

"If the girl had complaints, it would have been no issue to foist all issues onto the maid. We were already prepared for that in case anything came up."

The old man spoke the truth. Emma had been chosen as Alana's maid in part because she was disposable. There was no real chance of her dying, but she could have been punished for any issues caused, rendering herself no longer fit as a servant.

"Regardless, Alana is now far more guarded."

"Against you, yes. You need to find a way to make amends with her as soon as possible. If you need advice, come to me. We cannot let her slip from the prince's faction under any circumstances, is that understood?"

"Of course, Grandfather. On that note, I understand that she had Lord Fallon's niece assist her in replacing our asset."

"Did you orchestrate that?" The old man seemed a bit surprised, perhaps even impressed.

"Not at all. It seems they are simply friends. I understand that both are trying to form connections with each other on some level."

"That might be the best news I've seen regarding this. I'll contact Lord Fallon and see what we can do to make sure things go as well as possible. Young Alana keeps her secrets close to her chest, and if your reports are to be believed, she's got several that might actually be of any use."

"Indeed. Once we've brought her into the fold, she'll be a force for the whole country. We just have to make her understand how important her work could be." Rooke looked out the window toward the sky with a glint of hope in his eyes. "I suspected when I first met her that she might be worth our investment, and she's not failed to live up to that expectation yet."

"Do you think you can get the sky-metal source from her? Or at least that exploding material?"

"Doubtful in the near future. Honestly, I'm more interested in the sphere and whatever she did to it."

"What? Why?"

"You would have had to see it. It had . . . not an aura, but something almost like one. When I went to examine it, it appeared to be nearly reality bending. It has a shape that was defined to it, it's holding that shape, and that shape is a sphere so perfect that anyone who senses mana seems to get the idea that it is nearly absolutely perfect."

"Hmm, that is unusual. I may have to see it for myself at some point. Any ideas on how she managed to do that?"

"That's the best thing. I've got no clue as to what she did, or how, or even why. She claimed it was just a lamp. Even more, I think it actually is a lamp, and she made some kind of mistake somewhere doing one of the weird things she does with her magic and put together something special."

The old man stroked his beard for a moment before shrugging. "Well, I will need to see that then at some point. For now though, make your apologies and be sure not to pressure her unduly again."

"Yes, Grandfather, I will."

CHAPTER 42

◆

THUNDER

Several weeks had passed since our incident at the copse, and slowly things began to return to normal. The dead students were mourned, the survivors finally stopped getting asked to recount what had happened, and life went on. I sat in the back of Rooke's class, as normal, enjoying a lecture that was some weeks behind where I was in my own work on the "guide" when it began.

A peal of thunder sounded far-off, and from my seat I could see the rain start to fall upon the classroom windows. It was no big thing, no new action. The clouds showed clearly that it would rain today. I could even see the blue-white line as the rain traced its way across the sky.

My back tingled though; every hair stood up. I felt my heart rate quicken, and I gripped the pen in my hand tightly. As I looked around, everything seemed normal, seemed the same as it always had. Then why did I feel afraid?

Class continued on as it had, but by the end I was a mess. I stayed in my seat, trying to keep my composure as my heart felt like it would pound its way out of my chest. I was breathing fast and hard as I stayed where I was; everyone else left normally.

As Professor Rooke was cleaning up his things, he looked over at me, and I saw his eyebrows rise in concern. He quickly came over to talk to me.

"Alana, are you quite okay?" Normally, he was rather rough about things, but I could tell from his voice that he was genuinely worried.

"Oh yes, I'm fine, I just . . ." I tried to rise, but as I did, I found my legs shook like jelly.

A hand reached out to help me, keeping me from stumbling. "Come to my office and we'll talk."

We quickly walked through the halls. As we did, I saw the storm through the windows. Black clouds were building and pelting rain upon us; sheet after sheet of it fell to the ground and slammed into the glass. To the point that most of the world had lost its definition outside those windows. When we finally arrived, I was told to sit while Professor Rooke moved to his desk.

He looked me over. I was still having a hard time for some reason, my muscles not responding quite as I wanted them to. "Alana, if something is wrong, I need you to tell me."

I was still pissed at him for having my room searched, and we hadn't spoken much since then. He'd made a few attempts, but I'd rebuffed him repeatedly. While I'd not come to any harm from it yet, it was still an awful invasion of my privacy, and I was continuing to be a bit sore.

"No, Professor, I'm just fine." At that moment, a peal of thunder shook the room; as it did so, I gasped, drawing my arms up to protect my head.

"Alana, are you afraid of thunder?"

"No, that's stupid, why would I be afraid of thunder?" As if to contradict me, another round of noise sounded off, and I felt my anxiety level skyrocket.

That made no sense at all. I'd seen plenty of storms before, and they were no problem, so why now? This one was bad, sure, even worse than we normally got before the summer, but it was nothing terrible. It was stupid. I shouldn't feel any worry about this.

But I did. Every time the noise came, I felt fear. I hadn't recognized it for what it was before, but it was fear. As I saw the blue lines trace their way across the sky and leave light in their path, I felt afraid. I also felt ridiculous, I wasn't some puppy, needing help because of a bloody thunderstorm. I was me. I was a powerful spellcaster who'd faced death . . . more than a few times.

And then another bolt landed nearby, and I was afraid.

Professor Rooke looked at me with narrowed eyes. "Alana, Professor Endel said he instructed all those involved in the incident a while back to seek out and speak with someone. Did you do so?"

"Um . . . I spoke with Kala about it a bit." That was technically true. We'd discussed it a few times, but I really didn't like talking about that too much; mostly, I'd just kept myself busy with other things.

"That is hardly what he meant, and you know it." While there was a tinge of irritation in his voice, there was also a calmness, like he was reprimanding an errant child. "As it is, I have no classes for the rest of the afternoon, and I'd like you to stay here and speak with me a bit. Let us see if we can get to the bottom of things."

He went about making tea as I thought. It was interesting to watch him, since he used magic for the whole process, making the water and heating it, pulling cups and the like across the room to himself. I was still mad at him, and this was an obvious attempt to get closer to me. I needed to be careful here, but I couldn't well leave without a really good excuse.

"I don't think that's really needed." I said it, but it was apparently clear that I was still rather stressed, so he just handed me a cup of tea.

"Your words say that, but your movements say otherwise. Drink, this is a lovely herbal blend, and it will help you relax a bit. Why don't you tell me about how your classes are going?"

That was harmless enough I supposed. So I told him how things were, how I'd been getting good marks in everything. I shared that I really enjoyed Atali Dance, in particular, and even experimented with trying a few simple spells while dancing, though that was going painfully slowly. I wasn't sure why that was, but it might just be because I was so used to using sound as my medium of choice.

He nodded along, listening intently. He asked a few questions as he did so, but nothing particularly invasive. Had I had any other issues of note? What did I like about this subject or that? What hadn't I liked about them? Mostly, he just let me talk though. It also pained me to admit it, but the tea did seem to calm me down a bit. When I asked, he said that it was one he used when trying to wind down after a long day.

I was pleasantly surprised that he didn't breach the topic of my research. He also didn't ask about the incident in the Junkyard Copse, though he'd indicated that if I felt like it he would gladly listen. That was a bit refreshing, as I'd had to go over it with much of the student body. They were particularly interested in the attacker, and it seemed not many of us had seen her.

By the end of it all, I'd rambled for a few hours and the storm had passed. It had been hard at first, but I gradually calmed, even if just a bit, and when it finally stopped, so did we. Professor Rooke said that he had a few ideas about things that might help me, but that he thought Professor Endel would probably be the best to talk to. He also gave me a small bag of the tea he'd made, along with instructions on where to get it, should I feel the need.

"You seem more . . . kind than normal," I observed as I moved to go.

"I'm unsurprised by this development. It is . . . less than optimal for you, but I have faith that you will overcome it and continue to be one of the few students here who will make me proud. Now, you've missed enough classes, and if you don't hurry, you'll miss your dinner too." With that he shooed me out.

He wasn't wrong, and I was hungry. When I got to Hern's practical that night, I assumed he'd been spoken to by Professor Rooke, because he didn't mention me missing the period earlier in the day. He just continued on as if things were completely normal.

When I got back to my room that night, I had received a letter from Professor Endel. He wanted to have a meeting with me on my next off day, said he had a number of things to go over, and it would take a while. It was scheduled for after my Healing course that morning, which was something a bit worrying.

When I woke up that morning, Dora helped me dress. It was odd to have someone else dressing you, but I'd pretty much gotten used to it by that point. After she'd done the last of my many, many buttons and ties, I looked at myself in the mirror.

I was not unhappy with what I saw there. While I was a bit short, I assumed from my rough childhood, though it wasn't as bad as I might have feared. I was also filling out rather well with light curves that looked as if they would be quite nice in a couple of years. I was thinner than I'd been in the past, too, a mixture of food, having to do most everything by hand, and dance classes had kept me from gaining much fat at all, which was really nice.

Going through puberty again had been, and was being, an absolute bitch. It wasn't as if it was any surprise though. I was also quite happy to learn from some of the older bard girls that over the generations spells to alleviate the worst of it had been developed. I had quietly picked up those, since they were mostly small alterations to things I already knew how to do. Cleaning, a small healing variation for cramps, nothing big, but damn useful.

Those spells had small variations for each of the caster types. We bards had the best ones, being able to control many things without knowledge, but all had something. Teaching them to your junior students properly and well was the self-assigned job of the seniors, one they took with the utmost seriousness.

Small magical feminine products had also been invented some time ago. They were self-cleaning and could be acquired by simply asking for some in our dorm. The Order of the Lovers apparently produced and sold them at cost, but they were a bit pricey, as most magical items were.

I was surprised to learn that my Lovers' Mark didn't actually effect that kind of thing at all. It was specifically to stop pregnancy and did nothing else. When I'd questioned Kala, she'd given me a strange look and told me in no uncertain terms that while it was "possible" to stop your cycle, it was unadvisable unless you had very good reason. This world didn't use hormonal control, and screwing with that was a delicate mess that could backfire easily.

When I got to my Healing class, I was happy to see that our previous test subject had been replaced. He'd slowly been recovering his lost limb and, from what I could tell, had finally gotten it back completely. We had a new girl in her mid-twenties who had only one leg. I felt bad that she was going to be subjected to our many trials, but at least she'd be able to walk again without crutches at the end of it.

As it finished, I headed over to Professor Endel's office and was quickly let in. He had a number of things pulled out, and I could see that he had already put on his armor. I couldn't remember his previous set, but I thought this one looked a bit different.

"Good, you're here. Now, Professor Rooke told me about some of the problems you've been having, and I think there might be a way to help. I don't think you'll like it, but I want you to try."

I was a bit nervous already at what he'd said to me, but I nodded. "Yes, sir . . . if you think it will help."

He gave me a bright smile. "I do. It will also serve to help you in my class. Alana, if you'd come to talk to me right after that fateful day, we could have avoided some of the stress this is likely to cause, but I want you to know that no matter what happens, I will see that you are safe. Do you trust me?"

Now, I was really nervous. "Hesitantly."

"Good, good, now, see that armor? Put it on. It's a special one that Rooke made just for this at my request. He seems quite invested in you getting over this fear of yours."

I grabbed the armor and quickly began to put it on. It was like our practice ones and would fit easily over my uniform, so there was nothing wrong there, but it was not reassuring.

Professor Endel looked at me. "Alana, when a young man learning to ride a horse falls, it is imperative that he get back on and continue riding.

If he does not, he may come to fear the horse, and that won't do at all. We are fortunate in that you are particularly skilled for getting over this issue of yours, and together we shall see that you do." He clapped a hand on my shoulder in what I'm sure he thought was a reassuring way, but really made me want to run from the room screaming. "Now, I just need you to remember that you trust me, even hesitantly, to keep you safe for this."

CHAPTER 43

✦

ENDEL'S IDEA OF THERAPY

I was lead down to the training grounds, where I would surely die. Professor Endel led the way, a long metal rod hanging in the air behind him, some kind of spell to make it easier to transport. We got a few looks, as it wasn't often someone wore war gear just walking around, and I probably looked like death.

Once we got there, my teacher had the rod slam into the ground opposite us. It stood like a spear pointing upward toward the sky. He turned to me with a bright smile.

"Okay, Alana, this is going to go through a few steps. First, I want you to stand near me while I cast. Watch close, this might help you later on today."

I stood there. He was certainly going to do something with lightning, that was a given, but it seemed he wasn't going to point it at me, at least yet. He raised one hand to point at the spear, and a bolt flew from it with a *bzzt* sound. It was definitely lightning, albeit at a far, far lower intensity than I'd seen before. He let off several after seeing that I didn't bolt.

"Please don't shoot one of those at me, Professor," I said, shaking a bit as I'd watched him go a few times.

"Alana, please relax, I'm not going to shoot one of those at you today," he calmly stated, smiling.

"What do you mean 'today'?"

"Here's what I want you to do. First, I want you to sing us up a nice big storm." He totally ignored my question, and I got the feeling from the look on his face that I shouldn't keep pressing or I might find out.

"Okay . . ." I could do that, but I really didn't like where this was going.

"Then you're going to target that rod there with lightning."

"I've never done that before."

"First time for everything. I'm sure you'll be fine; just remember that I'm here with you, and that you'll be perfectly fine. If it helps, that armor is made specifically to protect against lightning."

"It doesn't."

"That's a shame, begin then." He gave a gesture up toward the sky.

I didn't want to, but seeing as I wasn't actually being given too much of a choice, I began to sing up a storm. I started small then slowly increased its power. I'd been doing these off and on for a while now and had a decent handle on them, so while it was still expensive mana-wise, it was manageable. I kept it growing slowly because honestly I didn't want to go to the next step.

"That's enough, Alana. Target the rod and let's see some lightning," Professor Endel yelled. My storm still wasn't big, only hovering over the arena, but it was strong, with winds whipping around us.

I waffled for a few moments, then began to think on how to do it. I knew that I needed to form a difference in charge, so I tried to focus on the idea of pulling there. I also knew, far too well for my taste, exactly what lightning felt like. I knew the sound it made, the heat, the flash, and the smell. I understood all of that and focused on it while I pulled the charge tight like a rubber band.

"Go on then!" I heard him, but I didn't want to, so I kept working on the spell, letting it take a little more mana, then a little more as I kept pulling. "Alana, do it!" I felt Professor Endel's hand on my shoulder again, pushing me forward toward this.

I didn't want to. I didn't want to. Why did he not understand that? Why couldn't he just let it go? Even my magic seemed to sense that this wasn't something I really wanted. That said with how much I was focusing and actually trying to set it up, the lightning was forming. Eventually, the hand on my shoulder gripped, and I let it go. It was like the rubber band snapping, an almost physical sensation.

KABOOM!

The arena shook at the force of the blast. My vision flashed just like one of those stupid bombs had gone off right in front of me. I, of course, panicked and screamed in terror at what should have been a significantly smaller strike, but some arm grabbed me and held me tight as the magic faded.

I tried to run, to pull mana for a scream to get this idiot professor off of me, but the magic didn't want to come. I felt almost faint and knew that if I cast again I would pass out. Even my body felt drained from the spell, and I nearly fell as my strength fled from my limbs.

I wanted out of here; this was insane. I couldn't hear it, but I could feel the rumble of my teacher saying something. I was also trying to blink the large line out of my vision while he held me there. Struggle as I might though, I couldn't get away, and there was no way I was letting myself faint next to this guy. Who knew what he'd do in the process of trying to "help" me?

"Calm down. You're okay. Everything is perfectly fine," I heard him say as my ears slowly stopped ringing.

"Let go of me!" I yelled, still not sure how loud I would be.

"Once you're calm."

I tried, but it was honestly not all that easy to stay calm while someone significantly stronger than you was holding you in place. That alone would have been enough to have me a bit worried, but this whole mess was too much. This was my first time casting that spell, and there was no way it should have been able to do that much.

"What . . . what was that?"

"That was a lightning bolt. Are you okay?"

I spent a few moments thinking, checking myself over for injuries. I was unhurt, but I was still shaking a bit and still weak from using too much mana.

"No, I'm almost out of mana. Why was it so big?"

"Because you put far too much mana into it."

That made sense. I'd messed around trying to find some way to avoid the exercise and put more and more power into it while doing so. That was dumb; it was possible to hold a spell, but for some reason I hadn't, maybe because I wasn't thinking? Or was it because I'd never done this one before? Whatever it was, it needed to never happen again.

"Can we at least go sit down?" I whined.

"Of course." Professor Endel led me over to one of the stands and let me plop down there.

From that vantage point, I got a good view of what I'd done. The metal rod had, of course, taken the full blast and was partially melted. All around it, I could see lines in the sand, too, here and there where the power had fled through it, melting the particles to glass as it went.

It took some time, but eventually I felt my heart stop pounding. The last of the ringing also faded, and before long I didn't even have an after-image in my view.

"I think I prefer tea and talking with Professor Rooke."

Professor Endel chuckled. "Oh? I'm sure he'll be happy to hear that. He seemed to think that you were still mad at him."

"I am."

"Well, would you like to go see the results?"

"No." I tried to stand up to leave, but my legs shook like a baby deer. "I want to go rest."

"I think you should stay sitting for a bit longer. You really put too much mana into that bolt."

"I'm fine," I declared as I made my way to the exit, holding the wall the whole way. I needed to cut this short before he came up with any other good ideas.

"Really, you should take a few moments to rest and think. Consider where things didn't go the way you wanted them to."

"Is there even a point to this?"

"Yes. That you don't need to be afraid. This isn't just their power; it's yours. You need to see it, understand it, and control it. Fear is what we feel when we think we can do nothing, but you can do something. You can fight back in a way that many cannot. You can learn to control this, to make it your own, to use it against others, and to protect yourself from it."

That really, really implied that not only was he going to try and force me to do more of these sessions, he would actually be throwing lightning against me at some point. I considered telling him to shove off, but . . . but I did need to get over this, and this seemed the best way and my only option. I couldn't just become a quivering wreck every time a storm rolled through.

I was a bit surprised that he didn't actually try to stop me from making my way to the exit, but he did not. He simply walked with me back to the doors of the school. I suppose that I'd actually participated in his little farce, so he was satisfied. You could couple that with the fact that there really wasn't enough mana left in me to do much, so we pretty much had to be done unless I was just going to watch him cast more.

Once I stumbled my way back to my room and Dora helped me remove the armor, I basically just fell into bed and passed out. It was my firm opinion that there were far, far too many of my teachers demanding my time on what were supposed to be my off days, and I considered if there was anyone who would even read that particular complaint should I try to file it.

*   *   *

As it turned out, nobody really cared when I pointed out that having me do actual work on our normal off days was insane. Professor Rooke did listen when I went to him finally, but that meeting didn't yield any results. I just ended up with another weekly obligation with Professor Endel, until such a time as he decided that I was no longer in need of his "therapy."

I heavily suspected that he was too interested in seeing how far I could take weather magic in this direction, which was influencing his judgment. That was because I spent several sessions just throwing lightning bolts at big metal rods. I did at least learn to control myself a bit better and not come close to passing out every time I did it. I was also getting more used to the lightning, at least when I was in control of it.

It was around midsummer that he pulled me aside after one of our weekly thunder fests.

"Alana, you seem to be well in control now. We can move onto the next step."

I narrowed my eyes at him. "What is the next step?"

He kept his smile big and bright. "Teaching you how to protect yourself against that which you fear."

Nope, no, no, no! Absolutely not! I turned on the spot and began moving as quickly as reasonably possible toward the exit, not even bothering to hear him out.

"Alana, I haven't harmed you so far, have I? Surely, I've earned enough of your trust for you to listen to what I have to say?" His guilt trip was not going to work. I was leaving. "If you succeed in learning this last bit, we should be able to end these weekly meetings. I know you don't like having them." That caused me to hesitate.

"I'm listening." I turned to look at him with a full-on glare.

"Good. There are a handful of techniques by which you can protect yourself from something like lightning, and I want you to learn them. The first is warding through magical items, much like the armor you wear when we do this."

I looked down at the armor. Professor Rooke had left it in my care since it was in fact made for me, and I suspected that the armor was rather valuable, even if it only really guarded against the effects of one element significantly. Learning to make that kind of thing wouldn't be too bad.

"All right, I'm happy to learn to make more magical items."

"The other two are a bit more . . . personal. You already know how to protect yourself from harmful spells, and working on improving that will help you not only here, but in the long run. I'd also like you to learn a shield for this, not unlike your current projectile shield. That's a bit advanced, as we normally don't work on putting anti-element shields up until your second year, and something as specialized as lightning would come in your third, but I think you can manage it."

I gritted my teeth. Those were, in fact, things that I wanted. It was just the idea of getting them that rankled. "I'm interested."

"Good."

I then wandered off to go find Kala and have her work on my ears. She did so on our evenings after these bits of training, so that I wouldn't lose my hearing. It was also our excuse to spend more time together during the very short periods we actually didn't have class.

CHAPTER 44

✦

CLARISSA

I smiled as Kala held my head, soft light flowing over it from her hands. It felt warm and close and made me want to find somewhere to sink into oblivion. These little sessions were needed, the light healing she was doing was to repair the damage from all the loud noises during my "therapy." Once we'd finished, both of us sighed and lay down on her bed to rest for a few moments.

"You ready for tonight?" I asked, finally breaking the silence.

"Of course. It should be fun at the very least." She held me close, since we both knew we'd shortly have to get up.

"Okay!" I popped up quickly; it made it easier not to lazily stay in place. "I'm off to get dressed. You should do the same, and meet after, okay?" That got me a little pout, but Kala nodded.

"All right then. I'll go make myself presentable." While I was a bit excited about our outing tonight, Kala was significantly less so, since she didn't like one of our companions and didn't really know the other.

Of course I didn't really know Clarissa either, save for a few things Dras had told me during our conversations before and after class. We were still both painfully busy with schoolwork, so that was about as much as we got to spend together. That said, we had both made some real attempts to stay in touch with each other as best we could.

I knew that Dras had kept up with his fire but was now also adding some cold magic to his repertoire. This was apparently a rather popular combination since they were similar to each other, just in different directions. Wizards had figured out that much at least and were abusing it as well as they could.

He was also super jealous that I was learning lightning-type magic. It was poorly understood and thus extraordinarily difficult for wizards to learn. Some more advanced war-wizards picked it up, and there were thought to be a few texts that explained important details, but if those existed, they were kept well hidden. When I told him that Professor Endel was teaching me as "therapy," he'd come to quick agreement with me that what he was doing also counted as him seeing just how far I could take it.

He even told me a few things about Clarissa here and there. For one, she was a noble, the third daughter of a baron and his fourth child to attend the academy. That was pretty odd, as it was stupidly expensive and hard to get into, but it seemed they were really skilled as a family. He knew that her initial attraction had been because he was quite a bit stronger magically than she was. But it had gone further from there, and from what I heard, they genuinely liked each other.

Clarissa had also gotten us tickets to see some exhibition at the training grounds for the apprentice knights. It had taken months due to the fact that they were really limiting the number of spectators. They were also thoroughly vetting everyone and holding them with almost no notice, so as to avoid any potential terrorist attacks. We'd found out only the previous day that we'd be going tonight, so it had been a real rush to get things ready.

I was personally excited. It'd been a good long time since I got to go much of anywhere that wasn't the local market, and even that was being discouraged. It was subtle, but once you got to looking, the signs that there were more and more attacks and that the kingdom was really struggling to keep up appearances became clear. I had heard no news of our war against the Lord of Shadows or his army, save that we were in one. That alone told me that things weren't going well.

That was all beyond my ability to do anything about though, so I settled for getting dressed. Dora was there to help, as she always was. I was unsure how much she knew about Kala and me. She said nothing though, and that was enough for me. I suspected that she was reporting back to Pinea or her family, but it hardly mattered, I'd shown her nothing of any real importance. I had been particularly careful not to make any more aluminum or even mention it around her.

Once I was properly ready, I headed down to meet up with Kala. The two of us talked about what kind of monsters we were likely to see when we got to the exhibition. Sadly, Kala knew many more kinds of monsters than I did, something I'd need to eventually get around to learning.

We met Dras and Clarissa at the doors to our academy. From there, the four of us took a carriage. It seemed even this was arranged by those in charge of the exhibition, but it was very nice. The inside was comfortable, with well-padded seats and some form of suspension to dampen the rocking a bit. I knew little about those, but it was possible to tell that there was something.

"So, how long have you and Dras known each other?" Clarissa asked, looking over at me.

"Around five years, I think. We met when we were both fairly young." I took a few moments to think about that night; it was a rather pleasant time in retrospect.

"That long? Were you in the same prep school or something?"

"No, he saw me hit a prostitute with a scream when she spilled food on me." That was not the expected answer, and Clarissa looked over at her boyfriend, who seemed to be trying to avoid eye contact.

"It was really funny at the time. I didn't really know many other casters, and I'd never seen a girl that young curse that fluently while slinging spells."

"So . . . you just went over and said hi or something?" I supposed it was more formal for nobles, but I didn't really know enough about how they grew up to tell.

"Yeah, actually. After that, we just sort of . . . ended up hanging out a lot. Alana taught me most of what I needed to get into the academy."

"I was taught by a wizard back home when I was little, so it wasn't like it was too much."

"Oh! You had a tutor too? That explains everything. Father hired mine when she first graduated, since she had high marks and needed a well-paying position. Where did your family find yours?"

I saw Kala trying not to laugh from the corner of my eye. "He was the old wizard who lived next to us in the village. He and my father were friends from way back when or something, so he taught me what he could."

I could see it dawning on the girl that I really was some village girl from way out in the middle of nowhere. To my surprise, that only seemed to cause her the briefest moment of pause. After which, she continued.

"I . . . see. Well, it's good to know that Dras found someone to teach him more about magic."

"What about you then? How did you two meet?" I asked in response.

"Oh, we met in our etiquette class. Poor Dras didn't know how to dance at all, and the two of us ended up getting put together several times. He was just so cute I couldn't resist."

"Let's move the conversation away from me now, shall we?" Dras interjected. "Why don't you tell Clarissa how you two met?"

"We were at a party that got ruined by a terrorist attack. After which, Alana told everyone to go jump off a cliff and invited me to join her to walk home." Kala really summed up that one in as few words as possible.

Clarissa gave me another long look. "You get into a lot of trouble, don't you?"

"I kind of seem to, huh?"

"Yup," said Dras.

"Absolutely," agreed Kala.

Not a moment too soon, we arrived at our destination. This led to something not dissimilar to a TSA search. There were multiple stations, all separated from one another through which everyone had to pass. You would stay with your group, and your group only, and everyone had to be checked against lists followed by a quick examination for any magical items.

It seemed a bit extreme to me until we actually entered the seating area. Once there, my definition of extreme was pushed up a few notches. No two groups were near each other, and between each there was both a physical wall and an obvious wall of enchantment. There were also the wards separating the arena and the spectators, which were so thick as to almost be visible. I could almost see a shimmer in the air there.

This was all on another level. It's like they almost expected there to be an attack. I knew that the academy was insulated, but this, this drove it home.

"Hey . . . Clarissa, is this level of protection normal?"

She furrowed her brow a bit as she looked around. "No, at least not that I've seen."

I considered adding some of my own to the area around us, but thought that might be seen as a threat by one of the many people I supposed were now on the watch for any odd behavior. Everyone seemed a bit put off by it all. Eventually though, the fights started.

The first one was a first-year apprentice against a spine-wolf. I'd seen these particular nasties before and so knew roughly what to expect. The fight was good, if short. The apprentice was quick on his feet, managing to avoid any of the many projectiles fired at him, ducking and weaving expertly until he could close in and deliver the blows that quickly ended the monster.

After that was a girl who used a spear. The only reason I even knew she was a female was due to the introduction from an announcer off to the side. She fought something called a pyre hawk. That fight was hard to watch, not because of anything awful that happened, just that both of them were really fast. The bird was also impossibly bright once it got going.

There were several others: one fought a mutated cat of some kind; it was big and rather scary. There was also another bird or two of varying varieties. I couldn't find any sort of pattern in what made a certain monster go a certain way, but they did seem to come in a finite number of species. It was also of note that not all the fighters won. Several, particularly the younger ones, would sometimes lose against their opponent, though the creature would be captured quickly by a few mages waiting on the sidelines for any such issue to arise.

"Ladies and gentlemen, now for our final bout of the evening. One of the knight instructors will be fighting a mountain lizard brought in just recently from the northern territories."

"Oh, that's a rare one. Those are particularly nasty." Clarissa spoke up, looking over to the rest of us.

"That name is familiar . . ." Was that the one Dad fought way back when?

The man who moved into the arena was decked out in gear. Runes covered every piece from his helmet down to his armored feet. Even if I couldn't read them from here. It was clear that he'd come for business.

His opponent was soon released as well, and I had to sit back in my seat. The mountain lizard was easily the size of a carriage. It looked most like a chameleon had had an angry love baby with a crocodile, which had then taken all the steroids it could find.

As soon as it entered the arena, the thing turned its head, seeming to recognize a foe when it saw one. It launched itself forward. I was expecting a tongue from its apparent similarity to a chameleon, but no, it seemed this beast preferred melee combat. It slashed at the knight, tossing him back with force—even through his armor, which sparked as the claws skidded across it lightly. He responded with a downward cut from his sword, which similarly did little to the beast as it flew back.

Their battle was the fiercest by far, and the longest. Both were heavily armored, and both were deadly quick. Eventually though, it was the knight's constant small cuts on the beast that slowed it bit by bit until it finally failed to keep up. Once its reactions were down to almost nothing, he managed a killing blow, by sticking his blade through the mountain lizard's eye. It was gruesome, but it worked.

"Why the eye?" I asked. That was just . . . brutal to watch.

"The hide is too thick. To succeed in actually killing it, one must hit through the eye, the mouth, or with potent elemental damage," Clarissa said to clarify. "Well everyone, ready to go home?"

I smiled as we made our way slowly back to the exit.

CHAPTER 45

✦

MEETINGS II

On our way out of the exhibition, we met Glen. The short knight apprentice was attending, too, it seemed and greeted us with a smile. It took me a moment to recognize him in what might be considered normal clothes, as opposed to the armor I'd seen him in last time.

"Hey there, long time no see," he said as he came over.

"Certainly has been. How have things been on your end?"

"Busy; what with the war and all, training has gone into overdrive."

I nodded in understanding. "What about Ethbert?"

"Still a bit scarred, but they're fixing that."

"Sad, but where are my manners? Glen, this is Dras, Clarissa, and Kala. Everyone, Glen was on my team in that botched training exercise. He's the only one who could stand after everything went south."

From there, we had some light, pleasant conversation. Most of it was a bit on the mundane side, but there were hints here and there that things weren't going as well with the war as would be hoped. There were barest cracks in the facade that the kingdom was trying to keep up.

I really wondered how bad things were for us to know here in the capital. From my years spent talking to Dras, I got the feeling that almost nothing affected life here. Even the years of starvation that had happened out in the greater part of our country had had little impact on this city. That concerned me to some level, as I knew that even if things were bad, really bad, we might not know until it all fell apart.

I worried about that on my way home, at least until it occurred to me that I had a good way to find out. I knew people who met travelers and who spent time among the lower city residents. All I'd need to do would be to go to them and ask.

And so it was that on the afternoon of my next day off, I headed out into the city. This was not something done without a bit of preparation, seeing that the academy was now also under heavy security, but I had an ace in the hole, so to speak. Kala had every reason to go and visit her order's temple here in the city, and nobody would gainsay a priestess from the Order of the Lovers going out with a companion in tow.

This, of course, implied that I was going to get a Lovers' Mark, which I already had. Or that I had some other "personal issue" that most of the guards, who were largely men, did not feel the need to ask or know. For this reason, they quickly let us leave, giving us all the information we needed on how to return. Getting back into the school would apparently be a bit of a chore.

"So, care to tell me what this little outing is about?" Kala leaned in as she took my arm. "You've been awfully tight-lipped about it."

"I'm a bit concerned that we might be watched in the school, and they decidedly don't want us talking about some things. It mostly comes down to the fact that I think the war is going much worse than we're being led to believe. I'm planning on asking Lucien and the others if they've heard anything. I'd like to know if the city is likely to be besieged soon. It will give me time to think about what I want to do."

"Think about what you want to do?" She seemed a bit concerned on that one.

"Well . . . the school has its evacuation plan and all, but honestly I'm not sure if that will be the best option if things are really bad. A large group of noble teenagers is likely to attract a lot of attention, so it might be best to go and hide among the commoners."

During the week after our little trip to the exhibition, I'd been delving into some of the aspects of the "guide" that I'd not yet reached. These were mostly involving light and sound, as well as the trick for hiding your runes. The last of which was honestly easier than I thought it would be. I still had a ways to go before I was ready for my next creation, but I had good feelings about it. By autumn, or winter at the latest, I'd be ready.

"You might be right. I think the priests will be going to the temple district if things start to get hairy. Listen, Alana I know you don't like the Shield, and going to stay with them is probably an idea that sounds . . . bad. That said, the school won't try to stop you since you're one of their wards, and regardless of what happens, I don't think anyone will attack their temple . . . so . . ."

"I know, I know, seeking shelter with them is probably the safest option. I've already put them on my list of places to hide." That seemed to relax her quite a bit, and we walked the rest of the way in companionable silence.

Lucien was, in fact, at the Starlit Sky when we got there. The bar itself was more somber than usual for this time of the day, and he smiled when he saw me, motioning me to the back. Kala gracefully allowed us to talk while ordering herself a cider.

"Long time no see, girly," he began as we entered the back room.

"You either, how's things?"

"Oh, you know, same as always. People come, they drink, the works. Jackson's getting married."

"Wait . . . what!?"

"Yeah, he and Lude. They were making eyes at each other for some time, and just up and announced it when he came back to town."

"Is he here? How come nobody told me?"

"No, he's not here, and you weren't told because . . . well, we're keeping where he is and what he's doing quiet." That stopped me in my tracks. "Relax, it's nothing bad. They reinstituted the draft, or did you notice? He's hiding out and avoiding being pulled into the army. The fact that he's a caster helps, more help is the fact that the little bastard has never stayed anywhere long enough to end up with people knowing where he resides."

In truth, I had not noticed. I supposed that perhaps there had been fewer young men on the streets maybe, but that wasn't something I paid too much attention to.

"Actually, that's kind of why I came. The academy is basically a walled enclave, so our news is what they want it to be. How bad is it really out there?"

Lucien sat down. "Bad, real bad. The people up at the top are trying to keep it tamped down as much as they can, but . . . Rumors are that several cities have fallen and a lot of villages. Those that were already having problems with rebels are almost now all gone. Things are keeping mostly to the eastern part of the country, but we're losing." He laughed for a minute. "When war was declared, I wrote you a letter you know, but I never could bring myself to send it. I think it's still sitting on my desk."

"Do you think the city is likely to fall?" Lucien looked bad, and my question certainly didn't help.

"Perhaps, but not soon, and we'll have plenty of time to panic if it does. They'll have to take most of the central section of the country to take the capital, and news of one of the central duchies falling won't be something suppressible. If things look like that might happen . . . I'm sure that the academy has its plan, but I've got one as well in case of an emergency. You'll be welcome to join me if you need to."

I nodded. After that things petered along for a while, but Lucien had said his piece, and I'd had mine. It was good to know that there was something if I needed it.

Bishop Theodore had had a long, very long, very tiring journey. First he had to make it well into a country that was currently at war, then he had to find and establish contact with his peers there. That done, he began the arduous process of trying to contact the leadership of that country and set up a meeting. He wanted to be quiet about exactly why he wanted to speak with one of their generals, if for no other reason than it was dangerous to let out any news about his irksome ward, but eventually he had to say that it concerned the man's daughter.

That had led to him being quickly given a meeting. Sadly not with the man he sought, but with family members who were available. The bishop was on his way to that meeting now and hating every moment of it.

These people took their operational security to a terrifying level. He'd been blindfolded, put in a cart and driven around for hours, and taken through tunnels, streets, and buildings. Now, he stood in a plain stone hallway and was being led to a door. They'd finally removed his blindfold, and he supposed that this was his actual destination.

Even this hallway was odd. He didn't recognize the architecture, and the stones were something unusual too. He recognized the large slabs of plain gray rock that had been cut perfectly into cubes. This type of stone though was generally only found in the far north of the continent, so what was it doing in one of the former empire's strongholds? It was weird, but that was not why he was here.

When he finally passed through the doorway, he was greeted by three figures. One of which was clearly a magic user of some kind, while the others seemed not to be. The youngest was a boy in perhaps his early twenties. He had two swords and an aura like silver flames, one strong enough to give even the well-trained bishop pause. Beside him was a woman, his mother likely. She seemed to be aging, but well, and had the air of a matron, well dressed and composed. The final individual was a man of prodigious size, with arms like small oaks and mostly gray hair; he smelled of fire and hard work, but lacked any aura to speak of.

"Good afternoon," the woman said. "I'm told you have information?" Her tone indicated that she hung somewhere between the grief of resignation and the small sliver of hope one would have for an unproven fate.

"I do, ma'am. We currently have a girl named Alana as one of the Shield's wards. I've come to see if she can be safely returned to her family."

At my words, the woman who could only be Alana's mother broke down in tears. She leaned on the older man for support, and if I was not mistaken I thought I saw even a small tear form in one of his eyes. The lad, on the other hand, seemed mostly to just lose the tension in his whole body.

"Shh, Amara, I told you to have hope, didn't I?" The older man patted her on the back, letting her calm so she could continue. "You're sure it's her?" he asked Bishop Theodore, his eyes serious.

"Her identity was confirmed by both a priest and a bard who I understand trained her as a child."

"Well, Bishop, you've certainly brought us the best possible news. When can you bring her here? Or do we need to send someone to pick her up?" The lady looked at me with a bright smile as she wiped her face.

"Ah . . . that's why I'm here. It's a difficult situation you see, as she's currently in the city of Lithere." That got me shocked looks.

"What in the world is she doing in the kingdom's capital!?" the old man asked, clearly shocked.

"Well, Mr. . . ."

"Barro."

"Right, it's a rather long story you see . . ."

I proceeded to tell them what I knew. The only real issue came when I mentioned who her kidnappers, those who had seen to it that she'd been separated from her family, were. When the young man who was Alana's brother John learned that it was their former lord's daughter, the room seemed to freeze, his hands clenched hard enough to split the knuckles of his gloves open. After he'd calmed, I continued, telling them how she'd escaped, ended up in the orphanage at Istlan, and then left there to go to the capital.

"Why in the world would she go there?" Amara asked, a sentiment echoed by everyone involved.

"Honestly, that was never entirely clear to me. She knew of a friend of one of her former teachers who lived there it seems, and thought she'd be better off with him, for some reason."

John rose from his seat. "I'll see what options we have. It'll take time to get word to Dad and Mystien though."

"Do it, and only tell those who must know. If they find out she's there . . ." his mother said, looking at him with hard eyes.

The young man nodded and left, and soon enough my escort came to return me to our local facilities. I pitied the little lord of Hazelwood a bit, but honestly he'd abused his power to the point where something like this was bound to happen eventually. I only hoped that his people would be spared from his poor decision's consequences.

CHAPTER 46

✦

THOSE WHO SHOW UP

It was late in the evening as I made my way back to the lab. It had taken far longer than I thought to work things out, but I was now fairly sure that I'd put together the code that I would need for my special project, far, far too long I thought as I looked at the autumn sky.

This one I'd mulled over for some time, happy that it was at least simple. Well, the function was simple, hiding the code wasn't, nor was the fact that I'd had to check for bugs myself. Nobody knew about this—not even Kala—it was too dangerous. I'd even kept the physical copy of the sequences needed on my person after I'd written it down, making sure there was no chance for any nosy maids or anyone else to see it.

I sat down in the lab with a pound of the silver mix I thought would work best and began my project. There would be four of them, for me, Kala, Dras, and Lucien, so I began by making the shape. It was a simple enough one, molded rather like a ball with a flat extending spiral piece. There were, of course, a few moldings that needed to be done for comfort, and I doubted that anyone would want to use one of these for too long, but they were for emergencies only, so that was fine.

Once each was done and I'd put a core in them, I began the process of actually putting in the sequences. These were simple enough, but even then they were pushing the limits of what one could do with an apprentice core. The lowest level like I had was weak, only able to do the most basic of things. I wasn't sure why that was, but probably to make sure that nobody without experience messed around too much and made something dangerous. I'd not bothered upgrading it so far, but soon that would have to change.

I added commands for converting sound and light and finally covered them with the obscuring sequence. Once each step was done, I needed to do some basic testing, and I already had what I needed for that. A little mana in each and a few illusions and I gave a big smile.

Making some small carrying cases was easy enough with the tools in the lab, and once my test was done, I simply burned the written copy of the instructions. This was something the army would decidedly want, and there was a zero-percent chance they'd take no for an answer if they ever found out about it. So I would make sure they wouldn't.

Now that I was done with all my cloak-and-dagger nonsense, I headed back to the dorms. I'd have to give these to their intended recipients soon, because even in the academy I was starting to hear whispers. Cities were falling, and some of the students were finding out about it because fathers, brothers, and friends died. One by one, parts of the kingdom were coming undone, and I had little faith that I could stop that.

I considered running, but to where? The lower city would be hit, too, if it came to that. I couldn't take the information I was gaining either, so that was no good. It would also mean leaving all of my friends, who were the only real connections I had right now in this world.

Even if I managed to get out, then I'd be basically alone in who knows what situation. Perhaps I could hide in a cave somewhere or the like, but that was unappealing. Any city or town I went to would likely be less well defended than where I was now, and I'd have to try and re-form a support network, so that was a no-go.

I could also try to support the kingdom, if that wasn't just as insane an idea. It would lead to too many questions like where I'd learned some of the things I knew. Best-case scenario, I would end up trapped in a little box working my fingers to the bone for some military organization. Worst case, they'd milk me for information for a while then just kill me, and that was far more likely. That didn't appeal to me either, so I thought I'd take a pass.

Joining the rebels? Too many unknowns. I didn't know anyone in that organization, and if I got caught, the kingdom would definitely execute me. I didn't think I would get caught, but why risk it? I didn't have a love of their tactics either, since they left too many innocents dead or hurt.

That left me where I was. Stuck between a whole host of bad options with no really good solution in sight. So I prepared, prepared to leave, prepared to hide, prepared to help my closest friends if I needed to. That was all I could do.

* * *

I had another session with Professor Endel. He wasn't actually insane in his method for teaching me defenses, which was a pleasant surprise. We'd been going over these for a month or two now, and I was improving in leaps and bounds.

His version of a lightning shield was fairly simple; it was just a plane that distributed the energy along it until it was harmless. Similar forms were used against fire and straight kinetic energy as well, but this one was tuned toward deflecting the potential of electricity. The way he described how he used it was to form a sheet, bubble, or whatnot, then concentrate on the idea of the difference in energy flowing across it rather than through it. Since electricity wasn't well understood, this was more a generalist approach.

I did understand what I actually wanted and that was to create a ground. So I imagined it rather as a bubble that was layered, an outer one that was very permeable to electricity, which helped it flow downward, and an inner one that was far less permeable to the energy, making it take the other path available, around and hopefully downward. At this point, I knew instinctively what I wanted it to do, and I was quite familiar with the power itself, all of which helped.

Mine was not nearly as powerful as Professor Endel's yet. His way of testing was to have me form it around a target, which he then hit with successively higher levels of his own lightning spell until it broke. Then I'd re-form it and we'd begin again.

He hadn't aimed a single bolt at me, though he'd had me form it around myself as practice. For that I was grateful. He had aimed other, far less powerful spells at me though. This was to get me used to having things shot at me, as well as for me to get more and much more intense practice at my own spell resistance.

"Can we stop?" I asked as he briefly paused in his rapid-fire assault of weak magical strikes.

"Are you asking because you're too tired to continue, or because you just want to finish up today's lesson?" He easily read the face I made in response. "Your enemies will not quit because you ask nicely, Alana. You will have to learn to make them." With that, he redoubled his attack.

The assault went on for nearly a full minute of me dodging and resisting. His little balls of force weren't enough to hurt me more than a slight twinge, but there were just so many. I tried to dodge and put up shields, only for him to switch to bits of discomforting heat or cold, which felt like putting my hand in ice water. As I tried to think of a way to get him to quit, I thought over his words.

After brief consideration, I began singing up a storm, letting wind and rain lash against him. I could see his smile as he pulled his own shields up and around.

"Good, but this will hardly stop me." At that, I let him have a weak bolt. "Excellent! Again!"

He and I spent a minute or two launching intentionally weakened spells at each other until he finally called it off. I was huffing and a bit weak from using a lot of mana; even weakened, my lightning spell was still unbelievably expensive.

"Really? You just wanted me to attack you?"

"You didn't just attack me, Alana." The teacher laughed as I plopped down in the arena sands.

"What?"

"You attacked me with lightning. It was weak, sure, but when we first started, you were afraid to even try it. Now, you're turning it into something you control. I'm quite proud of your progress in that."

"So . . . this is your attempt at giving me a cure?" I asked with a quirked brow.

"Hmm . . . there was a storm earlier in the week, no? How did you feel as it passed by?"

I looked down, playing with my fingers. "Nervous, like something was crawling up my back."

"But did you panic? Freeze up?"

"Well, I suppose not . . ."

"A cure is not something I can offer you, as I know of no magic to soothe such pains. Perhaps, in time, you may get over this problem completely; perhaps it will always bother you a bit. My goal is to get you to the point where you can function. So if you find yourself in the situation you were in before, you perform just as admirably and don't freeze up with terror."

"And to turn me into a walking weapon," I grumbled.

"I'll admit I'm curious how far you can go. It is seldom that I find a bard willing to put forth even a bit of effort, and your circumstances allow me to push you to new heights. Thank you for that."

"I didn't exactly volunteer."

"You showed up. You had the chance to run, to not come to these lessons, to not even learn the basics of weather magic, but you did. You did go and learn what I told you I thought best. You did come to meet me even though you knew I was going to do something unpleasant. Here you are now, going through training I'd expect of a trainee actually preparing to go to war. You did volunteer, even if you didn't realize that was what you were doing."

"I mean . . . all I did was just show up."

He knelt down beside me, looking me in the eyes. "Alana, it is not the strongest, the fastest, the smartest who decide things. The world is ruled by those who show up."

CHAPTER 47

TEACHER CONFERENCES
AND FUTURE PLANS

It was late summer, and my first year was slowly coming to its end. So I had to meet with Professor Magnolia. I hadn't had much to do with him in the past bit other than our General Bard class, something that was, to be quite honest, really boring. He would be the first of my professors who'd be having a talk with me, being that he was in charge of the bards.

"Well, Alana, what are your thoughts so far?" he asked as he looked up from a sheaf of notes, ostensibly on me.

"Um . . . on what exactly?"

"Your classes, are you happy with them?"

"Yes, sir, I suppose I am."

"Well, let's go over them. You're doing quite fine in your general courses. You are perhaps more limited than your fellows, but what you are using is far more advanced and well honed. Frankly, I'd like to see a little more flexibility from you, but . . . I suppose I shouldn't push too hard."

"Thank you for that."

"Well, I would, but then there's the letters I'm getting from some of your other professors. Both Hern and Rooke have implied that if I were to take you from their classes, they might resort to "extreme measures" against me for it. Endel is also insisting that you remain in his class. He does say that he doesn't think that you have what it takes to be a front-line battle-mage, but we need every combatable caster we can get, so he's keeping you as well."

"Do I get a say in that?"

"No. Let's see then . . . your History scores are abysmal, but it's required. On Math though, you seem to be dozing in most of your lessons and still able to answer everything with ease . . Your instrumental courses are fine, Atali Dance . . ."

I dreaded where he was going with this. We didn't have exams as such, so our teachers would report to that student's adviser about their progress and assignments. I felt like I was doing well in most of my classes, or at least acceptably. That is, except History. I didn't know why but it was just so boring, and everything just sounded the same to me. I honestly tried to think about it as little as possible.

"Professor Etia is happy to keep you for both her dance class and her language class, though she does want to meet with everyone in them both . . . I think that about covers it."

"You left out both Proper Etiquette and Healing . . ."

"Oh, so I did. Well, you're doing fine, you have to continue in both anyway, and we're having almost nothing from Proper Etiquette because everything is canceled, but neither sent me any notes saying 'She's a failure! How is she here!' or anything like that." Professor Magnolia made fake panic hands as he said that. It was kind of endearing.

"I still have to meet with all of them, don't I?"

"Yup, here's your list of appointments." He passed me over a piece of parchment with times and days written, all of them in the next week.

"Wonderful."

"Have fun, and send the next one in, if you don't mind." There were several other students waiting in line outside his office door. They looked a mix of worried, from the younger students, and tired, from the older.

Most of the meetings went roughly how I expected them to. We chatted briefly, and I confirmed that I wished to stay in their classes. For Endel, it was almost a hand wave. Rooke had a brief chat with me where he actually asked about my personal time, but little else.

Then there was Professor Etia. I'd never been in her office before and found, to my delight, that it was large and open. The floor was covered in a thick rug and while there were a couple of books, from what I could see they seemed little more than the normal reference tomes.

"Come in, sit with me," she said as I entered, in Atali of course.

She motioned me over to a small alcove off to the side, where there were two chairs and a little table. There she went over a few simple sentences with me, holding a brief conversation in her native tongue. I was still stumbling through the language, but I understood most of what she said, and that I was welcome to continue learning that particular subject.

"Your accent is thick, but not the worst I've had so far. We'll continue in your language for now." She said after she'd finished up.

"Ah yes, Professor. So I suppose we'll be talking about dance now?"

"Indeed! I hope you'll be joining me for next year."

"I plan to. I still haven't gotten down casting through it yet." I had been trying, but it was difficult, and I had a lot of other things to study.

"I'm sure you'll get there in time, perhaps I should even focus a couple of lessons on it . . . Regardless of how that turns out, I'm glad to see you're continuing."

"It's a good way to keep in shape. Also nice to have something to take my mind off the war."

"That I understand, my dear. I even considered heading back home once or twice."

"But you're staying?"

"Yes. I'm not much part of any government's forces, so it's doubtful that anyone would care about me very much either way, and the opportunities here were too good to pass up."

"Is a job teaching that good?"

"Not really, but your land has a number of powerful casters who might be tempted to join me, at least for a time."

While our language class did cover some of the basics of Atali society, it was all surface level. So I wasn't too sure about what all she was talking about. She saw my look and nodded, explaining.

"Within Atali culture, mana is one of the most important things. Those with it, and with it in large quantities, are valued, those without . . . less so. For that reason, we are encouraged to marry young and have many children. The problem arises in the fact that young elven men with large quantities of mana are viewed as hot commodities. Many will have a wife and several mistresses. The more powerful they are, the more they'll have."

"I see . . ."

"I do not like to share. Among my own people that would be an issue, as most who might match me will have one or more other mistresses. But as prudish as I might find your humans, you are far more dedicated to monogamy."

"You're being really rather forward about this, Professor."

"I see no reason not to be. What if one of my students has a brother or friends who would make a good match? Would I want to miss out on that just because I tried to hide my desires? That's sort of preposterous, Alana." She waved as if that much was obvious.

She was a bit weird. No other professor I'd ever known would have had this conversation with a student. That said, I couldn't say she was wrong either. She knew what she wanted and had no issues asking for it.

The insight into the elven way of thinking was also a bit shocking. They were so forward, even more so than the nobility about how important mana was to them. It really seemed to her that the first, and potentially only characteristic in a husband was how powerful he was.

"But wouldn't anyone you marry here be a human? We don't live nearly as long as you do I thought?"

"That thought did cross my mind. While there are a number of elves who care quite a lot about how 'pure' their bloodline is, I am not one of them. The fact is that I will easily outlive any human man I marry, but how is that a bad thing?"

"Huh?"

"I'll stay young and fresh while he lives, which I think most men will like. I can leverage that even if I think he has more mana potential than myself to try and get someone capable of being amazingly powerful." She tapped her chin as she spoke.

I, on the other hand, was rendered speechless for a few moments. "Ah, okay. Well, Professor, I seem to have lost track of time. Do you mind if we cut it short here?"

"Oh, so we have. Do be well, Alana."

With that, I quickly fled from the room. I knew that the elves had a weird culture, but that was all just a bit too much. I wondered if I had felt the same way before being reborn. I think it would have probably been a little less jarring. I'd spent so long here, that I'd really lost a lot of my flexibility to adjust for other cultures.

I hiked back to the dorms where I joined up with Kala and headed off to the baths. They were the best place to sit back and relax, and with our schedules, that was something we all needed. She sat next to me in one of the larger, hotter tubs and put her head on my shoulder.

"So, you know we have a few days off when they do the next rounds of entrance exams, right?" she said, leading the conversation.

"I do, and I'd like to have a meeting with you, Dras, and Lucien, if you're up for it."

She pouted a bit. "You always include them in everything."

"Not everything, but in this I will. We all need to talk about what to do if things go wrong."

"Why Dras? You barely even talk to him nowadays."

"We talk, and . . . I feel a bit responsible for him. He's here because I helped him make it, and I want to make sure that no matter what he has an out if things go wrong."

Kala absently got a handful of water, which she poured over my head. "Fine, but when we're done, we go do something fun. I want at least a little bit of time away from the gloom and doom while the newbies see if they can make it in."

"I know what I'll be doing while exams are on," Pinea spoke as she walked in, slipping into the water opposite us. It was seriously rude to just join without asking, but I somehow doubted she cared.

"Oh?" Kala asked.

"I'm going to go and get myself a dancing outfit!" she beamed.

"Are . . . do we need one of those?" If that had been added to supplies, I'd never gotten the memo.

"What? No, Professor Etia said that she'd wanted to put it on the supply list when she took up the class, but the dean had forbade her from doing so for anyone under their last year. I really want one though, so I'm getting one. I even found a tailor who'll make it for me. You have no idea how hard that was."

"Yeah, I can imagine. Your family would probably be scandalized if they saw you in something like that."

"Which is why they will never know. Want to come with me?"

"Yes," Kala answered for the both of us while I was trying to find the proper way to turn her down. "It'll be just the thing. I also want to see what all of the fuss is about."

"Great! Do you want one too, Alana? I'm sure you'd look great in it."

"Absolutely not. Someone would see it, and then they'd make a big deal of it, and it would be a whole thing. I'll come with after our meeting because Kala thinks it'll be fun, but I'm taking a hard pass on this one." I made a big X with my hands in front of me. Sadly, that gesture was slightly lost on these two, but they understood the refusal for what it was."

"She can be a real spoilsport, huh?" Pinea asked.

"Yup," Kala answered.

CHAPTER 48

✦

EMERGENCY EQUIPMENT AND PINEA'S SCANDALOUS OUTFIT

I managed to get Dras to join us at the Starlit Sky, alone, while our soon-to-be classmates were proving their worth. He complained and whined, and asked what in the world I wanted that was so important. But in the end, he did trust me enough to just bloody join us. That was a relief, since I really did want him along.

"Mind if we all head to a back room?" I asked Lucien as we came in.

The old bard quirked an eyebrow at me, but he knew me and knew that I had business to discuss. He led us into his own private office. This room wasn't really built with the idea of having four people filling it up, but it would suffice for the short time we needed it.

"So, mind telling me what this is all about?" the old man asked as I set up sound blockers and a black-out curtain over his window as well.

"I have something for you three. In case things go really, really wrong, these will help." With a flourish, I put the three carrying cases I'd made for them on the desk.

"And these are?" Dras asked, picking one of the boxes up and opening it carefully.

"I'm not going to tell you exactly, but they're a tool that will help us group up."

"You're not even telling us what they do?" Lucien asked, looking confused.

"Let us simply say that if the wrong person found out about these . . . well, I doubt we'd all be alive for too much longer."

"Alana, please, please don't just carry around weapons like it's nothing." Kala looked nervously at the little carrying cases.

"They're not weapons and not dangerous to us or anyone else, probably. Here, I'll show you what to do."

It took a bit of goading, but I got Kala to help me demonstrate. I slipped the little ball into her ear, working the spiral-like bit around to hold it in place. It was ugly, and probably uncomfortable as crap, but these were for emergencies, and I didn't really have the skills to make them too much better than I had already.

Making light was a rather simple and well-understood sequence of runes, as were the runes for changing exactly what color that light was. It did have issues when you got into extremely high wavelengths, but that might be a safety measure built into the core, or just the limits of its abilities to form them, I wasn't sure. That didn't matter for me. What mattered was that it didn't have any issue at all making much, much larger wavelengths.

Detecting light was also a simple and well-understood sequence. The thing was that nobody knew the purpose of the lower ranges. Sure, there was some evidence that if you made a light detector that picked up really big wavelengths, it would detect things sometimes, but it was discounted.

Either nobody had found out that those were able to send messages really far, or the people who did had been really, really quiet about it. I suspected that one or more of the other people from Earth had done something similar in the past. The elven king was a shoe-in for this, as he'd run an absolutely massive empire.

My only issue had been the sound-to-light and light-to-sound conversion. I did not know a ton about how radios were designed, but I did know that they were light. I also knew that they were within a certain period of like 80 to 110 MHz, because that's what the radio displayed. That was enough to kludge these together.

I'd gone with a design that messed with the amplitude of the wave to communicate the frequency of sound to be played and put in a controller that kept it at a constant volume. It worked at roughly 100 MHz, and without some of the definitions already provided in the "guide," there was a zero-percent chance I'd have been able to figure out the wavelength for that. For reference, right at three meters.

With all this, I'd made these little radios. They had one station and one volume setting. I'd also set them up to broadcast about as strongly as

I reasonably could, starting about two meters away from themselves and pointed only outward. I had heard that radio towers were dangerous or something, so that felt prudent.

Those features, along with the rune hiding, had pushed the limits of what I could do with an apprentice-level core. I mean it had really pushed it, most apprentice-type items were painfully simple, doing only one or two things. These with their complex parameters and far more complex functions had come right up to the limits, we were informed of in our classes. Perhaps if I were a bit more elegant with my design, I could have added in another feature or two, but I doubted it.

"This is really unpleasant, Alana," Kala complained as I showed the others how to wear it.

"Many things are unpleasant, but they are for emergencies only." I turned to the other two. "Okay, so, if things fly headfirst into a pile of manure, you put these in and pump them full of mana. Um . . . they probably won't work underground, and maybe don't stand too close to anyone while using them."

"At a full charge, how long will they last?" Lucien picked his up and looked at it wearily.

"I'm not completely sure on that, as I've not had a ton of testing time, but less than half a day." They all looked at me tiredly. "Look, I don't know if these will ever see use. They might not even be helpful if they do, but they're the best thing I've come up with so far, and I think they might save our collective bacon later on."

Everyone took their radio and looked at it. Kala took hers out of her ear as soon as I wasn't looking. Lucien seemed to be thinking hard, with a furrowed brow and all.

"Is that all you needed?" Dras asked.

"Yes, just . . . keep it on you okay?"

"All right."

Everyone agreed to keep them on hand, though I had to frown and pout at Kala to extract that promise. They also agreed to keep them hidden, particularly after I reinforced that they really, really could cause us far too many problems if known about.

As soon as we were done, Kala physically dragged me down the street. I knew the tailor we were going to, as I'd been there a couple of times before. I sincerely hoped that Marcus was doing well.

A small bell rang as we entered the shop, and the assistant came to greet us.

"May I help you, dears?" she looked us over as we walked in. I got the feeling she recognized me slightly.

"Yes, we're here to join our friend Pinea. I understand she's getting a fitting today?" Kala answered for us.

"Ah, one moment please." The woman disappeared into the back for a few moments before returning and waving us along.

I saw Pinea in all her barely dressed glory in the fitting room we were led to. The outfit was mostly done, save for the flourishes. Kala was stunned and seemed to be trying to pick up her jaw from the floor. The tailor supreme himself was working on pinning pieces here and there to get the fit exactly as he envisioned it. I briefly wondered if he remembered me.

"Kala, Alana, I'm so glad you came. How do I look?" Pinea was all smiles.

At her words, Marcus turned and looked at us briefly. I thought I saw a slight eye twitch as he looked at me. He certainly remembered me, and that I had absolutely destroyed one of his works.

"Um . . . well . . . if you wear that you will . . . certainly get attention," Kala stammered. "Is that the standard uniform?"

I tried not to laugh at my dear, sweet Kala. She'd been told that the standard outfits were not much. I do not think that she'd been expecting what was effectively a bra and small panty decked out with bangles and flowing bits, much of it in nearly sheer silk. What wasn't covered in the decorations really wasn't much, and that for this world was almost impossibly scandalous.

"It is. What do you think, Alana?" Pinea beamed at Kala's reaction before turning to me.

"It's lovely. The green tint is perfect on you too. The real question is: Where are you ever planning to wear it though?"

"Probably mostly in my own room and while alone or with others from our class." She frowned as she considered, knowing well that this was not the dress expected of a young noble girl.

"You should get one too." Kala leaned over and whispered in my ear.

"Not going to happen."

"It'll be fun. You know the dances too . . ."

"I'll happily dance with or for you any time you want, Kala, but I am not getting one of those." I looked at her and the deep, potent pout. "At least not now . . . Pinea implied that they'll be required in our final year of the course. Also, if you like it so much, why don't you take Atali Dance next year?"

She considered that for a few moments, looking first at Pinea and her clothing, then at me. She kept frowning, tapping her chin.

"I kind of want to now, but . . . I'm jam-packed lesson wise. You'll have to teach me." She gave me a grin.

"Perhaps, but I'm not the elven professor who's been at this for . . . who honestly knows, decades, centuries maybe?"

"Well, you're done," Marcus declared as he pulled the last bit in with a small spell.

The clothes were, for all their briefness, a work of art. The fabric hung just so, pulling along the bits of Pinea's curves that it touched, bunching and flowing. The top was perfectly fitting, with several chains and similar bits hanging here and there. The bottom had less of those, but the two panels in front and back that revealed the pale flesh of Pinea's legs hung nearly as perfectly as those on our teacher's clothing.

The girl in question marched over to a mirror and examined herself thoroughly, turning this way and that. She even began a few of the moves we'd been working on in class. That was a bit too much for Marcus, who turned away before speaking.

"Miss Pinea, I agreed to this against my better judgment because you have been a customer for a long time. I will ask, however, that you control yourself in my shop. I do not want anyone to walk in and see this scene."

"But, Marcus, it's magnificent. I'll make sure to tell people where it's from when they ask." She was all smiles as she looked at herself in the mirror, seemingly oblivious to the scandal she would almost certainly cause, or just uncaring.

"Please don't." He did seem exasperated by the way the girl was acting in his presence. "I'm going to return to the front."

Once he'd left, she turned to us. "It's so scandalous. I love it!"

"Pinea, please don't do anything dumb and cause a riot."

"I won't cause a riot."

"You know that your Lovers' Mark is showing, right?" It peeked out from behind part of the skirt, just barely, but enough to be understood for what it was.

That put a damper on her and quick. Pinea might be a bit of a shit-stirrer. I was convinced that she was more than a bit of a pervert. She wasn't stupid though, and that was something that nobody did, not ever. It was a hard rule that that particular tattoo was only acceptable to show to those men you were actively trying to sleep with. It was so much so, that even though I'd worked in a tavern that catered to prostitutes, I'd not seen one out in public ever.

There wouldn't be a problem if she wore this in our dorm. Even in class, since we were all girls, there would be no issue. If, however, she were to take that outfit out in public, she would basically be advertising that she wanted to sleep with everyone present. Even she wasn't that insane.

"I should go get changed," she said, finally realizing what she'd been doing to irritate the long-suffering tailor so much.

"Yeah, I agree," I quipped.

"Um, could you two help me?" It was nearly impossible to get yourself into and out of the many, many layers that upper nobility wore on your own, which was why . . .

"What? Where's your maid?" Kala looked about, finally realizing the absence.

"I . . . left her outside. If she'd seen that outfit, she'd have told my father who would . . ."

"Have lost his mind?" I interjected.

"Yeah . . ."

Both of us, shaking our heads, went to go help her.

CHAPTER 49

✦

LENGTHENING SHADOWS

I sat in my command tent, going over today's reports. We were well on in our war, and things were going mostly to plan. I had command of our best war wizards, and unlike the standard battle-mage, we specialized in large-scale artillery type spells, mostly water. To say that my unit alone was a force to be reckoned with was no exaggeration.

Things had been going well, as we'd expected. The kingdom of Bergond was nowhere near our strength. That was primarily because of their abuses toward their own people during their previous war, as well as the fact that many of their subjects were all too happy to throw open the gates and let us take over when they learned about Lord Durin's laws. There had been a few fights, to be sure, but nothing too bad on our end.

As I went through the various sheets of information, a soldier moved to the front of my tent and announced his presence.

"Sir, permission to enter?" He was respectful and forward, traits I rather appreciated.

"Granted. Some development?" I asked as he moved in front of my makeshift desk, really just a wide board between two stands.

"Yes, sir, a group nearly walked into us a few moments ago. Our scouts found them before they made it all the way to the camp, but they came far too close for comfort."

"Soldiers?"

"I . . . don't think so sir. The group is primarily women, with a few guards and the like. There was a spellcaster with them, ostensibly their leader. She surrendered but is more powerful than we'd anticipated."

"Interesting, are there others with magic among them?"

"One of your unit is guarding them; he said he saw nothing more than a few minor talents, but that is no sure thing, so he's advising caution. Their caster has been restrained as per standard protocol, but . . ."

"That is imperfect, and it is advisable to learn more. If she's powerful enough that one of mine sent you to me, I suspect that he thinks that I should see her."

"Yes, sir," the man said, nodding. My unit wasn't actually under his command, and even generals would have trouble giving me a direct order, but he wasn't wrong.

"Bring her in then."

It took only a few moments before she was led in. Around the woman's hands and feet were shackles and small floating magical items. The items actually included each cuff in them and served to form a shield around her blocking several types of elemental energy that would even stop kinetics to a degree. These were, of course, powered by the prisoner herself, who would be forced, at sword point if needed, to constantly put mana into them. This served to limit her abilities to some extent as well. A dark bag to limit vision was the final piece, simple, but quite effective in most situations.

Even these measures were considered nothing more than a stopgap. While they could likely restrain a weak or inexperienced caster for a long time, it wouldn't be forever. A powerful caster would be at least delayed for a few moments by them though, hopefully long enough for someone to arrive to put said individual down.

In most cases, they were also not used to their fullest extent. Casters were valuable to most and knew, if they surrendered, that they would likely be spared, noncombatants more so, and women even more than that. If a wizard or bard girl was content to surrender to you, she would almost always be kept in very good conditions. Food would be ample, safety and comfort guaranteed, often better than a common soldier or low-ranking officer would expect. There were, on the other hand, no second chances with casters. If one tried to escape or fight you, she would be killed. Casters were simply too dangerous.

This prisoner was visibly tense as she was led in and to a chair. I was as I studied her aura as well, because there was no way that . . .

One of the soldiers pulled off the hood as a courtesy. We were going to be interviewing her, of course. I looked at her and she at me. I had to blink a few times.

"Oh, Mystien," Veska purred, barely missing a beat. "If you wanted to blindfold me and chain me up, all you ever had to do was ask." That comment was enough to visibly surprise her guards.

"Goodness, still at it then?" I sighed. "Why are you here, Veska? I'd like the truth, and straightforward if you don't mind."

"Oh, fine. I fled Hazelwood with my people when the war started up. Which was in my personal opinion the safest option, since I expected you and that monster of a man to rip off the gates, followed by the lord's head."

"As I understand, Verren did kill him, violently to boot."

"Well, that's news to me. Anyway, after we fled, that asshole of a noble sent some of his men after us. Seemed he was irritated that I'd made a break for it. So, we've been moving westward, hoping that this war will be over soon, and we'll be well and out of the way when it does."

"Congratulations. It's not over yet, but you're now on our side of the lines, as is Hazelwood. You can return there if you want. We will have to check your things and hold you for a while though. I'm sure you understand."

"That's more than acceptable. I don't suppose you could arrange it so that my tavern is returned to me?" She gave me a bright smile.

"I cannot say that for sure, unfortunately. You may need to rebuild."

"Well what about a trade? I've got some information I'm sure you'll want . . ." She hesitated a bit. In some circumstances, this might well backfire, but it was clear that she thought that I wouldn't try to force her to spit it out regardless of what she did.

"What kind?"

"I did get some small bits and pieces about your apprentice, or was it really . . ."

"Everyone out." I snapped, causing her guards to look at me with surprise. My voice was hard and cold as ice, and after the moment it took them to process, they all quickly made their way to the door.

"Mystien . . ." she stammered as I set up privacy wards, obviously surprised as I let my aura loose a bit.

"You will not play games about this. Tell me what you know, and do it now." The air grew heavy and drops of condensation began to form on every surface. This was no joke, almost nobody knew just how dangerous that girl would be in the wrong hands, beyond that, she was also my best friend's daughter. I would carve a mountain in two if needed to get her back to us safe and sound.

"Of course, of course. Here's what I know . . ."

Veska wove me a full story about how Alana had been kidnapped, escaped, ended up with the Shield and disappeared after that, to where she didn't know though. It seemed plausible to some extent. If she were captured by some half-wit soldier who didn't know all that I'd taught her, she could easily enough get away. I also doubted that she'd be willing to stay in an orphanage for too long with how much she'd grown even under my tutelage. I did regret, by the end, that I hadn't joined in killing Hazelwood myself, but the past was the past.

My heart was pounding as I was finally taken from Mystien's tent to the one where they were holding me. The setup was simple but nice for an army camp, with a very nice cot and even a table with some snacks. I was even allowed to be in here without my blindfold, which was quite kind of them, not that I'd be doing anything inappropriate.

I plopped down on the cot and let my breath out. My heart was thundering, every muscle tense. Perhaps teasing him about the girl was a bit too much. That said, while he'd let a bit loose, he'd never raised his voice, nor threatened. He'd just told me exactly what he wanted and showed that he meant it.

He'd make a really good father. He'd absolutely take care of any of his own children if he was willing to go so far for his apprentice. Perhaps when this war was over . . . I mean I'd always had a bit of a soft spot for him, and I was fairly sure he liked me too. Would this interaction spoil him on me though? Did I even have much time? I was getting a bit beyond the years that most women would be able to seek such things. Hmm, so many things to consider.

Of course I'd spilled everything I knew. I would have anyway, and he could have probably found it in what files I'd managed to bring with me, but it was the action that counted. I knew he'd want the girl back and smiled that I'd guessed correctly. It was a real shame that I'd not been able to procure her for myself. If I could have handed him her, safe and sound, well . . .

My feet skimmed along the ground as I ran. It had been days tracking my father and we were still behind. The miles flew behind us and we surged forward.

Sadly, because of his assignments, my father was mostly out of contact with the main body of the army. I could have gone there, but there really was no point, he'd be out and about, taking on targets that had been assigned to him and his unit by the Lord of Shadows himself. These were places and people who really needed to go, and he was the man for it.

Dad could suppress his aura until it was practically nothing and could behave as a simple farmer because, well he'd been one much of his life. He'd chosen a few who were similar to join him. Together, they could get into places a normal caster or physical magic user had no chance of going. Once inside, they could do what needed doing. It was better that way, less killing overall.

My own unit was with me for this delivery mission. There were only a few of us, and we were still learning, but each was an up-and-coming soldier in his own right, each well suited for his job. They'd stood with me when we fought against the empire's army, and they were standing with me now, even if they didn't know why I was going, and even if they knew that it was mostly personal business. We all suspected that we'd be called to the front soon enough anyway, with how things were going.

The camp was easy to spot. It was near a main road, like any of the kingdom's normal camps. It was small, but the soldiers were in mostly standard uniforms, milling about here and there. The only thing that would have alerted anyone was that they seemed to have more than normal sentries on duty, and if you could smell it, there was no alcohol.

We approached, not in a rush, but quickly enough. All of my father's men had met me before, so I led, helmet in my hand. From a distance, I could even recognize the men on duty as they smiled at me, finally loosening their auras just a bit. I confirmed by pulsing my own once before approaching.

"News? Orders perhaps?" the man asked as I walked up.

"News, but only for Dad."

"All right then, he'll be by the fire at this time, head on."

I found him with ease. He sat there, looking for everything like a normal conscript of our enemy. He was a bit older than they'd normally want, with a bit of gray slipping into his dark hair, but still strong and well built.

"This is unexpected. What's the occasion, John?"

"We found her."

Dad put his drink down. "Where, and in what condition?"

"The kingdom's capital, and from my understanding, perfectly fine. I'll give you the details in private."

"Later. We've got a few things to mop up here before we join up with the main host again. If she's in the capital, we'll be there soon enough." He gave me a grim smile. Behind him, if one climbed up a small rise, you could see the border to the central duchies. Before long, I'd hold my little sister again.

CHAPTER 50

✦

INCOMING

School continued on. We got a new batch of students, and I was really starting to get a good feel for guessing who was a noble and who wasn't. There was just no denying that during the worst of the previous war, food had just been poor for those not in the nobility, and the students were therefore short in stature. I thought that the new first-years displayed more of this than our year, but that might have just been prejudice.

We had had a couple of days off while they were prepping the dorms and moving everyone in, which was pleasant. It wasn't a real break like we'd have gotten on Earth, but it was just enough for us to breathe a bit. I spent the time mostly with Kala, taking in the fresh autumn air in whatever empty part of the grounds we could find. We had invited Pinea to join us for one of our outings, but she'd had to go spend the break with her family.

Soon enough, the break ended and we were pushed back to the grindstone. Classes were much as they had been. There was no need to do much of a review as nobody had actually been out of practice for long. We did get a small surprise as we entered Professor Hern's class though.

"Good afternoon, everyone. Now that you're in your second year, you'll all need to begin advancing your cores toward the journeyman level. This is a lengthy process, and we don't think most of you will finish before your final year here." His eyes flitted toward me on that last remark. I'd probably have a year at most to get it done before Hern and Rooke started whining about me.

"Professor, does that mean we'll have to go meditate in that room again?" one of those closer to the front asked timidly.

"Thankfully, no. You will have to meditate, but the location is not as important."

He began to explain the process in detail. First we'd have to meditate to enter our own cores, then focus on one of the options therein, which would bring us back to the same location we were in before, allowing us to build more structures. We were told that we would emit a faint blue glow while doing so, some kind of side effect of the magic.

The "guide," of course, spoke of this as well, though I hadn't tried it. In the description, it was clear that this was a quantitative increase, not a qualitative one. Basically, we'd be building a lot of the same structures we already had in order to increase the ability of the core to function. These increases came in two forms: the ability to hold longer rune sequences (codes) that would work and the ability to hold more mana in an item.

Our current version was called the apprentice level by the teachers here, but the "guide" maker thought of it more as a beta or a proof of concept. It wasn't ever meant to do much, because it was just the maker proving that it could be done. It was one hell of a proof of concept though. Even with the severe limits on how much it could do at once, it was still a game changer for most people.

There was similarly a note on the blue glow. Whoever had written the "guide" had noted that he didn't actually know where it came from, but it reminded him of the Cherenkov radiation he'd once seen while touring a nuclear reactor. I'd had to read that sentence multiple times to process it completely, because apparently that was something people could do.

I had not been working on increasing my core, mostly because I was generally exhausted and a bit lazy sometimes. I did have to acknowledge that it would be good to do though.

That night, I decided to go about actually beginning the process of building it up. As soon as I started, I realized why he only really expected us to finish years in the future. I dove in, navigating through to the proper places and selecting what I needed so that I could see the next stage and initiate construction.

It was massive, absurdly, enormously massive. I'd thought that the original was something to worry about, but this was on a whole other level. It looked like a lot of the structures from the first one were repeated and somehow connected, but I really didn't know enough to understand exactly how or what all that meant.

I briefly considered trying my trick to speed things up with some of the larger structures that I could see, but I simply lacked the understanding of circuitry for anything like that. It was too big to internalize anything more than the basic functions. Still, those would help speed me along markedly.

I walked into Atali Language and knew immediately something had happened. Rather than pulling out their materials or looking forward, everyone was huddled up, whispering. I slipped next to Dras, looking about as we still had a few minutes before class began.

"Something up?" I asked.

"You're not in on all of the rumor mills, are you?"

"Sorry, no."

"Well, word is that an army has been spotted to the north and another south. They're making moves against the central duchies there."

"That's bad, Dras." I felt the blood drain from my face as I looked at him. If they were this close, they'd be here soon, or they'd lose soon. There were only those two options.

I had a small panic attack there. While I didn't see them nearly as often in my dreams, I doubted I'd ever forget the faces of the villagers as they slowly starved. How the children would come and sing with me hour after hour for a mere bit of bread. Would I have to see that again? Would the capital that had been so safe turn slowly into a horror-scape with hollow eyes and skeletal bodies? Dras must have noticed that I seemed off, because he placed a hand on my shoulder, making me jump.

"Hey, don't worry. Even if everything goes wrong, you're not alone. I'm here, and you remember that Lucien and Kala won't abandon you either, right?"

"You still haven't seen what'll happen, Dras. What the city will become and quickly if things go bad."

"I know. That aside, we'll make it through. I'd bet money that the academy has plans for just this kind of thing."

"Yeah, but everyone else . . ."

"We can't do anything right now, and we don't know that we need to. Just do your best, and when you're needed, if you are, help how you can."

Around that time, Professor Etia entered the room. She sighed as she looked out at everyone. "Well, it seems news has spread. I see no reason to lie to you. The central duchies have indeed been attacked. We must assume that the kingdom's enemies are on their way to the capital and respond accordingly."

"So what do we do?" one brave boy in the middle of the room asked.

"You? Nothing as such. The lot of you are all too young for this fight, so stay out of it. It is likely the school will be closed off though, so just be ready for that."

She tried to bring her class back to order, but it was useless. There was too much on everyone's minds and too many people who wanted to make wild speculations. Then there were a few like me. We just sat there, staring out the windows. That was oddly peaceful, and while it didn't help to pull me out of my memories, it did quiet things in my mind.

The first few flakes of this year's many snowfalls were floating down from the sky to try to stick to anything they could.

When I got back to my dorm that night, I found two letters. The first was from Endel; with these new developments, he was being assigned extra duties and would no longer be available to teach me about lightning magic. The other were from Lucien, the Shield, and Professor Rooke, all imploring me to not get involved in anything stupid and offering support should I need it.

I tossed those to the side and walked down the hall. It was only a few doors down that I found Kala's room. Her maid looked a bit bothered as she opened the door, and it was soon clear why. Kala sat on her bed, her face ashen.

Moving to her side, I did the only thing I could. I sat down with her and hugged her tight. Together, we sat there in silence, letting the time whittle away until sleep overcame us both. As I felt it creeping up on me, I heard her breath shift into an easy and even rhythm.

I was alone back in Orsken. Half the houses were destroyed, the other half open to the elements. Bodies were strewn across the street. I saw friends, neighbors, even Rod was there. I walked alone through the graveyard, seeing all the people I knew as a child dead and laid out.

It was then that a soldier approached me, wearing the armor of the kingdom. I couldn't rightly see his face, but I knew that it was twisted in hate. With a scoff, he pulled up his sword, preparing to strike me down with all the rest.

I couldn't move. I deserved this, for all the people I'd failed, everyone I'd let die. They were all gone now and soon more would join them, and there was nothing I could do. As the blade went to fall, a ball of flame struck him dead center in the chest, sending him sprawling. As I watched, it consumed him, and he melted away to nothing but smoke.

"Hey!" Dras yelled as he moved over to me. "Didn't I tell you that you weren't alone?"

More soldiers were coming, moving out from the edges of town, slinking toward us. Even as they were though, I started to see those I knew. Kala stood beside me, holding my hand. From a patch of darkness filled with stars, Lucien stepped forth. Charles and his overlarge eyes patted my shoulder, giving a kind smile. From the edges of my vision, I could see others I knew as well, people who weren't really close, but were there flitting in and out.

As our enemies approached, my friends and I struck, tearing into them.

As I woke up I blinked, committing the dream to memory. That one was happy, something I'd had precious few times in the last bit, and I didn't intend to let it go. Kala opened her eyes soon after I'd opened mine. She looked much better than the previous night. I wondered if she'd had a good dream too.

CHAPTER 51

◆

THE CALM

I looked down from the window of my dorm. The city was currently in two states. While the streets were nearly dead to all traffic, the walls looked like someone had kicked an ant nest. Men were running here and there, ostensibly setting up barricades and defenses, or delivering supplies to caches along its length. With a sigh, I took another drink of my tea.

As far as things in the academy went, there had been some changes. Classes were cut so that we were now using almost no mana in them. The reasoning for this was simple: as much mana as possible had to be flooded into the school's wards. We didn't know if we'd be attacked, but it was safe to say that if the city was the academy would be a rather large target for capture.

The only classes I was now using any mana in were my Healing and Combat Spellcasting courses. These were considered to be so important should the time come that practical experience was deemed invaluable. Even in those though, we were going through a lot more theory than actual spellwork.

I'd taken time to make a few adjustments. First and foremost, there were a few things I was going to have with me at all times: some gold coins hidden in a hollow in one of my shoes, my radio in its carrying case, and my spindle. The last of which was now mounted on a necklace. These were the only things I really considered crucial to have; the rest was nice, but not really that important. I did put a rather plain dress and the armor Professor Rooke had made for me in easy to get to places though, in case things started happening and I had time.

* * *

For the moment though, the central duchies were holding. Nobody honestly thought that that would last forever, but there was hope. The real hope was that perhaps the enemy army would have supply issues like we were sure to have soon. Of course, that was more of a pipe dream; no chance they'd come all this way without proper supply lines.

I slipped out of my room and made my way down the halls, heading for my next class. I still had plenty of time, but getting out and moving sounded like a wonderful idea. It was so quiet. Everyone seemed tense and worried, so conversations never growing much beyond whispers in the halls.

We'd also lost a good number of our older students. Many of those boys who'd been of age, almost all in their final year, had left the academy to go and help with the preparations and the fighting to come. They'd been extended that option and told in no uncertain terms that they'd be welcomed back when classes resumed.

Those of us who were left behind could only worry and grit their teeth as their friends, family, and lovers had been pulled into the effort. Particularly, because it was becoming increasingly clear how much had been hidden from public knowledge. We were now getting a few rumors about how so many of the forces sent out in this war had never returned or had been beaten so badly that they could no longer function in their current forms. Letters informing students of their loved ones' deaths that had been kept hidden to keep morale up were now being delivered, one after the other. There was simply no reason to conceal them anymore.

I sat through my classes, but it all seemed a bit forced. The teachers' hearts weren't in it, nor were the students. We were just learning to keep ourselves busy while those who had the power to do so made decisions that would spell the doom or deliverance of our country. Afterward, I went up to one of my favorite spots at the top of a tower with Kala to watch the stars.

"What are you thinking?" she asked, leaning over and resting her chin on my shoulder.

"I'm wondering if we should stay here or not."

"Mmm, you're thinking that it might be better to go hide in the temple district or perhaps with Lucien."

"Yeah. When things start getting hot . . ."

"If . . ."

"When. We're going to be sitting in one of the biggest targets."

"Fair. Then why haven't you whisked me away yet? I assume you don't plan to go alone."

"This is still probably the best place to be. The wards are strong, the teachers are bound to be tough, and there are still a lot of escape routes. Who knows what it'll be like somewhere else?"

"And yet you're worried about it."

"Of course."

"Well, mind if I make a suggestion?" I leaned on her as she asked, nodding. "Let it be; there's no point in worrying about something. You've already made some plans, at least basic ones. Now, trust that they'll do the best they can, then depend on the rest of us. There's no point trying to handle it all alone."

We lay there, looking up at the sky for a few minutes in silence. "Do you think the country will survive?"

Kala blew out air with a huff. "Honestly? I kind of hope it does, if only for stability's sake, but I doubt it."

"And when it falls? Do you think that we'll be okay?"

"I mean, probably. Yeah, they might go after the royals and their immediate families, but we're just a priestess and a bard. Who'd care about us either way so long as we don't make any big waves?"

"One second." I sang up a silence bubble around us, and Kala looked at me with a raised eyebrow.

"Giving us a bit of privacy?" She leaned forward a bit and I stopped her with a slight glare.

"Yes, because I'm not supposed to talk about what I'm going to reveal."

"Oh."

"Did you know I met Crown Prince Lief a few years back?"

"Seriously? How?"

"Well, let's just say Dras and I ended up going on a brutal, little adventure during an attempt on his life, and we ended up with him for a day or two. He's . . . well, he was a bit naive. Generally, a pretty good person though. He . . . helped solve an issue that had been hanging over me for a while. Then I was told, in no uncertain terms, that we were probably never going to talk again."

"I'm not entirely sure what to say to that, Alana. It's not every day that you learn two of your friends were all close to a potential king."

"Two? I thought you hated Dras," I chuckled.

"Hated? No, I was just jealous of how close he was to you. He's all right, I suppose."

I laughed, "Yeah, and he's matured a good bit here recently too. When we were young, he was just this little spitfire wizard who liked to hang out in all the wrong places."

"Like a bar that caters to prostitutes and other dregs?" She mimed fainting.

"Just so. What kind of horrible person would frequent such places?"

"I can only imagine someone of terrible moral standing. Indeed, I'd hate to associate with such characters!" Kala loudly proclaimed.

"Well, it could be worse. At least, they wouldn't be boring. Can you even imagine spending time with a bunch of . . . I don't know, priests or something? The mere thought of the lectures could put me to sleep."

"Oh, my sweet, you have no idea the horrors that lie that way."

The two of us sat there and laughed for a bit. It was refreshing, I'd been stressed and not had a good one for far, far, too long. Soon enough though, we ended up going back to our stargazing.

It was nearing time for us to head back inside and actually sleep when I heard a ringing. Kala popped up, her hair falling over her shoulders as she looked around. It took both of us a few minutes to realize what was going on as a series of lights appeared near the city wall. The sound of the explosions took another moment or two to reach us.

The world seemed to stop between the rings of the alarm bell. Somehow, the enemy had made it all the way to the capital's wall without anyone knowing. Had the central duchies fallen? Had they just been bypassed? It was impossible to know.

The two of us watched in stunned silence for a few moments. We looked on as flash of light after flash of light flowed over the walls, some of it seeming to bounce up and around them. It seemed the wards were holding back whatever magics they'd released against us. Even then, it was still shocking to watch.

Kala's hand grabbed for mine, holding it tightly. I was sure that my face mirrored the terror and surprise written now on hers. Both of us watched with wide eyes as the assault continued, unsure of what to do.

Then there was another bell, this much closer. The whole tower below us shook as the academy's alarms went off one by one. With a quick look at each other, we both began to move.

The stairs seemed to fly by as we took them at speed. Neither of us yet knew exactly what the situation was, so the go-to would be to head to the dorms rather than try to evacuate immediately. They had the best protections and thickest walls in the school, so were the elected place in case of an emergency. There were also plenty of escape routes from them as well, so we'd not be trapped if we did need to evacuate.

The sound of the school's alarms felt like it was nearly shaking the building as we breathlessly made our way into the halls. They were mostly empty at this hour, and those who had been out of dorms seemed to have already made their way back as we ran along.

Our school may not have been overly complex in layout, but it was surely big. It was only a few halls until we came to the main atrium, across from which was the path home. Around the halfway point though, there came a nearby booming sound, followed by a cloud of dust.

My heart seemed to freeze in my chest as a dozen men ran inward from the front entrance. Each and every one had at least a minor aura, and they were all in solid black armor. I instantly regretted not casting invisibility over us, using my radio, or a hundred other possible protections I could have tried, but it was too late.

"Remember, men, capture only. Minimal damage, particularly on the students. We want everyone alive," a man at the front said as they stepped in. His eyes locked on us as ours did on him. "We have our first targets."

I'm not sure if anything good has ever happened after the words "we have our first targets," but for us this was decidedly a bad beginning. Here, in the atrium, we were close, painfully so, to one of the emergency exits. It being nearly below our feet and the entrance easily within view, if closed.

This situation was not viable though. There was an approximately zero chance of us getting out of this without a fight, and the chances of us winning said fight were not terribly much better. We did have one advantage: they were out to capture, but we had no such restrictions.

"Come nicely now, girls. I'd really rather not have to get violent if I don't need to," their apparent leader said as his men began to spread out, closing off several of the exits.

Kala and I both responded at once, her tossing an angry purple beam forward as I started singing my shields into existence. While she attacked, I set up the defenses. We might be able to manage to hold them back if we could buy enough time.

The leader ducked expertly under the purple beam, though I could tell from here that it had also smashed into whatever shield he'd had up, sapping much of its power. He could probably have survived whatever Kala aimed with even passable spell resistance, but taking unnecessary hits was beyond foolish.

His men responded quickly as well. Most of them aimed at Kala, some kind of kinetic restraint spell if I had to guess, but my shield was up by the time it arrived and well-tuned against kinetics. Two aimed at me though, one opting for water, the other for a cold attack. The water splashed away just as any other projectile would have, but the cold grazed my arm with harsh chill.

Cold was an excellent nonlethal against a bard, and I had to internally compliment the choice. If they hit me right, or enough, I'd be gasping for breath as if I'd jumped into a frozen lake. That would end the fighting in a hot second, so I needed to do something about it and quickly. With that in mind, I tried to add my self-heating magic into my current defenses. It probably wouldn't stop their attack fully, but every bit of help was important.

To be quite frank, we were outmatched. The soldiers that we were up against were all more powerful than us. It was the fact that they wanted us unharmed, and they needed to keep an eye out for other entering combatants, that meant that we didn't fall in the first seconds. Without those, we'd be either dead or brought low almost instantly.

With that said, we did have a chance. If we could do something distracting enough or hold out for the teachers who would inevitably arrive, we might get out of this. That in mind, I began the process of starting up a storm. The idea was that it might manage to distract them, or I'd get lightning added to our attacks if we could hold on.

Our enemies had other plans though. Even as I started working on the storm, they battered my shields. Those who had seen the cold spell pass had already switched and were also becoming a bit of a problem. It had only been about ten seconds, but each brought us closer to being able to do something about this mess.

"Pulse the shields down," their leader said, his voice indicating his irritation at our continued resistance.

His men responded with perfect synchronization. The majority immediately started sending waves of kinetic force at us, slamming into the shield with potent force. Several though, the leader included, had small objects float up from their belts, hovering in the air beside them.

As the concussive magic hit again and again, my shields finally began to falter. It was instinctive that it would draw in, pulling closer to me as I struggled to protect myself. As it did so though, it passed by Kala leaving her exposed.

It was too late that I realized that she was no longer safe. One of the waves came in and smacked her, sending the young priestess flailing. I watched in horror as Kala fell and several of the little floating objects sped at her. I had been unable to expand the shields again quickly enough. Most missed, but two hit home, and I saw that they were small syringes, propelled like darts. One got Kala in the stomach, the other hitting hard in the back of her shoulder.

The pulses refocused on me, leaving her out of their fire as the man closest to her threw another of their restraint spells forward. It hit Kala, expanding over her like a net as she tried, and failed, to stand back up.

My face must have shown how shocked and terrified I was because their leader spoke again. "Merely a sedative. Surrender now and you'll be fine."

I couldn't respond as I needed to keep singing to work on my shields and the storm growing overhead. I did consider it though, we would probably not be hurt, they'd even said they wanted us all alive. That thought passed quickly as Kala turned to me, her eyes struggling to stay open.

"Alana, run," she said as her head fell forward.

That got a visible reaction from the leader of this little group, whose eyes immediately turned sharp. "Primary. Shut. Her. Down."

Oh, shit was the first thing that flew through my head as two of the men I could see held up fists glowing with a pale blue light. They'd stopped playing it safe and were now all in, and I was out of time. Sound died in the room as the light flowed forth, whatever spell they had killed it dead. This was unlike what I'd done to the other bard during our test; it didn't just block sound in a shield but stopped it completely. My spells began to fail as my song did, sending a trill of pure fear up my spine. This group had come loaded for fighting bards.

I closed my eyes. There was only one gambit I had left to play, and it was a long shot at best. I'd only ever gotten the most elementary of basic magic to work this way, but there was nothing like panic to inspire you to go above and beyond.

A number of the little syringes hit my disintegrating shields, being stopped for the last time as I stepped forward and began to dance. I had to abandon defense and focus everything upward. My storm could hardly be called ready, but it would have to do. As I brought my hands up and into position, I pushed all the mana I could in, releasing it in the form of a widely splitting thunderbolt.

The world shook as it fell, splitting over me like an umbrella and flying toward my attackers. Even through my tightly closed eyes, I could see the bright flash of the point-blank lightning arcing toward them. I doubted it would do any lasting damage, but sincerely hoped it would be enough.

As soon as it passed, I opened my eyes, bolting forward to grab Kala from where she lay insensate on the floor and running with all my might for the girls' dormitories. The spell binding her fell away as I scooped her up, all of the men momentarily disoriented from the brilliant flash and strike of my attack.

I had no time to gloat at that working as I pumped my legs faster and faster, driving myself forward toward what would almost certainly be safety. At the very least, the others there could help in the fight. I wanted to put up some invisibility or illusions, but I was on the last dregs of my mana. I was also struggling to carry Kala. She was just slightly taller than I was, and while my adrenal gland had been smashing the go button for the last couple of minutes, there was only so much that it could push from my body.

As I was nearly there, something blurred past me, stopping just ahead of where I was. One of the men in their assault team must have been a physical magic user, and he now stood before me. He'd opened his arms wide, planning to catch me in a hug rather than risk hurting me by tackling me from behind. That was at least a small kindness.

I had no chance to dodge as I was already going full tilt; momentum would push me into him. There were only a couple of seconds before his arms would wrap around me and that would be it. I had no mana, and my body was pushed to its limits. There he stood though, just over the line that denoted the girls-only area of the school, standing in the big oak door like a goalie.

As said line began to glow an angry blood red, it occurred to both of us that he'd fucked up. A small bolt issued forth from the ward, pounding into the lower part of his abdomen. The man blurred again as he doubled over in pain, falling forward. It was just barely enough for me to jump as I approached, clearing his prone form by the slimmest of margins, my feet grazing it.

From there, it was a clean shot into the dorms proper. It was only about twenty feet into the entry, but it felt like a mile. As I passed into the open space at the bottom of our tower, I saw Professor Sasha, my Proper Etiquette teacher speaking to a group of assembled students.

"ATTACK!" I screamed, hoping to get aid before I collapsed.

The professor only took a moment to process, her eyebrows climbing up her head. After only a beat, she sped forward, taking something from around her neck and pushing it into the tower entry. The panel where we added mana to the wards was there, and the small opening was sealed instantly by a formidable-looking barrier, opaque and sizzling with energy.

I lay on the cold stone floor, sucking in air as hard as I could. My lungs burned from the efforts of the last few minutes. My arms and legs spasmed painfully every few seconds, their objections to my run while carrying another being made clear. I could even feel the beginnings of tears in my eyes as I tried to move.

"Are you hurt? What happened to Miss Kala?" It was Professor Sasha who made it to me first, and she'd knelt down to check us out.

"Okay . . . drug . . . sedative . . . trying to capture us." I answered as I gulped down more air. The group of steadily more panicked-looking girls was gathered around.

"They were after you two?" She looked confused for a moment.

I was pretty sure they were definitely after me since their apparent leader had identified me as "primary." They'd also stopped holding back at that point, which was some real supporting evidence. Of course, I was nowhere near stupid enough to admit that though.

"All . . . of . . . us . . . many men." The air almost froze as the panic attacks began among my classmates.

The professor, on the other hand, kept herself well together. "Everyone, prepare for evacuation. Get to the emergency exits. If we're not contacted quickly, or if the ward shows any sign of issue, we will move."

Pinea and another girl helped me toward the exit, while Kala was being carried by several more. One priestess was working hurriedly on her, trying to neutralize the drug that had put her out. As we got there, Pinea looked over at me.

"How did you escape?" she asked.

"Lightning bolt to blind them, then ran. One almost got me, but he crossed the line into the girls' area and something hit him."

She almost smiled, "I can't believe that actually worked. I've never seen it go off before."

"What was it?"

I knew that there was something there, but like her I'd never seen it. The male students avoided the whole area like it was cursed or something, never straying more than ten or fifteen feet toward the mark on the floor.

"Couple of decades ago, some of the girls got tired of boys breaking into our dorms for pranks and the like," the other girl helping me answered. "So a handful of the fourth-years put in a ward there. Any boy who crosses it, with a few exceptions, gets hit with several years' worth of cramps. It stopped the male students from bugging us and made the dean laugh his ass off, so they left it."

Now it was my turn to try and not smile. To think that I'd be saved by the frustrations of classmates long past.

I wanted to bolt from here as soon as was possible. Unfortunately, I had a few problems. First of all. I was running on fumes of mana. And if I got caught out again in any kind of fight, I was done. Second, Kala was still recovering. The priestess had gotten the drug out of her, but even without it, she was nowhere near fighting shape yet. There were also the twin issues of needing to let Dras know I was bolting and all the bloody people now hanging around at the emergency exits.

We were still waiting on the administration to show up or whatever, though who knew how long that would last. As it stood, there were no sounds of fighting, or any indication anyone was trying to get into the dorm. That would normally be rather comforting, but our invaders had somehow managed to get into what was supposed to be our very secure school, so I was feeling less than confident that the next set of wards would stop them.

There was a series of tones from the entry, and Professor Sasha went to go undo the wards. Apparently, that particular series indicated that the staff was here and everything was secure.

We were shortly called to the main room. Our main emergency exit was in our baths, a roomy and well out-of-sight room. The dean stood there, appearing rather more tired than I'd seen him before. He was normally a rather amused-looking old man, like everything around him was a joke. Now though, his eyes had bags, and he seemed to be his actual age.

"Do we have any missing?" he asked as his eyes flitted over us.

"No, sir, what happened?" Professor Sasha asked.

"We were attacked. We're not sure how they got into the city, much less the school, but we think that they're gone for now, and we're calling a few guards go aid with things here," he said, rubbing his forehead.

These statements brought a whole series of questions from the room. There were demands to know if we were safe, who attacked us, and what they wanted. The whole dorm was basically in a stir about the night's activities and wanted to have a full rundown of things.

"Enough." Dean Lorrae let his aura fill the room, instantly silencing everyone. "From what we can see, they are obviously from the army attacking the city. There is also evidence that they were here to capture students, ostensibly as leverage against their families. We do not believe that there is any danger at the moment, but we will be investigating tomorrow. For now, several teachers will be staying in the dorms for the night, so everyone can rest. We'll also be organizing shifts for the older students and staff to back them up."

That all sounded well fine and good, but I had my own problem. They'd designated me as "primary" as in "primary target," and that was no good. I needed out of here and as quickly as I could manage it. If I stuck around, either the staff would eventually figure out what our enemies were after, which couldn't end well for me, or they'd come back, which might well end worse. I didn't know why I was being sought, but I suspected they might have gotten wind of some of my research and decided that I needed to work for them, or at least be taken from the kingdom as a safety precaution.

Therefore, I needed to go hide, at least until I could figure out what they wanted. There were a few things I'd like to take along, gold, some personal effects, my armor, Kala. Sadly, that would all have to wait, because my chances of getting out of here bone-dry on mana were practically zero. I might manage to if I told the school that I was going to head off to the temple and got an escort, but that would be just putting up another target. I needed to take a page from my old friend Jackson and make tracks *before* the heat got any higher. Before I could go though, I'd need to sleep for a couple of hours.

So I headed up to my room like everyone else and went straight to my bed. I feared that I would have issues getting to sleep, but the day's events had been quite a bit, and I fell right out like a light. My dreams were a bit fitful, seeing again and again the people coming after me, catching me, or prison cells.

Eventually, I stirred, sitting up and finding my room pitch-dark, which suited me just fine. A quick call of "illuminate" fixed the darkness, and I set to work. I packed my things, donning my armor and prepping a bag with some clothes and my other necessities. I put on one of my dresses over the armor, trying to hide what it was, a poor camouflage, but it would do from a distance.

I also wrote a few notes: one to Dras telling him I was heading off, but would meet with him again later; one to the school authorities, telling them basically that I thought that there was too much danger and was leaving; and finally one for Dora. I left a glowing review for any future employers and a few gold coins to make up for my swift exit.

I heard the door open and the subject enter my chambers just as I was finishing up the last one.

"Am I to assume that you intend to flee the school, Miss?" Dora asked as she looked me over, seeing my clothes and packed bag.

"Yes, Dora, I do. Will you try to stop me?"

"No, Miss, I quite understand your decision. Have you packed everything?" She was taking this remarkably well, but I suppose she was a professional and would return to Pinea's family afterward.

"I have a few sets of clothing that I'm having to leave. Other than that, I've got everything. This is for you." I handed her the note and the money.

"You're quite kind. Most wouldn't have thought of their staff."

"They should. Anyway, Dora, if you would please cover the fact that I've left until the rest of the students get up I would be quite appreciative."

"Of course, Miss. I wish you the best of luck." With that, she moved out of the doorway, letting me pass.

I deactivated my lamp and began to hum. By the time I was past her, I was quite invisible and silent as a passing breeze. There were a few people here and there in the halls, but none were really equipped to deal with my level of stealth, another point against staying here.

Kala's room was just so close that slipping to it and in was almost trivial. I moved to her bedside and woke her gently.

"What's up?" She took a moment to look me over as I dropped my spell. "Ah, leaving, are we?"

"Yes, and you need to get ready to go too. It's not safe here for us anymore."

"Seriously? Sure, they came after us, but they were after the whole student body."

"Kala, please trust me, I'll explain on the way, but we need to go now." That got her attention and got her to start moving quickly. I helped where I could, putting her things in a bag and helping her into a warm traveling dress.

I was happy to see her follow my lead in leaving a couple of notes explaining her absence. She even left one for her temple, on the off chance that we didn't end up there for a while. Neither of us really wanted to cause problems with our getaway, but some would doubtless appear anyway.

I gave her a brief primer on hiding her aura, took her hand, and started tossing on the stealth. We moved down the stairs silently and made our way quick as you will to the baths. I could see just the faintest bit of energy coming off of her, but to anyone not paying attention, it was unlikely to register. There were still a few tiny bubbles coming off of me, too, but there was little to do about it.

As we slipped into the baths, I was amused to see that we weren't the only ones to have had the idea. There were already several girls behind a small silencing wall who seemed to be getting a firm reprimand by one of the teachers. There were gesticulations and pointing, and if I could read lips, I'm sure I'd have seen the standard admonitions being repeated. Again though, they weren't prepped for the amount of stealth I was bringing to the party.

I waited until the professor had turned her back to activate the secret door. It was simple enough, just pushing a bit of mana into the right place. As I did so, the wall slid back and we hurried in. I thought I saw a smile flash on one of the girl's faces who could see our exit, but hopefully she wouldn't say anything. I closed the door behind us, and we began our trek through the tunnel.

Within a few hundred yards, we found a faintly glowing barrier. We'd been told of these back when the emergency policies had first been handed out. It was a simple-enough spell. It functioned as a one-way door. You could leave, but once out, there was no coming back in. It also appeared as a black surface to the other side, though we could see through the spell.

On the other side was a tunnel, much like ours. The passage was about ten feet across and the same in height, clearly designed for people to move quickly along it with smooth floors and walls. It had one light near the doorway, since light on our side wouldn't be visible over there but was otherwise empty.

I quickly pulled out my lamp and we passed through. After a few minutes walking in silence, Kala squeezed my hand. I dropped the invisibility. The floating light would have given us away anyway, but I had been nervous.

"So, care to tell me what this is all about? Not that I mind running off with you too much."

"Kala . . . I'm sorry I got you into this."

"I suppose you'll have to find a way to make it up to me later then. What am I into?"

"Um . . . so after you called my name and went down, the leader told his men I was their primary."

"Oh." She stopped walking for a few seconds. "That's bad."

"Yeah. I would have wanted you to come along anyway, but . . . they know who you are, so . . ."

"Well, nothing we can do now. If we get to the temple, the Order of the Lovers can protect us, or the Shield for that matter." With that, she started up again.

"I'd like to stop by Lucien's first. The Shield is my official guardian, so it seems likely that order will be the first to get checked if they realize I'm not at the school anymore. The Starlit Sky isn't much better, but I'm fairly sure it's more off the record. Lucien said he had somewhere to hide, too, so I think it's good to investigate."

Kala frowned. "Alana, I think we should go based on where we come out. If we come out closer to the entertainment district, we head to the Starlit Sky, if we're nearer the temples, we head to the Order of the Lovers."

I pouted a bit, but she was right. "Okay, but let's not tell the Shield, okay? I think their asshole bishop might just lock me in a room if he finds out there are soldiers after me."

She snorted and put her hands on my face. "Deal, and feel free to continue pouting like that. It's terribly cute on you."

Our course decided, we made our way swiftly down the tunnel. I was glad I brought along my lamp, it would save me a decent bit of mana depending on how long this trip took. A quick check confirmed that it was nearly full. That was great. I had no idea how long exactly that charge would last, but saving anything right now was a good choice.

CHAPTER 54

RETURNING TO THE LOWER CITY

The walk down the tunnel was good, if a bit boring. It was a wide, quiet, and easy trek, probably because this was where all the panicked students would be going if things went tits up at the school. I also had no need to use any mana for it; consequently, I had time to charge up what I'd lost. I briefly considered tossing some things up around us, but it seemed rather unlikely that we'd run into anyone else for the duration, so I held off.

Kala and I silently agreed that talking for now was off the table. Both of us had our ears pricked for anything major going on, of which there was mercifully nothing. It eventually got a bit eerie, with only the sounds of footsteps and echoes and the pale glow of my lamp. After a few minutes, Kala did take my hand, though if that was because of the spookiness or just because she was Kala was anyone's guess. The warmth was comforting though, so there was no reason to complain.

The whole walk probably took well more than twenty minutes, not that there was any way to tell the time down here. It seemed that we'd gone a good long way, crossing most of the city. I'd expected as much from an escape route. It hadn't occurred to me that it might take us out of the walls, something that began to worry me slightly just as we got to the end.

The end of the tunnel was much like its beginning, with a simple stone arch and the familiar one-way barrier. The stones were plain, much like you'd find in any part of the undercity, each fitting perfectly into their neighbor. The other side actually looked like part of the undercity, with walls that were slightly misshapen and only one clear path leading out. Rather than a magical light though, there were some small glowing mushrooms illuminating the room, a good way to hide that a mage would use this.

If this exit did go out into part of the undercity itself, that could be a problem. We didn't have a guide, and I certainly didn't know it well enough to guess too much, though it would serve as a good way to obfuscate the location of the exit. A blocked-off doorway, even one with a magic lock, probably wouldn't arouse much suspicion in the locals.

Kala gave my hand a squeeze, and we looked at each other before stepping through, making our way out and into what we hoped was a clean getaway.

Someone had been clever and placed mushrooms along a winding path that avoided a few turn-offs here and there, along with some arrows pointing and labeled "Exit." I was sure that nobody who frequented the tunnels would mess with any of those, as such things would be absolutely vital to anyone lost down there. Among those who had to work in unpleasant jobs like rat-catching, there seemed to be some sense of camaraderie. This path also had the advantage of being fairly easy to walk, tall and wider than average for an undercity passageway.

Our exit, like many exits from the undercity, was a thick wooden door. We approached cautiously, looking at it for a few moments. There were sounds on the other side, faint, but very odd for this time of night. After a brief consult, I cloaked us up as best I could, and we opened the door from a distance.

It was now clear that we could hear into the night. The sounds were fighting, not too far off if I had to guess, punctuated with the odd explosion. That was a most unwelcome finding, but there was nothing we could do, nor for the fact that wherever we did go, we needed to leave through here, preferably before dawn came and made life that much harder.

"I don't like it," Kala offered.

"Me either, any other ideas?"

"Sadly, no."

We moved fast into an alley, then out into a larger street. I was unsure of our exact location, but the shops on either side seemed to give away that we were somewhere in the more mercantile part of town. If I had to guess, we were well away from the main street, though that didn't really narrow us down too much.

What was odd that I could see—once we got into that street—was the second light in the sky. The moon was there, as normal. Joining it though was a pale yellow glow, pulsing slightly in the distance over the city. It looked almost like something was pushing there, trying to slam against the glow.

I squinted for a few moments and felt the lightest of drops on my face. It seemed to be drizzling, even though there was not a cloud in the sky . . . I looked over at where Kala would be if she were not invisible.

"I . . . I think someone's firing a water cannon at the city."

"That's . . . a lot of water."

A few seconds passed, and the glow from what I guessed were the city wards got brighter and brighter until they seemed to burst. A stream flew over us, screaming toward the center of the city, toward the castle. I could see another burst of light as whatever protections they had there went off, blocking the attack. It soon faded though; the stream seeming to trickle down and away.

"But, why?" Kala asked, we still stood by the alley, watching.

"To drain the city's wards. Hitting the castle was a bonus, but our normal protections . . ."

"Alana, we need to get off the streets . . . now."

"Totally agree." With that said, I picked a direction.

I could sort of see the center of the city, and supposing that we were somewhere in the mercantile district, we had only a few choices. I was fine with either until we got somewhere that we knew, so we set off in the way that seemed the quietest.

It was only a few streets, plodding along and keeping an eye out for anything until a group of armed men came trudging along. There were about twenty in total, all in dark-colored civilian clothes, each with a spear, ax, or some other weapon. They filed along at a fast clip, while Kala and I slid well from their path. The man in front had a torch and sword and seemed to be ushering the group along.

"Come on, hurry it up, lads. Last runner said the fighting was worst around the main street." He motioned to grunts of approval.

As they made their way past, we looked on after them. My guess was rebels, but there was honestly no way to tell. Frankly, it didn't matter. We neither wanted the risk or to waste mana on fighting them here if they were. If they were city defenders, I'd be even more hesitant to go after them. Men defending their home can be scarily dangerous, even without magic to aid them.

Figuring out which way was the main concourse helped though. With that and knowing where the city center was, I could sort of guess the general direction to the temple and entertainment districts. It looked like we'd be heading toward Lucien's after all, as it was just barely closer.

I silently began to move in the direction that should lead us to more familiar parts of town when far behind us there was a murderous sound, one I was all too familiar with. The lightning bomb was well and far away, but as the bright blue glow flashed across the sky, I froze for a moment, every hair standing up. My breath hitched for a second, and I felt my hands begin to tremble ever so slightly.

Kala's other hand rested on my arm as she leaned in, bringing her face close to where my ear was. "Alana, it's okay. You'll keep us safe, but we need to keep going," she whispered.

That was enough. I did add my lightning shield to our current protections, a large strain, but an important one, and we made our way forward. There were a few more explosions from the monstrous magic items. But thankfully, the area we were in seemed fairly quiet for now.

After about five or so minutes, we came upon the site of what must have been a rather nasty skirmish. Men were dead on the street, their blood pooling in the moonlight around them. A cart that had been in the street was pin-cushioned with arrows and crossbow bolts. A few weapons had even been discarded on the street, mostly broken, or poor quality and caked in gore.

I wanted to vomit as we made our way through the site, carefully avoiding the wet spots on the ground. It was then that I noticed him, a man laying against a lamppost, barely awake. His breathing was labored, and he had a nasty wound in his side, slowly leaking his lifeblood out and onto the cobblestones.

I also recognized his face. The thick beard of Sorn the cobbler was matted, and his eyes stared blankly forward, but there was no mistaking who it was. He tried to call out for help, then to rise, but it seemed futile. I could feel my eyes widen a bit as I looked upon him, once so kindly as we rode in a cart to the city, him jabbing me about working for him and now fading as I looked on.

"I know him," I said. "Can you . . . ?"

"No." Kala sounded almost pained, her voice straining a bit.

"What?" I turned toward where she stood instinctively, flabbergasted.

"He's . . . obviously a combatant, and the battle is still going. It would violate the rules of all of the orders to aid him at this moment." I could hear the sadness, but acceptance. This was how things were, how they had to be to maintain neutrality.

"Hello? Is someone there? Please . . ." He must have heard us and called out, his pained voice begging for aid he knew would probably be wasted.

"If I do?"

"I won't stop you, but be careful. We don't know what repercussions that will have."

I began to hum. I wouldn't do much, but the least I could do was seal up his wounds enough for him to survive. As the magic flowed forward, I could feel it latching on, stitching and pulling shredded bits of flesh into place, carefully reconnecting them. Sorn sighed in relief as some of the pain must have faded a bit.

"Who's there? I can't see you," he asked as I finished. "Are you one of ours?"

I wasn't sure how to answer the latter question, but as for the former, that one was easy. "I'm a friend."

"Truly, my shop is only a couple of streets from here. Can you help me, or let someone know where I am?"

Kala and I both sighed in stereo. It was hard to say no to that, but saying yes . . . saying yes would get us caught up in this mess.

"I'm afraid not, but . . ." I kicked a broken spear over to him, close enough that he could reach it to use as a crutch, "Good luck, Sorn."

"No, no, it was too much of me to ask. Thank you." He picked up the spear and began to help himself up as we carried on. Now knowing roughly where his shop was, I could easily guide us. I nearly missed him looking up and asking as we turned the corner, "Wait? Lad, is that you!?" It was something that brought a much needed smile to my face.

The rest of our way was free and clear, and as I turned onto the street where my one-time home lay, I was in exceedingly high spirits. The two crowds of men funneling into the streets from nearby alleys killed that good mood. Clearly, the next fight would be here.

✦

CHAPTER 55

PROCLAMATION

I looked on as the two forces slowly moved toward each other. For some reason, I was expecting a mad rush, but there was none. Nobody seemed to be running forward screaming madly and swinging. Probably because everyone who'd done that was already dead.

Both sides here had at least some level of military training; that much was clear. I supposed that most of the rebels, because I had to believe these were such, were in the previous war. The kingdom's soldiers, too, seemed a bit hesitant. They weren't up against some wild mob, but men who knew how to form into ranks, slowly advance, and utilize all of the tactics that they knew.

Kala and I kept back. We were well and away from the front of the action, which looked like it would go down right in front of the Starlit Sky and had a fair view of both sides. If either started to retreat, we might find that some men fled down the alley we were currently in, but because of the way they had entered, we weren't really in their midst.

Kala wouldn't get involved due to the rules of the various temples; that much I knew. It was a heavily enforced rule, it would seem, that no priest could step in on either side. I knew that Kala would protect us if any of the soldiers attacked without provocation, but for now, she seemed content to watch.

For my part, I wasn't sure I really wanted any part of this either. While I had a number of friends who were nobles, I couldn't say that I liked the nobility as a whole. The same with the royals. I liked Prince Lief well enough, but their governance frankly kind of sucked. On the other hand, who knew what this Lord of Shadows was like?

So we watched as the groups inched toward each other. The kingdom's men certainly had better, or at least more matching equipment. I was no expert on armor, but they seemed to have more: each man outfitted in a standard set of mail, a shirt-like piece with some arm guards. The rebels, on the other hand, had a smattering: some in cloth armor, some without, except the men at the front, who were clad in mail. Mostly, they had spears or improvised weapons, staffs, clubs, and a few crossbows.

The rebels though had the numbers advantage. Having perhaps thirty-five or forty men to what I would guess was twenty-five on the kingdom's side. I wasn't sure how much that would help, but they seemed quite confident. Many of their number were older and held themselves like they knew what they were doing.

The action seemed to drag on for a minute or two, neither side willing to engage, and then it exploded. Spears thrust forward and twisted; some went wildly up or to the side as their line of attack was blocked. Men screamed in pain and fell back, the whole exchange having taken only a few seconds.

As we looked on, the scene repeated itself again and again. Men would move forward, attack for only a few seconds, then everyone would fall back. It was hard to tell, but I couldn't see that either side had an advantage as of yet.

I tried to think of what to do. There was no way into the Starlit Sky until their bout was over, since we were certainly not crossing those lines. If only I had a way to contact Lucien . . .

Feeling like a complete idiot, I fumbled and pulled out my carrying case, slipping the earpiece in as I kept one eye on the fighting.

"Hello?" I questioned after turning it on.

"Hello, I'm glad to see you're using it now." The voice on the other end seemed young, male, and lightly calm.

"Um . . . who is this?" That was definitely not Lucien, nor Dras, and Kala was here with me.

"Charles. Lucien gave this to me while he prepped some things underground. Said it was a communicator of some sort. I'm quite surprised; it sounds like you're just beside me."

I had to take a few moments to process. One, Lucien had recognized my radios for what they were, and two, he'd handed it over to Charles. I supposed I couldn't really object to that. Charles did seem the dependable type and was definitely on our side, whatever our side was.

"Okay, Charles, where are you? We're near the Starlit Sky, but there's a lot of fighting outside right now, and I'm not sure what to do here."

"I'm on the roof . . . ah, there you are. I can kind of see the distortion where you are. Um . . . are you alone?" That guy's eyes would never cease to surprise me. Then again, he did seem to have most of his aura focused there.

"No, Kala is with me. I don't suppose you have any plans on getting past this mess?"

"Honestly? I'd just wait it out. This isn't our fight, and getting into it will only cause us more problems."

While I followed his advice, I scanned the rooftop. There he was, sitting quietly in a shadow. I probably wouldn't have noticed him at all if not for the slight bit of aura surrounding the twin points as he looked down at us. It seemed he'd really been working on whatever his skill set now was, something involving stealth and spying if I had to guess.

I hadn't really noticed the sky getting lighter and lighter as we moved, but now that I was looking up, it was obvious. There were pinks and a few streaks of the palest blue now beginning to stretch where there'd been only deep night before. As the skirmish nearby continued slowly, a golden ray peaked over one of the nearby buildings.

As the sun rose, pouring its brilliance onto the bloodied street, a voice sounded. It was an older man's tone, calm, confident, strong. It was the voice of a leader.

"My brothers, hear me. I am Durin, the Lord of Shadows."

The fighting stopped, all of the men looking around for the source, but his voice seemed to come from the air itself. It wasn't painfully loud or overpowering, like from a speaker, but rather like he was standing nearby and giving a speech. Magic was certainly involved.

"I know that many of you are afraid, afraid for your families, afraid for your lives, but know this, my armies are no barbarians. We do not seek to raid, rape, pillage, and destroy. No, my friends, we have come to liberate, to lead you to a brighter future.

"I desire that none of you men, disregarding if you have supported me or not, to perish. No, no, I bade you to put down your arms, to let me and my men free you from the oppression of those nobles who sent you here to die. Those who cared not for your lives, only that they could buy a bit more time, those who left you here.

"So I implore you all to lay down your weapons. Those who surrender will not suffer any harm from me. Those who try to avoid the fighting will come to no harm by my hand, nor the hand of my men. For my men were drawn from those like you, those who were beaten down, ground under those who thought themselves your betters.

"This as well to those who support me within the city walls. I would ask you brave men to fall back for the time being, to allow your enemies this chance to do what is right and put down their spears. For now, let them have a brief time—to consider and to see reason—to end this pointless fighting.

"For my armies have already breached your wards. We shall fell the gates in short order, and we shall take this city. I do not desire to harm any of you, but no resistance to us will be tolerated. Surrender now, return to your homes, your shops, or seek shelter in the temple district, and I shall show you mercy. Fail to, and you shall have none. Consider and make your choice."

When it ended, the silence was deafening. All across the city it would seem that men and women had stopped all they were doing to listen, and now they took a second to think.

An older man stepped forth from the group of rebels. He was well built and had a thick beard and pale gray hair. He raised a hand forward to show he'd put down his weapon as he spoke to the opposing side.

"Allow us to gather our wounded and leave in peace, and we will cease fighting for now." He stared at the soldiers opposite him, eyes hard.

The man who spoke from the ranks of the kingdom's soldiers was younger, but no less resolved. "I'm not authorized to make a truce, but . . . it seems we have our own wounded to tend to. So if you're happy to ignore us as well . . ."

With that, their fighting ceased. Injured men were carried, a few had to have improvised stretchers made for them, but they all began to back away. It was weird. This lot had been going at each other viciously just a few moments ago, but now all they had were cautious looks toward one another as they retrieved their friends and backed away.

I wondered if the whole city was going through this now. How many of the men of the kingdom would leave the walls and just go home? Could their commanders even stop them at this point, and what would happen if they did? Would the Lord of Shadows keep his word?

Did it even really matter though? If he had enough magical talent on his side to broadcast his voice over the whole of the city, he might well just be able to destroy it. We were already losing, everyone knew that, and him offering peace like that . . . He didn't need to. He could have just kept on grinding us down. But he did offer, and I thought that many would accept.

I barely heard it when Charles landed beside us. The only sound was a light rattling from the chain-mail vest he was wearing over what had to be the most boring brown-and-gray outfit I'd ever seen. A few things stuck out as I looked him over though. There were pockets all over the clothes, and what looked like the outlines of a few knife sheaths here and there.

"Come on then, girls. I'd wager Lucien will be thrilled to see us all."

I sighed as I dropped the invisibility spell and followed him across the road. There were a few puddles of blood here and there, some crossbow quarrels left behind, and a broken spear. As we opened the door, I turned and heard it. The sounds of fighting, at least in this part of the city, had ceased. They were replaced now by a deep rumble from far away. It was the sound of an army readying itself to end this siege.

CHAPTER 56

✦

TO THE TEMPLE DISTRICT

While the outside of the Starlit Sky looked calm and normal, the inside was anything but. The windows had been blacked out with curtains and people huddled in, mostly women and children. Those men who had avoided the draft were up to a few moments ago waging war on those who hadn't. I recognized a few, nodding here and there to them as they tried to find somewhere to sit with friends or family, old regulars who'd been here even when I was young.

Jackson was running things so far as I could see. He looked to have aged a decade since last we'd spoken and smiled as I came over.

"So . . . what's with?" I gestured to the people all around us.

"Simple thing that. Most people understand that few really want to tangle with a caster. So when the fighting in their neighborhoods got too bad or their homes were set aflame, a few came here to seek shelter."

"Wouldn't the temples be safer though?" Kala asked, quirking her brow.

"Sure, if you could get to them. You two haven't been around the last few days, have you?" Both Kala and I shook our heads in unison. "Well," he continued, "it's been pretty rough. Though if everyone is respecting the truce that the Lord of Shadows called, for I suspect a lot of them will head toward the temples."

"All right, where's Lucien?" If we'd need to move again, talking to him would be the fastest way to sort it all.

"Downstairs."

Kala stayed behind with Jackson. There were several wounded among those who'd come here seeking shelter. That wasn't honestly the worst idea. While they may not have been invited like me, the old fart was not a bad guy, and even now I wouldn't want to tangle with him. I was unfamiliar on the exact rules she had to follow for her particular order, but the people here seemed to be noncombatants in every sense, so there should be no issues.

The basement was the same as always, save for one thing. There was a door supposedly leading into the undercity down here. It had been there silently for a very long time. Lucien had even warned me against trying to open it when I first expressed interest in the tunnels.

It now stood open, unsealed by the man who'd built this bar, who'd plugged up that hole in the first place. Lucien himself was nowhere to be seen, but what I could see were wards around the opening, keeping it all contained. They surrounded a small spiral staircase, leading down into the depths.

Taking out my lamp, I began to descend. Interestingly, the lamp was not needed for long. At first, it was almost unnoticeable, but there was a slight, almost blue-black glow to the walls in places. In other places, there were points of faint light or gentle swirls of the same. The lower I went, the more attached the patches became, until soon it looked like the stone instead with the patchy part. I didn't dare touch whatever was causing this. It was obviously some form of magic.

After what felt like five or more stories worth of stairs, they ended. The room I came out in took my breath away. The ceiling, the walls, every surface was covered in the same thing that had been in the stairwell. Except here, in this room that had to be fifty feet across, it looked like I was standing in an infinite sky.

Swirls of galaxies adorned the walls in myriad colors and shapes. The space between was dark, but even that darkness seemed to hold some faint light, stretching between in an almost three-dimensional effect. There was one small pulsing bit that looked like it was supposed to be a nearby star, round and with an almost swirling effect.

"It's magnificent, isn't it?" Lucien stood in the middle of the room, looking around. There were small patches of light glowing around his feet and a path leading from the stairwell to where he now stood.

"Beautiful, what is it?"

"Starlight mold. It's harmless, in case you were wondering. I found this place years ago, took the name of my bar from it. I sealed up all the other entrances to down here, but we're deep, and it should be safe regardless of whatever they do on the surface."

"Why? Why hide it?"

"This stuff is like so many other beautiful things, Alana." He motioned to his feet, and I could see that, very slowly, the small glow there was retreating. "It's fragile, just coming down here will damage it severely. It will take years for it to recover just from our walking here. If we were all to come and hide here . . ." He set his jaw, looking mournfully again at the vista all around him. "It will be worth it though."

I realized that he'd kept this place for years. Letting it grow and flourish into the wonderful place that it now was. He would destroy it though, for those he cared about, letting the colony of magical fungus collapse from our very presence. This was what he would sacrifice for those he cared for.

"I'm glad you got to see it like this. We should hurry and bring Jackson down, too, before everyone else. I'd like him to see it once." With that, he began to walk back over to me.

"Well, he should, but let's not bring everyone down yet. Looks like there's been a truce."

"Really? That won't last long I imagine, but it's something. Let the innocent get out of the way."

As we ascended, I turned to talk to the older bard. "How did you know they were communication tools?" I asked. "Charles said you told him that, but I don't think I ever explained exactly what they did."

"They go in your ear, girl. That's so obvious, it's painful. Also, I don't want to know where you got military-type magical items like that. It hurts my head just thinking about it."

"Okay, fair enough. Why Charles?"

"Because he's good at what he does now. He's also rather discreet. Finally, he really likes you."

"I'm a bit young for him," I replied sarcastically.

"I don't mean in that way. Though in the future, perhaps. You're not there yet, but you've never been a bad-looking girl. I reckon in a few years you'll be quite attractive. Don't rush it though; youth is a gift." He still seemed a bit sullen, even if it were possible we'd have an out now.

"Back on the subject."

"Back on the subject, I think he views you lot what saved him as his best friends. He seems more fond of you in particular than the other two though. Could be because you're a girl, could be because you remind him of something else."

I sighed, shaking my head.

* * *

Kala decided she needed to head back to the temple district once we returned. There were a lot of people who'd seen seeking shelter here that had already left for that particular quarter of the city, and a number more who were waiting to go with her.

That left me in a bit of an odd spot. I really wanted to stay with Lucien and the others, but at the same time I wanted to be near Kala. I was hoping that she might opt to stay here for the duration, but realistically that was never going to happen and I knew it. With a sad smile, I turned to my friends at the bar and bade them keep themselves safe.

Our group consisted of around thirty people. There were only a couple of older boys mixed in with the women and children. They were too young to be drafted and had opted instead to stay with their families instead of joining either side.

About halfway to our destination, we encountered a small issue. At one of the crossroads, it seemed a checkpoint of sorts had been set up. There were around twenty guards in the standard-issue armor of the kingdom, all lined up and going into and out of a few requisitioned houses.

One of these men, older, with a slight belly, moved in front of our group. "Attention, due to the recent attacks, all citizens are required to return to their homes."

"We can't, that's why we're heading for the temple . . ." one of the women in our group began.

"I'm afraid not. You all need to turn around and go home." He stood back, crossing his arms like a middle manager. He seemed to be in charge of turning groups like ours around, and based on the way he spoke, he also seemed to think he could just order people to go back to a war zone or burned-out husk.

I took only a second to hum together the most basic of my shields, one that would protect me from crossbow bolts and the like before I spoke.

"Sir, the people here are not soldiers, and they are seeking shelter with the orders, certainly . . ."

"Little girl, you don't seem to understand," he said, cutting me off before I could even finish. "You're not coming through here."

I saw red. This tiny little tyrant reminded me of all the people I'd ever met just like him. He was the man given just a smidge of power and determined to use it. He was the poor leader that everyone below him dreaded. He was just like our former mayor, Malke.

That last though flowing through my rage-filled head was what stopped me from doing anything I might regret. Sure, this guy was petty and being stupid. I could also probably wipe the floor with him and all the little soldiers he had here with some effort. If I did so though, if I really hurt or killed them, then I'd have to live with that. It would be so easy to send down a thunderbolt and fry him, but it would also haunt me if I did so.

A hand rested on mine, and I turned a bit to see my dear Kala smiling. It was not a nice smile, but her light touch had brought me fully back to my senses.

"No, little man, you don't seem to understand," she began in a sickly sweet voice, and the man puffed up. She didn't give him enough pause to speak again before continuing. "My lovely friend here is a trained battle-mage, I am a priestess, and these people with us are refugees who I am escorting. We will be passing to the temple district, and you would be heavily advised not to lay a finger on any of them. Understood?"

"I . . . um . . ." he sputtered, seemingly unable to come up with something to say to that.

"Good! Come along everyone." Kala gave a bright smile as she began to casually walk us past the man whose mind still seemed to be trying to process.

I was gathering mana up just in case as the group walked, and it was fortunate I was doing so. One of the older boys with us, probably fifteen, stupidly chuckled as he walked by. That was enough to illicit a response from the would-be guard.

The pair were both acting absolutely foolish. The guard grabbed him, intending to do something, it didn't really matter what. As he did so, the boy pulled back, falling to the ground. From there, I wasn't sure if it was Kala, or myself who hit him with a spell first. Hers was a small bead of the purplish light she seemed to favor as a visual cue. Mine, of course, was a simple concentrated scream, as I didn't want to kill the guy.

It had been a while since I'd used that against someone without any resistance to magic. In a second, he was bleeding from his ears. He was also lying on the ground, somewhere between being curled up in the fetal position and shaking like he was having a seizure. I was fairly sure I hadn't put that much into it.

The other soldiers bristled before a voice from one of their own spoke. "Do nothing. He was warned." From the look, it was another of the older soldiers.

"But . . ." one of the men began, looking at the downed guard.

"But nothing, those are casters, and I don't fancy being turned inside out. He was warned that they were under the priestess's protection. He grabbed the kid anyway. Let him be."

"He should live . . ." Kala looked to me, and I nodded to that statement.

"Thank you for that." The new leader nodded politely as we finished passing by.

Once we were through, the kid came up to the two of us. "Hey, thanks for that," he tried to give a big grin, only to be met with glares.

We all collectively spent the rest of the walk to the temple district telling him just how stupid he'd been. His mother was nearby and began piling as much of everyone's luggage as she could on him, informing him that if he had enough energy to screw around, he had enough energy to work.

CHAPTER 57

✦

QUARRELS AND HELPING OUT

As we approached the temple district, which now had a gate made of interwoven vines, Kala turned to me. "Alana, a bit of privacy please."

That was a bit concerning, but easy enough. I furrowed my brow as I sang the spell into place, making a bubble around us.

"What's wrong?"

"We need to talk. Alana, there are rules for priests, and rules for those who seek shelter with us. If you enter the temple district, I need you to promise to follow them."

"Um?"

"We do not heal soldiers while battles are still going, nor support any side over the other. The man last night, I know he was your friend, but you can't do something like that again."

"I . . . he wasn't even fighting though."

"I know, and I know that you didn't take sides in the fight. You were just helping a friend. That's why it's technically okay, but it skirts the rules we priests must live under, and once we go in, you can't do that again." She had a very serious look on her face, and we stared at each other for a few minutes.

"Why didn't you tell me this before we left?"

She looked away, "I . . . didn't know if you would come if I told you. I'm sorry, I thought it was best."

I couldn't hear them, but the people with us looked aghast as my hand made contact with her face. "You tricked me? Did you really think I wouldn't have come if you just asked? But no, you had to bring me here, where you knew I wouldn't turn around, where I wouldn't have a choice before you told me what needed to happen! All because you 'thought it was best'? Seriously?"

Kala held her face where I'd slapped her, looking like she was about to cry. "I just wanted you to be safe."

"I know. That's not the problem. The problem is that you took away my choice, Kala. That's not how you treat people. It's why the Shield ticks me off so much, because that's the kind of thing they do."

That seemed to resonate with her, causing her to wince. "I didn't mean to hurt you, please . . ."

"I'm mad, but I'll get over it. Just don't do anything like that ever again." I huffed a bit, but knew that I wouldn't stay angry with her for too long. A quick look at her and I felt my own pang of regret. "Sorry for hitting you."

"I kind of deserved it." She looked away a bit.

"Maybe, but I still shouldn't have done that. It was wrong, and . . ." I was at a loss for words on that one. Striking her had been completely out of line, even if she had deceived me, and even if I was unbelievably pissed at her.

"That doesn't change things though. If you come in, you still have to promise that you won't get involved in the fighting. If you won't, we'll figure something out, if we can."

"I won't get involved anymore, Kala. Come on, let's go."

Normally, I'd have held her hand while we went, but I was still a bit cross. Perhaps it was that my interactions with the Shield had soured me a bit on people insisting that they knew best and trying to force it on others. Regardless, that, mixed with how I felt about my own loss of control, put me in an awkward place.

I'd never struck any of the people I'd gone out with before in my previous life, nor would I have let them hit me. The very idea of being in that kind of relationship seemed disgusting. Now, I had to deal with the fact that I'd lost it and actually done something like that. The very thought made me feel slightly ill.

I dropped the privacy ward as we moved toward the gate, getting strange looks from both those with us and the few men stationed there who could clearly tell that Kala was a priestess. I decided to bottle up my storm of emotions for now as we made our way and entered this section of the city. The refugees were quickly being interviewed to help them figure out where to go while Kala and I talked.

"I should probably check in with the Shield," I said, sighing. "If I don't, they're likely to show up at some point and cause a whole scene."

"Oh, I suppose that's for the best," Kala mumbled a bit, looking slightly dejected.

"I'll ask them if I can help the Order of the Lovers, or at least come by later. If that's okay with you?"

She immediately brightened back up. "Of course. See you later then."

I gave her a brief hug before heading off, something that seemed to surprise her a bit.

When I made it to the Shield's temple, I found the place in a riotous state. It was packed with injured and confused people seeking a place to go. There were a few assistants at the gate helping those who needed healing get inside and those who didn't find other sections of the district where they could go. Seeing how busy everything was, I got in line and watched while I waited.

There were very few men here, and they were mostly injured. The ones in line had rather small injuries while the more serious ones who showed up were rushed inside for healing. It seemed that the men who were okay were being assigned locations depending on age and family status. Those with families were mostly being sent to a section between the Shield's headquarters and that of the Order of the Vine.

Women with their families but without adult men were being sent to a similar but distinctly separate section near the men. Those who were alone were sent to an area near the temple of the Lovers. There were apparently some concerns about assaults, though with how dangerous I could see a priest being if they found such a thing, it was probably a minor concern.

After waiting for a few minutes, I well understood what was the current state and had only to wait for my turn. Since I had little else to do, I turned to one of the women near me. This lady was probably in her mid-thirties and had a few rather nasty-looking burns on one of her arms. Those would hurt, but they were far from life-threatening, and so she would have to wait to be seen.

"Excuse me," I asked, giving her a small wave.

"Hello, dear, did you need something?" She looked outright exhausted but was quite polite.

"Um, would you like me to fix your arm?"

"Can you?"

I reached out and hummed "Twinkle, Twinkle, Little Star" and watched as her arm began to regrow new skin. Her injury was not all that bad, so it quickly faded into a light red mark. Of course, that got several of the people around looking at me, including the person who was directing everyone.

"Miss, are you a caster?" he asked, leaving his position for a moment to come and see me.

"Yes."

"I hate to ask, but are you willing to lend aid? If your parents are here, I'd like to speak to them. We could use all the help we can get." Even the temples wouldn't order someone underage to work for them, but they could ask.

"They're not around. If Eleanor is around though, she's probably who I should go talk to. It's rather complicated."

It took him a few seconds to process that statement, and he smiled just a bit. "Of course, go into the temple and to the wing just on the right. She should be in there directing some of the older children on helping carry water and the like." He pointed me toward the temple. While a few groaned that I wouldn't be seeing to them, most seemed to understand that I should probably be helping in the most efficient way possible.

It was surreal walking through today. A lot of people were injured, revealing some rather important facts. Mostly, that none looked like soldiers. Similarly, there were far less than I would expect for a city of this size embroiled in fighting. The other big thing was that most of the wounds looked like they'd been inflicted on the edge of the fighting. Some had arrows or burns, or other nasty things, but they all seemed like something that a bystander would get, not a soldier in the thick of it.

Finding my old guardian was easy enough. She stood in the midst of a swarm of teens, directing each one of them here and there to clean things like sheets or bandages, or else to deliver water or other supplies to the various parts of the temple. There were a handful who seemed to be coming and going with notes and reports, which she hurriedly leafed through before sending the next adolescent off on a mission.

"Hi, Eleanor," I said as I approached.

"This is hardly the time for . . ." She looked up from the paper before her, fixing a glare on me that shortly turned to a wide-eyed gawk. "Alana? What are you doing here? Why aren't you at the academy?"

"It got attacked by a bunch of men trying to capture students. I didn't think it was safe, so I fled. Long story, I'll tell you later. Kala and I got here just a bit ago, and I decided to come and check in with the Shield. If possible I'd like to go help her over with Order of the Lovers," I rattled off at speed. The other teens were giving me a look now too.

Eleanor moved one hand to her face and began to massage the bridge of her nose. "I'd nearly forgotten what an incredible little headache you can be."

"That's not fair. I'm not really little anymore. Anyway, where should I go then?"

"I think I can answer that one best," a thick masculine voice said from behind.

I turned to see Rosk. It'd been years now since I'd laid eyes on him, and he'd grown his hair out a bit. The look was quite fetching on him. He, too, looked like seeing me was dredging up a mix of memories.

"Oh?" I asked, putting a finger on my chin and tilting my head a bit. It was ludicrous, but the most obvious "innocent act" I could put on.

He seemed mildly amused rather than bothered. "Yes, we're having some issues at the Order of the Vine's temple that you are well suited to help. As for healing, we've mostly got it covered here for now. Will you do so?"

"Of course," I chirped.

"Good, do you know where their temple is, or do you need someone to show you?"

I knew almost nothing about the Order of the Vine, but I'd seen a temple that fit that general aesthetic and described its location to him. The temple district wasn't that big regardless, so it was nearly impossible to get lost. He nodded, and I hurried off before someone tried to force me into cleaning bedpans or something else odious.

I was given a scribbled note and sent on my way. It would be easy enough to look at it, but it was sealed and my peeking might well be noticed, it would also ruin whatever surprise I was in for. I walked along the quite busy street to the walled-off complex with the vines around it and found a man standing near the entrance. He wasn't a caster, I thought, but a brief flash of aura told me he was either hiding it well or a minor talent of some kind.

"I'm afraid we're closed for the moment, Miss. As you can tell, there's quite a bit going on." He gave me a kind smile, but one that told me in no uncertain terms that he was really too busy today.

I proffered my note, which he quickly read and then gave a deep laugh. "Well, seems you're going in after all. See Jorus, he's the priest whose beard doesn't quite reach his chest."

He let me pass with what certainly had to be the strangest instruction on finding someone I'd ever heard. Then again, I knew almost nothing about the Order of the Vine. There was only one guy in my class who was with them, and he seemed rather aloof to everything. I was pretty sure we'd never even talked.

Once I got in, I began to quickly understand. Finding the priests was easy enough, since they all had auras. There were a couple of women who were both rather young and four men. Three of the men had ostentatious, belly-length beards, where the third had one that was only around half a foot long. They were alternating between discussions with themselves and with a few attendants.

"Are you Jorus?" I asked, walking up to the shorter-bearded man.

"I am indeed. What brings you here?" he asked, raising one eyebrow. I knew he could see that I was a caster, so he didn't dismiss me outright.

"I have a note." I smiled brightly as I passed it over.

It took him a few moments to read the text before he began to chuckle. "Oh, that will be useful indeed."

CHAPTER 58

THE ORDER OF THE VINE

Jorus passed the note to the other priests and quickly led me off.

"So, what do you know about the current situation?" he asked.

"Lots of refugees, ongoing fighting outside the district, anything else specific?"

"That about covers it. We of the Order of the Vine have been given the task of trying to keep the people fed for now while this all settles down. Something that has been a bit of a task. That little letter from Rosk explained that you would likely be of great help. You've done something like this before?"

"I made bread during the famine a few years back. We have enough food, right?" His words chilled me. I'd seen starvation, the slow hollowing of cheeks and creeping gauntness that swallowed whole families.

He apparently heard the fear in my voice. "Oh don't worry, my dear. We've enough for quite some time. The issue is getting it all prepared and out to those who need it. People are coming in so fast that we've not yet managed to get the system fully up and running to handle it yet. The districts store of grain may be large, owing to the fact that we knew this army was coming, but making grain into bread, porridge, or the like takes cooks and stoves."

"So the bottleneck is in preparation, not supply?"

"Never heard it put like that, but I suppose the neck of a bottle is a good way to explain it. Yes, we have enough for everyone but can't get it to them fast enough. It takes weeks to starve, but being hungry will lead to things like violence, theft, and all kinds of other problems we don't want."

"Okay . . . why is the Order of the Vine in charge of this?"

"Hmm? Well, we specialize in magic involving plants. Though force-growing fruits and vegetables is rather bad for the plants and soil."

Finding volunteers to sing with me so I could utilize the gestalt effect was easy enough. People was the one thing that we had in spades right now. With them in place, I'd sing up several loads of bread and then take a short break to recharge.

It was notable that my capacity in this had increased dramatically since I was little. Back then a basket or two of bread would be around my limit. Now, I was managing five with gestalt before I needed a break, and that was a short breather compared to what I needed before. I frowned a bit when I realized that at my current state I may well have been able to feed my entire village. If I'd been as good back then as I was now, perhaps it would still be standing, and with my weather ability, I may have been able to stop the drought too.

"You look bothered." Jorus had approached without me noticing as I was finishing up this load.

"I was thinking about the past." It wasn't a subject I often broached, particularly with strangers.

"Well, you look like you might need a short rest, and I think you'll find me a good listener. Would you tell me the story?" He plopped down next to me. The whole of the Order of the Vine's compound was covered in grass and short plants like moss and clover, so sitting anywhere was quite possible.

"Not much to tell. Back during the last war with the empire, our crops failed." I joined him, finding a nice section of moss that was surprisingly comfy. "I could make bread even then and did as much as I could to try and feed the people living in our village."

"That was very noble of you. Most children would struggle under that burden."

"It wasn't really effective. I tried, but it was never enough, and with the situation how it was . . . Starvation is a horrible thing to watch. I was thinking that if I'd been then as I am now, then perhaps I could have done a lot more."

"I see. We all wish we could have done more. Everyone who's been through something like that thinks about what could have been if only they were a bit stronger, faster, or smarter. Sadly, we cannot go back and do those things we might have. I myself saw some of the horrors you speak of in that same time and often think similar things." He looked out at the distance, considering the past as well.

"You were there too?" I asked, quirking an eyebrow.

"Yes, my order generally deals with issues involving the wilds. Managing areas so that they do not overtake civilization and are not overtaken. We try to maintain the balance there, since so many magical plants and animals are greatly affected by both cities and forests. In times of need, we do what we can to aid our fellow man. I did all I could to help fields and orchards during that time, though it was seldom enough." Jorus seemed happy to explain what he and his did, giving me a light smile.

"Well, Rosk, the priest who wrote to you was with us at the time, and I never saw him do anything like that."

Jorus nodded. "The magic to affect plants is subtly different from the one that affects animals and humans. It takes time to learn and can be detrimental if you aren't trained in the art. It's a careful thing, though potent if used well."

Our break ended, and I began to sing up the next batch. Jorus elected to stay. There were several apple trees nearby, and while he sang along with us, he wove his magic into them, causing them to first bloom, then bear fruit. The apples looked a bit small, but they were there, nonetheless.

As we stopped and a few of our gathered assistants went to retrieve the bounty of fruit, we retook our places on the ground.

"Mind if I ask you about something else?" The priest did seem to be a good listener, and I needed advice from someone as uninvolved as possible.

"Not at all." He smiled through his beard, leaning back a bit.

I told him about the situation between Kala and me. How she'd tricked me into coming to the temple district and how I was monumentally mad that she hadn't even asked me about it. I also told him how I felt about hitting her in response, an action that still gnawed at my conscience a bit.

"So, any advice?" I asked once I'd finished.

"Hmm. Think about if you want this to end your relationship, about how bad you view this. Then act in accordance. As for your actions, I think you already know what to do there." His advice was the sort of non-advice that you sometimes needed to hear. I already knew what I wanted, and I certainly didn't need someone else to tell me that.

I smiled. "Thank you."

The two of us worked together off and on until sunset. At that point, he walked me back toward the temple of the Order of the Lovers. We carried our baskets for them as we went, chatting lightly about what wild plants made the best seasonings. Nobody bothered us a bit, probably because of the obvious priest robes.

"Well, I'll leave you here for the night. The Shield may think you should stay with them, but as an unaccompanied young woman, the Order of the Lovers is the right place." He winked at me. "I'll come by in the morning to retrieve you. If you're willing to continue helping?"

I nodded my agreement and went in. I knew where Kala's room was and could practically walk there by habit at this point. At my knock, she opened the door and I entered.

The two of us looked at each other for a few moments in awkward silence, before we both began speaking.

"I'm sorry, I . . ." I tried.

"I shouldn't have . . ." she began. When I stopped, she laughed, nodding with a "You first."

"I'm sorry I lost control like that. It was wrong. Please forgive me." There wasn't much more to say as I bowed my head. I'd been completely out of line, regardless of how angry I'd been.

"Of course. I will insist you not strike me ever again, but I know I betrayed your trust here. Will you forgive me for tricking you into coming?"

"I won't, and I already have. Please don't do that again though. I've had a lot of people trying to trick or force me into doing what they want my whole life. It's terrible."

"Promise I won't. Now, come sit down and tell me how your day went." Kala plopped onto her bed and patted a spot beside her.

We talked for some time about how everything had gone, and how we felt about all of it, before finally falling asleep in each other's arms. It was the best way I'd yet found to enter the land of dreams, and I was happy to do so every chance I got.

On the other side of the city, a general walked into the tent housing one of the special operations forces. This group was set up and trained specifically in the capture of priority targets, and the forces had been sent against several noble households to secure their members with no casualties.

General Verren was tired. He'd had to spend the whole day dealing with several enemy knights and was both physically and mentally exhausted. That said, some things were important enough to keep going.

"Report," Verren said as he came in. The tent itself was warded against eavesdropping, so he had few concerns on that front.

"Mission failed, sir. We had to retreat to keep from coming into conflict with the academy's staff." It was the unit's leader who answered for them, standing straight as he gave the bad news.

"Damn, was there anything gained?"

"We made contact with the primary, General. Unfortunately, she displayed abilities beyond what we were prepared for and managed to escape."

"What? Explain." The aging man gave them all a hard look, seeming to think that they may have made some foolish mistake.

"Well, sir. We were attacked with some kind of weather and lightning magic. The latter of which was a great distraction. We were also unprepared for the target to be able to cast without sound. It's not unheard of in bards, but a rather niche ability. Finally, sir, we're not sure what happened to Roland, but he still can't quite walk right."

Verren began to laugh hysterically. "The little spitfire. Well, I'm glad to at least confirm her presence and safety. Any chance we can make another assault?"

The team leader blinked at the sudden change. "I'd advise against it for the time being. They've got their guard up fully now, and any attempt is likely to be met with the whole staff descending upon us. That's a mixed lot: some are very dangerous, particularly their dean."

"Hmm, you're right there. We'll have to wait until the city is captured properly. Well, men, we've got plenty of missions for you lot now anyways. There are a number of noble estates that are in need of a visit from those with your particular skills."

Verren left both happy and frustrated. He now had confirmation from a source close to him that his daughter was alive and well, and able to meet one of their more skilled teams and escape apparently. It would have been best if she'd been captured, of course, but it was hard not to feel a great swelling of pride at his little girl's skill. At the very least, he took solace in the fact that soon she'd be with him again.

CHAPTER 59

PALACE SHOWDOWN

I looked out over the town. The castle's wards were still holding for now, but even I realized that that wouldn't go for too much longer. It had been just more than a week since the city wards had failed and the fighting had started in earnest, and we were losing badly.

Our enemies had known the city well and had plenty of contacts within. They knew which noble houses were likely to surrender in hopes of getting a better deal with them and which they'd have to destroy. Their strikes had been surgical and violent, wiping out the strongest leaders still present in the walls.

We had gotten a few wins. Lord Fallon had been away from the central duchies, trying to stomp out some rebels in the north when they'd arrived, and he seemed our best chance for relief from this assault. We'd also managed to take out several of their units, mostly non-magic-using soldiers, and some of the rebels who were still assisting them.

I sighed and turned. Dean Lorrae had opted to join us in the castle. Normally, this would be unthinkable, as he would need to stay with his charges until the end, but he was too valuable a target and much needed to reinforce our defenses in real time. The current plan was to keep the students at the school until its wards started to fall, then evacuate en masse. Hopefully, most of them could escape.

"How much longer can we hold?" I asked, looking over toward the old man who normally wore a mischievous smile.

"That depends. A few days more at most, but I'll admit that that's a generous estimate. I've already started holding my mana for when we have to flee."

"I'd prefer to fight."

"I know you would, lad, but there's an army out there, and regardless of how good you are, you can't fight an army on your own. No, it's wiser now to hold them in case Fallon makes it back, or to escape and see if we can't go find him."

"You're right, but we'll have to leave so many behind if we run. Don't you have family too? I know my cousins and friends will likely be killed or at least held after."

"I've a few grandkids, but they can take care of themselves. Well, some of them can, a few . . . Sadly, not all of my children's children turned out well."

In the middle of our conversation, there was a brilliant light that flew up over the city. The pale green projectile flew higher and higher until just below the clouds. Once there, it exploded with an ear-shattering noise. That was a first, whatever it was certainly had some energy to it, but had not come even near the castle. It also looked like something our wards would stop with ease, so I saw no point to their doing it.

"Their attack . . . missed?" I mused, cocking my head a bit.

"That wasn't an attack, my prince. We should get to the courtyard." Lorrae looked over toward two of the nearby servants. "You, go and inform Their Majesties of where we're headed, and quick, and you lass, to the princess, fast as you can."

I watched the pair rush off as Lorrae began to move. It was unknown to most, but the courtyard was our evacuation spot. It was secured by a separate set of protections from the rest of the palace and readied for the dean's plan.

It took us only a few moments to get there, and once we had, he began to cast. The spell he was making was one unlike any I'd seen before, and several of the intricacies would have been lost on even a skilled caster. I could do nothing but stand back and wait.

And wait . . . and wait . . . and wait . . .

I looked around. There was only one knight here with me for the moment, my guard for the day. "Where are my parents? Or my sister, they should all be here by now." Something seemed wrong.

Two things happened in quick succession. First, a blast of water slammed one of the nearby towers, the one I'd been in only moments ago, sending debris flying. Second, there was an explosion from deep in the castle, one that shook everything nearby. Dean Lorrae was still casting and didn't flinch.

"Stay here and guard him with your life; we'll need the exit ready," I said to the guard as I turned and sped off. He sputtered and tried to follow, but he was skilled at surviving and protecting, not speed, and I easily left the courtyard before he had a chance to stop me.

I ran through the halls of the palace like an arrow, the edges of the world starting to blur as I moved. There was no time to spare as I bolted toward my parents' chambers, dodging past servants, almost all of the knights were already at the walls for defense.

The guards who should have been standing outside the royal chambers lay dead on the ground, the doors they had stood before burst open. Inside the results of the explosion could be seen, scars from a lightning bomb slashed the walls. The king, his crown fallen to the ground lay there. He'd not died from the blast it seemed, but rather a knife that bloomed under his chin, pointing up into his skull.

The queen had survived, too, but was being held aloft by the neck by some kind of magical tentacle or rope. A girl the prince knew vaguely stood before her, one of his sister's retainers. The obvious source of the spell.

"Aw . . . no more? How disappointing." I barely registered her as she cast my mother's corpse aside, tutting.

My sword, an enchanted blade gifted by an elven ambassador appeared in my hand as I screamed in incoherent rage. The blade burning a brilliant blue as it drank some of my mana. I bolted at the caster who had barely the time to turn as I bore down on her frail form.

Her spell was faster through, turning and speeding toward me at an almost impossible rate. Several passes were made in the course of only a few seconds. She lost several of her little tentacle ropes as my blade slashed through them and my mana burned against hers. In that time though, she had a moment to fall back and begin focusing on me properly.

She didn't have power, but she did have skill. This . . . what was her name? Gwenna? She could cast under pressure and in ways that would irk even the most skilled of battle-mages. None of her spells had the pressure that one would expect, but they were cast perfectly and with extreme speed.

Had I not screamed to alert her, or not rushed in blindly in anger, I would have easily overpowered her before she could do anything about it. She was no physical user and didn't have the reaction speed to do much with as short of an alert as she might have gotten. Foolishly, I hadn't used any stealth, giving her the moments she needed to react.

On our third pass, she managed to hit me with some kind of force, knocking me back a little. That was enough for her to get those bloody ropes in play and well around me. It took all of them to wrap me up, but they did, holding tight to my limbs as the last wrapped around my throat.

"Aww . . . so close, you nearly had me there, Little Prince. Too bad, too bad. Now look at me, I like to see . . ." As she was taunting, walking toward me, she stopped looking down.

Below her arm, in the area of her ribs, a small stick protruded. As she gasped, a second joined it. I watched the girl stumble a bit, her eyes wide at the intruders poking out from her dress. Not only had she focused her all on me, but she'd devoted all of her little spell to hold me in place. Now, she grasped and reached, trying to pull out a pair of crossbow bolts.

I could see that I was not alone in having come to check on the royal couple. In the doorway stood a man who looked more like a snake, holding some monstrous contraption with two slots for quarrels.

Emil ran over to me as the wizard's spell failed. Gwena was busy with trying to deal with her own issues. With one of my arms over his shoulder, he began to drag me out of the room, moving as fast as he could. I was still gasping for breath as we made it to the end of the hall and he helped me down the stairs.

"Need to kill her, she killed . . ."

"No, sire, we need to go. The castle's wards are down, and we don't have the time to waste. We must flee now. If it is any consolation, I doubt she'll survive."

At this point, my legs were working a bit better, and I could help as we moved. I didn't like it, but he was right. There was little else I could do here.

"That monster will probably just pull them out and plug the holes. I should have cut off her head."

"Ah, perhaps, but what about the poison?" I could hear the amusement in the man's voice as he waxed, almost gleefully, on the situation.

I looked at the spymaster and tried not to laugh. No self-respecting knight or battle-mage used poison. Even among common soldiers, it would be derided. Emil though wasn't a knight, a battle-mage, a priest, or any kind of mage at all. He was a commoner and had no issues with anything that worked.

A few people had thought us mad to have a commoner as our spymaster and in such a proximity to us. Mostly, those were nobles and the like who objected to them on a fundamental level. On the other hand, he was simply the best at what he did and loyal to the royal family for all we'd done for him.

Once I'd recovered enough, I picked up the man and took him with me as I ran back to the courtyard. We arrived in moments to find it much as I'd left it, one knight and one caster. The old wizard looked at me as I approached.

"Where are . . . ?" he began.

"Not coming, get us out," I said sadly, from my voice I could tell he understood.

"Very well, everyone close in."

Normally, the knight would have been left behind, Emil too, but as the rest of the royal family was not joining us, there was no reason not to take them. As a spell formed a shell around us, I thought hard. I'd known my sister had some issues with me, but murdering our parents seemed too much. She had either totally betrayed us, was captured, or was perhaps dead. It didn't matter which now, but I'd need to find out.

The shell that encircled us now looked not unlike an opaque egg. As it came together, I felt a sort of weightlessness overtake me, and then we began to pick up speed. Up and up we went, letting the castle shrink below us as we climbed toward the bright white clouds. I could see the whole city as we turned, flying at incredible speed northward and away from the doomed capital of Lithere. It didn't even feel like we were moving, just seeing it all pass below.

I was dizzy, and incredibly angry as I pulled on the damn bolts that arrogant little bastard had shot at me. I was going to kill him. First, I'd wring that little prince's neck, then I would skin the spy. Perhaps I could stretch it out and use it for a book cover when I was done? Questions for later.

I'd even fallen over while they fled, the disgrace. First thing first though, I needed to stop my bleeding. That was easy enough in the short term, and a small covering of force wrapped around the shafts. I'd tried to pull them out at first, but they were deep, and a few touches had reminded me how bad of an idea that would be.

As I tried to rise, I found I was having trouble moving. Arms and legs were fine, but curling myself, I just couldn't. That was no good, had he hit something? Just one more sin to his name, but no matter, I could just use magic.

A little mana gone and I floated up, able to get my feet below me again and tried to walk forward. It was hard, and I was short of breath as I made a few paces, then faltered again. Once more, I stumbled and fell.

This was bad, very bad. I felt a cold fear creep up my spine as I considered my options. I seemed to be hurt far worse than just a simple wound. What to do? What to do? I just needed to stay where I was. We'd won, and soon our forces would get here and heal me. Yes, that was it, just keep the bleeding down and I'd be fine.

I gasped. It was so hard to breathe, like someone was pressing on my chest. I tried and tried, but I just couldn't get the air to go in. The muscles wouldn't move. The cold fear washed over me as I realized that something was very wrong. I needed a healer and now. I tried to stand up again and couldn't. I tried to scream, but only a bare squeak escaped.

I thrashed, trying to get attention. The pain was growing by the moment, spreading through my chest as I focused all of my will on just pulling in one more breath. Without thinking, my hands grasped for my chest and legs. I was so scared, it hurt so bad.

In only a few moments, I found I couldn't move my arms or legs either. The pain was all consuming, and I wept as numb fear took me. The only thing I could hear was the deafening beating of my heart.

"Papa, big brother, help me."

The beating stopped.

CHAPTER 60

✦

REUNION

We had finally finished. It had been several days to take the city once we got in, ending in the assault on the palace. That part, at least for me and mine, was almost routine. The wards were disabled by some internal agent, and from there, the assault was just the slog of cutting through the knights. It was vicious, hard, and bloody, but it was also something we'd done a hundred times. This lot had been better trained, but there'd been only so many of them. Having too many people in your secure holding tended to end in someone betraying you.

While it may have been just a bit irresponsible, both Mystien and I went to the Bergond Academy of Mages, which would need a new name shortly, ostensibly to secure the location. We'd managed to take and secure the palace before our move, even if that operation had taken the better part of the whole night. Those still alive there had all either surrendered or been forcibly stopped, and now all that was left was the paperwork.

"Thanks for coming along," I said to my old friend as he walked next to me.

"It's been too long since we've been able to work on something together, Verren. I also know that school better than you're likely ever to. Any word on the situation there?"

"Looks like most of the students and staff fled into the lower city. We've caught a few of the dumber ones and those they left behind to keep the place looking active."

That had been a whole situation. Several of the noble kids had nearly gotten themselves killed, but others simply didn't know a thing about commoners or where they lived and were easily picked up because they looked like the lost rich kids they were.

"What word on . . . ?" He didn't even finish the sentence before I shook my head.

"I haven't gotten any reports that detailed yet. We'll know shortly after we get there."

After that, our walk was quiet. The former kingdom's premier and only school for casters was close enough, and when we arrived, the place was abuzz with activity from our soldiers. They'd locked the whole facility down and were combing it for anyone who was hiding or anything of import that needed to be logged.

We approached and were questioned, but that was a formality. Once they'd established who the two of us were, we were quickly shown to the officer in charge of the documentation and prisoners.

"Greetings, sirs, anything you need?" He was a formal sort, and we'd not worked together much before, but if he was put in charge of this job, there was no doubt in his competence.

"Yes, can you please provide us with a list of current students, along with those who've been captured or whose whereabouts we currently have?"

The documents themselves were a mixture of those from the school's own records and ours. They'd been so kind as to mark several different situations. Some of the older boys were labeled as having joined the defense, some were marked as captured, and a large number had been marked as evacuated. None of those really mattered when I got to Alana's name, it was there with a marking beside it "missing, presumed fled" along with another girl in her year. Some other students had the same designation so I looked up at the officer.

"What does, 'missing, presumed fled' mean."

"That was the school's designation, but it seems to mean that the student in question disappeared before the main evacuation and is therefore unaccounted for."

I tried not to grit my teeth at that answer, then went back to the records. The other girl was marked as a priest, but I didn't know if they'd escaped together or separately, and asking about her specifically was a risk.

"Please take me to where the staff is being held."

Going through each and asking them about each and every one of the missing students was tedious, but it kept most of my cards out of play. I also learned a number of things. The man who taught the Magical-Item

Creation practical class seemed to guess who I was looking for and sighed when I got to her name.

"She's the one you want, isn't she?" He looked sad as he asked. "I understand, particularly if you've seen some of the weird stuff she does."

"Like what?" It was Mystien's turn to talk. He'd been mostly silent, content to watch, but this seemed to have him very interested.

"She came up with a few things we didn't quite understand. An odd fire spell, some kind of orb that she claimed was a lamp . . ." He seemed to pause for a moment, leaving some things out. "You lads must have got wind that she's sharp, but she's a child. If you find her, and you probably won't, I'd ask you not to hurt her."

I could answer that. "I have no intention to harm her at all. We just want her found."

He nodded, seeming to conclude that there was no more he could do.

Her adviser, and in fact the adviser for all of the bards, was around too. He had his own opinion when we got to Alana.

"Doubt you'll ever catch her, not unless she wants to be caught, or just makes dumb decisions."

"You're not the first to have said something like that, why?" I asked, thinking back to the other professor's words.

"Well, it's no secret, but she's some kind of illusion prodigy. Full body invisibility, realistic images, and copies. During her exam, she fooled the whole staff into thinking she was somewhere she wasn't, Rooke thought it was teleportation. The dean could see through it, but if you're at his level, why would you even care about her?"

I resisted the urge to rub my temples. "What about the other girl in her year, the priestess?"

"Oh yes, they were fairly close from what I understood." He didn't have much more than that though, which was irritating.

Sadly, we couldn't ask any of the fairer members of staff, because they'd all scattered like flowers on the wind. That action was smart on their part, but a pain for me personally.

"Your daughter is an invisible tree in a forest, and she keeps moving," Mystien said after putting up some basic privacy spell.

"I know, I'm not sure if I should be proud, or irritated at her."

"Eh, be irritated at me. I'm the one who taught her basic running and hiding."

"Fine, I'm irritated at you then. Next we try the temple district. The Shield definitely had contact with her, and while they might not let us in just yet, I'm betting we can at least get a message sent if we ask nice. Who knows, maybe she ran off with that priestess to hide there."

"That's not a bad thought."

"First though, I need a drink."

"Fair enough, come on then, I know just the place. It's even on the way if you squint a little at the map."

I chuckled and followed. On our way out, my son joined us. He'd come by after finishing up his own duties, ostensibly for the same reason we had. We all three agreed that the temple district was the next good place to look, and that we all wanted a short break.

Since all of us kept our clothing rather plain, we looked like little more than common soldiers, and with a bit of suppression on auras, we appeared as little more even to those who could see such things. We made our way through the streets, which were being patrolled by our men now, and around to a seedy-looking bar nestled among a mixture of similar establishments and brothels.

As we passed into the entrance of the Starlit Sky, I could see the place was packed. A number of people were here to get food and stay at the inn, as large swaths of the city were either in ruins, or a complete mess. Even with the crowd, the barman, an older man with a sizable belly, let out a deep laugh.

"Well, look at you, you miserable old bastard." His greeting to Mystien was followed by another laugh and a fist slamming on the door to the kitchen. "Oi, hurry up and get on out here, we've got customers!" he shouted to one of the staff.

After days of staying with the temples, I was relieved when the fighting finally ended. It may have been only that evening that the palace fell, but the city was finally fully at peace. For my part, it was time to take a step out of the Shield's area before they tried to lay claim to me, again. So I returned to my old stomping grounds at the Starlit Sky. I was visiting Kala a lot still, so I'd know if anything came up, and we had plans for her to make some careful inquiries about the academy in a couple of weeks. I didn't know if it would still be running, or if we'd still be students, but I hoped to continue my education.

For now though, I was content to make food for all those seeking shelter and sustenance from Lucien. The money was nothing but pocket change, but it was a fun job to do, and he was relaxed to be around.

As I was finishing up preparation on some more loaves to feed our mass of hungry folk, I heard a banging on the kitchen door.

"Oi, hurry up and get on out here, we've got customers!" Lucien shouted, in what may have been the rudest way he'd ever spoken to me.

I threw the door open, scowling as I exited. "Hurry up yourself you fat, old . . ." It was then that I saw my dad, brother, and Mystien, standing there like it was nothing. They all looked a bit older, but almost exactly the same as I'd seen them last.

The old bartender tried to keep himself upright through the laugh. "Seems you finally came to collect your wayward apprentice? She seems surprised to see you."

Dad was the first to recover. "A-Alana? Is that you?"

I had thought long and hard what I would say to my family when next we met. I'd had years to consider, and knew exactly the first thing I wanted to speak to them.

"SPINDLE!" I loudly declared.

Mystien looked confused.

Dad began to weep, something I'd never seen before.

John laughed so hard he fell and smacked his face into the floor. He was still a bit of an idiot.

I walked down the hall of my newly conquered palace. I didn't intend to live here or anything. I already had a much more secure home, and taking it would be both in bad taste and make me look like I was establishing myself as a new king of this country, neither of those were desirable. No, keeping myself close to my men, above, but also humble, that would lead to their continued loyalty.

It had been years since I'd stepped in this place, but following the path to the royal chambers was easy enough. I could have had others deal with this, but I wanted to see it on my own. It was therefore that I'd ordered them left as they were until I arrived.

When I reached the room in question, only one other was inside. Princess Sophia stood there in all her glory. She'd taken time to clean herself and dress well for this meeting, regardless of the fighting going on around her. It was the things like that, the careful preparation regardless of situation that made her stand out.

"My dear," I greeted her as I entered. It had been some years since we'd spoken in more than infrequent letters. "You seem a bit bothered. Hopefully, you can forgive me the deaths of your parents."

"I'm not bothered by that at all, my lord. They would have sold me off like a common cow to whomever had made the best offer." That much was true, sadly the lot of a princess was often to be married for some financial or political gain. "Did you know that you were the only one who ever asked me what I wanted?"

"I suspected as much." I followed her eyes, my own landing on a corpse I didn't recognize, a young woman frozen in death, her face a mask of pain and fear. "One of yours?" I asked.

"Mmm, I told you of her in one of my letters. The one who I had issues reigning in. It's a shame really; she was loyal."

I wrapped my arm around her shoulders comfortingly. "Ah, my dear, you know I would have had to put her down anyway. One cannot leave a rabid dog, no matter how loyal, to run amok. She served her purpose."

"I know. Still, at least you would have been merciful about it."

I nodded and gave her a light kiss on the cheek, causing her to blush ever so slightly. "Well then, come, my dear, we've much to do. There are so many things that need to be set right."

ABOUT THE AUTHOR

Wandering Agent is the North Carolina–based author of the Melody of Mana series as well as other fantasy and isekai stories.

Podium

DISCOVER
STORIES UNBOUND

PodiumAudio.com

www.ingramcontent.com/pod-product-compliance
Lightning Source LLC
Chambersburg PA
CBHW031934110726
47902CB00001B/174